GODDESS OF CHAOS

A Dragonheir Novel

By

Sarah Edgerton

Lake Charles, LA

THE DRAGONHEIR TRILOGY

DAUGHTER OF CHAOS
WARRIOR OF CHAOS

TO ALL THE GIRLS, YOUNG AND OLD.
EMBRACE YOUR INNER CHAOS AND USE IT AS A
SOURCE OF STRENGTH. YOU ARE A GODDESS.
DON'T LET ANYONE TELL YOU DIFFERENTLY.

The Order of Dragons

Chaos Dragons - Chaos Dragons are the most powerful Dragons to exist. They created the unnamed world and the Elemental Dragons. Their scales are colored in exquisite shades of purple from the deepest violet to the richest amethyst. Their eyes are an intense violet. They can wield all magic.

Chaos Dragongoddess: Nimerah
 Chaos Dragongods: Ragnar and Amram

Fire Dragons - Fire Dragons command the flames, breathing forth infernos from within. Their scales are colored in shades of crimson, orange, and gold. Their eyes are like the flames with red and specks of gold intertwined. Their secondary power is shapeshifting.

Fire Dragongod: Vukan

Water Dragons - Water Dragons embody the mysterious waters, conjuring torrents that can both cleanse the senses and engulf their victims. They can manipulate water in any form. Their scales are colored in shades of cerulean, turquoise, and sapphire. Their eyes are dazzlingly blue. Their secondary power is telepathy.

Water Dragongoddess: Anahita

Earth Dragons - Earth Dragons are one with nature. They can connect to the earth itself, shaping mountains, summoning tremors, and upheaving the landscape. Their scales are colored in shades of greens and mossy hues. Their eyes are green like the forest trees. Their secondary power is strength.

Earth Dragongoddess: Dhara

Air Dragons - Air Dragons are ethereal and intelligent. They can harness the power of the wind, creating gusts and whirlwinds that sweep through the air. Their scales are colored in shades of gray and silver. Their eyes are sparkling silver. Their secondary power is empathy.

Air Dragongoddess: Ilmari

Light Dragons - Light Dragons hold power over the light of the world. They can illuminate any space at any moment. Their scales are colored in shades of iridescent white that reflect the sun. Their eyes are bright white. Their secondary power is healing.

Light Dragongod: Endrit

Darkness Dragons - Darkness Dragons embody the essence of night, harnessing shadows and plunging the brightest day into absolute darkness. Their scales are colored in shades of gray and black, making it easy to disappear into the veil of night. Their eyes are an unsettling onyx. Their secondary power is teleportation.

Darkness Dragongoddess: Tamasvi

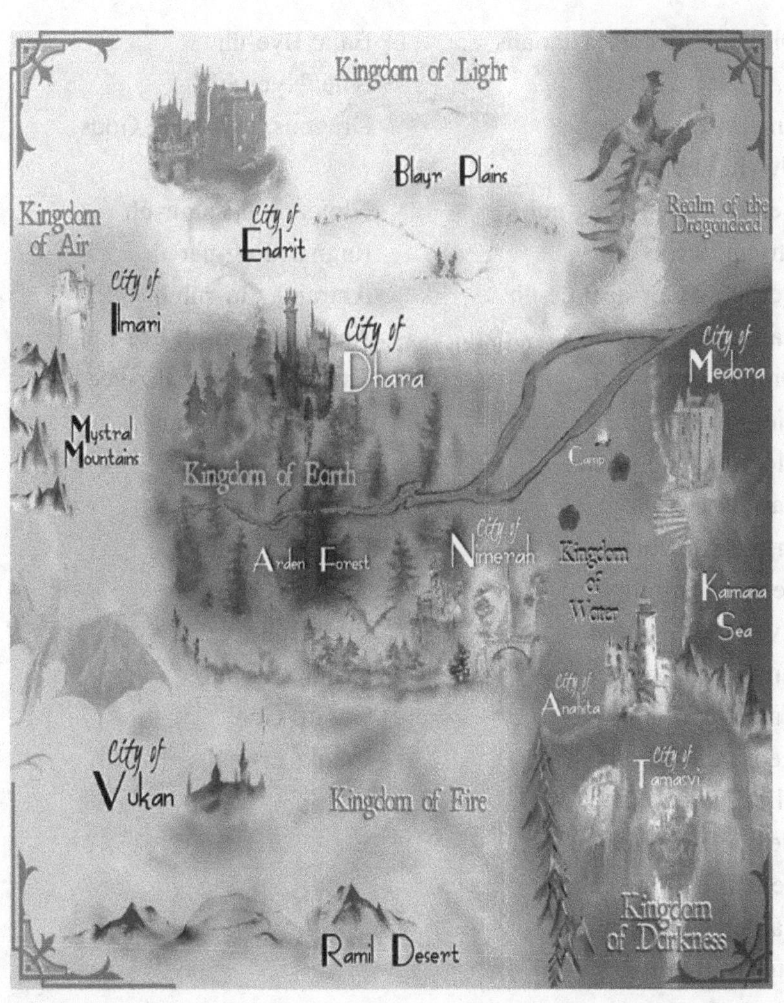

Kingdom of Light
Blayr Plains
Realm of the Dragonblood
Kingdom of Air
City of Endrit
City of Ilmari
City of Dhara
City of Medora
Mystral Mountains
Kingdom of Earth
Camp
Arden Forest
City of Nimerah
Kingdom of Water
Kaimana Sea
City of Anahita
City of Vukan
City of Tamasvi
Kingdom of Fire
Kingdom of Darkness
Ramil Desert

Pronunciation Guide

Dragonborns and Humans

Emera: Eh-mair-uh
Dwyn: Dwin
Benigno: Beh-neeg-noh
Struan: Stroo-uhn
Cordelia: Cor-deel-ee-uh
Calian: Cal-ee-uhn
Dhruv: Droov
Fin: Fin
Morwen: Mor-wen
Zari: Zar-ee
Erjon: Air-yon
Senna: Sen-nuh
Avani: Uh-von-ee
Anwir: Ann-wur
Valda: Val-duh
Kedron: Ked-ruhn
Elio: Ee-lee-yoh
Hestia: Heh-stee-yuh
Tellus: Tell-uhs
Calder: Cahl-der
Eteri: Eh-tair-ee
Leora: Lee-or-uh
Orpheus: Or-fee-uhs
Zepherin: Zef-er-in
Nyx: Nix
Shula: Shoo-luh

Baia: Bye-uh
Nile: Nye-uhl

Dragons, Including Gods

Nimerah: Ni-mair-uh
Ragnar: Rag-nar
Amram: Am-ruhm
Anahita: Ann-uh-hee-tuh
Tamasvi: Tuh-mahz-vee
Vukan: Voo-kuhn
Ilmari: Ill-mar-ee
Endrit: Ehn-drit
Dhara: Dar-uh
Gawen: Gah-wen
Bud: Buhd
Risna: Riz-nuh
Ghoul: Gool
Irmak: Er-mahk

SUMMARY OF BOOK TWO

Emera Edevane, Captain Calian Westbow, and the other Dragonheirs are in the City of Ilmari within the Kingdom of Air. Emera has a haunting vision of Amram killing her friends, claiming that they will die if she tries to stop the Dragongod. She eventually reveals this vision to Calian and her friends.

The Dragonheirs meet with Queen Eteri to discuss their plans. Kedron arrives with news that Queen Hestia of the Kingdom of Fire will join their cause.

With the help of Calian, Erjon, and Morwen, Emera attempts to block Amram from her mind. In doing so, she learns how to shift into her Dragon form. After she can transform back into her human form, the three of them witness a Dragon called Hadeon being resurrected.

A battle ensues and Emera takes flight in her Dragon form. She is weak, thinking that using her magic to transform is taking energy from her. She goes after Valda but ends up getting hurt. Calian uses magic to heal her. He's then visited by Tamasvi, the Goddess of Darkness. The goddess reveals that Nimerah is dying, and that Emera is the only person powerful enough to heal her.

Emera gets back into the training ring but realizes quickly that she is having difficulty with her magic. They decide to train without magic. Meanwhile, Emera still tries to find a way to keep Amram out of her mind.

Calian meets with the monarchs joining their cause, including Queen Hestia. The queen shows Calian a vision of what could happen if Amram is able to raise his army. After that happens, Emera meets the Winged Warriors for the first time, including Zepherin, Erjon's brother. Zepherin teaches Emera how to fight like a warrior in case she cannot access her magic.

They leave for Medora to find Nimerah. Not long after leaving, the Dragonheirs run into Valda, still alive, and her Dragons. A battle ensues. Senna is killed by Anwir, and Emera leaves with Valda to prevent any more bloodshed. The next morning, the others continue their journey to Medora. Calian is surprised, and not happy, that Queen Hestia has insisted on joining them. Zepherin does as well.

The group stops to rest in the Kingdom of Earth. Calian, Fin, and Kedron teleport to the City of Dhara to retrieve an amulet like Fin's. They are met by Kedron's sister, Nyx, who helps them maneuver through the palace. Calian and Fin, by disguising themselves, gather information from King Tellus himself while Nyx and Kedron look for the amulet. Things go badly. They teleport back to the forest.

During this, Emera is taken to the Dragonrealm of the Dead. Valda brings Emera to Ragnar's Sanctuary. There, Emera is shown a statue of who she learns is the Dragon Slayer, the one responsible for killing Amram during the War of Three. After she sees the statue, she goes to her room and is visited by Amram again. Because of this, she discovers a secret doorway that leads to a hidden library. There, she runs into Elio. Elio, it turns out, is an ally and works for Hestia. He wants nothing more than to stop Amram. He reveals a second part of the prophecy to Emera where a Dragon Slayer and his mate will kill the Dragongod once and for all by using the Dragon Slayer's blade. Emera and Elio agree to help each other. He will locate Nimerah, and she will get the blade from the statue of the Dragon Slayer.

After their exchange, Emera discovers that she and Calian are Dragonmates. The reason Calian has Dragonmate wings and she does not, is because a deal was struck between Valda and Anwir that if Anwir helps Amram, Emera belongs to him.

Emera travels with Valda, Anwir, Gawen, and Bud to resurrect a Dragon. The Dragon's name is Risna, and Emera believes that Risna is actually an ally. Risna cannot transform back into her human form as punishment from Amram.

Back in the Arden Forest, the group breaks apart. Calian, Fin, and Hestia head toward Medora. They come across what seems to be an abandoned town. Once they cross over a bridge, the town changes. It is called Khaosar, and it is a hidden town full of people. They meet Anahita, the Goddess of Water, who takes care of the town. Anahita reveals that Calian really is Vasuman, the son of Vukan and Hestia, as well as the Dragon Slayer. They leave for Medora soon after.

Back in Ragnar's Sanctuary, Emera discovers a prisoner in a dungeon: Vukan, the God of Fire. They escape with the Dragon Slayer's sword, but not before Emera is wounded. They travel to Medora where they stop at her parent's home to rest. Calian, Fin, and Hestia arrive. Calian meets his father for the first time since learning who he is. Calian is told that Emera has been poisoned. Calian heals her a little bit, but only enough for her to feel comfortable. She needs chaos magic from Nimerah to heal completely. If she doesn't get it, Emera will be a human forever.

A small group heads off toward a small island where Nimerah is. Vukan stays on the beach while Calian, Emera, Fin, and Morwen search the island for Nimerah. They enter a cave and survive three tasks that eventually get them to an open chamber where they see Nimerah. However, Nimerah is dead. Nimerah's Dragon form vanishes and is replaced by Amram, who is not back in the flesh. He's been within Valda the entire time, waiting for what he needed to become whole again: Nimerah's body. He syphoned Emera's magic and in doing so, took most of her soul. A battle ensues and Emera is killed.

They take Emera back to Medora where they mourn her death. Hestia says that Calian will see his mate again.

CHAPTER ONE

EMERA

I'd never thought much about death. From a young age, I was taught that on a human's final day, their body would just give out. Their heart would play its final beat, and their mind would drift into nothingness. There would be no grand light or eternal palace awaiting their soul. Only Dragonborns had the luxury of an afterlife.

So, one could understand my surprise when my blurry vision cleared, revealing not only Dragonborns, but also humans standing next to me in what I assumed was the afterlife. "So, in death, we are all the same," I whispered.

I studied their faces, all calm and peaceful, having no fear of their deaths. There were many of us, all different shapes, sizes, and skin colors, just standing and waiting. No one looked familiar as I made eye contact with several of them. Most cast their gazes upward toward the sky where twin moons surrounded by dazzling stars brightened the otherworldly plane below them, illuminating their skin. Sleek black mountains loomed in the distance; their peaks covered in glistening snow.

Minutes passed before I forced my gaze away from the mountains to a long white bridge suspended over a sparkling river. The stones of the bridge were amethyst with intricate carvings made to look like scales. The bridge was familiar in appearance, but I failed to remember where I'd seen it before. I slowly shifted my eyes from left to right, surveying the landscape. In fact, everything around me was familiar, but I couldn't quite place who I was, exactly, or the particular setting I stood in. It felt like something out of a dream.

I journeyed over the bridge and paused midway to look below into the tranquil blue water. My reflection stared back at me, but it was a face of the past. Exhaustion hung on my features. Whereas my fellow travelers glowed in their white satin attire, I did not. My skin was sallow, and my once vibrant hair was dull. My green eyes peered back at me, no longer the violet they once were. Despite the other humans and Dragonborns having illuminated skin and clear, vibrant eyes, I still looked…Well…Dead. I shifted my gaze back toward the bridge and continued across at a leisurely pace.

Where the bridge ended, a flight of stairs began, the same color of amethyst as the walkway on the bridge. As the stairs ascended upward, they split, each side curving around a towering statue of the Dragongod, Ragnar. On either side of the statue were fountains with sapphire blue water sprouting into a small pond at the Dragongod's clawed feet.

"I know this place," I whispered.

A young man with bright yellow hair and bright blue scales leaned toward me. He was maybe a couple of years older than me and, unfortunately, missing an eye. He also had a large scar from his eyebrow to his chin. Despite the damage to his face, he also looked familiar.

He gulped nervously as he tugged the collar of his pristine white satin shirt. "Are we…dead?"

I did my best to ease his anxiety with a comforting smile. "We are. But do not be afraid of this place."

"Why do you say that?"

"Because something deep inside of me tells me that I've been here before." I closed my eyes and concentrated. I was losing my mind. Everything was familiar, but I couldn't quite place a name to what I saw.

The man's mouth gaped open as he took a step away from me. He started to say something else, but he was cut off.

"This place is the realm between worlds."

Both the man and I turned our attention up the path of the stairs. The steps met again at the top and opened into a courtyard where a woman in a simple black satin dress stood, her raven black hair swaying in the warm breeze. Recognition seized me. I knew this woman. It was Tamasvi, the Goddess of Darkness.

"Welcome to the Dragonplane of Existence," she said, her tone soothing and peaceful. "I am here to guide your souls to their final destinations." The moment the goddess said we were on the Dragonplane of Existence, the fog within my mind began to clear slowly, and I remembered bits and pieces of my life in the living world. I remembered her. I remembered this place. I remembered my death.

I pushed past the young man and jostled through the crowd of newly departed souls. Taking two steps at a time, I rushed up to Tamasvi. I had every intention of throwing my arms around her, but she stepped aside suddenly, revealing another person behind her.

Senna.

I stopped dead in my tracks. Funny, considering that's what I was. And so was she. And it was because of me! The battle at the mountains flashed momentarily in my head. Valda, Anwir, the dagger. I scanned Senna's face for any signs of anger. Did my friend blame me for her death?

As if reading my thoughts, Senna wrapped her arms around me, pulling me into a warm embrace. Her satin white dress was soft against my skin. "Don't you dare think it."

A sob caught in my throat. I swallowed it loudly. "I'm so sorry."

"My death was not your fault, Emera. I knew what I was signing up for."

"I tried to bring you back. I really tried."

"I know you did." She released me, stepping away and turning to Tamasvi. The Dragongoddess of Darkness only smiled before nodding and then leading the way back into the courtyard beyond the stairs. By then, the other souls had climbed the staircases and were ushering themselves behind her. Senna and I followed.

When I finally set foot on the beaten stones of the courtyard, I was met with weathered marble and intricate mosaics, framed by a palace towering behind it. Dragon motifs were carved into detailed designs, swirling around the columns and archways that outlined the courtyard.

From the mountains to the trees, the Dragonplane of Existence's landscape resembled the Dragonrealm of the Dead. But whereas the Dragonrealm of the Dead was barren, this place was a harmonious blend of nature and artistry with lush gardens that provided a tranquil setting for meditation and reflection. Souls sat on the stone benches that were scattered throughout the courtyard. Some engaged in quiet conversation while others read books or wrote in journals. The group of souls I was a part of meandered the winding pathways that converged at another set of stairs, leading toward an exact replica of Ragnar's palace. The palace I had been held captive in.

I quickened my pace and fell in step behind Tamasvi. "I don't understand," I said. "If this is the Dragonplane of Existence, why does it look like the Dragonrealm of the Dead? It wasn't like this when I was here. At least, not the parts I can remember."

"The first time you came here, you were only here through your mind. Nimerah and I agreed that it would be best to tailor the scenery to what you were familiar with."

"I would have managed just fine."

"Perhaps."

When she reached the door to the palace, she turned and held up her slender hand, signaling the other souls to stop. Then, she addressed us all. "When we go inside, you will be ushered into a large sanctuary. From there, your soul will be weighed. Should you feel any guilt or despair for your mortal life, you will remain here until your affairs are in order and your soul is at peace. Only then will you cross into the DragonEmpyrean. Should you accept your mortal life as it was lived, you will immediately cross into the DragonEmpyrean." She winked at me, and I looked away quickly. I didn't want to cross over. I needed to finish what I'd started with Amram. I needed to go back.

Tamasvi opened the wide double-doors, and we all strolled inside. There was an abundance of light emanating from the sconces on the walls, and the air was clean and smelled of Twilight Orchids. I inhaled deeply and let the fragrance stir within my lungs before releasing it.

Just as Valda had done, Tamasvi placed her palm on an engraving of a key at the center of the door at the end of the hallway. "Vylar, mir'draconar."

"Open, my friend," I whispered, repeating Anwir's translation.

The doors opened, and all the new souls stepped into a vast chamber. Their eyes widened in response to the large violet crystals that hung from the ceilings, suspended by magic and radiating a light much brighter than what I remembered in the Realm of the Dragondead. The chamber was also circular, but there were no murals on the walls that told of the unnamed world's tumultuous history. Cast in vibrant light at the center of the chamber was the large throne, but this time, it was constructed of ivory instead of obsidian. Just like the obsidian throne in the Dragonrealm of the dead, the ivory was crafted to look like Dragonscales and mimicked the form of a Dragon, but here it was welcoming instead of foreboding. Its feet also mimicked the appearance of a Dragon's feet, and atop the high back was a Dragon's head looking downward with its wings closed below it. The angle of the wings was the same, made to appear as if they were draped around an unseen object. I had guessed they were to drape around souls. I was right.

Tamasvi held her hand out to a soul behind me. "Please, sit," she said.

I looked back and found an older woman, her salt and pepper hair falling below her shoulders, walking gingerly to the throne. She looked at Tamasvi who nodded her head and smiled. The woman smiled back and sat on the throne. As she settled in, her lips parted in surprise.

"Do you hear that?" the woman asked everyone. "There's a gentle hum. It's beautiful."

The souls started looking at each other curiously. Tamasvi's smile widened just as an ambient energy appeared above the woman, weaving a luminous tapestry around her. Beams of golden light shimmered and danced in the air. Everyone watched as the memories of her life unrolled like scrolls, casting vivid reflections of kindness and compassion. The woman inclined her head, acknowledging her past deeds—the good and the bad. Suddenly, the energy transformed into wings of pure light and wrapped around the woman. The wings lifted her from the throne. As she ascended, her form underwent a gradual transformation, melding with the radiant energies that embraced her. The light faded and she disappeared entirely.

"Will that happen every time?" I asked Senna who now stood beside me.

"No. Sometimes, there is no light. And if there is no light, then the soul stays."

"Was there a light for you?"

She chuckled. "I didn't even sit because I knew there wouldn't be any light for me. I know I have unfinished business."

I turned toward her and searched her face. "Which is?"

"You."

I didn't know what to quite make of that, so I remained quiet and focused my attention back toward the throne. Tamasvi's hand was already extended, guiding another soul to the throne. The man with yellow hair walked past me, his face angled so that I couldn't see his expression. Whatever it was, I'm sure he was nervous because his shoulders shook.

He stepped before the throne but hesitated to sit. Tamasvi still smiled, waiting patiently. Everyone there knew that no one would disobey a goddess, especially if she was standing right there. The man pivoted slowly and sat down. My eyes darted through the crowd at the souls who watched in keen interest, wondering how long I'd have to stand there and watch. I had business to take care of.

When I turned my attention back to the man on the throne, I gasped, finally recognizing him. "Nile Ford?" I blurted. All eyes shifted to me, which included Tamasvi's. I ignored their stares. "What? How?" Forget that in my past life he'd been a jerk. It was jarring to see him here. Dead.

He leaned forward and squinted. "Emera? I'm sorry. I hadn't recognized you before. My memory here is hazy."

"Yes, it's me. And I understand. My memory is coming back in pieces. What happened?"

He hung his head. "There was an attack," he answered. This was not the Nile Ford I once knew. This man was hunched over, his shoulders slumped to make himself appear smaller. He was timid and unassertive.

"Medora?"

"City of Anahita."

My heart pounded violently within my chest. It was a phantom response, considering I was dead and didn't have a pulse. "Morwen," I breathed. Waves of worry flooded my body.

"I'd never seen anything like it. The Dragons were… They were…" He swallowed a visible lump in his throat.

Tamasvi stepped forward. "I do not believe it is your time, Mr. Ford." She scanned the crowd for Senna. When the goddess located my friend, Tamasvi signaled for Senna to step forward. "It is time. And take him with you. I will be there shortly."

Nile's one eye darted back and forth between Tamasvi and Senna before speaking again; this time his words burst from his mouth like water breaking a dam. "I was a coward, I know. I fought until I was so tired, I couldn't fight any longer. The Dragons were everywhere."

Senna stepped forward and placed her hand on Nile's shoulder. "You'll see the Empyrean one day. But until then, I need you to come with me. There is someone you should meet." Nile nodded and stood. He followed Senna to a door at the back of the chamber.

"You must go with them," Tamasvi said. I didn't say anything. I just followed Senna and Nile, leaving the other souls behind to learn their fates.

We exited the chamber and stepped into the largest garden I had ever seen. At least, it began like a garden, but it stretched on endlessly, eventually transforming into what seemed more like a forest.

"Come," Senna said.

Under the soft glow of the moon and twinkling stars, we strolled through the garden. Celestial blossoms in light hues of lavender and purple bloomed all around us, including more Twilight Orchids. The air was rich with the scent of them, which eased my body into a peaceful state of tranquility. It was quiet except for the sound of leaves rustling in the breeze. We passed a large fountain and turned, entering a glade bathed in moonlight. At the far end of the glade, stood a tall silver willow tree, its branches blanketing the ground below it. Beneath its canopy sat a woman with flowing purple hair. Her violet silk dress was a stark contrast to the silver of the whispering willow above her.

"Nimerah?" Senna called out.

My Dragonmother's eyes fluttered open. There was an astounding violet glow to them, accompanied by a warm smile. She rose to greet Senna and Nile, not seeing me coming up the path behind them. "Welcome," she said to Nile.

Senna beckoned toward me. "She's here."

She, meaning me.

Nimerah's neck turned slowly, and our eyes met. "My

daughter," she whispered. Her lips parted slightly, but they quickly spread into an endearing smile. My mother rushed toward me and wrapped her arms around me tightly. "My darling."

"Hello, Mother."

Nile looked at me and then my mother. He was completely flabbergasted…And I loved it. Before I could stop myself, I winked at him from over my mother's shoulder. As much as I understood what Nile went through, it was still difficult for me to completely forgive him for the nasty things he'd said to me back in Medora.

My mother dropped her arms and took a step back. "And who might you be?" she asked, her eyes narrowing on Nile.

"Uh…Nile…Nile Ford." Nile was clearly shaken up. He started to back up little by little. "I can't do this." He turned quickly and ran, zig-zagging his way back to the palace.

Senna sighed. "I'll get him."

Nimerah laughed. It was music to my ears.

"Do you get that reaction often?"

"You'd be surprised." Her brows furrowed as she studied my face for a moment. The goddess let out a heavy sigh. "I'm so sorry, my daughter."

"Why are you apologizing? You did nothing wrong."

"If I had been strong enough, I could have saved myself

and you."

"You are a Chaos Dragon. And my mother. You're the strongest Dragon I know."

A faint smile tugged at her lips. "I don't think it's fair to say that I hold that title." She lifted her palm and cupped my cheek. "Not anymore."

"Agree to disagree."

She chuckled. "I have something for you."

"Oh?"

Movement behind me caught her attention. "But it will have to wait. It appears that your friend is back."

"The term friend is a stretch."

Senna marched back toward us; her arm interlocked with Nile's. His face was pale and sweaty.

"Gave me a good run. Found him outside a small shed just east of the palace."

"A-a-pologies…y-y-your…" Nile stammered. I'd never seen him this shaken before.

"Nimerah will be just fine." Her demeanor changed abruptly, her eyes flashing with recognition. "Now, let's get down to business. Weren't you the boy that dared Emera to steal a ceremonial basin and dagger? The ones which were to be used for Partition ceremonies? The ones dedicated to the Dragongoddess Anahita?" She leaned toward him and lowered her voice. "The ones that started my daughter's activation before it was supposed to. You're that Nile Ford?"

Nile looked nervously at me.

"All is forgiven, mother. I think it turned out well." I looked down at my almost translucent hands. "Well, all things considered."

My mother straightened her back. Nile let out the breath he'd been holding captive in his chest.

Senna took a step forward, drawing Nimerah's attention away from Nile who was clearly about to pass out. "Nile fought Amram's Dragons at the City of Anahita. He could have valuable information as to how to fight against the Dragons. That is, if he doesn't try to run away again." She twisted his arm slightly.

"No! No! I won't run again." Nile pulled his arm inward and massaged his elbow.

"Really?" my mother said, her eyes locked onto Nile's. "Well, looks like you might be of some use to us."

CHAPTER TWO

CALIAN

"Come in."

The war room of my mother's palace in the Kingdom of Fire was illuminated in a soft glow from the flickering candles, casting shadows on the papers scattered across the table. I glanced behind me as Fin entered the room. I turned my back to him and hunched over the documents I'd received from Kedron. The documents he'd risked his life for.

"Well?" Fin asked.

"It's pretty much as we expected." I scrutinized the documents detailing Amram's impending strike against the Kingdom of Darkness. My eyes darted across the intricate details, absorbing the seriousness of it, and my heart sank. Since Emera's death, Amram's army had tripled in size. He'd resurrected countless other Dragons and had the armies from the Kingdom of Light and Earth at his disposal. The kingdoms had been more than willing to join Amram's cause, proclaiming their allegiance in the name of Amram's children—Endrit and Dhara—who had joined Amram in the war.

His first plan of action had been setting up his command within the palace in the City of Endrit—a gift from Queen Leora. He then asserted his authority over the City of Dhara and planted his forces along the border of the Arden Forest. King Tellus and Queen Leora were traitors, and I couldn't wait to drive a sword through their chests. Or maybe a dagger through their throats. I hadn't decided.

Fin leaned over the table, obstructing my view. "You've been in this room all day."

I peered up at him. "Really? I hadn't noticed."

"Funny. You need a break."

"It's crucial that we determine Amram's patterns and weaknesses. If there are any. The key to our defense lies here in understanding the nuances of his planned attack against the City of Tamasvi. If we don't…" My voice trailed off. Fin knew what I was going to say.

An elongated pause filled the space between us. My friend—my brother—was choosing his words carefully. I couldn't blame him. I had been a real Dragonass as of late. But it was to be expected. It seemed like every second we delayed striking out against Amram, the more people—particularly humans—he killed. While Fin debated what to say, I looked back down at the portion of the map that haunted me most.

Fin sighed. "I don't know how many times I have to say this, but the Kingdom of Air wasn't your fault."

I snorted in response. After taking Dhara, Amram's forces seized control of the City of Ilmari, and ultimately, the Kingdom of Air itself. Queen Eteri and her Winged Warriors had put up a tremendous fight. They'd killed three Dragons and wounded more. But in the end, they just didn't have the power to overtake them all. It cost Queen Eteri her life. She'd left the camp almost immediately after we'd buried Emera, anxious to be with her people. Erjon and Zeph had gone with her. Thankfully, they made it out of the city alive.

Fin straightened and placed his hand on my shoulder. "Despite what you think, Erjon doesn't blame you."

I slammed my fists on the table. "He should! His kingdom is in ruin and its queen dead. His mate!"

"And that is war, Cal!"

"You should be with Morwen."

"She knows I am needed here."

"Fine," I spat. I pushed back from the table, grabbed a vase, and threw it across the room. The door opened just as the vase shattered into jagged pieces on the wall. Right next to my father's head.

"Bad time?" Vukan asked as he closed the door behind him. I hadn't heard him enter.

"Maybe you can talk some sense into your son. He won't listen to me." Fin closed his eyes and took a couple of deep breaths, fighting to maintain his composure.

"You cannot blame yourself, Vasuman," my father said softly.

I didn't feel like arguing, so I turned my back and continued my inspection of the documents. After a few minutes, a warm hand rested on my back in an attempt to provide comfort. But comfort wouldn't come. I didn't deserve it. I swallowed a sob that formed in my throat.

My father's voice, low and gentle, filled the empty air. "What have you gathered, my son?"

Happy that he'd changed the subject, I traced my finger over the maps, connecting the dots of Amram's recent targets. His paths of destruction included mostly human dwellings including towns and farms. "Amram seems to favor certain regions, mainly inhabited by humans. If we can predict his path in any way, it might be possible to strategically position our defenses to minimize the impact to the City of Tamasvi."

Fin appeared at my side and pointed to the northern border of the Kingdom of Darkness. The tip of his finger sat on a dot marking a small town situated between two tree lines. "What if Kedron and I position ourselves here. At the first sign of his army, Kedron will teleport me closer to their front lines. I'll infiltrate their ranks, gather intelligence on their movements, and have Kedron report back to you. Then, we can position ourselves along the border."

A light knock at the door broke the awkward silence between us. "Come," my father commanded. The door opened slowly and Queen Hestia, my mother, poked her head through the door.

The queen of the Kingdom of Fire studied our faces. "Am I interrupting?"

"Not at all," my father said and took my mother's hands in his. He pulled her in and kissed her gingerly on the cheek. A sharp pain cut through my chest as if I had been stabbed with a dagger. It was just another reminder that I'd never have that. My mate was dead. And here I was, left to pick up the pieces and fight for a world that I wasn't convinced deserved to be saved. I shook my head, trying to rid myself of the negative thoughts that continued to plague my mind. Of course, the world needed saving. It's what Emera would have wanted.

"I just thought I'd check in. See if there's anything I can do to help." She crossed the room and took Fin's place beside me. Our eyes connected. I watched as hers darted back and forth, up and down. She searched my face for something. I didn't have a clue.

"You will find nothing," I whispered.

She smiled in return. "My son, I have found everything."

As much as I'd grown to love my mother in the short time of knowing her—remembering her—I'd also grown impatient with her cryptic statements. She picked up on my frustration because she chuckled and turned her attention to the documents, inspecting them. "The Kingdom of Darkness will be next."

"Seems to be that way," Fin answered. He'd found a bowl of fruit on a nearby side table. He tossed an apple in the air before catching it and taking a bite. "Just as all signs point to him leaving the Kingdom of Fire last," he commented between chomps.

Hestia glanced at Fin and then me. "You seem pretty nonchalant about all of this," she said to Fin.

"Not at all. I just don't let my emotions get the best of me. What is it that Erjon is always saying?"

"Emotions get you killed," I said.

"Exactly." He looked point-blank at my mother. "Emotions get you killed."

I waved my hand in frustration. "Let's focus on the matter at hand, please."

"Amram seeks to close off all the kingdoms, isolating us from our allies," my father explained, his brow furrowed in deep concentration as he analyzed the map. "His strategy is to divide and conquer, which will leave us vulnerable."

My mother leaned forward; concern etched on her face. "How do we counter such a strategy?"

"I'm not so sure we can," I replied wearily. "In any other situation, I would say that we should create a united front against the enemy. Coordinate with the other kingdoms, share intelligence, and fortify our borders collectively. Maybe then we'd stand a chance."

"But he's a god," my mother said. "It's different."

I hung my head in response. How could we defeat Amram without Emera?

Fin swallowed his last bite of apple and tossed the core into the fireplace. "What Kedron has gathered so far is that Amram has not left the palace within the City of Endrit. His goons are doing his business."

My mother leaned against the table and crossed her arms. "So, that is who attacked the City of Anahita." Her words sounded like a statement rather than a question.

"Which is why they were able to fight them off," my father mused. Until that point, he'd been unusually quiet. "Look at this." He held out a document that had been buried.

I snatched the paper and searched it for anything out of the ordinary. "It's a list of towns they've already hit. What is it I should be looking for?"

"A third of the way down. See the name? Fin was right. That town leading into the Kingdom of Darkness is their next target. See why?"

"The town has a series of tunnels connecting it to the neighboring city. Then those tunnels eventually lead to the City of Tamasvi. How did I miss this?"

Fin yawned. "Easily overlooked when we've been at this for days." He rolled back his shoulders. "We've been receiving new intelligence every day. Everything is starting to blur together, so don't beat yourself up, Cal."

Hestia picked up on Fin's exhaustion, and like any mother would, she started fussing. "Okay, you two, off to bed."

"But Mom!" Fin cried out; a smile planted firmly on his face. "Well, if you insist." He nodded at me and headed for the door.

But no one was going to bed just yet. Because at that moment, Kedron appeared. "Wait," he said and held up his hand to stop Fin from leaving. He leaned over, bracing his hands on his knees. I'd never seen Kedron so out of breath from teleporting. This was serious.

"Kedron?" I asked hesitantly. "What is it?"

"Calian," Kedron began, his voice shaking. "Amram has taken the Kingdom of Water. The City of Anahita has fallen, and…" he stopped and looked at Fin.

Panic twisted Fin's face as he demanded, "What of Morwen?" He grasped his chest, right over his heart, where his Dragonmate wings rested beneath his shirt.

Kedron finally stood. "Alive when I left."

Fin crossed the room quickly and grabbed the collar of Kedron's crisp black shirt, pulling his face close, anger flaring in his eyes. "You just left her there? Why didn't you get her out?!"

"Now, now, Fintan," my mother said. "Don't say anything you'll regret. What was it you said earlier about emotions?"

"I don't plan on killing him," Fin hissed.

"She told me not to," Kedron said. He didn't make any attempts to free himself from Fin's grasp. In fact, he could have teleported away, but he didn't. Kedron, and everyone else in the room, knew that Fin wouldn't hurt him. He was just…scared. An emotion I knew all too well.

I stepped toward them and put my hand on Fin's shoulder. "You know good and well that Morwen would not abandon her people in a time of need," I said. "Kedron is not to blame."

Fin's hand opened slowly, and his intense expression softened. Once he'd let go of Kedron, he backed up and hung his head. "I'm sorry."

Kedron plopped down in one of six plush red chairs at the long rectangular table on the southern side of the room and dropped his head back. "Do not apologize. I understand."

Normally, the night was my refuge. But after hearing Kedron's news, I found little comfort in it. I paced anxiously, a knot tightening in my stomach with every step I took around the battle room. I circled the table a couple of times before my father spoke.

"How could this have happened? King Elderbrook's forces were strong. The Dragonborn had the power of water at his disposal." He pointed to the documents we'd been analyzing. "Besides, every move Amram's made has been to get them closer to us. The Kingdom of Darkness was next."

Kedron sat up. "The documents were a ruse. Their aerial

attack on the City of Anahita caught us all off guard. Morwen commanded me to warn the surrounding towns so that citizens could escape. I was able to warn most of them before my instincts told me that something was wrong. So, I headed back to the city and teleported into a private room below the palace. The king was dead, and the queen was injured. Thankfully, her injuries were nothing too serious. A healer was with her." He turned to Fin who now leaned against the wall with his arms crossed. "I tried to reason with Morwen. Tried to convince her to go with me. She wouldn't leave."

Fin only nodded. "Of course, not."

"We cannot let this attack go unanswered," my father said.

My mother clasped her hands together. "Calian? Your thoughts?"

I slammed my fist down on the table once more, my head still reeling from the news of Calder's death. "I am such an idiot! Of course, the Kingdom of Water would be next. And now King Calder is dead." A heavy silence settled in the room.

Fin looked at me square in the eyes. "I ride for the Kingdom of Water." He left the room, not daring to look back. I wasn't going to stop him.

Kedron shook his head. "No, I will teleport him there."

My mother and I exchanged somber glances before I addressed Kedron. "You need to rest," I said.

He leaned forward, took a hefty sigh, and stood. "I need to get Fin to Morwen." He started for the door, but I cut him off.

"No," I said gruffly. "Morwen can handle herself. Sleep tonight. Tomorrow, you will go to your father and warn the king of Amram's plans. I don't care if those documents were false. We will not let what happened to the City of Anahita happen to the City of Tamasvi."

Kedron opened his mouth to argue, but he thought better of it. He pursed his lips, stepped past me, and exited the room.

"Get some sleep!" I called over my shoulder. I ran my hand through my hair, hoping I could wipe away some of the anxiety from the day.

"I'll go and convince Fin to sleep tonight before riding out to the City of Anahita," my mother said. "I'll then see to it that Kedron gets some rest as well." She rested her hand on my cheek. I closed my eyes, placed my hand on top of hers, and leaned into the warmth of her palm against my skin. Breathe in, breathe out. Breathe in, breathe out. After a few minutes of breathing, the tension in my shoulders lifted slightly. I opened my eyes and dropped my hand. Hestia leaned in and tenderly kissed my cheek before she left the room.

I turned to my father. "We will end this. I don't know how, but we will. We have to."

CHAPTER THREE

EMERA

Unlike being concealed in the living world, the palace library's location was visible and available to everyone, including the souls that had yet to transition to the DragonEmpyrean. In fact, the room that Valda had held me prisoner in, didn't even exist. In its place was the entrance to the library. As we stepped through the double doors, the hushed murmur of conversation and the soft rustling of pages greeted us. Instead of the dark, damp hallway I'd stumbled upon, this one was light and airy. I breathed in the comforting scent of old books instead of the musty odor I had been forced to grow accustomed to. Candelabras and swaying chandeliers cast a warm glow on the rows of neatly organized bookshelves. Tapestries and artifacts decorated the walls. Directly across the room was a huge fireplace, and hanging above it was a beautiful violet bow and quiver of arrows.

"Ragnar loved to hunt," my mother said, noticing my gaze upon the immaculate weapon. What I wouldn't give to hold the bow in my hands. To shoot a slew of arrows once more.

I continued following Nimerah. She nodded occasionally at the souls who filled the large space. In one corner, two older souls sat at a table, engaged in animated conversation. Laughter punctuated their discussion, and I smiled after noting that one was a Dragonborn whereas the other was human. My eyes swept the room, lingering on the individuals of various ages and backgrounds, an even mixture of human and Dragonborn. Their faces, brightened by the soft glow of reading lamps and candles, were at ease with those around them. The library was a communal space where human and Dragonborn souls found common ground within the pages of books. There was no fighting. No division. Was this possible in the living world?

"What are they doing?" I whispered to my mother.

"Some are trying to make peace with their previous lives, researching how to atone for their transgressions. Some are trying to decipher the meaning of life, hoping it will give them clarity and understanding about who they were and where they are. Some are just waiting."

As we navigated through the aisles, I observed the lone souls. Some browsed the shelves, meticulously selecting books with a thoughtful gaze, while others sat in secluded corners. My eyes lingered on a young soul crouched in front of a shelf, debating on which book about horses he was going to choose. A breath caught in my throat. Was this soul the young boy from Dhara? The one who took good care of Zari when Calian and I had gone to find Avani? I shook my head, hoping I was wrong. "Won't they all go to the DragonEmpyrean?"

"Eventually."

I nodded, more so to myself, and clung to the hope that the young soul would soon leave this place. Despite the amazing wonders of the Dragonsoul Plane, it was no place for one so young to spend eternity. I tore my eyes away from him, knowing deep within my heart that it was the same boy. I also knew that Tamasvi took good care of him.

Nimerah ascended a spiral staircase to the upper level of the library. At the top, a soul sat nestled in a comfortable chair, whispering to herself. Her eyes darted between the pages of the book in her hands, occasionally pausing to think. I wondered if she was trying to figure out the meaning of life.

We came to a wooden door that was slightly ajar. My mother pushed it open, revealing what appeared to be a small study. There was a long table with six chairs. Nimerah lowered herself into a chair at the head of the table while I sat to her left. Senna, still having a hold on Nile, guided him to the chair at the opposite end of my mother. Senna then took her seat across from me. The interrogation was about to begin.

"Spill it," Senna ordered. My mother remained silent, patiently waiting for Nile to disclose any and all information he harbored.

Small beads of sweat formed along Nile's hairline despite the room being chilly. With a haunted look in his eye, he took a deep breath. I leaned in, desperate to hear anything that would help us defeat Amram.

"The Dragons came out of nowhere," he said, his voice trembling. "They breathed fire and caused havoc. Buildings crumbled to the ground, and people were running in every direction."

Senna shifted in her seat, leaning back and crossing her arms. She nodded, gesturing for Nile to continue.

Nile's one eye locked onto mine. "I had just joined the king's guard. We were on patrol when we heard the roars and saw the flames. We rushed back to the city, and the streets were chaotic. The Dragons were vicious, spewing fire everywhere. I had never seen anything like it.

"What did you do?" I asked.

"We tried to help the civilians, evacuate them to safety. There was a Dragonheir there. Dressed all in black with light hair, but I can't remember his name."

Senna and I glanced at one another. "Kedron," we said simultaneously.

Nile snapped his fingers. "Yes! That was it! He did this thing where he appeared and then disappeared. He would take people with him. We tried to get as many out as possible, but then more Dragons appeared. They were relentless, attacking without mercy, and there was so much destruction. I saw people…" his voice trailed off and he hung his head.

My mother finally spoke. "Then what?" I didn't miss the edginess of her tone.

Nile took a shaky breath. "We fought back, but our weapons hit their scales like pebbles against a dam. I watched my fellow soldiers fall. And the screams…" He paused, closed his one eye and covered his ears. "One minute, I was running toward a group of people, and the next, fire erupted between us. Their screams of agony still ring within my ears."

"It sounds like you did everything you could, Nile. Their deaths are not your fault," I assured him.

He slowly lowered his hands and opened his one eye. It could have been the lighting, but it seemed different. Colder somehow. "I know, but it's just...It's hard to shake off the images, the fear. I wanted to run back to the palace, but my limbs were tired from all the exertion. The Dragons had all but decimated the city even though they never landed. Who knew they could cause so much destruction without setting a clawed foot on the ground? I found refuge in a hole beneath the rubble. I stayed there. And I shouldn't have." Nile hung his head once more, but this time, his shoulders shook from the audible sobs of embarrassment and guilt. When he looked up, I expected to see tears. But there were none. "I called you a cowardly human. You were never a coward. I was. I couldn't understand how a human could have so much bravery, trespassing into a church at night to steal from a Dragonborn. Whereas I, a Dragonborn myself, did not."

The image of me sticking my tongue out and saying I told you so in a whiny toddler's voice flashed in my mind. I wasn't going to do that, but a small part of me wanted to.

Senna let out a deep sigh. "As horrific as all that sounds, did you see anything useful?" I opened my mouth to say something, but she held up her hand. I looked at my mother, stunned. Was she going to allow Senna to speak to Nile that way, considering all he'd been through? Regardless of him being a spineless coward, he'd been through a lot. But Nimerah didn't move, nor did she speak.

"Look. What you went through was terrible—traumatic, even," Senna continued, "But we need something—anything—that will help us defeat Amram." She continued talking to Nile, but as I watched my mother, Senna's voice faded into the background until it all but disappeared completely. My mother wasn't just staring at Nile, she was trying to figure him out. Did she know something that we didn't? I had no magic of my own, thanks to Amram, so I couldn't tap into my empathic abilities.

"Again, I don't know," Nile said, pulling me back into the moment. "I didn't see much. At one point, the screams stopped, and all I heard were the flames. When I emerged from my hiding spot, only half of the palace was still standing."

"Tell me about the Dragons you saw," my mother interrupted, her voice low but firm. "Tell me again about their arrival. What color were their scales?"

Niles hesitated for a moment, searching for the memory. His fingers began to lightly tap the table. He probably buried it deep within him to suppress the horrors of what happened. I couldn't blame him.

"They were red."

Nimerah's eyes narrowed. "Interesting," she murmured. "Because the accounts from the lost souls that arrived here shortly after the attack happen to paint a different picture. And most of the Fire Dragons were loyal to Ragnar in the war. Are you sure about the color?"

A bead of sweat formed on Niles's brow, and a subtle shift in his demeanor betrayed his unease. "Well…Um…Things were chaotic. I could have gotten a bit confused. It could have been red or…maybe…it was more like a dark green splattered with blood."

My mother stood; the chair creaked as it slid away from her. "But you mentioned earlier that the Dragons never landed. Why would one be covered in blood?"

Senna and I glanced at each other. Something was wrong, and my mother knew it.

Nile's eye, once seemingly innocent and trustworthy, now sparked with menace. Then he chuckled. "And they say Amram was the clever one."

My heart raced beneath my chest. I knew that tone.

"What's your play?" Senna hissed.

A sly grin spread across Nile's face, and he winked at me.

Nimerah's eyes flashed with anger. "You will not harm her."

Harm me? I was already dead.

"Yes, I will. I'll shove this blade right between her lungs and suck her soul dry." He withdrew a shiny black dagger from his shirt and twisted it in his palm. With a flick of his wrist, he threw a torrent of water toward me. How the hell did he have magic? I fell to the floor just in time for water to crash into the wall behind me. Nimerah and Senna looked at me, their eyes wide before each of them were swept backward by the wave of water.

"Get the souls out!" I shouted.

My mother lifted herself to her knees. "I will not leave you here." She looked at Senna who nodded and darted through the open door, screaming to the other souls to vacate the library. But Nile didn't care what Senna did. He was focused on me. He continued to blast water magic at me, but I managed to dive and roll out of the way each time. I didn't have my magic, but I had Zeph's training. The only problem was that my clothes were now soaked. My white silk dress was heavy, making my movements slower. Water dripped into my eyes, blurring my vision.

Nimerah crawled to my side and took my hand.

"He's not dead," I huffed.

"Not at all." She glanced toward the door.

"This is just too much fun," Nile taunted.

I quickly surveyed my surroundings, trying to figure out a way to escape. "The table," I murmured. My mother nodded. We put our hands on the table's legs and shoved with all our strength. Thankfully, Nile hadn't moved an inch since the start of the attack, so the table slammed into him and pinned him to the wall. He was stunned, which gave us enough time to dart out of the room.

I ran down an aisle just as a wave blasted through the door. My breath caught in my throat as I watched the wave take my mother over the railing. Her back slammed onto the floor of the first level. Through the bookcase, I watched Nile step out of the room, waving the dagger slowly in his hand. What was it about that stupid dagger?

"Filthy human, filthy human. Come out and play." His voice was like nails on a chalkboard. I shuddered.

"Why are you doing this?"

"Because I volunteered. Valda needed someone worthy to finish you off."

"Valda? How…Wait…You knew?"

"Of course, I knew."

The dare. It was all Valda's doing. She just needed an excuse to be there past midnight, and who better to do her dirty work than Nile.

Some might think that I was a fool for suggesting such a thing. But I knew Valda. She found pleasure in prolonging the suffering of others. She enjoyed the anticipation and fear her victims had from not knowing when their demise would come.

"Why don't you just fight me and get it over with?"

"She was right. She said tormenting you is fun. I think I'll do it a tad longer before I finish you off with this dagger." And there it was. He had no plans of ending things quickly. He wanted to drag it out as long as possible, just as Valda would want. He was so confident in his power and superiority that deep down he believed he had nothing to fear from me or anyone else here. His overconfidence was pure lunacy considering there was a Dragongoddess in the palace—and I didn't mean Nimerah. If I could keep him talking long enough, Senna could get to Tamasvi.

The panicked cries from the souls drifted out of the library until silence remained. I still hadn't heard my mother, and I couldn't see her from where I was. Could Nile hurt a soul? I needed to get to her.

I clamped my hand over my mouth to steady my breathing so that he couldn't detect my location. I crouched low and quietly maneuvered between the bookshelves, my footsteps muffled by the thick carpeting beneath my feet. I desperately called to my water magic—yes, even though I knew it to be futile—to ease the erratic beating of my heart. Could Nile hear it, too? There was no time to find out. I needed to move. I had to get to my mother and out of the library.

Despite my attempt to remain calm, panic gripped me. What if a soul died in this plane? Would they just cease to exist at all? A shiver coursed through me, and I forcibly gulped down the lump of fear that had risen in my throat. All I could think of was my mother. A faint sound echoed behind me. It was the soft whisper of footsteps, drawing closer and closer. Nile was nearby.

"Come out, come out, wherever you are," he sang softly. "I think it's time that I plunge this dagger into you and watch the final light fade from your eyes."

I took a quick step around the bookshelf and lowered myself once more, placing my hand on the floor to detect any sign of movement through vibrations. There was none, so I summoned what courage I had left and moved, edging toward what would hopefully be the stairs. In my attempt to get away from Nile, I hadn't paid attention to my exact location. After a few steps, I stumbled upon what looked like the chair the soul had been sitting in at the top of the staircase. I inched closer. Sure enough, it was the same chair. I was so relieved that I'd almost forgotten about Nile.

A low chuckle echoed close by, chilling me to the bone. My breath caught in my throat as I turned slowly around, searching for the source of the sound. And then I saw Nile, his one eye gleaming with hatred as he emerged from the shadows. His presence seemed to suffocate the very air around us, and his gaze fixated on me with intensity and a wicked smile spread across his face. He'd found his prey.

I turned and ran down the staircase. My mother was lying on the floor unconscious, but before I could get to her, bursts of water flew past me, causing me to lose my balance, and tumble down the stairs. A sharp, searing sensation erupted against my flesh as I crashed into the metal railing. An explosion of pain radiated outward to my fingertips.

My heart hammered against my chest as I got to my feet. Ignoring the pain, I ran straight between two large bookshelves. They were the same ones I'd run through to find Elio. A breath hitched in my throat from the memory of his lifeless bird form hanging from Valda's hand.

I scanned the nearest shelf, hoping to locate a weapon of some sort. Then I saw it: a heavy bust of a Dragon sitting on a nearby shelf. With trembling hands, I lifted it from its resting place and held it to my chest. I needed a better spot to strike from. But before I could make a move, Nile appeared out of nowhere and lunged forward, the razor-sharp blade glinting in the dim light. I staggered backward and tripped, the bust falling to the floor and breaking into pieces.

"Dammit!"

Nile's lips parted into a wolf-like grin. "Gotcha." He drew his arm back, but before he could bring the dagger down, I rolled away. When I faced him again, the library doors swung open loudly.

"This ends now." Tamasvi's voice rang throughout the library. Instantly, she was next to me. She took my hand, and just as Nile hurled water magic at us, The Goddess of Darkness teleported to my mother, took her hand, and then teleported again. We reappeared at the northern side of the room where Senna stood in the doorway. Tamasvi pushed me toward Senna. "Get out of here!" The goddess then turned and ran toward Nile, her silky black hair whipping back and forth in the air, shiny silver daggers adorning her hips.

I turned to Senna. "Take my mother and get her out of here."

Senna leveled her gaze. "You're going after them, aren't you?"

"Absolutely."

Senna's eyes narrowed. "Give him hell." She lifted Nimerah as best she could and dragged the goddess out of the library.

When I turned back around, water and debris were everywhere, yet I couldn't see Tamasvi nor Nile. Just then they both appeared out of thin air, standing on opposite ends of the room.

Nile could teleport? How? As if reading my thoughts, Nile glanced back at me, winked, and said, "Do you like my new gift? It's from my future father-in-law himself."

My mouth dropped as Nile pulled back the collar of his shirt, revealing a pair of violet Dragonwings.

Nile chuckled. "We've been mated since my activation."

Heat flared beneath my skin. This was just my luck. And it explained everything. It explained why Nile had magic. He wasn't a soul here after death; he was sent here by Valda and Amram. It also made sense now that he didn't transition to the DragonEmpyrean—not that he would, anyway, being the horrible Dragonheir that he was.

The two continued to appear and reappear in such quick succession that my head hurt from watching them. Tamasvi was visibly frustrated. Each throw missed Nile by an inch. She finally raised her arms, and the library went pitch black.

It was good for Tamasvi, who could see in the dark. Bad for Nile, who couldn't. And me.

If Nile found me, I would be done for. I needed something to defend myself. "Think, Em," I whispered to no one. "What can I use?" I closed my eyes, picturing the library as I had entered. My memory sparked, there, across the room! With my arms out in front of me, I slowly maneuvered to the other side of the library, bumping into fallen furniture and sloshing through the water, until I felt the fireplace. I grabbed the closest chair, positioned it, and climbed towards my objective. With bated breath I wrapped my fingers around Ragnar's bow. Expecting it to take a great amount of muscle to dislodge it from the wall, I heaved. I was wrong. I fell back, crashing to the floor along with the chair, the bow and arrows thankfully landing on top of me. What I wasn't thankful for was the noise when I hit the floor.

"I told you to leave," Tamasvi said, suddenly appearing at my side. She lifted the darkness around us, putting us in a bubble of light.

I gasped for air as I rose to my feet, completely winded from the fall. "I…don't listen…very well," I managed to choke out.

"Clearly. I don't know what your plan is, but—" A powerful wall of water slammed into Tamasvi, propelling her into the wall; a sickening crunch echoed around me at her body's impact. The darkness throughout the library lifted. She slumped to the floor, and my mouth gaped open in horror as I watched her body become still.

CHAPTER FOUR

EMERA

"No!" I screamed. Nile burst forward, and I didn't know if it was my adrenaline or Zeph's expert teaching skills, but I waited until he was close, squatted, and then swung my fist up. I winced from the pain that shot through my hand when I connected with his face. Nile staggered back and began massaging his jaw.

"You Dragonbitch!"

Well, that was a new one.

I tightened my grip on the bow while reaching for an arrow. I only had two, so I needed to make them count. I looked back over my shoulder at Tamasvi. Her eyes were closed, but her chest rose and fell. So, she was alive. I turned my attention back to Nile, who teleported again. He materialized and vanished with unnatural swiftness, but I refused to believe his movements were unpredictable. There had to be a pattern. He was the mate of a General. Everything about Nile was calculated down to the last detail. Even teleporting. And if she trained Nile…

With determination, I scanned the library, my senses now heightened in anticipation of where he'd appear. Higher maybe? Sure enough, he looked out over the railing and down at me. His eyes blazed with fury. I'd really made him angry.

Good.

A smirk played upon Nile's lips. "Time to end you with this." He held up the dagger.

I sighed and rolled my eyes. "Enough with the stupid dagger!" Undaunted, I sprang into action, my mind racing with strategies to outmaneuver him. With a swift motion, I knocked an arrow and released it toward him. But before the arrow could find its mark, Nile vanished into thin air, his form flickering before it was no longer visible. And now, I was down to one arrow.

He reappeared on the second floor of the library. He peered over the railing and locked his eyes onto mine. "Stupid dagger? This stupid dagger is going to end your existence once and for all!"

"You make it sound special," I hissed, trying to keep him talking. Maybe Tamasvi would wake up.

"It is special. Only three were made. One was destroyed in the war, one is lost, and this one, which is for you." He twisted his wrist, letting me get a good look at it. The blade was forged from a rare, obsidian-like metal that gleamed at every angle. The hilt was wrapped in leather that was engraved with Dragonscales. Embedded in the center of the hilt was a small violet gemstone.

"See this gem? That is your undoing. The dagger not only takes life, but it traps the soul of its victim, leaving an empty shell behind. I'll take the last remaining drop of your soul, and when I destroy the blade, you're gone for good. No DragonEmpyrean for you." Then he teleported.

But this time I was ready. I knew he was going to materialize beside me. It was his pattern. When fighting Tamasvi, Nile had teleported away, gained his composure, then teleported back. So, this time, when he reappeared beside me, I kicked his stomach. He flew back into a tall bookshelf, causing an avalanche of books to bury him after he fell to the floor. As the dust settled, he didn't move, so I turned and focused my energy on Tamasvi.

"Tamasvi! Please get up! Please!" I knelt beside her and

shook her body. Time was of the essence. I couldn't be gentle. "Get up!"

The Dragongoddess groaned and her eyes fluttered open. I stood abruptly; relief flooded my veins. Tamasvi sat up slowly and her eyes drifted past me. "Emera," she croaked and pointed her finger.

Letting intuition guide me, I simultaneously whirled around and drew back on the bow. I didn't hesitate to release the arrow. Nile stood behind me, his arm drawn back. But before he could stab me with the dagger, the arrow lodged itself into his heart. He gasped and stared at me, shock resonating on his face. He grabbed the arrow and pulled it from his chest. Healing magic—another gift from Amram's chaos magic—flowed over the wound, but surprisingly, it didn't work. The wound didn't close.

The light in his one eye faded slowly, and he dropped to one knee and then the other. He leaned his head back, keeping his eye locked on mine, and opened his mouth to say something. But no words came. Instead, his body fell to the side, unmoving, and his lifeless eye remained open.

I glanced back at Tamasvi who stood in a fighting stance, dark tendrils pouring from her hands. She was in no condition to fight, but maybe she wouldn't need to. I turned my gaze back on Nile's body lying motionless on the floor and stalked toward him, cautiously placing one foot in front of the other. I raised my fists to protect my face. I wasn't taking any chances.

"Nile?" I said softly. I lifted my foot and nudged his body. "Are you…alive?" Really, Em. What kind of stupid question is that? Regardless, Nile didn't answer. He didn't stir at all. "Why didn't the healing magic work?"

The doors to the library flung open, crashing against the walls. I flinched but still kept my eyes locked on Nile who remained still. After a few seconds, my mother appeared at my side. "So…That happened," I said.

"Is that Ragnar's arrow?"

"Yes." I lifted the bow.

Nimerah's eyes drifted from Nile to the violet bow I held, and she shook her head, clearly confused. "I can't believe the poison lasted that long."

"Excuse me. Did you say poison?"

"Ragnar always laced his arrows with poison. He used it to guard this place. After the war, evil didn't dare tread upon this plane, so the bow and remaining arrows were put on display."

"Poisonous arrows were put on display in a library? A deadly weapon was put on display…in a library?"

My mother angled her head toward me with an

incredulous look upon her face. "There is no greater weapon than a book. It seemed like a fitting place."

I started to say something but decided against it. I was still reeling from the fact that I'd killed Nile. If Valda didn't hate me enough already, she was going to loathe me now. I'd just killed her mate. I shuddered from the revolting notion of them being mated.

"Ragnar would basically marinate the arrows in a cauldron of poison." My mother gestured to my hands. "I'd suggest washing up before you eat anything." I couldn't tell if she was being serious or not. Better safe than sorry, though.

"I think it's time we speed up our plans," Senna said from behind us. She held the dagger up and inspected it.

Tamasvi nodded. "The palace is not safe. That dagger is supposed to be in my possession in a safe location. Somehow, Nile was able to retrieve it. If he can do that under our noses, there's no telling what else Amram will do. We need to move the souls."

"Agreed. We will need to dispose of the body," Senna said, her gaze on Nile.

"I will do that," Tamasvi said. She was already walking toward the dead Dragonborn. "I will meet you back at the lake."

Nimerah nodded. "Yes. The lake."

I leaned toward my mother and raised my hand. "Um…What's at the lake?"

* * *

The moon remained suspended over the realm, its gentle glow illuminating all beneath it and reflecting in the crystal-clear surface of the lake. I figured it would have set already, bringing with it the morning sun, but maybe it never did and darkness prevailed. This was Tamasvi's realm, and she was the Dragongoddess of Darkness. One of her symbols was the moon; maybe here the moon resided in the sky for eternity. It was a lovely thought.

Senna, Nimerah, and I stood at the lake's edge. My heart was heavy from the life I'd just taken. Even amidst the tranquility of the serene night, where I found solace when alive, my heart ached. It ached for my parents, whom I knew were recovering from their daughter's untimely death. It ached for Calian, whom I knew was putting the weight of the unnamed world on his shoulders. And, selfishly, it ached for my death. Here I was, standing next to a beautiful lake on the beautiful Dragonsoul Plane of Existence, but I longed for the living world.

I took a deep breath and peered down into the water. My sallow skin and dull eyes reminded me that I was truly dead. Even though I moved around freely here, I was not free. I had only a fragment of my soul. From the corner of my eyes, I glimpsed Senna sitting beside the silver tree. She was dead, too, but she was vibrant. A tear streamed down my cheek as memories flooded my mind, memories of Senna with Avani. I wiped the tear away with the back of my hand. Fate had been cruel, tearing Senna away from Avani too soon.

I dropped my head back as a soft breeze sang its lullaby, each note gently caressing my cheeks. For a moment I closed my eyes. I didn't move, didn't speak. It wasn't until my mother wrapped her arm around my shoulders that I let my mind come back to the present. I rested my head on her shoulder, and despair took hold of me once more. Like Senna, I had failed to save my mother as well.

"I'm sorry," I whispered.

But the goddess simply shook her head, her eyes filled with understanding and forgiveness. "You have nothing to be sorry for, my daughter."

Footsteps drew our attention away from one another. Tamasvi strode toward us, her previous simple dress, which had been torn in several places during the fight with Nile, had been replaced with a black silk gown. It flowed in the breeze as she walked, and there was no doubt that she was the goddess of the night.

"It is time," she said.

I looked at my mother, then Senna, then Tamasvi. They all knew something that I didn't. Secrets made me nervous.

Senna stood from her spot on the ground and nodded. She took a position next to Tamasvi and across from my mother. The three of them formed a semi-circle. My eyes darted quickly back and forth. What was going on?

Senna turned toward me. "Your heart is burdened with my death, and it shouldn't be. You are not to blame. I knew my fate."

I scoffed at her words. "Just because you made it your life's goal to defeat Amram, doesn't mean you were going to die."

"Yes, it did. My father employed a seer, so I was made aware of my short life span long before I'd met you."

I was instantly numb. Senna knew she was going to die young. How did one come to terms with that?

"He'd seen several paths, but they all ended the same. I didn't know exactly when, but I knew that I wouldn't make it to my twenty-fifth birthday."

"Senna," I breathed, my voice shaky. "I'm so sorry."

Senna smiled, and it lit up her face. She was radiant, even

more so than before. Oh, no. Was it her time?

Tamasvi took a step forward. "It is time for Senna to travel to the DragonEmpyrean."

I shook my head. "No. Absolutely not. I just got here."

"My final task was you knowing that I don't blame you for my death, and that I am not afraid of what is to come. In fact, I welcome it." She held out her hands and looked into the sky. Her entire body started to glow and a beam of light I'd seen in the chamber emerged from above. I held back the tears that pooled within my eyes.

"There's a gentle hum now. It's soothing. Can you hear it?"

Beams of golden light floated on the breeze, and I watched as the memories of Senna's life flashed before us all. Just like it had done with the woman, the energy transformed into wings of pure light that wrapped around Senna. The wings lifted her from the ground, and she ascended upward. Senna's body gradually transformed, melding with the radiant energies that held her. The light faded and she disappeared.

I sniffled. Senna was gone. For good this time. But knowing she was at peace was reassuring.

"And now, it is my turn."

"Excuse me?!" I turned to Nimerah. There was no way I

had heard her correctly.

"Mother," Tamasvi said to Nimerah. Was it odd that I just then realized Tamasvi was my sister?

Nimerah nodded and looked me in the eyes. "Daughter, I give you, my soul."

I leaned back. "What does that mean? What does *give you my soul*, mean?" I looked at Tamasvi, my eyes pleading.

"Did you notice how you look different from all the other souls here?" Tamasvi asked softly.

"Yes."

"It is because only a fraction of your Dragonsoul remains. Amram took the rest of it when he took your magic. I cannot send you back to the unnamed world without a soul."

I let go of my mother and took a step back. "Amram resurrected evil Dragons. Surely, they had no souls." How could an evil Dragon still have a soul?

She took a step toward me. "Amram was able to resurrect the Dragons because their souls were bound to their bones."

I shook my head furiously and crossed my arms like a petulant child. "No. If I take your soul, then you can't cross into the DragonEmpyrean."

Nimerah rushed toward me and grabbed my shoulders. She leaned forward so that our eyes were level. "I knew all along that this was my fate. Ragnar had proclaimed it through one of his numerous prophecies. I willingly give you my soul so that you can return to the living. Then, you can reactivate the blade, and the Slayer can kill Amram once and for all!"

I refused to believe this was the only way. "You're a powerful Chaos Dragon! Can't you just snap your fingers and kill Amram?"

Nimerah sighed deeply. "I cannot. We are designed with a unique vulnerability. It requires both chaos magic and a well-forged weapon to end our lives. This is how Ragnar was ultimately defeated."

"Magic and a weapon? Together?" I asked.

The Dragongoddess laughed. "The sword, along with your chaos magic, is designed to exploit that vulnerability in our physiology that magic cannot by itself."

I looked from Tamasvi to Nimerah. I had no idea what my mother had said, but I decided to just go with it. "What about the blood? Chaos blood is needed to resurrect a Dragon."

Tamasvi and Nimerah looked at one another. What weren't they telling me? "That is where I come in," my sister answered. "Despite being an Elemental Dragon, I am still the daughter of a Chaos Dragon, therefore, I have a kernel of chaos blood within me. I am giving you my blood to send you back. But it will come at a cost. I will have to give most of it. Best case scenario, I will be weakened."

My breath caught in my throat. "And worst case?" I feared I knew the answer, but I had to ask anyway.

Tamasvi looked at me intently. "I die."

I backed up until I hit the tree behind me.

"If that happens, it is imperative that you come back to usher in the new souls once Amram is defeated. If you don't…Well, let's just hope that everything goes according to plan."

"No, no, no." I push myself from the tree and past both goddesses. "What will happen if I don't come back?"

Tamasvi paused, thinking. "I am unsure what will happen. Souls could overcrowd this plane. Some may even fall back to the living world where they will reside in torment for the rest of time."

I gulped. "Okay, so let's make sure that doesn't happen."

"Come," Nimerah commanded. "I must tell you one more thing. The amulet—my amulet —that your father gave to you."

"Yes, I know. I must give it to a human."

"My amulet can be given to any soul that is worthy, human or Dragonborn. Remember that." With trembling hands, my mother reached out to me, and as our fingers touched, a warmth spread through my body, a sense of peace unlike anything I had ever known. At this moment, I knew she was willingly giving me her soul. The air hummed with a subtle Dragonmagic, as if the Dragonplane and all the souls that inhabited it were holding their collected breaths. An array of emotions swept through me; fear mingled with awe, and sadness entwined with gratitude. My mother was making the ultimate sacrifice for the unnamed world.

Then, a surge of energy pulsed between us. A luminous violet thread connected our bodies, and along that thread, my mother's soul, ancient and compassionate, flowed from her to me. And then, without a word, she wrapped her arms around me, and warmth flooded my body. I held onto her tightly and buried my face into her shoulder. As the energy settled into my body, I felt a gentle pull, a sensation of weightlessness that seemed to draw me away from her.

"Goodbye, my daughter," Nimerah said into my ear, her voice barely more than a whisper. "Thank you for everything." And with that, my Dragonmother kissed my cheek before fading away for all of eternity, leaving Tamasvi and me alone by the edge of the lake. Tears of sorrow stung my cheeks as I embraced my mother's soul. I would defeat Amram and carry my mother's legacy with me wherever I went.

CHAPTER FIVE

EMERA

"We must hurry," Tamasvi said, and she headed toward the palace.

I started to follow, but then the most unusual sensation seized my mind and body. I swayed slightly. For a brief moment, I contemplated requesting a momentary reprieve so that I could rest and replenish my energy. I was emotionally drained from what had just occurred. And to be truthful, I didn't feel quite like myself. Was it because two very important people just crossed over? One to the Empyrean and the other out of existence? No…that wasn't it.

As if reading my mind, Tamasvi answered, "Are you all right, Emera?"

"I can't quite put my finger on it," I told her. At a time such as this, it was best to be upfront about one's feelings.

Tamasvi stared blankly at me. She opened her mouth but then closed it slowly.

"What is it?"

"Your…tone…The way you're speaking…"

"Yes?"

"It's…Wow…You sound like…Mother."

Well, that was quite preposterous. "How is that even possible?"

"A Chaos Dragon's soul is strong, and your soul is a shred of what it once was, so it makes sense that hers would be the dominant personality."

"So, what you're saying is that I am her? And not me?"

"I think you're still in there, but you're more Nimerah than you are Emera…if that makes sense."

I nodded. It would explain why I didn't feel like myself. I felt different. My thoughts weren't so scattered. My heart beat softly and in perfect rhythm. There was a sense of peace that filled my body, like through the right determination, I would be able to fix any problem. "And to even the balance, I must retrieve my soul."

"Yes. Which is another reason we must hurry. Nile's target was you, so it's safe to assume that any other Dragon that dares to enter this plane will also be here for you. We need to get you back to the living."

"Let us proceed, then." I followed Tamasvi as she turned down a different path that led to a small shed on the eastern side of the palace. It looked like a forgotten relic, weathered by time's relentless passage. Its gray stones bore the scars of eons, while moss and vines twisted and knotted along the walls. The windows reminded me of hollow sockets, peering out from beneath the creeping foliage. Yet, despite the decay, there was an undeniable allure to the ancient structure.

Tamasvi pushed open the large door made of pure obsidian stone and continued inside. I followed, unsure of what I was about to step into. But whereas the outside was old and unwelcoming, the inside was the opposite.

"Welcome to my private sanctuary." Inside, the atmosphere was of an otherworldly beauty like I'd never seen before. But I had seen it, in a way. After a few seconds, recognition flooded my mind. The interior of Tamasvi's sanctuary was adorned in dark hues, where the walls were decorated with intricate carvings of a nighttime scene. A large moon shone brightly over a woodland area where creatures grazed on the grass beneath their hooves. Soft candlelight flickered, casting dancing shadows that played across the smooth, obsidian surfaces. A sense of tranquility permeated the air. I breathed deeply, letting the peacefulness stir within my chest.

At the heart of her sanctuary was an altar, crafted from polished black marble with veins of silver and gold. Upon the altar were a basin and a dagger. Both were exquisite, made of moonstone.

Tamasvi grabbed a silk shawl from a secluded velvet chair in the corner of the sanctuary, its cushions a rich black velvet. My sister—again, it was so weird to think of her as such—wrapped the shawl around herself. She walked to the altar, gathered the basin and dagger, and sat on a rug next to a low table. She motioned for me to sit opposite her.

"Are you ready?"

"Does it matter?" I looked around the sanctuary. For what or whom, I didn't know. My eyes landed on a curious glass case. Again, my heart told me that I recognized it, but my mind knew that I didn't. "What's that?"

"Your baby chamber."

I almost choked on my own saliva. "My…what?"

"You were told that you were not born of this time…Weren't you?"

I turned away to hide my irritation. I thought I was past all the secrets. Closing my eyes, I breathed in and out a few times before looking at Tamasvi. "No."

"Hmm…Well, you were born just before the end of the war. I've been hiding you here ever since. Our mother wasn't in a long slumber because of the energy she expended during the war. She'd given birth to you, and after that, she used what remaining energy she had left to freeze you in time. Then she fell into an almost eternal slumber to regain her strength and her magic. I've been watching over you ever since, hence the rumors that I died."

I stared at the glass case. It looked somewhat like a coffin, but it was made purely of glass. Inside was a violet velvet cushion. It was a bed.

"Were you expecting an egg?" Tamasvi asked.

I threw my head back and laughed. And laughed. And laughed. Gods, it felt good to laugh again. "No. Well…Maybe? How did you wake me up?"

"My mother left a vial of her magic mixed with crushed starlight," Tamasvi said, the corner of her lips pulling into a warm smile. "Look. We are losing time as we speak. So, we must go now."

"But I…" My voice trailed off, swallowed by the gathering darkness as a swirling black whirlwind formed around us. The air grew thick and oppressive, weighing on my bones. My hair whipped wildly into my face, stinging my skin, and I clawed at it desperately to keep it from obscuring my vision. The wind roared in my ears as I tried and failed to see Tamasvi. I could barely see through the inky vortex, shadows and shapes causing me to become a bit disoriented. My heart pounded in my chest.

And then, as suddenly as it had started, the whirlwind ceased. The oppressive darkness lifted, leaving only silence behind. My eyes widened in bewilderment as I took in my surroundings. The world around me had transformed. I was no longer in Tamasvi's private sanctuary. Instead, it was replaced by a familiar landscape. I was back at the camp and beside the lake.

I took a step forward, my legs unsteady, and looked around me. "This is…impossible," I whispered to myself, trying to steady my racing thoughts. But deep down, I knew that in this place, the impossible had become all too real. "It's…"

"Your resting place."

I stood at the edge of the freshly turned earth. I lifted my chin and marveled at the early morning sky. It was a soft blend of pink, lavender, and peach hues, spreading across the horizon. Wispy clouds drifted lazily, catching the first rays of sunlight. The air was cool and refreshing, full of birdsong signaling the start of a new day. My heart swelled with a bittersweet mix of emotions. Then I looked before me to where we'd laid Rehema to rest. Next to her was my own grave.

Memories flooded my mind—laughter shared, tears shed, and moments cherished between us. Part of me wanted to cry, but the other part of me— my mother's part—remained calm.

Tamasvi stepped beside me.

"Wait."

"Nervous?"

"No. I just…I'm not sure what to do when I'm alive again. At the present, there is a war within me. I am me, but then I am not. How will I defeat Amram if I cannot contain this imbalance within my body?"

"You must focus and use this." She pulled out the dagger Nile had used.

"And how can a dagger defeat him if Calian's large sword won't do it?"

"Calian's blade will kill the body, not the soul. The dagger will do just that."

"And if he has no soul, he cannot be resurrected."

"Precisely."

I eyed her skeptically. "Why didn't we know about this dagger sooner?"

"I knew of the dagger. Three, actually. The one that killed Ragnar was destroyed during the war. One of them was lost, and I've been trying to find its location with no luck, so I stopped. Then, there's this one, which I've kept hidden all these years. Once your Dragonblood activated, I started searching for the lost dagger again…as did Valda. Thankfully, she hasn't found it either. I had planned on giving this one to you, but you died. It's been in my…What had Senna called it? Shed? Anyway, the blade is called Velarnal Soulzar, Velzar for short."

"Soul Reaper," I whispered. I knew the blade was not for calling rainbows and sunshine.

"When you face Amram, plunge it into his heart just as Calian's blade hits true. Calian's blade will kill the body…"

"And this dagger will reap Amram's soul."

"Exactly. Then you destroy the blade."

"And Amram is gone forever."

Tamasvi smiled. "Now, let's bring you back to the living."

I watched the trees sway gently in the breeze as I waited for Tamasvi to start. A feeling of dread filtered through my body. Would this work? What would happen if Tamasvi didn't make it? I shuddered at the thought and hoped for the best.

Tamasvi stood over my grave, the black dagger in her hand. We each stood barefoot on the soil, which was soft, as if the earth itself anticipated my resurrection to come. The goddess placed the dagger against her arm, its blade glinting in the moonlight. With a swift and precise motion, she drew a line across her skin, letting her blood flow freely onto the ground.

As the crimson liquid seeped into the earth, Tamasvi began to chant, using the ancient Dragonlanguage that I'd heard before. "Arthar, Emera. Mir'seklor. Varalor ol unkarnar vorlin. Rise, Emera. My sister. Savior of the unnamed world." She repeated the phrases over and over as she continued to let her blood spill from her vein. I wanted to reach out to her, to stop her from continuing. Her skin was becoming increasingly pale, and the light was fading from her eyes. But before I could say or do anything, my body began to fade, and the ground trembled beneath my feet. I held out my hands and shivered from the sight. I could see through them.

Suddenly, the ground shifted and cracked, and I watched as my lifeless body emerged from the grave. One last drop of Tamasvi's blood hit the ground, and she fell to her knees. I tried to step toward her, but I couldn't. Instead, I was pulled toward my body that remained suspended within the air. I closed my eyes and held my breath as my soul and body met. When I opened my eyes again, I was radiant and renewed, my eyes blazing with chaos power.

I landed gracefully on what was once my final resting place. A breeze whipped my hair across my face. Stunned, I grabbed a fistful of it and held it before my eyes. My hair was now violet. Gone were the wavy strands of fire red hair. They were replaced with an alluring shade of deep violet. I gasped. My hands were no longer covered in the pale skin I was used to. There was color now, a light golden hue, like I'd been bathing in sunlight for an entire afternoon. New scales, a mixture of vibrant colors just as I'd had before, ran up my arms. Two amulets were hanging around my neck. One was my mother's. The other? It had to be Amram's. I pushed the thought away. I'd figure out why I had it soon enough. Right now, I was elated. "We did it," I whispered. "We actually did it."

With an almost inaudible cry, I stepped forward to embrace Tamasvi, but I dropped my arms when I saw her lying cold and lifeless on the ground. I raced to her side, held out my hands, and channeled my healing magic. "Tamasvi, wake up. Please wake up." How many times would I have to see her like this?

The familiar golden glow flowed from my hands onto

Tamasvi's arm. The cut closed, but I knew she'd lost a lot of blood. I closed my eyes and forced as much healing magic as I could into my palms. The glow intensified, becoming warmer, and I moved my hands over Tamasvi's chest. I watched intently as color flooded back to her cheeks, and her breathing evened out. Her eyes fluttered open. She must have been a bit disoriented because she teleported away from me but only a few feet.

Tamasvi shook her head, and the tension in her shoulders lessened. "Thank you, Emera."

My magic rescinded from my fingers, and I held them out in front of me to inspect them. "I thought Amram took all of her magic?"

"He took her body, nothing else."

"Well, that was foolish of him." I twisted and turned, looking all around me. "So, what do we do now?" I asked.

Tamasvi looked up. "I go back to the Dragonplane."

"And I hope you will travel with me."

Tamasvi and I turned to see a man with a round stomach and flowing blue robes. His glasses sat perched on his nose, and his mouth widened in a warm smile.

"Priest Benigno!"

"Hello, Emera."

I walked quickly to him and—as if it were natural—took

his hands in mine. "What are you doing here?"

"A little birdie told me. Or you might refer to her as a queen."

Hestia.

As if right on cue, the priest finished his thought. "Queen Hestia had a vision of your resurrection. She knew that I tutored you and that I could be trusted," he puffed his chest out slightly, "so she located me to ensure someone was here to greet you. Someone she could trust not to reveal your resurrection to the enemy. The Dragongod Amram wouldn't think to keep track of me." He smiled. Now that I have found you, I am to escort you to the City of Anahita. Queen Hestia's vision was somewhat hazy, but she said I'd need to take you there.

Morwen. I would see her. "Okay, then."

"Well, that's it then," Tamasvi said as she smoothed out the layers of her black dress. "I will head back up and Emera will head south with you." She turned to me and clasped her hands around mine. "Emera, dear sister of mine, your path is a dangerous one. When you feel lost, remember to embrace your darkness without fear, for within the shadows lies the profound sanctuary of self-reflection."

"Wiser words were never spoken," Benigno whispered.

In the blink of an eye, Tamasvi was gone. I stood there,

not sure of what to do next. I gazed at the sky, taking in its beauty.

"I was told that your mate will soon be arriving in the City of Anahita as well," he said with a smile.

I looked at him, confusion sweeping through me. "Who?"

CHAPTER SIX

CALIAN

Just after the sun welcomed the day, my mother burst into the war room and woke me from my slumber. I lifted my head groggily from the table. A thin sticky string of drool clung to my lower lip, so I turned my head and hastily wiped it off with the sleeve of my black shirt.

"You could have knocked," I said quickly. Heat warmed my cheeks from the embarrassment.

"Good morning to you, too," my mother drawled with a smile. She crossed the room, sat down, and crossed her legs. Normally, her attire consisted of pants and a flowy top, but today, she opted for a red shimmering dress that was…What did the ladies say? Bejeweled? I shook my head. I wasn't up-to-date on any of the kingdoms' fashions. I was just fine in my riding pants and black cotton shirts.

My mother shifted her weight and propped her elbow on the armrest of the chair. "I've had a vision of great importance. I've called everyone here to discuss it."

I stood and stretched, leaning left then right, my arms over my head until the stiffness in my back receded. After a few pops from my spine, I felt better. "Okay," I replied. "Positive or negative."

"Maybe we should wait until the others arrive."

"Negative. Got it."

My stomach growled furiously, urging me to appease its demands for food. "What if we did it in the dining hall instead? I'm famished."

My mother uncrossed her legs and leaned forward. The jewels of her bodice tinkling together, mimicking the sounds of bells. "I'm not sure that's wise. The staff will be present."

"They serve, and then we send them out."

The door burst open, and Fin strolled into the room, chomping on an apple. My stomach growled again, begging for a bite. I ignored it.

I grimaced. "You're still here."

Fin leveled his gaze. "I'm still here. But not for long. I'm not staying."

Honestly, I didn't have it in me to argue. I wanted him to remain in the Kingdom of Fire and oversee the city's plans to prepare for an attack. But if it were me, I'd want to leave, too. I'd do everything in my power to get to Emera.

I turned my attention to the map on the table. Nothing had changed since the previous night. The City of Anahita still lay in pieces while the City of Tamasvi was poised for the taking. We still didn't have a plan as to how to defend the city from Amram and his army.

My father entered the room next with a plate full of food. My stomach twisted and turned in agony as soon as the aroma from the sweetened meat hit my nostrils. He held out the plate to me. "Take it. I figured you'd be hungry."

"Starving," I said all-too-eagerly. I snatched the plate and dug in like a wild animal.

My mother cleared her throat. "Manners, Calian."

"Yeah, Cal. Don't be disgusting," Fin said as he threw the apple core into the fireplace. "There's a god present." He flexed his arms, attempting to showcase his muscles. "As well as a queen and your father."

I rolled my eyes. A god my Dragonass.

Once I'd finished my meal, I discarded the plate on a nearby table. I'd deal with it later. At the moment, we had more pressing issues than me making sure it found its way to the kitchen.

"So, about this vision," I said to my mother. She started to say something, but the door opened once more. I threw my head back. "Who is it now?" I groaned, my patience wearing thin.

"I believe I have every right to hear this conversation."

When I first arrived at the palace, I was welcomed by an opinionated human woman with short curly black hair, dark eyes, and fire tattoos up and down her arms who called herself my adopted sister. At first, her brash attitude and disregard for manners had me reconsidering if I'd willingly call her my sister, but the more I was around General Shula Sunniva, the more I realized how much she was like my mother. She was fearless. She cared deeply for her people. She was headstrong. I couldn't wait for her to meet Erjon. A smile tugged at my lips from the thought.

Shula pushed past Fin and took a seat, her red fighting leathers almost blending in with the red velvet of the chair. When our eyes met, she raised one of her slender brows as if commanding me to sit. I rolled my eyes and pulled out a chair to her right. As I sat, my mother took the seat at the opposite end from Shula, while Fin and my father sat in the remaining two seats. We were quite the group: a god, a queen, a general, an assassin, and a so-called Dragon Slayer.

My life had changed so much since I was picked up off the streets by Anwir. The thought sparked an annoying question that had been plaguing my mind since I'd arrived in my parents' palace: How did I end up on the streets?

I locked eyes with my mother. Her eyes darted back and forth as she scanned my face. She knew my mind was troubled. I pushed aside all thoughts of my past and took note of Kedron's absence. "Where is Kedron?"

"He already left for the Kingdom of Darkness," Fin answered.

My mother straightened her back. "Please, come closer," she said, motioning toward me.

I eyed her curiously, but did as she said.

"I'm going to show you what I saw. Just as I did in the City of Ilmari."

"Wouldn't it be easier to just tell me?"

"You might see something useful," Shula remarked.

"Fair enough."

My mother turned in her chair as I scooted mine toward her. She reached her hand out slowly and pressed two fingers softly to my forehead. Like my first experience with a Dragonmeld, the room went pitch-black and eerily still.

When I opened my eyes, I stood next to the palace within the City of Endrit of the Kingdom of Light. I was outside beneath a bright blue sky decorated with puffy white clouds. Beyond the palace were rolling hills in all shades of green, covered in grass that swayed back and forth in the wind. I understood that Queen Leora had handed over her palace to Amram, but it just seemed comical considering a being of such corruption was hiding in a welcoming land of sunlight and open spaces. I suppressed the chuckle in my throat and approached the palace's gleaming walls.

The gate was wide open as priests meandered back and forth in prayer. The guards on foot didn't show any sign that they could see me, so I just walked on by. I checked behind me just to make sure I wasn't being followed. Nope. I was all clear.

I recognized the palace grounds from my previous visit with Anwir so long ago. There were bright Lightenion sunflowers everywhere. They were planted in configurations designed to symbolize a thousand suns.

Once through the gardens, I paused at the entrance of the palace. It was an architectural masterpiece, one of my favorite palaces in the unnamed world. Once I stepped inside, sunlight flooded through the windows, and I had to cover my eyes for a moment to adjust. How was it possible for the inside of the palace to be brighter than outside? I looked left and then right until an invisible thread of energy pulled me toward the throne room.

I continued down the main hallway. The marble floors glinted like molten gold and were so polished that I could see my reflection. Interesting how someone else couldn't see me, but I could. I was a ghost. A phantom.

The white stone walls were still as pristine as I'd remembered, adorned with tiny scale-like crystals designed to catch the sunlight and create a kaleidoscope of patterns across the marble floor below. Tall pillars supported thick archways that led to airy chambers filled with warmth and light. At least, that's how I remembered the chambers I'd stepped into when I'd visited with Anwir so long ago. With Amram being here, I assumed they would be musty and cold.

After passing several chamber doors, I finally stood outside the two large gold metal doors that led into the throne room. How did I get inside? Could I walk through walls? Only one way to find out. I took a few quick steps toward the entry doors…and almost fell backward once I ran into them.

So…No. I couldn't walk through walls or doors in a vision. Noted.

To my luck, the doors opened, and one of the queen's advisors walked out with a priest. I slipped through the doors and pressed my back against them once they closed. I first studied my surroundings in case something went wrong. I might have been a ghost so far, but I didn't know how Dragonmelds worked. Would I somehow become visible? Better to be safe than sorry.

I looked upward to see golden silk banners hanging from the ceiling. Their folds caught the sunlight and cast it to the white walls and marble below. Sitting on the golden throne wasn't Queen Leora, but Amram himself, with Anwir kneeling before him. Queen Leora was nowhere to be seen. My breath caught in my throat when my eyes landed on the dark figure before him.

"No," I whispered.

Kedron laid lifeless on the cold marble floor, dead.

With a cruel grin, Amram lifted his hand, looking at something that glinted violet. As the object shifted, my breath caught. His hand wrapped tightly around an amulet and with a force laced in anger, he squeezed until it shattered into countless fragments. Amram stood and stalked toward Kedron's body. The Dragongod callously tossed the broken pieces onto Kedron. "Thank you for returning my amulet to me."

My blood instantly boiled; heat flared beneath my skin. I opened my palms, but I couldn't produce any flames.

Amram turned to Anwir who remained on his knee. "Once

my daughter has ended the lives of both King Elderbrook and King Tynan, we will resurrect the remainder of my forces and unleash them upon human settlements."

"When will the general return?" Anwir asked, his eyes on the floor.

Pride shone on the god's face. "Within the week. She is regrouping her forces after her attack on the City of Anahita. By then, Nile will have gotten rid of both Emera and her mother once and for all."

My heart skipped a beat. I didn't know what he meant by 'ending them both once and for all.' My mother had promised I would see Emera again. Panic flooded my body. The beating of my heart quickened, and I felt my face flush. What if my mother was wrong? What would we do? We needed Emera's magic to ignite the sword. I needed my mate.

Anwir stood. "Then we will eliminate the humans quickly."

Amram chuckled, low and cruelly. He placed his hand on Anwir's shoulder and squeezed. His voice, cold and calculated, cut through the air as he all but whispered. "I don't want to simply end their lives, Anwir, I want them to suffer."

Then the god looked ahead and stared straight into my

eyes, into my soul. I looked to my left and then to my right. Sure enough, Amram was looking right at me. He saw me. His eyes narrowed. "I want them to know fear."

I swallowed hard and watched Amram and Anwir disappear into the darkness while the vision faded away to black.

Back in the war room, I slowly opened my eyes and steadied my breathing. The eyes of everyone else were on me.

"So?" Fin asked.

"We must hurry," I all but whispered. I swallowed the lump that clogged my throat. "Amram's forces will march on the City of Tamasvi within the week."

Shula stood abruptly. "We must prepare our own forces for battle. We will surely be next." I had to hand it to her. Maybe it was my lack of experience in dealing with them, but I figured most humans would cower from the idea of a Dragon attacking. Shula didn't. It seemed that her bravery knew no bounds. Maybe Emera was right. Maybe they were all worth fighting for. Until now, I'd only been concerned with stopping Amram and preventing the deaths of the people I loved. Maybe it was time for me to do better. Be better.

"Cal?" Fin's voice jolted me from my thoughts. It seemed

that lately, I withdrew inside my head more and more.

"Hmm?" I stood and made my way toward the map. I had no intention of studying it. I just couldn't look at everyone at the moment. They demanded my guidance, and I didn't know what to do. I fixed my gaze on the intricate lines that marked the territories of the kingdoms. My mother joined me at the map, her brow furrowed in deep concentration.

"You need to leave," she said, her voice low but firm. "Emera's resting place holds the key we need. The third amulet, the one I assume Amram was holding, is the one you buried with her."

Fin's brows furrowed. "I thought you buried Nimerah's amulet with Emera."

"I buried her with both."

"Even more reason you need to leave, my son."

My fingers tightened around the edge of the table, causing my knuckles to turn white from the pressure. "I gathered that," I murmured. "But I can't leave. Not now, not when the fate of our kingdom hangs in the balance."

Mother reached out, placing a reassuring hand on my shoulder. "You're not alone in this, my son," she said, her voice steady. "We'll stand by you, no matter what."

I shook my head; my confidence faltering under the weight of their expectations. "What if something goes wrong?" I turned and stared at the others.

Shula's voice cut through the silence like a knife, her tone sharp and commanding. "That's why we need Kedron to spy on Amram," she declared, her eyes blazing with determination. "We cannot afford to let Amram retrieve the amulet before we do."

My mouth gaped open. "You knew?"

Fin stood from the table and leaned against the wall behind him. "Your mother gave us a little summary of the events while you were…wherever you were."

"Then you know what happens to Kedron. I will not send him there to die." I didn't care that Hestia was right. Even if Amram reclaimed the amulet, making their chances of victory slim at best, I would not command Kedron to forfeit his life.

No one moved. No one made a sound. "I will go to Emera's resting place," I huffed. "But I am not having Kedron spy on Amram."

"Very well," my father said. He'd been so quiet the entire time. "Please, come sit back down."

My mother and I both took our seats at the table once again.

As the severity of the vision settled upon me, my mind raced with military tactics and strategies. We needed allies.

"We need Anahita," I all but yelled. "Her knowledge and power could be invaluable to us."

My father's eyes widened. "Anahita? You've met my sister?"

Fin crossed his arms. "If it weren't for the history lesson Amram laid on us, I wouldn't have guessed you were siblings. You're so…outgoing and manly…and she's so…"

My father's eyes flashed. "She's what?"

Fin gulped. "A very lovely and welcoming woman," he added quickly.

Hestia's eyes narrowed in thought, her lips pursed in consideration. "Don't let him fool you, Fintan," my mother said. "Vukan is well aware of how secretive and rebellious Anahita is. But there is no time to analyze one's character. Calian is right. Anahita would be very useful to us. However, he shouldn't go alone." Her gaze drifted to my father. "You should accompany him."

Vukan's brow furrowed in concern, his gaze flickering between my mother and me. "But what about you?" he asked his wife with a worried tone. "I can't leave you here alone, Hestia."

My mother offered him a reassuring smile, though the anxiety in her eyes betrayed her own fears. She took a quick breath and straightened in her seat, manifesting whatever bravery she could muster. "The Kingdom of Fire can handle Amram's army if it shows," she assured him, her voice unwavering. "But I don't believe it's going to happen yet. Amram either lacks the strength to annihilate the entire world, or he's up to something else entirely. Which is where I think the amulet comes in."

Reluctantly, Vukan nodded. He leaned forward and clasped his hands on the table. "Very well," he conceded. "I'll go with Vasuman…Er…I mean, Calian."

I accepted Vukan's offer, knowing that our journey would mean him being apart from my mother again.

"I'm going with you," Fin interjected.

I leaned back and crossed my arms over my chest. "I thought you were going to Morwen."

"It'll be a small detour."

I stared at him. He'd been insistent on returning to his mate. What changed?

Fin smiled. "You need my help persuading Anahita. I can be quite convincing."

I snorted and waited for a better answer.

My friend sighed. "Morwen would want me to. Without Emera, you're the best chance we have at defeating Amram. Leaving the safety of the palace exposes you to other threats. You need all the protection you can get."

Shula slapped her hands on the table. "Now that that's settled," she said loudly, "I have something to show you before you leave.

One after the other, we exited the room. My parents headed toward the throne room while Shula motioned for Fin and me to follow her. I didn't know if I should be scared or intrigued. Knowing Shula, it was probably a bit of both.

AMRAM

I settled upon Queen Leora's pathetic excuse of a throne. My fingers curled around the armrests as the shadows I commanded writhed and danced around me. Anwir stood several feet to my left, picking at his teeth with the makeshift toothpick he'd created from a bone. I winced at his disgusting display.

"Can't you do that elsewhere? It will be dinner soon, and I am, unsurprisingly, losing my appetite."

His back straightened, and he deposited the toothpick in the pocket of his green shirt. The same color that matched his horrendous green scales.

"Of course." Anwir glanced at me tentatively, casting a wary look in his eyes. There was a hint of an unspoken question lingering on his lips.

I rolled my eyes. "What is it, Anwir? You've never held your tongue before. Why would you start now?"

Anwir approached me with a respectful bow. "What is our next move? With the Kingdoms of Air and Water in ruins and their monarchs dead, surely, we can now focus our efforts on the Kingdom of Darkness."

I nodded. "Indeed, Anwir. Those siding with Emera's cause will tremble before us, and their feeble attempts at resistance will be crushed beneath the weight of my power."

"And what of the Kingdom of Fire?"

I narrowed my eyes out of frustration. "The Kingdom of Fire remains a thorn in our side," I hissed. "But their time will come soon enough."

Anwir nodded. "And then the humans."

"Yes. Once we've taken the kingdoms, we shall unleash Dragonhell upon the humans, and none shall be able to stand in our way."

He remained silent for a couple minutes.

"Get on with it."

"Why do you seek the amulet?"

I paused, debating on how much I wanted to share. Despite Anwir's annoying persona, he was a loyal servant. "The amulet is not merely valuable, Anwir. It is the key to my very long existence."

Anwir's eyes widened, curiosity sparking within them. "I'm not sure what you mean."

"Of course you don't." I leaned forward. "My soul, Anwir. A piece is bound to the amulet. As long as it exists, my soul is immortal."

"Yet you were killed."

"My body, yes. But not my soul. As long as there is a body to return to, I can live for all eternity."

"I have not heard of an amulet with such capacity or your long-lasting lifespan. I assume you did not tell Ragnar or Nimerah?"

A sinister grin curled upon my lips. "It was my contingency plan, dear Anwir." I thought a bit more about his question. "And also, because Nimerah turned out to be a traitorous Dragonbitch."

Anwir narrowed his eyes slightly.

I waved my hand dismissively. "Oh, please, Anwir. You've said worse, I'm sure."

Anwir shifted uncomfortably. His confidence always seemed to wane in my presence. "And do you have an idea of where your amulet is?"

I did not, and knowing Nimerah, she'd probably tucked it away in some obscure place in case she died.

"Sire?"

Ah, yes. Anwir. "Not yet, my friend. But once I do, I will disclose the location to you." That was a lie. I had no intention of telling him. Power was not meant to be shared. It was meant to be seized, to be wielded by those strong enough to claim it. Anwir was not strong enough.

Anwir seemed pleased with my response. "Are there any other amulets?" he asked. His tone feigned innocence, but he no doubt wanted an amulet for himself.

"Yes. But my amulet is the only one of importance. The others do not contain the souls of Ragnar or Nimerah. Now, leave me. I must think."

Anwir nodded, and as he slithered away, a smirk twisted my lips. Sleazy creature, he was. Always scheming, always plotting to raise his status. Little did he know, he was merely a pawn, a disposable piece in my game. I reclined upon the throne, the shadows embracing me like old friends. The path to victory, a world of only the strongest Dragonborn with humans for slaves, was paved with the blood of those who dared to oppose me. And with each step, I grew stronger than ever before.

CHAPTER SEVEN

CALIAN

We exited the palace into the midday heat. The sun blazed overhead, causing my fire magic to hum beneath my skin. Like calls to like, I guessed. Most of the Kingdom of Fire was illuminated by the sun. Parts of the kingdom were barren wastelands with rocky terrain, but most of it was covered with golden sands and the occasional shimmering oasis. Despite the sun appearing as if it were overbearing with sweltering rays of heat, it was quite mild. I'd break a sweat just as easily in the Kingdom of Earth as I would here in the Kingdom of Fire.

The City of Vukan was, as I'm sure Emera would phrase it, a shimmering jewel nestled in the heart of the kingdom.

When I'd first arrived, I'd marveled at the glistening golden walls that encircled the city. They were decorated with intricate carvings and shimmering mosaics that depicted Fire Dragons and warriors—human and Dragonborn. After setting foot inside the walls, my brain frantically searched for memories of the sprawling city, including my time as a thief within its labyrinth of narrow streets and bustling markets.

I stared past the soldiers into the city beyond. The architecture was—and I wouldn't dare utter the word to Fin—breathtaking. It was a blend of cultural influences of the people in the kingdom. There were graceful arches and ornate domes. The buildings were crafted from what appeared to be sandstone and marble. The mosaic pieces of various hues caught the light and cast patterns on the ground. The children were fascinated by them.

It wasn't until I'd reached a particular market called the Grand Bazaar that I'd paused. The innermost market square was home to merchants who sold their wares amidst the scent of exotic spices and the sound of lively music. People would come from near and far to find everything from fine silks and rare jewels to enchanted artifacts and mystical talismans, each item imbued with the magic of the desert. Anger flared within my chest at that moment. Despite how much my affection for her was growing, Hestia Sunniva had let me wander the streets, begging for food and stealing from merchant carts. And for what? Even now, as I followed my sister to wherever the Dragonhell she was leading us, a seed of resentment for my mother remained planted in my Dragonsoul. She still hadn't explained why she cast me out of my home.

We continued on, eventually reaching the sprawling military grounds adjacent to the palace. Fin and I followed Shula while she nodded occasionally at soldiers who practiced sparring. Most of the sparring was hand-to-hand combat, but there were other pairs wielding their magic.

Shula led us past the numerous sparring rings—truly, there were too many to count— and down a narrow path past all the barracks. She kept turning her head to make sure we were following, a sly smile adorning her face. I snorted each time she peeked back, growing more impatient with every step. We finally slowed down at a carefully guarded and fortified enclosure. Fin and I glanced at each other; a feeling of unease settled within the pit of my stomach.

"Welcome to Wolf's Hold," Shula said. She spread her arms wide and twisted her body, showing off the enclosure like it was her most prized possession. "This strategic location serves as the training and breeding grounds for the formidable Lightenion war wolves of our kingdom."

Fin started choking on the piece of jerky he'd been chewing on. I clapped my hand on his back hard enough to dislodge the meat from his throat.

"You…Wolves…What?" he managed between coughs.

"Come see for yourself," Shula said with a wink. She faced the two guards and nodded. Without a word, they opened the gate. She turned back and faced me directly. "You might want to be careful, Deceiver."

I felt my brows furrow from confusion. "Deceiver?"

Fin stroked his beardless chin. "Isn't that what the wolves called Emera when they attacked her?"

Shula shook her head and pointed at me. "No, they attacked him. They've been waiting for Emera. According to them, they were forced to fight for Amram against their will during the war. Regardless of what you might believe, the wolves have a strong moral compass and a sense of justice. It's why I love them. It's also why they refuse to align with evil."

"A moral compass?' Fin asked, deadpan.

Shula threw Fin an exhausted look. "Yes. The wolves saw Amram's actions as inherently wrong and at first, refused to bow to him. But through his magic, they were forced to. When I moved here, a group of them moved with me, seeing an opportunity to escape. More soon followed. It's quite impressive, considering they also value their independence, but they're waiting for revenge. Many of their pack were killed during the war."

"What does that have to do with me?" I asked.

"They don't trust you. Regardless of you killing Amram, you were Vasuman during the war. They think you're deceiving the gods by pretending to be Captain Westbow instead of the Dragon Slayer. They see it as dishonorable."

Fin chuckled. "Wolves have honor?"

I ignored him and continued. "It's not like I chose to forget my past."

Shula held up her hands in surrender. "Their words, not mine."

Fin rolled his eyes. "This is all ridiculous. Wolves can't speak."

Shula smiled. "To you, maybe." Then she turned around, and we entered. It was an unusual site to behold. Spacious training yards and sturdy barracks accommodated the needs of both the soldiers and the wolves. We stopped once we'd gotten to a vast training arena, ringed by elevated platforms where higher-ranking officers could observe the wolves in action.

"It's an arena," Fin whispered in awe.

"Appears to be." The arena was vacant, so I took a slow walk round it, inspecting everything from the floor covered in fine sand—ideal for the wolves to dig their claws into—to the thick metal gates that no doubt led to their cages.

"What do you do here?" I asked Shula without so much as a backward glance. I needed to see how sturdy the doors were. Could they really keep Lightenion Wolves barricaded?

"Typical training. Mock battles, Agility exercises. Under the supervision of their riders, of course."

I turned abruptly.

Fin whipped his head to Shula. "Riders?"

"Of course. How do you think we ride into battle?"

Fin scrunched his nose. "Oh, I don't know. Horses? Like normal soldiers?"

Shula laughed. "Oh, Fin. We're far from normal here."

Fin scanned the arena before adding, "Clearly."

"Come on, you haven't seen the best part."

We exited the training arena and headed left toward rows of shelters constructed of thick metal.

Fin paused. "Is that…where they sleep?" His voice was barely a whisper.

"It is, but they aren't in there. The riders went out for a stroll today."

Fin looked to the sky. "Oh, a stroll. Of course. Why not? It's such a pleasant day."

I chuckled to myself.

Shula ignored Fin and walked toward one of the shelters. "Want to see inside?" Without waiting for an answer, she opened the gate. I leaned inside. Each enclosure was spacious with ample room for the wolves to rest and recuperate between training sessions.

"The trainers themselves are a skilled and dedicated group. I selected them myself. I wouldn't dare go riding with anyone that I didn't believe could handle a wolf."

I swore Fin was about to pass out. "You are a rider?"

"Yes."

"But…you're…How do I put this delicately? You're…" He gestured his hands toward her.

"I'm what?"

"A human," I interjected, rolling my eyes. "How do you keep yourself safe?"

Shula put her hand on her hips. "The bond between a rider and a wolf goes beyond mere training; it is a partnership."

"That doesn't answer my question."

"I can speak to my wolf."

"How is that possible," I asked. "You're not a Dragonborn, let alone an heir to Anahita."

Shula crossed her arms and gave me a look like it was obvious. "Mother did it."

"Ah, of course," Fin sighed while rolling his eyes. "The all-powerful Hestia Sunniva."

Shula advanced toward him, "You say her name with that tone, and I'll have you meet Orcus in a manner which you would find grossly unpleasant."

Fin backed away with his hands up. "Down, girl! Down!"

My palm met my face before I could stop it. Fin was insufferable at times. "He's just joking, Shula. You have to admit, it does sound far-fetched…" I glanced at Fin and mouthed the word no to keep him from using far-fetched as another dog joke. He grinned but kept quiet. "As I was saying, it does seem a little too easy for mother to whip up a potion, and you can speak to dogs…um…I mean wolves." Fin cackled. "Shut it, Fin!"

"You're making this too easy," he quipped.

Shula remained quiet for a moment, carefully selecting her next words. "If you tell Mother that I exposed her secret, I will feed you to Orcus. Do you understand?"

"Aw. I love the family bonding moment. So precious."

"Shut it Fin!" both Shula and I yelled simultaneously.

Fin plopped down on the ground. I looked back at Shula. There was a war in her eyes. Should she tell me? Should she not? At least the idea of betraying our mother's confidence weighed heavily on her and that she took our mother's feelings into consideration.

The distant howls of the wolves met our silence. Shula looked behind her then back at me. She'd made her decision. "Calian," she began, but I held up a hand to stop her.

As if reading my thoughts, Fin interjected. "Shouldn't we go somewhere more private? Y'know? For the private conversation. Emphasis on the word private."

Shula considered Fin's words. "Come."

We followed her to another shelter just south of the wolves' training arena. It was made of the same thick metal like the other shelters, but it was larger. Without hesitation, Shula placed her palm on the door and said, "Vylar." After a deafening click, Shula turned the handle and entered the shelter.

Fin and I entered, but we both stopped abruptly. Shock rippled through my body, igniting my fire magic. Beside me, Fin shifted uneasily, his gaze fixed on the large, sleeping form of Orcus, Shula's wolf. The massive white Lightenion wolf was nestled on a voluminous plush pillow just a few feet away. Despite its peaceful slumber, the wolf's presence made both of us nervous.

"Meet Orcus," my sister whispered. I took a quiet step

forward. Then another. Orcus was massive, his fur a bright shimmering white that appeared silver when the light of the shelter hit him just right.

Fin turned to me, his voice barely a whisper. "Will he eat us?" he asked, eyes never leaving the wolf.

"It's safe," Shula assured him, though she kept her voice low, not wanting to disturb the beast. "Come. Sit. Let's talk."

We sat at a nearby table. I eyed the room slowly, taking in as much as possible. Orcus's shelter wasn't a cage, it was a small room. There was a bed for Shula, a circular table with four chairs, and a small fireplace.

Shula took notice of me and asked, "You thought it would be all stone floor and dark shadows. All riders have a bed inside the shelters. It helps us bond. The other shelters are smaller because, well, the wolves are smaller. Orcus is the alpha.

"Yeah, that part is obvious," I murmured. As I watched, the wolf twitched in its sleep, a low growl rumbling from its throat. I saw Fin's hand instinctively reach for his daggers. I placed a reassuring hand on his shoulder. If Orcus woke up suddenly, he probably wouldn't appreciate daggers being pointed at him.

Without taking my eyes off of Orcus, I joined my sister

who had already taken a seat at the table. Fin did the same although he placed himself the furthest away from the sleeping wolf.

"Our mother was born in the Kingdom of Light. She is not from this place, and she's gone back to visit many times over the decades. In fact, she knew my parents. When they died, she traveled back to the kingdom to retrieve me. She officially adopted me just a few months after I turned five. Anyway, that's beside the point."

At that moment, the wolf stirred, lifting its head and opening one of his piercing gold eyes, and for a moment, I felt as if it were looking into my Dragonsoul. Then, with a soft huff that seemed almost like amusement, he laid his head back down, closing his eyes.

Fin let out a breath he seemed to have been holding. "Just a big pet," he said quietly as if attempting to reassure himself that he was safe. "Just a big, fluffy, human-killing pet."

"You're one of the bravest men I've ever known. You've fought Dragons for crying out loud. But that," I pointed at Orcus. "That scares you?"

"I had a bad experience."

"But it's just—"

Fin's eyes flashed with warning. "I had...a bad...experience."

"Okay, okay." I turned my attention to Shula. "So, mother is not of this kingdom. What does that have to do with anything?"

"For starters, it explains why you have such potent healing powers. That comes from her line."

"Her line?" Fin asked. "She's not a Dragonborn."

"Not technically, no. Her Dragonblood never activated, which is why she's a sorceress. But the Dragonmagic is still there in her blood. It was passed on to Calian."

"Still doesn't explain the wolves."

Shula sighed in annoyance. My lack of patience with her was wearing thin. "When she married your father, she was given a gift—a kernel of chaos magic."

I blinked slowly in disbelief. "Chaos magic?"

Fin leaned back in his seat. "It would explain a whole lot, Cal."

"It explains everything," Shula replied.

Fin sat up straight and angled his body toward me. "You have a primary power and two secondary powers. You're the descendent of Vukan, so the primary power being fire makes sense as does the shapeshifting. But healing? On top of that, you're stronger and faster than an average Dragonborn. It's obvious that the chaos magic that runs through Hestia's veins was passed onto you. Gods, Cal! I bet you have other powers. If healing is another secondary, then you have to have light magic."

"Our mother's magic is what allows me and the others to communicate with the wolves, to form bonds with them."

I could feel my brows furrowing as I struggled to grasp the enormity of what this all meant. I ran my hand through my hair, trying to come to terms with my abilities being rooted in chaos magic. "But why? Why would our mother be given chaos magic as a gift?"

"To protect you," Shula explained, her voice firm. "To ensure that you were born of chaos and forever shielded from harm."

Fin whistled softly. "Ragnar knew all along. He knew you were destined to bring down Amram. But you needed chaos magic to do it."

I shook my head. "I can't defeat him alone. I need…" My voice trailed off. I needed Emera.

From outside Orcus's shelter, the howling of wolves grew louder. We all turned to Orcus. With a contented sigh, the wolf began to stir, its nose twitching. Orcus's eyes opened slowly, and with a leisurely stretch, he extended his front paws forward, arching his back. A low growl—reminiscent of a human groan—escaped his throat.

Now fully awake and invigorated, the wolf rose to its feet.

He was massive. He padded across the room in what seemed like only two strides—he was that large—with a sense of purpose, ready to pass a final judgment on whether Fin and I were friend or foe. I held my breath as I watched Orcus's muscles tense, preparing himself to attack at the first sign of danger. He stopped beside Shula, and with a tentative growl and narrowed eyes, lowered himself into a defensive crouch, curling his lips back to reveal sharp white teeth. He analyzed us for a few short minutes. He must have been satisfied with his assessment because his eyes softened.

Shula reached out her hand to stroke the wolf's fur coat. Her gentle caress assured Orcus that we meant no harm. Shula and Orcus looked at each other; it was obvious they were speaking telepathically.

"What is he saying?" Fin asked.

"That you smell like day old roadkill."

Fin sniffed his armpits while I rolled my eyes.

"You said that you're able to bond with the wolves because of Mother. How?"

Beyond the shelter walls, howls erupted, loud enough to rattle the small windows and make the hair on the back of my neck stand up. The pack had arrived back in the enclosure.

"She concocted a potion containing a drop of her blood

that a rider takes before attempting to bond with a wolf," Shula said with a smile. "She says some fancy words, and that's it. I mean, it took her awhile to get the potion to do what she wanted, but after some trial and error, it finally worked."

"She needs to be careful," Fin said. "Tampering with chaos magic. I doubt any good can come from that."

Shula's eyes flashed. "We needed protection. So, she did what any other monarch would do. She found a way to give her kingdom a fighting chance. We've been smuggling in wolves ever since."

I let out a hefty sigh. "How does it work?"

Shula smiled. "Let me show you." She stood and exited the shelter with Orcus following closely behind her.

Fin and I exchanged looks but left the shelter after the wolf. We walked back toward the training arena. As we got closer, we could see wolves of various shapes and sizes entering their shelters. Instead of following their wolves, the riders closed the metal doors and made their way to the training arena.

"You are in for a treat!" Shula exclaimed over her shoulder. "You are going to witness the bonding ritual."

"What happens if a bonding fails?" Fin called to her.

Her silence was telling.

*   *   *

It took no time for us to be seated on the upper balcony. Orcus stood guard at a closed gate as we looked down into the arena. Before we'd taken our seats, Shula had explained that should a bond fail, then there was a chance the wolf would attack. If so, Orcus would step in and prevent any unfortunate deaths from occurring. Fin wasn't so sure about the whole ordeal, as made apparent by the "fingers crossed" comment he'd made.

A soldier stepped forward into the arena, his gaze sweeping across the open area until it fell on Orcus. The wolf nodded and stepped away from the large gate he guarded, and it opened. A wolf of gray and white fur sauntered through. It approached the soldier, and their eyes locked. A look of serenity befell the soldier's face as if the wolf called to his soul.

Fin's eyes widened. "Where is his armor?"

"Conleth doesn't need it."

Fin and I exchanged looks as if to say, "Yeah right."

Shula had also mentioned that the journey ahead of the soldier and wolf was one of mutual respect and understanding, so I kept that in mind as I watched the bonding unfold.

Conleth had come prepared, bearing an offering that symbolized his willingness to enter into the bond. With careful, calculated steps, the soldier placed the offering at the midpoint between him and the wolf and retreated a few steps. It was a piece of hunted prey. The wolf approached the offering and nuzzled it before sniffing and licking it. Once satisfied with the offering, the wolf devoured it.

Fin snorted beside me. "Always a smart idea to appeal to one's stomach."

Shula leaned toward me. "This is the beginning of respect, of observing and learning from one another, of finding common ground," she said in a hushed tone. I didn't know why everyone was talking so quietly. We were well above the arena.

The rest of the crowd watched, enraptured, as Conleth withdrew a small vial from his pocket.

"Conleth will take the portion Mother created. The wolf has already taken it."

I looked at my sister.

She answered with a sly smile. "It was in the offering."

The arena held its breath as the potion gradually took effect within both Conleth's and the wolf's bodies. A visible aura enveloped the pair, linking them with strands of light that weaved around and through them. As the aura grew brighter and brighter, the wolf and Conleth drew closer to one another, their eyes open but seeing beyond the physical. When he reached the wolf, Conleth held out his hand. The wolf grazed Conleth's fingers with its nose before stretching its legs forward and lowering its chest, bowing before him.

"It is done," Shula said, standing, as the other riders burst into applause.

"That's it?" Fin asked.

Shula nodded. "That's it. See? No accidental deaths today."

Fin smiled, but it didn't reach his eyes. "Lucky us."

I slapped Fin on the back. "I think you should be next."

Fin's face paled.

"Kidding," I said just as my father joined us. He nodded at me. It was time to leave.

CHAPTER EIGHT

CALIAN

After a day of furious flying, my father landed just outside the dirt path leading into the village of Khaosar.

"*Khaosar* means Chaos in the old tongue," my father mused. That's exactly what my mother had said when we'd first come upon the hidden town.

We didn't waste time as we hurried to the bridge. Before stepping onto the worn-down stones, my father stopped. I knew what he was thinking. Were we safe? Why did it appear abandoned? But I knew better. I waved him forward with a slight smile. Just like the first time I'd stepped onto the bridge, everything around us changed. The town had remained the same since our last visit. It was alive with people bustling around. A light breeze brought with it the laughter of children playing in the streets. The crystal-clear lake still glittered beneath the sun's rays. Most of the crops were there, but some had been harvested.

We strolled beneath the gated archway into the town. My father marveled at the buildings, commenting on the immaculate white stone and intricate carvings.

"There's so much history here," he said softly. "I've missed so much."

"But no more," I assured him. "Now, you'll help usher in a new future."

"They've hidden themselves from the outside world. Very smart."

I smirked at his comment. I wondered what their reunion would be like. Brother and sister reunited once again. Would there be tears? Laughter? Something else?

We continued past the quaint homes. I wished Emera was with us. She would love the swirling patterns of the ivy-covered walls and the colorful flowers poking out of the bushes that lined the streets. Unlike our last visit, the townspeople smiled at the sight of Fin and me. Or maybe it was because they recognized my father. He did stand out in a crowd.

"Did you receive such a welcome when you were here last?"

"No," Fin said and laughed, "Because what normal person would cross that bridge into a run-down looking village?"

The god chuckled. "Fair point."

Father's eyes widened once we set foot on the black stone roads of the central square. He dipped his hand into the fountain before pausing to admire the statues of Nimerah and Ragnar. His gaze lingered on Ragnar for a few minutes before he turned to me. It could have been the glistening of the sun, but I was positive a tear sparkled in his eye.

"Almost there," I said. But instead of turning toward the inn, I headed east. With my father close behind, we weaved in and out of a couple of alleyways, trying to follow our previous route. It took me a few missed turns and backtracking, but I'd finally found the large wooden door marked with ancient runes and symbols. Before I could knock on the door, someone cleared their throat from behind.

I turned and greeted the Goddess of Water. "Hello, Anahita."

"Nephew. Human." She gave Fin and I curt nods, but her eyes remained focused on my father. I winced. Thick tension was building inside of Anahita, but how the Dragonhell did I know that? I mean, I saw it plainly from the strain of her face, but I also felt it—the animosity growing within her.

The sensation was foreign, and I had no clue how to rid myself of it. I closed my hands into tight fists, forcing my nails to dig into my palm. A warm liquid broke through my skin as I struggled to remain calm and take control of what was happening. Then it finally dawned on me that this was what Emera felt when she tapped into her empathic abilities. A distant memory flashed before me of the time she'd felt the pain and suffering of the soldiers who'd died for her. She had doubled over in agony. I only had a kernel of chaos magic, and I was ready to throw myself to the ground and gasp for air. She was stronger than I'd given her credit for.

And no wonder Erjon chose to suppress his empathic abilities. This was torture.

My father's fiery eyes flickered uneasily as he gazed at his sister, anticipation mingling with apprehension in his eyes. He wasn't sure of what to say or do, that much I could tell.

Anahita crossed her arms, over her dark blue leather vest, the same color as her leather pants. She took a few steps forward, her black boots creating deep imprints in the dirt. Even the jingling of her silver boot buckles were menacing. Although she was moving closer, her expression remained somewhat hidden by the shadows of her long wavy hair that framed her face. As she drew nearer, the wind whipped the blue curls behind her, exposing her eyes. They locked onto my father's, and I saw a mix of emotions playing across her face—relief, disbelief, and beneath it all, a simmering anger. She closed the remainder of the gap between them, and without warning, she lunged forward, her fist connecting with my father's cheek in a swift blow. He staggered back, stunned.

"I was told you were dead, yet here you are. Explain yourself," she demanded.

Fin leaned in and whispered. "You'd think she'd be a bit happier."

My father's eyes softened, but he didn't reply. He was carefully contemplating his response.

Anahita took another swing, but the God of Fire was ready. He leaned away before her knuckles could split open his lip. "I mourned for you!" she thundered. She took another swing. Then another, barely missing each time.

Finally, my father spoke, his words tempered by remorse and understanding. "And for that, I am sorry. It wasn't by choice, Anahita," he replied, his voice tinged with sorrow. "I was imprisoned in a darkness beyond my control."

"Valda captured him and tortured him beneath Ragnar's palace," I translated.

The Goddess of Water fully acknowledged my presence,

throwing me a look that thanked me for the explanation. She looked at my father and paused, her demeanor softening slightly as she absorbed his words. "That doesn't change the pain I endured in your absence."

I snorted. I couldn't help it. Was she really going to blame my father for something out of his control? "He was captured, imprisoned, and tortured for decades. Your anguish is no comparison."

The angry facade fell, and tears formed in her eyes. My father cautiously reached out to her. With a hesitant sigh, she accepted his hand. He pulled her in, and they stood for a few minutes in a deep embrace.

I cleared my throat, causing them to part. Anahita wiped a tear from her rosy cheek. "What do you need?"

"We need your help."

*　　　*　　　*

"For the last time…No."

We'd been at it for hours. Although we were deep within her hidden room, I knew the sun was setting. It was time for us to leave for The Kingdom of Water.

My father sighed deeply. "And for the millionth time, your people will be fine."

Anahita leaned back in her chair and crossed her arms in front of her. "You cannot guarantee that. Hell, Vukan! You're the most powerful of all the elemental gods, and you were captured! I cannot put their lives at risk."

Fin's eyes narrowed as he unfolded his arms and pushed off from the wall he'd been leaning against. "Yet you'll put the rest of humanity at risk without hesitation? What kind of leader is that?"

Anahita whipped her head toward him. "I never said I was a leader," she said, her voice low.

I stood and waved my arms around. "Look around you! This entire town exists because of you. Humans live here They rely on you…"

She interrupted me. "Which is why I must stay."

"Which is why you must show them how to be compassionate for others! How do you think they will feel watching the world burn around them while they are safe inside this bubble?"

"Let's keep our voices down," my father warned. "We are not here to force Anahita to do anything she doesn't want to."

Fin gawked at him. "Excuse me?" He pointed at my aunt. "She's a powerful Dragongoddess, and you're not going to make her help humans like me?"

"I can't make her *because* she is a powerful goddess. And look at her. You try to make her do anything." A smile tugged at the corner of his lips.

I shook my head in disbelief then locked eyes with Anahita. "I can't believe this. The whole world will burn, but you'll do nothing to extinguish the flames."

"How poetic, nephew." Then she pursed her lips. She was done with the conversation.

"You're a coward." The words were out before I could stop them. The goddess's eyes widened in surprise, as if I'd just slapped her. She opened her mouth to respond, but she then closed them. "Yeah. That's what I thought." I turned my back on her and left.

Being outside didn't help my mood. The sun had already dipped down behind the trees, making way for the first stars. The air had started to cool, making the crickets and grasshoppers come out to play their songs. Even the townspeople had lit their candles to illuminate their homes in preparation for nightfall. We lost time arguing with a scared Dragon for nearly half the day.

A deafening roar echoed around me. "Speaking of Dragons," I said to no one. While I twisted and turned, straining my neck to see how close it was, Vukan, Fin, and Anahita burst through the wooden door. All three of them wore a different expression on their faces. My father's brows were furrowed with confusion. Anahita's eyes were wide with panic. Fin cursed, clearly annoyed.

I glanced back at Anahita. "I take it you've never heard a Dragon that close before?"

"No. We must get to the bridge just before the barrier."

The Dragon roared again.

"Yeah. Uh…I don't think that's coming from the sky," Fin commented. My father and I nodded in agreement.

We took off in a dead sprint. My father, Fin, and I kept pace with Anahita, weaving in and out of streets and alleys until we were back on the familiar road that led to the bridge. We looked onward through the barrier. A giant purple form emerged in the distance. A sliver of hope bloomed within my chest. Maybe it was Emera. I'd give anything for it to be my mate and not whom I dreaded. However, as the creature drew closer, all hope that it was Emera vanished. A gasp of disbelief escaped the lips of the small group of humans and Dragonborns that had gathered behind us. We all held our breaths as the Dragon began to change. Was this Valda? Or was this Amram. I willed it to be the former.

"A traveler must be in human form to enter," Anahita explained. I wasn't sure if we should be thankful for that bit of magic or not. A Dragon was large and destructive, but it couldn't wield magic as effectively in that form. Suddenly, the smoke engulfed the giant body, but through its thinnest wisps, I watched as the monstrous scales melted away like molten metal, revealing a female form. And it wasn't Emera's.

"Valda," I growled.

The people behind us screamed. Just the way she walked sent shivers down my spine. She was a predator stalking its prey. Anahita's eyes flashed with anger. Beside her, my father stood rooted to the spot, igniting flames in his hands.

"I never thought this day would come," my aunt murmured, her voice barely audible over the crackle of fire and the pounding of my heart. "We believed we were safe— hidden."

But there was no denying the reality unfolding before us. Through the barrier that protected Khaosar from prying eyes and unwanted guests, we watched silently as Valda strode purposefully across the bridge, a wolf-like smile spreading across her face. She opened the purple knee-length leather jacket she wore, revealing rows of shining daggers within. More daggers were secured at her thighs, a stark contrast to the purple leather pants she also wore. I glanced down and cursed myself for not being more prepared. I had Vultesh strapped to my back. That was it. At least Fin had his bow and quiver of arrows.

As Valda drew nearer, the air crackled with magic and tension. The barrier between Khaosar and the outside world trembled with the force of her chaos magic. I stared into her eyes. There was no mistaking her intent—she had found the hidden town, and she would stop at nothing to burn it to the ground.

With a silent exchange of glances, Anahita, Vukan, and I knew that the time of Khaosar's hiding was over. I unsheathed Vultesh and gripped it tightly in both hands. Anahita closed her eyes briefly. When she opened them, they glowed a vibrant blue.

"She's enjoying this," Anahita whispered as Valda closed the space between us. The Goddess of Water clenched her hands, ready to defend her home and face the darkness head-on. To protect all the innocent lives that lived in Khaosar.

"We will do this together," my father said, his eyes glowing red by the flames that blazed within them.

"You need to calm down," Valda said as she took her first step off the bridge. She now stood in the town, which had grown eerily silent.

"We're perfectly calm," I replied.

"Calm?" she laughed. "Tension is rippling through you. Lonely nights will do that to you, though," she purred as she slid her gaze down my body and up again. "I can help with that." She looked at Fin. "Fintan."

"Valda. Stylish as always."

"I do try."

I released the blade and summoned my fire magic. Balls of fire formed in my palms, growing larger with each surge of magic I infused into them.

Anahita stepped between Valda and me. "Leave."

Valda cocked her head to the side and said, "And what if I don't want to?"

Anahita's words cut through the air like a razor-sharp dagger. "We'll make you."

"Good luck," Valda sang, twisting her arms and channeling her chaos magic. She released a burst of what looked like jagged purple lightning bolts. The chaos magic crackled around us, and the wind picked up. Valda was calling in a storm. Lightning crashed in the distance, followed by thunder. Valda's eyes glowed with malevolence as she faced all of us with an evil smirk. She raised her hands, and the air itself seemed to shudder in response. Dark purple tendrils of chaotic energy snaked out, threatening to devour everything in their path. The ground trembled beneath our feet, and I fought to maintain balance. What were we going to do?

Around us, the residents of the town screamed and scrambled frantically to their homes for safety. Some of them stepped back out into the streets with household items as weapons. Some of them called elemental magic to their hands and took fighting stances, readying themselves for an attack on their homes.

"Fin," I yelled. "Hang back. You're the last line of defense for the townspeople."

Fin nodded and retreated behind me. He stood a few feet in front of the nearest house, his bow up with an arrow ready to be released.

My father, hands now wreathed in flames, stepped past Anahita and me. He raised his arms high, calling upon every fiery fiber of his being. The flames in his palms grew higher and higher. He twisted and turned his wrists, the flames now circling around him in a blazing inferno. Valda merely laughed, weaving her chaos magic to counter the flames. Her chaos magic tendrils lifted into the air and wrapped themselves around the flames. Valda couldn't extinguish my father's fire completely, but she'd diminished what she could. Eventually, she'd overpower him. I tried to advance, but Valda snapped her fingers and vines erupted from the ground, took hold of me, and threw me into the crowd of fleeing townspeople. I landed with a resounding thud; my breath knocked out of me. I coughed and gasped for air while I got back up to my hands and knees.

Throughout all this, Anahita had been holding out her arm toward the nearby lake, which was just outside the town. Her eyes glowed with water magic. With a commanding gesture, she summoned a great wave up into the sky that turned and surged toward Valda. Valda dropped her hold on my father just in time to create a shield of wind. The wave hit the shield and rolled off. Once the wave had diminished, Valda seized hold of the water with her magic and transformed it all into ice shards, hurling them back toward Anahita. Screams of agony escaped Anahita's throat as the ice shards passed right through her core. She dropped to her knees. I needed to get to her.

As I got to my feet and ran to Anahita, my father threw fireball after fireball at Valda. I silently thanked him for the distraction. I knelt beside my aunt and placed my hands on her stomach. A bright golden glow emitted from my palms, and her wounds began to heal.

"Go," she said hoarsely. "I'll be okay."

I nodded and leaped to my feet. I turned just in time to see my father being hurtled past me. I stepped forward, and Valda smiled. Drawing upon the small essence of whatever chaos magic I had, I wielded a power I'd never known I possessed. With a wave of my hand, I summoned four whirlwinds, one of each element. Fire was the largest, but the others followed behind it. I guided each whirlwind until they had Valda surrounded.

The skies darkened as lightning crackled overhead; my air magic having cultivated a small lightning storm. Valda's confidence wavered. It was brief, but I saw it. I still didn't have the amount of magic needed to overpower her, but she was taken enough by surprise at what I could do, that she hesitated.

"How are you doing this?" she yelled.

I didn't answer. As each of my whirlwind's reached their peaks, I forced my whirlwinds to converge upon her. My brow sweated from the concentration I was using; I didn't know how long I could keep this up. It wasn't just physically draining to use so much magic at once, it was mentally draining.

Finally, all four whirlwinds consumed Valda. There was no way her form would survive all four elements consuming her. I was so elated that I didn't notice one of my hands slowly falling. It was all that Valda needed. A sudden surge of chaos magic burst from within the whirlwinds. She seriously lit up like a violet star. The chaos magic eviscerated all of my own magic. She snarled at me, and with a deafening roar, her transformation into her Dragon form began.

My father and Anahita now stood at my side. We all exchanged grim glances, realizing the direness of the situation. Valda's transformation was almost complete when they both turned to me, and with urgency in their voices, said simultaneously, "Go!"

"Go, my son," my father said, his voice gruff. "You must get to the Kingdom of Darkness. We will take care of Valda."

Anahita, having finally understood the grave situation the world was in, nodded in agreement. "We cannot let you risk your life any further. It seems you are the last hope to stop Amram. And if she's this powerful, I can only imagine what her father is like."

"You can't defeat her alone."

"Maybe not," my father said. "But we can hold her off long enough for you to get away."

"I've already lost Emera. I can't lose you, too."

Valda's roar interrupted the moment. My father rested his hand on my cheek. "Calian. I will see you again." Reluctantly, I nodded, knowing that they were right. This was all bigger than us, and to defeat Amram, I needed to live. It angered me that, according to some stupid prophecy my grandfather wrote, I was more important than them. Because I wasn't.

With a heavy hostile heart, I turned, motioned for Fin to follow me, and ran toward the stables, weaving in and out of the Dragonborns who had come to assist my family. Dhruv was already galloping toward me. I jumped onto his back and took the reins. "Go!" I shouted. Dhruv turned toward Fin, pausing just long enough to let him hop on. Then he raced off through the streets. Innocent men, women, and children continued to hide in their homes, peeking out to see the attack.

Meanwhile, Vukan and Anahita prepared to face Valda alone. Flames danced around my father, while water surged around both him and Anahita in a protective barrier. But movement from the town took me by surprise. The numerous Dragonborns that had been guarding their homes were moving forward and taking fighting stances behind my father and aunt. I smiled in the small comfort that my father would not die alone.

I continued to watch the battle behind me even as Dhruv raced out of the town. When he was finally far enough away that our lives were safe, I forced him to stop and turn. I needed to see. Were they going to make it? Could they defeat Valda on their own?

With a thunderous roar, Valda lifted into the air and from her snout, blazing fire descended up on those still left fighting. She soared overhead and unleashed chaos upon everything in her path. Buildings crumbled under her massive claws, and flames continued to incinerate everything in sight. There were no more torrents of water or large walls of flame. Were my father and Anahita dead?

Just when I thought there was no hope, two large Dragons appeared in the smoke, flanking Valda. They were a massive red Dragon and a smaller blue Dragon.

"Go get her, Father," I whispered.

Fin's hand rested on my shoulder. "They'll survive."

In my heart, I knew they would. But it didn't ease the sick feeling in my stomach. The Goddess of Chaos had done what she'd sought to do. With each swipe of her claws and blast of her fiery breath as she retreated, the town descended further into ruin. When smoke finally obstructed my view, and I couldn't see my father or Anahita any longer, I commanded Dhruv to turn away and head for The Kingdom of Water, my heart heavy with guilt and sorrow. Anahita wasn't the coward. I was.

CHAPTER NINE

ERJON

Tuuli was dead. Emera was dead. My mate was dead.

Prior to the attack, we had been married in secret. Eteri had no heirs, so the union was a logical plan to ensure the crown passed into trustworthy hands. She trusted me, so naturally, she chose me to be king regent in the event of her death. I never wanted to be king. The title was a burden I had no intention of bearing. I had already lived through enough traumatic experiences that all I was good for was the decision-making needed to maintain a prosperous kingdom. I was perfectly content with being Eteri's top advisor.

Truthfully, I didn't think her death would be so sudden. Yes, war could claim the lives of anyone at any given time. No one was special in times such as these. Nevertheless, I'd let my emotions get the best of me yet again, and I had hoped that my mate and I would live a fruitful existence. Dare I say, one with children and grandchildren.

But that would not come to pass. At this point, the gods were telling me that I did not deserve joy. I did not deserve happiness or the comfort of love from others. I should be angry at the concept, but I did my best to suppress any emotion that would interfere with logic. The kingdoms were at war, fighting each day to see another tomorrow. We needed logic and control to survive. Not emotions.

Emotions killed people.

The rhythmic beat of hooves pulled my focus back to reality as our group advanced toward the Kingdom of Fire. The loss of my mate weighed heavily on everyone's mind, but unlike the others, I refused to show outward signs of grief.

To my left, Avani rode with determination in her green armor, poised and ready for any threat that dared to interfere. She kept her eyes forward most of the time, but occasionally let them drift to the skies, scanning the clouds for any signs of a Dragon. I understood the need to be prepared, but Zepherin and his Winged Warriors guardsmen maintained a vigilant watch as they soared overhead, their presence a necessary precaution in the midst of constant Dragon attacks. They had a better vantage point from their location, so Avani's constant glances into the sky were pointless. Avani did not know the exact reason for the guardsmen's presence—to oversee the safe travel of their King Regent.

To be quite honest, I protested Zepherin's plan for me to escape the city in secret. Eteri had put her trust in me to rule the kingdom, but as we rode south, I could not shake the feeling of being hunted. The dragons, relentless in their pursuit, sought vengeance for the loss of The Great War. But I was not one to be hunted. A small smirk played on my lips. I was a predator in my own right, using logic to maintain the upper hand.

Logic told me that we were not alone. It was inevitable that a Dragon would attack. "We must reach the Kingdom of Fire before the Dragon finds us," I stated flatly, my tone betraying no sense of urgency. Urgency would only provoke panic. Panic would get us killed. Being in a somewhat secluded area with not a town in sight meant we must be diligent and cautious. The path was chosen for its areas of coverage. In the event of an attack, we would be able to find refuge.

Zepherin, however, was less than pleased with my chosen path. He descended from the sky and maintained a position to my right. "As I said before, this is not a good idea, Erjon."

Zepherin had warned me prior to escaping the city; it was pointless for him to do so again. "We should've taken the western route. It would've been faster."

"Possibly."

"That's all you have to say?"

I adjusted the collar of my gray silk tunic. "Arguing is futile."

Zepherin flew beyond my horse and me. He landed on the path ahead, causing my steed to stop abruptly. I was glad that I had secured my saddle before riding out, or I would have fallen off. "Was that necessary?"

"What is wrong with you?" At this time, the rest of the Winged Warriors had landed, and all the other horses had stopped.

"Must we have this conversation now?"

Avani nodded in agreement beside me, her gaze fixed on the path ahead. "Erjon is right. The decision was made. Now we press on."

"Look here, little brother. I understand what you've been through, but to choose a longer path that risks the lives of everyone else?"

"Do you hear yourself right now, Zepherin?"

Zepherin's eyes widened. "Excuse me?"

My expression remained unchanged. "The western route

was a dangerous choice. There were numerous Dragon burial sites scattered throughout the mountains. Amram is not finished resurrecting his army."

"Those sites very well could've been empty considering the amount of Dragons that attacked the city. We would have been to the border by now."

"Stop it." A gust of wind blew the sand at our feet. Avani placed her hands on her hips. "If you two don't stop arguing, you're going to get us killed." She faced Zepherin and said, "Your brother has lost his mate along with his father, mother, sister, and friend. I think you can cut him some slack." She turned to face me. "And you. Your brother sees himself as your protector. He wants nothing more than to ensure your safety because he loves you. He also bears the burden of a significant loss. Whatever is up both of your Dragonasses, you need to pull it out."

Zepherin remained tight lipped. He jettisoned back into the sky. I pursed my lips. The conversation was over.

We rode onward, our steeds thundering through the last of the Arden Forest. The day stretched on, each passing moment filled with tension. The horses ran as fast as they could. To my mild surprise, we never caught sight of a Dragon. One never caught up to us. Zepherin's frustration only grew as we continued on our journey unimpeded.

Zepherin landed several feet before us, this time giving enough time for the horses to slow before stopping. "The skies are clear," Zepherin muttered, tucking his wings in with restless energy. His demeanor had softened just a tad. "They must have taken another route. The Warriors need rest. Once we clear the forest, we'll have half a night's worth of traveling out in the open at night. To some, darkness seems like enough coverage. But it's not. Dragons have impeccable eyesight."

Zepherin waited for my response, but I said nothing, my mind already focused on the challenges that lay ahead once we entered the Kingdom of Fire. I had read of the creatures that inhabited the desert plains. Some of the creatures were not as formidable as a Dragon, but they were deadly, nonetheless.

*   *   *

As the sun dropped below the horizon, the Warriors were quite anxious to take flight. The horses were well rested, fed, and watered, so I did not argue. The sooner we crossed the border, the better. Just before the battle in the City of Ilmari, Eteri's spies confirmed that Amram's plans of attack did not include the Kingdom of Fire at present. Despite the excuse that Amram's forces were working their way southward, I had a nagging suspicion there was an underlying issue. Something gave Amram pause where the Kingdom of Fire was concerned. I needed to find out why.

We finally reached the border to the Kingdom of Fire. Once we crossed over, cheers erupted from the Winged Warriors in the skies.

A quick movement in the distance caught my eye. A shadowy form appeared and disappeared almost instantaneously. I held up my hand, signaling the others to stop. The horses halted abruptly while the Winged Warriors remained suspended above. Zepherin and his lieutenant, Naseem, landed beside me as I dismounted my steed.

"What is it?" Zepherin asked, his eyes focused straight ahead. "Your expression is unreadable as always, brother."

"The journey has been long and arduous," I replied.

A piercing cry echoed several yards away. It was a high-pitched sound that instantly sent a shiver down my spine. I took a deep breath, let it stir within my chest, and released it. Fear was just an emotional reaction. Death was inevitable. There was no use in fearing it.

I turned to Zepherin. "But it is far from over."

Zepherin nodded at his lieutenant. They crouched for a

split second before ascending into the sky at full speed. While they relayed the danger to their Warriors, I addressed the riding party. The night air grew still as they all maneuvered their horses to hear me better.

"Listen closely," I began. "Unknown creatures inhabit this terrain." Some of the soldiers straightened in their seats as if my voice had cut through the darkness like a blade. "Ahead lies a threat unlike any we've encountered before. I have read reports and first-hand accounts of deadly creatures lurking in this kingdom."

By the light of the moon, I watched the soldiers exchange nervous glances, their hands instinctively tightening around their weapons. Avani showed no hint of fear or hesitation. She only nodded, ready to fight.

"Our mission remains unchanged," I continued, willing my tone to remain even and calm. "We will confront these creatures head-on and eliminate the threat they pose to our lives."

Beside me, Avani nodded again, her eyes now glowing green as she channeled her earth magic within her. With a subtle gesture, vines and roots quietly snaked out from the ground, curling around us like protective serpents.

"We have the advantage of magic on our side. But we must remain vigilant. We will not know the extent of destruction these creatures can do until we discover what they are."

As if they heard me, the Winged Warriors hovered above us in an aerial attack formation, their bows drawn and ready to strike.

"We will approach from the air first," Zepherin called down.

I nodded. "And I will come with you." I put my hands out and called to my air magic. I did not need wings to guide me. Being a Dragonheir, I could manipulate air itself and force it to carry me.

With that, Avani whistled and gestured for the soldiers to stay. I was a fool for doing it, but I tapped into my empathic magic to check their emotions. With silver tendrils, I reached out to them, cocooning their hearts. I felt the steady pounding of anticipation, but there was only a hint of fear. They were ready. My tendrils withdrew, and I flew toward the unknown threat.

As the Warriors and I neared the creature's location, a low growl rumbled. Emerging from the shadows of two large boulders, came a grotesque sight to behold. This creature was neither wolf, nor lion. It was a mutated and mangled mixture of the two. Its fur was matted with blood and its eyes gleamed with feral hunger.

"What is that?" Zepherin asked.

"A dunescourge," I said.

Zepherin cleared his throat. "That sounds terrible."

"An understatement. The dunescourge is a deadly creature that prowls the desert sands at night. From my studies, it is as tall as a Lightenion Wolf, but deadlier. It used to be a beautiful creature with sleek fur. But over time, it has become more savage and isolated, even from its own kind, only caring for the next hunt. Its fur is now matted and ragged, but it is intelligent and cunning."

A pair of menacing eyes glowed as the dunescourge finally stood fully lit by the moonlight, terrifying in all its depravity. It snarled its fangs, which were elongated and razor-sharp, that protruded from its mouth.

"Their teeth are capable of tearing through flesh and bone with ease."

"That's reassuring," Zepherin replied.

The creature took a few more steps and looked up, letting out an ear-deafening roar.

Zepherin noted the color of the creature's fur. "No wonder it's difficult to see with fur the color of the desert sands.

"Precisely. It serves as camouflage."

"How do we kill it?"

"As a nocturnal predator, the dunescourge relies on its

senses to hunt. Its hearing is acute, capable of detecting the slightest rustle of movement. It moves in near silence as it stalks its prey before pouncing with unmatched speed. More than that, this creature does not rely solely on brute strength, but also cunning strategies to outwit its prey."

As if it heard me, the creature backed up into the shadows, camouflaging itself once more. Zepherin turned to the Warriors. "Half of you will position yourselves just north of the rock formation, and the rest of you will do the same on the south. Erjon, Naseem, and I will hover directly over the boulders to get a better view of what we're up against. Have your bows ready."

The soldiers nodded and did as they were commanded. Zepherin, Naseem, and I assumed our positions as well. I dropped down slightly and angled myself to see the dunescourge, but my inspection was short-lived because I caught a glimpse of another figure several feet away.

"Avani," I whispered. I turned my attention back to the dunescourge. Its twisted form prowled below.

Silently, Zepherin raised his bow, signaling the Warriors to ready their weapons. As one, they notched their arrows, eyes fixed on their target below.

"Remember your training," Zepherin called out, his voice carrying away only as far as his warriors before being whisked away by the wind he was creating to stay suspended in the night sky. "Recall how we coordinated our movements and attacks. Focus on the vulnerable spots, such as its eyes or throat."

With a chorus of determined nods, the Warriors descended upon the dunescourge. The creature snarled and lashed out with claws and fangs, but the Warriors remained out of reach.

In a coordinated assault, each Warrior unleashed a volley of arrows, each shaft flying true toward the dunescourge. However, the monstrous creature was unsurprisingly agile, dodging and weaving out of each arrow's path. Despite their best efforts, not a single arrow found its mark.

The Warriors were undeterred. In quick succession, they circled and swooped, harassing the creature from all sides. Some flew in close in an attempt to distract the dunescourge, while others remained back, raining down arrows. The dunescourge grew increasingly frustrated, its roars of anger echoing through the air. Yet still, the Warriors pressed on.

"This is not working," I said. I flew closer to the dunescourge, and with a quick rush of power, sent it careening into the boulders behind it. The creature slumped to the ground.

Zepherin laughed. "That was easy."

"Too easy," I murmured.

Sadly, yet unsurprisingly, I was correct. The beast rolled over and got back to its feet and launched itself into the air right in front of me. I had no time to react as its massive paw swiped through the air and connected with my chest, sending me hurtling to the ground several feet behind me. Pain tore through my chest, and I glanced down briefly to see blood where the beast's claws ripped through my shirt. There was no time to check the wounds. I propped myself up on my elbows and watched as the beast stalked toward me.

From above, Zepherin called out and sent an arrow flying. This time, the arrow hit its mark and the dunescourge roared in pain. It whipped its head back to Zepherin, who hovered just above the boulders. The creature leaped into the air toward Zepherin just as he nocked an arrow and released it.

In a heart-stopping moment, the dunescourge twisted and turned in mid-air, evading the arrow with ease. Zepherin ascended into the air just before the beast caught hold of his ankle.

Movement caught my eye. I turned to see Avani inching closer to me. I glanced at the dunescourge. The creature was too distracted by Zepherin and the Winged Warriors to notice that Avani had approached from behind. With a swift motion of her hand, Avani summoned her earth magic. She crouched low and touched the ground, calling it to her bidding. I watched the ground pulse slightly beneath her fingertips.

The dunescourge twisted its head suddenly, detecting Avani as she focused her energy, channeling all her earth power. With a fierce cry, Avani thrust her palms forward just as the creature ran toward her. Her eyes glowed a fierce green as she sent a wave of jagged rocks hurtling toward the dunescourge. It roared in defiance, and lunged at Avani, but it was too late.

The rocks slammed into the dunescourge, and it released an ear-splitting shriek. The monster stumbled before backing away slowly, blood dripping from jagged wounds in its flesh. Anger flashed in its yellow eyes as it hunched on its hind legs and curled back its lips, its sharp teeth on full display.

But Avani was relentless. And I was in awe.

Drawing upon the very essence of the desert itself, she lifted to her feet and summoned forth a torrent of sand, enveloping the dunescourge. The creature thrashed and roared, its claws tearing uselessly at the dust cloud as it was assaulted by the small sandstorm. And then, Avani lifted her arms like she was lifting the ground.

The earth trembled furiously beneath her. Any other

person would have lost their balance and fallen to their knees, but Avani stood firmly in place. The ground erupted below the dunescourge. Rocks and stones rose up like vines to ensnare it.

We all watched as the creature struggled against the rocky prison, its cries of rage echoing all around us. And then, with a final, thunderous crash, the rocks fell upon the monster. It flailed and roared, refusing to die beneath the rubble. I shot into the air and hovered just above it. With all the force I could muster, I sent a heavy wind, strong enough to crumble a building, down upon the rocks and stone, pushing them into the creature. The dunescourge's bones cracked and broke instantly from the force. The creature fell silent, its twisted form still and lifeless.

Breathing heavily, I lowered to the ground beside Avani. Her eyes returned to their normal shade of green.

"That was incredible!" Zepherin yelled, landing next to Avani and slapping her on the back. He held up his hand in front of me. I eyed it curiously.

Avani smiled and slapped Zepherin's hand in the air. Zepherin sighed and shook his head at me.

CHAPTER TEN

ERJON

We continued our journey through the vast expanse of the desert. No one uttered a solitary word after our confrontation with the dunescourge. The only hint of noise was the soft padding of the horses' hooves on the shifting sands.

Avani had done her best to heal my wounds, treating them with a medicinal herb from her kingdom. I was very grateful, considering the heat of the desert made my dripping blood sticky.

As we ventured further south toward the City of Vukan, the darkness seemed to close in on us. Despite our attempts to remain focused, the unending sandy landscape started to play tricks on our weary minds. Well, they played tricks on the minds of my fellow travelers. I was still of sound mind which was to be expected. My ability to focus was far stronger than anyone else in our party.

A soldier named Fei glanced nervously at his companions, all of their faces drawn with tension. They were all feeling it—the eerie presence that was carried with the light night breeze.

"No need to be afraid, Fei," I said without so much as a glance in his direction. "Your fear will only distract you from thinking clearly. You must learn to either control your emotion or suppress it."

Avani snorted. "Easy for you to say."

I did not entertain her response. I had more important things to think about. Like the fact that we were not alone.

Suddenly, a low moan drifted in on the breeze. The horses whinnied in fear. "Oh, I hate being right."

Avani twisted in her saddle toward me. "First, no you don't. And second, right about what?"

"We're not alone out here," Fei muttered.

I tightened my grip on the reins because—and I would not dare admit it to anyone—the beat of my heart started to increase. I scanned the horizon, searching for any sign of danger, seeing nothing but endless sand and darkness.

"Must be the wind," Avani said softly, although I knew she did not mean it.

In the distance, a structure jutted out of a large sand dune. The closer we got to the structure, the more the moaning died down, giving us a reprieve from the constant noise in our ears. After several more minutes, the structure took the shape of a forgotten relic. A castle that lay half-buried beneath the dunes.

Its stone walls, worn and weathered, bore the scars of countless windstorms and decades of neglect. The windows gaped like empty eyes; their frames eroded. A large doorway faced us, seeming to invite whatever nighttime creatures dared to enter. A single gate, once grand, lay shattered and broken, its iron hinges rusted over.

As we approached, the Winged Warriors descended, landing next to the castle wall.

"This is as good a place as any to stop and rest for the night." Zepherin said. "Looks like we can take refuge here."

An audible gulp from Fei gave me pause. Although emotions were a hindrance in most situations, caution was necessary when considering one's safety. "We do not know what dwells within it." Surely, Zepherin took more care of his Warriors.

"We'll go check it out. You can stay here if you're…"

"Do not dare utter your next word—"

"Scared."

I huffed, annoyed by his use of the term. "You are mistaking caution for cowardice."

"Am I?" he called over his shoulder as he and a team of Warriors strolled toward the forgotten structure.

"You're going in, aren't you?" Avani said with a laugh. "Don't worry. I'll stand on guard out here." A quick smile graced my lips but only for a brief second. Avani was by far the youngest of our group, but she was one of the strongest. I had every confidence that she would handle leadership with ease.

I paused and watched Zepherin closing in on the mangled gate. I contemplated not going in. Yet I could not shake the idea of how useless our journey would be if we were all killed because of Zepherin's curiosity. Therefore, with a hefty sigh, I dismounted my horse and followed my brother into an empty abyss.

Zepherin and his men were already through the front door. Following the glowing light from the torch, I proceeded forward to join them. Amidst the decay, hints of the castle's former grandeur remained. Carved stone arches, though worn by time, still remained strong and unyielding to the weight of the sand on top of it. Weaponry hung on the walls. This was no castle for a king. This was a fortress.

"This place smells like death," murmured Naseem, his voice a low rumble that seemed to echo through the empty halls.

The others nodded in agreement, but I could not fathom what else they expected. The castle was old and buried. There was no telling what beasts had taken refuge and then died within these walls.

Without a word, Zepherin raised his torch and moved onward. He pushed through a set of wooden doors that creaked open, revealing nothing but darkness. As we followed, venturing deeper into the abandoned castle, a sense of unease settled over me like a heavy blanket. I shook off the feeling and forced my empathic shield into place.

Suddenly, a chill breeze swept through the corridor, carrying with it a faint, ethereal voice that seemed to whisper in my ear.

"Erjon," it said softly. I looked around in confusion, expecting Zepherin to be standing there with an immature grin on his face. But I did not. The men didn't seem to hear it and continued to search the rooms as we walked through them.

"Erjon," the voice whispered again, its tone soft and pleading. "Come closer, Dragonchild." I whipped my head back and forth. My empathic shield vibrated from the terror that pounded on it. Even my heart skipped a beat as I turned toward the location of the voice. It was a large wooden door with words written in the dead Dragonlanguage carved above it. When peering up at the door, my senses tingled with a mixture of fear and curiosity.

"Erjon!"

I whirled around. Zepherin stood behind me.

"What are you doing?" He pointed at the door. I looked down and saw that my hand was already on the doorknob.

"I…Uh…I do not know."

"You don't know?" Zepherin's brows furrowed. "You always know."

"What is it with everyone thinking that I know everything?"

"Because you act like you know everything."

Had I not heard that same line before?

Zepherin raised his torch above the door, illuminating the words scrawled there. "You were mumbling something. Was it this?"

"I was not mumbling anything."

"Oh, you were mumbling all right," Naseem argued.

"What does it say?" Zepherin asked, still inspecting the language. "I'm not familiar with those words."

"You would not be. They are from the dead Dragonlanguage."

"Huh. Really? Do you know what they say?"

"They say, Draol, valmornulzor lith crulon et velarnal Soulzar avorolzor et sekalnolzor."

"You're seriously going to make me ask you to translate it?"

"To the depths of darkness our souls depart."

Naseem whistled. "That's some heavy stuff."

I rolled my eyes. "Of course, you would say that."

"Well, let's see what these depths of darkness are, shall we?" Zepherin took hold of the handle and attempted to open the door. He pulled with all his strength, but it would not budge."

"Let me try." Naseem took Zepherin's place. I had not the slightest idea as to why Naseem thought he would be able to open the door if my brother could not. Naseem was far inferior in not just intelligence but in physical strength as well. Naseem pulled and pulled, but as I had predicted, Naseem was unable to open the door.

"You must say the words while you open it."

Both men turned and looked at me, annoyed expressions on both of their faces.

"What?"

"You could have mentioned that." Naseem groaned.

With hesitant steps, I walked toward the door. I gripped the handle tightly, closed my eyes, and whispered, "Draol, valmornulzor lith crulon et velarnal Soulzar avorolzor et sekalnolzor." Heat filled my palm, and the handle glowed a vibrant gold. I pulled, and the door opened easily. Stairs leading downward appeared before us. The shuffling of footsteps behind me indicated the apprehension of the others. Only Zepherin and Naseem did not move. What Naseem lacked in intelligence and strength; he made up for in bravery. I would give him that.

"Erjon." The voice was louder than a whisper this time.

"Do you hear that?" I asked Zepherin.

"Here what?"

"Nothing."

He furrowed his brows before ordering the other two Warriors to remain at the top of the stairs. He followed me down the steps.

"Erjon," the voice said more forcefully this time. I followed the sound of the voice, drawn deeper into the castle. Each footstep echoed like a thunderclap in the silence as I progressed down the steps.

At the bottom of the stairs was another dark and musty hall. I walked forward, toward the beckoning voice, rounding a corner and stepping into a large chamber.

"This hall is as spacious as a cavern," Naseem said with awe. He strained his neck to see farther into the dark. "Are those…skeletons?"

Naseem was correct. Before us were rows and rows of skeletons still wearing their golden armor.

"This room is a mass grave," Zepherin said. "Spread out. Let's see what we can find."

The three of us took off in different directions, inspecting the large chamber. Why were there so many skeletons? Who were they? Surely, more of the Dragonlanguage would present itself. The voice came yet again, beckoning me toward another set of stone steps on the right side of the chamber. I ascended them quickly, hoping to discover answers to my questions. Instead, I came upon another door. But this one was different. "Whatever resides behind this door is important," I said to no one. I pushed it open and came face to face with an apparition—a spectral figure clad in tattered robes, its form flickering like a candle flame. Its eyes, empty sockets devoid of life, seemed to peer into my soul with unwavering intensity. My breath caught in my throat.

"Do not be afraid, Dragonchild," the ghost whispered, its voice low and heavy with the weight of time.

"Who... who are you?" I stammered, my voice trembling. I cursed myself internally for the lack of control.

"I am one of the fallen" the ghost replied, his voice hollow and filled with sorrow. "I am the general of the soldiers who lie entombed below, we who perished in the War of Three."

My mind raced with numerous questions, but before I could utter a single word, the ghost beckoned me forward, its outstretched hand glowing. None of this made any sense. Ghosts were not real. Our Dragonsouls departed the world to the Dragonplane of Existence. Those Dragonsouls that were not worthy of such deliverance were bound to their bones.

My eyes widened in confusion and the haunting illusion that unfolded before us.

There was not a trace of moonlight to be seen through the thick smoke from the flames that engulfed part of an unknown city. We stood on a balcony of the castle, a great fortress as it had been in his time, overlooking the death and carnage below. Dragons soared over the fortress, their fiery breath destroying the land while incinerating the bodies of the fallen soldiers.

"Unbeknownst to my soldiers, we were tasked with guarding a precious weapon until reinforcements joined us. I wanted to fight, to face the beasts that killed my men," the ghost lamented. "But I couldn't. I knew we were outnumbered. Despite my desire to join the battle, I gave the order for a small group of us to stay hidden, desperately guarding the weapon with our lives even if meant appearing like cowards. This castle was the last remaining fortress left standing along the border. We were the City of Vukan's last defense. As you can see the small city of Idalia stood just south of us. I failed to protect either of them." The ghost turned to me.

"It appears you had no choice," I said.

He pursed his lips. "Come," he replied.

We turned and reentered the fortress, descending the stairs into a large chamber. I watched in silence as the past unfolded. My empathic ability opened up fully, and I struggled to remain calm as the weight of the soldiers' sorrow washed through me. A large group of them sat huddled around a fire pit.

"We are cowards," a soldier whispered, his voice filled with anguish.

Another soldier nodded. "But what can we do? We cannot take down a Dragon."

"We live," commanded a large man standing behind them all. It was the man whose ghostly form now guided me. "We barricade ourselves down here and live. We live until the reinforcements show."

Several men laughed. One stood and yelled, "There are no reinforcements!"

Fire burst from the general's hands, and he threw it forward, nearly incinerating the soldier who had made the outburst.

"You dare question my judgment?" he thundered.

The soldier cowered back. "N-n-no, sir."

"I know the fires of battle burn within each of you, but now is not the time for rash action. We were given an order to stand down, and we will continue to do so."

"And who gave that order?" a soldier demanded.

"The God of Fire himself," the general answered without so much as a glance in the soldier's direction. The general stroked his beard and then tugged on his armor. He gazed up at the ceiling, choosing his words carefully. He addressed the soldiers. "Our strength lies not only in our swords, but in our strategy. Reinforcements are on their way, but until they arrive, we must bide our time and remain here." He strode over to the soldier who had called him out and placed a hand on the young man's shoulder. "Sometimes, our survival hinges on our ability to outlast our enemies and not engage them head-on."

The soldier nodded, but it was clearly evident that he did not believe his general.

The general refused to acknowledge the distrust and addressed his soldiers once more. "Remember our oath, soldiers. We fight not only for ourselves, but for our kingdom. Stay vigilant, stay hidden, and trust in our allies to come to our aid. Together, we shall reemerge and reclaim this land. For Nimerah!" He thrust his hand up into the air upon yelling the Dragongoddess's name.

"I lied," the ghost whispered.

"Obviously."

"I forced them to stay with me. You said earlier that I did not have a choice, but I did. I could have let them fight. I could have guarded the blade alone. I could have given them honor. Instead, we were all labeled cowards and traitors."

"What is the purpose of showing me this?"

The ghost turned to me as the vision beyond dissipated. "I seek redemption." He took a step forward and I followed, exiting the void. We were back in the castle. Back in my time.

"I am unsure of how I can give you that."

"Find the small chest beneath my resting place. There, you will find what you need to defeat the Dragongod Amram. And when you need our aid, we will come. You know where to find us." And upon his final words, the ghost vanished.

I contemplated his words for a moment before joining Zepherin and Naseem on the other end of the chamber. Naseem had located a journal while I was…*searching*. While Zepherin and Naseem read the pages for more information regarding the dead soldiers, I scanned the bodies for the general. Even though all that remained would be a skeleton, the clothing would give away his rank. Once I spotted the familiar uniform I had seen in the ghost's vision, I left the other two standing and went to retrieve the weapon. The general laid face up. Wasting no time, I carefully used my air magic to lift the skeleton and place it gently to the side.

"What in the Dragonhell are you doing?" Zepherin asked, appearing at my side.

"Yeah, Erjon. Moving the remains? That's disrespectful," Naseem mumbled. He stood opposite me, his head angled downward with a look of horror on his face.

I ignored them and lifted the leather bag that was hidden beneath the general. I opened the bag and withdrew a silver blade.

"What is that?" Naseem asked.

"How we will end this war," I said. I put the blade back in the bag and headed out of the chamber. "We must get to the City of Vukan as soon as possible."

"I second that," Zepherin said with a cough. "My lungs can't take much more of this decay. We rest for the remainder of the night. Then we head out at first light."

We headed back up the narrow stone stairs to the mid-level of the castle. Zepherin exited through the front door to gather his men. I needed to speak with Avani. Only she would have enough sense to believe what I had just witnessed.

When I returned to my horse, Zepherin was addressing everyone. The troops had gathered around him, their faces weary but curious. "Alright, listen up," he said, rubbing his hands together to warm them against the chill of the night. Despite the mass grave in the chamber below, the castle would provide more warmth than we would get out in the open desert. "We're going to hole up in this creepy old castle for the remainder of the night. I know, I know, it looks like something out of a nightmare, but trust me, it's better than sleeping out here with the dunescourges. Besides, we just did a thorough search of the place, and all is clear."

He pointed toward the castle's entrance. "Grab your stuff and follow me inside. Find yourself a good spot to sleep and try not to think about the ghosts," he joked.

Oh, if he only knew.

"Naseem and I will take the first round of watch duty."

Some members of our party exchanged nervous glances, but they trusted Zepherin's lead, so they shuffled toward the castle with tired steps and bags flung over their shoulders. As they crossed the threshold, Zepherin clapped his hand on my shoulder.

"Good luck catching some shut eye," he said with a wink.

And with that, Zepherin led his men through the entrance of the castle. It was then that I turned to Avani who fed her horse one last apple before patting its neck. "I have information to share with you," I said.

CHAPTER ELEVEN

EMERA

We arrived in the City of Anahita the morning after my resurrection thanks to my mother's Dragon form being incredibly fast. We landed outside of the city so that we didn't draw attention to ourselves. The army would be watching and waiting for any sign of a Dragon. We didn't want to cause any alarm.

The City of Anahita was nestled between rolling hills off the coast of the Kaimana Sea. Just north of its towering walls was a meandering river, leading into the sea. Many smaller vessels utilized the river as a trade route between the palace and Medora.

As we approached the outskirts of the city, my heart clenched with a mixture of dread and disbelief. Smoke billowed against the sunny blue sky, casting a shadow over the landscape below. The walls of the city still stood; I couldn't make out anything else. Once we entered the city, the full extent of the devastation hit me. My father and I would travel to the city twice a year, and although it had been some time since I last visited, I still remembered what it had looked like. Now, it was vastly different.

The familiar streets, once bustling with life and laughter, lay in ruins. Buildings had crumbled under the weight of destruction, now nothing but charred remains. The air was thick from the smoke and ash, which stung my nostrils and slowed my breathing.

My gaze darted from one heartbreaking sight to the next. And for a few seconds, tears pooled in my eyes as I stumbled through the debris-strewn streets. But I straightened my bag and summoned my water magic to drown out the sorrow.

We turned toward the marketplace, where my father and I had once sold our wares, it was deserted and desolate. Anahita's temple stood like a hollow shell, its spires fallen and stained-glass windows shattered.

"This is worse than I thought," Priest Benigno murmured.

"We will help make this right," I assured him.

With every corner we turned, every familiar landmark I passed, the ache in my stomach grew. The people picking up their scattered possessions served as a painful reminder of how war affected everyone.

"These poor people," the priest whispered.

"They will rebuild their lives," I answered. "It will be a long and painful process, but they will find the strength to heal." Upon my last word, I saw a lone figure standing among the wreckage. It was Morwen handing food to a survivor of the attack. The woman she was helping had eyes that were hollow with grief and despair. My empathic magic swelled within me and reached out beyond my body with its familiar tendrils. They wrapped around the woman and anguish washed over me in relentless waves. In that moment, the weight of the woman's sorrow took over and threatened to drown me. But I pushed my power through, and soon, her breathing eased; she looked like a weight had been lifted.

"Morwen," I breathed.

Morwen turned and our eyes met, and for a moment, time seemed to stand still. My breath caught in my throat as Morwen studied my face. Her brow raised as she angled her head to the side. She was unsure of what to say or do. Well, I was supposed to be dead, so I couldn't blame her.

Priest Benigno held back as I carefully walked toward Morwen. Once I'd closed the gap between us, I stood silent before her, my violet hair whipping back and forth in the wind.

"Emera?" Morwen whispered, her voice trembling. She wiped a tear from her cheek with her tattered sleeve, her blue dress was blood-stained, dusty, and torn.

I nodded. "It's me."

Morwen stepped forward. "But... how" she asked, her voice barely more than a whisper. Her eyes scanned my face, my body, and my hair.

"My mother."

Morwen finally looked past me, having finally caught a glimpse of Priest Benigno. "Then perhaps there is still hope for us yet."

I nodded and reached out to her, and she took my hand in hers. We embraced amidst the ruins of her shattered city. For the first time since I'd met her, Morwen rested her head on my shoulder and cried. Thick tears dampened the fabric of my dress. My knees buckled from the extent of her sadness, but I remained strong.

Morwen raised her head and stood back.

"Morwen, let me introduce you to…"

"Priest Benigno," Morwen said warmly, cutting me off. She wiped a tear from her cheek with the tattered sleeve of her blue dress. "It is nice to see you again."

The priest nodded. "Likewise, Princess Morwen."

Morwen smiled, but it didn't reach her eyes. "Let's get back to the palace. There is someone I want you to meet." I'd never met her father before. Would he accept me with open arms? I sure hoped so.

With my hand in hers, Morwen guided me through the city streets. The elegant bridges I'd played on as a child still arched gracefully over the waterways. Debris littered the running streams, once clear blue and vibrant with life. Now, the waters were murky. I managed to see some of the same vibrant fish swimming around which gave me hope. I glanced up at the buildings of what used to be gleaming white marble. The marble was now tinged with smoke and ash. Yet, beneath the stained color, were the intricate carvings of sea creatures and flowing waves.

"We're here," Morwen murmured.

I gasped. The once pristine palace lay in ruins. Half of its domes and spires lay crumbled and charred. I pushed down the burning lump in my throat. I wasn't about to say anything. Morwen needed me to be strong.

The surviving half of the palace stood defiant. Pillars of white marble, though weathered from the battle, still towered over the city. The courtyard was eerily silent, considering the amount of people wandering in and out of the palace. Some were cleaning the destruction while others were helping the injured. Peeking through the debris was a blue Waterion Lily, the official flower of the kingdom. It served as a reminder that not all was lost. Life still remained.

"When did this happen?" I asked.

"A few weeks ago."

My jaw dropped. Everything before me indicated the battle had been more recent than that.

As if reading my mind, and maybe she had been, Morwen said, "It has taken a lot of time and effort to clear the wreckage, tend to the wounded, and bury the dead."

Walking through the rubble, I saw a group of soldiers patrolling the remaining corridors of the palace, their weapons drawn and eyes alert for any sign of danger. Nile Ford used to be one of those soldiers. I wondered if Morwen knew anything about him. The soldiers passed, revealing servants working tirelessly to repair what damage they could. We nodded in understanding as we walked by them.

Morwen led us into the throne room. I expected to see King Elderbook delegating people to specific duties, but he wasn't there. Instead, Queen Baia Elderbrook stood by the shattered remnants of the king's throne. She looked annoyed as she listened to her advisors prattle on and on with the day's damage report. Where was the king? Shouldn't he be listening to these reports, too?

Before Morwen could utter a word of our arrival, the queen noticed our small group. Her eyes blazed with fury when she saw me. "What is the meaning of this?" Morwen's mother demanded, her voice sharp. She waved her hand, dismissing the advisors. Instead of leaving, they backed up a few steps.

I met the queen's gaze with confusion. I had no idea why she was so angry with me.

"Maybe we should wait until the king is present," I whispered to Morwen.

"The king is dead," the queen spat.

A new lump formed in my throat, but I swallowed it and straightened my back, pushing back my shoulders.

"Mother, this is…"

"I know who you are, Emera Edevane. And if you are standing here in the flesh, it means you are not dead as presumed. Therefore, it's within reason to believe you sat idly by as our city burned to the ground," she seethed, her voice laced with contempt. "You being here puts this city at risk, despite being a powerful Dragongoddess as the rumor says you are. Leave this place at once, before you bring further harm upon us all." She turned her back to us all and addressed her advisors.

Morwen faced me and Priest Benigno. "I apologize for my mother's harsh attitude." She sighed softly. "She is…"

"Heartbroken," I finished. "And understandably so."

"She has lost her husband, the king, to a violent threat they stood no chance against. She has every right to be angry. With time, her soul will heal."

"Why is she still here?" Queen Baia appeared suddenly at Morwen's side. My heart truly ached for the queen.

"I am here to learn," I replied with determination.

Queen Baia eyed me suspiciously. "Learn what?"

I glanced at the priest then back at the queen. "How to defeat Amram."

"Ha!" the queen scoffed. "I'm afraid you're too late."

"For here, maybe." Queen Baia was taken aback. I sighed. "I'm sorry. I truly am. But I *did* die, and although it was too late to help here, the Dragongoddess Tamasvi brought me back so that I can put an end to all of this."

"We needed you sooner."

"Mother. Amram is nowhere near finished. He will stop at nothing until we kneel to him and the humans are extinct."

Queen Baia's demeanor softened slightly, and she sat on the floor with a look of defeat on her face. Morwen knelt at her mother's side. "I know you are tired, Mother. Do not let your fear and grief cloud your judgment. Amram may have destroyed our city, but he has not destroyed our spirit."

The queen looked up at me. "Were you really dead?"

"Yes."

"How are you here now?"

"My mother sacrificed herself. She gave me her soul so that I may live."

Queen Baia sighed. "So, Nimerah is dead."

"Yes."

"Then you must have her power?"

"Yes, but there is another pressing matter. Amram has my soul, and I will need it if I am to defeat him for good."

Priest Benigno stepped forward. "Hmmm," he murmured softly. "I believe I have an idea. On how to help you get it back. But I will need access to your library, Your Majesty."

"What's mine is yours." The queen stood gracefully. "Now, if you'll excuse me. I have a kingdom to run."

I took note of the sideways glance she gave Morwen. It dawned on me that Morwen should be queen. If her father died, Morwen was next in line for the throne. I opened my mouth to ask, but Morwen shook her head dismissively. A conversation for another time, then.

Morwen led us through the empty corridors and into the library. After a Dragon attack, I expected there to be books and pages strewn everywhere with upturned tables and bookcases leaning against the walls. But I was pleasantly surprised to see that the library remained mostly intact.

Shelves stood slightly askew; their contents having been disturbed by the tremors of the battle. Servants moved around in hushed tones, doing their best to restore the books to their proper places. A lingering scent of smoke hung faintly in the air, but it didn't deter from the soft light that filtered through the stained-glass windows.

In one corner of the library, the ceiling had a small fracture. However, I doubted much needed to be done to reinforce the ceiling's structure and stability.

"What are we looking for?" I asked.

"A specific text called The Dragon's Mindforce: Delving into the Depths of the Dragonpsyche."

"Good gods, that's a mouthful."

The priest chuckled.

"Who is the author?" Morwen asked, her eyes darting back and forth between the sections of books.

"You mean, who *was* the author? It was Dragonpriestess Maren Ondine. She was an academic scholar at Lir Winslet."

"Ah, that is where I studied," Morwen said. "And I know exactly where we can find the tome, which is not here."

I had never heard of the Dragonseminary called Lir Winslet, so I figured only wealthy people within the city attended classes there. By the way Morwen was walking toward the library's entrance, I gathered that we would be heading to this school.

Priest Benigno blushed. "If you'll excuse me, I have…um…private matters to attend to."

"Go down the eastern stairwell. Two doors on the left."

Once the priest had gone, Morwen led me out of the hall into the corridor. A couple of plush chairs sat beneath a window.

"We will only be gone for a day. Should Calian arrive, I'll make sure mother conveys our whereabouts."

"Hmm? Oh! Calian. Yes. As I told Benigno, I look forward to seeing him again."

Morwen shifted in the chair and crossed her ankles. "Look forward to seeing him? He's your mate, Emera."

I started to twirl my hair again. "I know that."

Morwen placed her hands in her lap. "I just thought you'd be more excited."

"Who says I am not?"

Morwen gave me a look. She didn't need telepathy to know what I was thinking.

I raised my hands in defeat. "This sensation within me is difficult to explain. I am me, but I am not. My mother's soul doesn't yearn for Calian like mine does." I winced at the word yearn. "To be quite honest, it makes me wonder if we're still…mates…at all."

Morwen leaned forward and dropped her gaze to where my heart drummed calmly within my chest. "Have you looked?"

"Huh. I didn't even think to do so." I grabbed hold of my collar and pulled it to the side.

Morwen gasped. "They're gone. Your Dragonmate wings are gone."

*　　*　　*

"We need horses to get to the Dragonseminary?"

We'd decided to stay overnight in the palace and rest. The next day, Morwen led us out of the palace. Neither of us had said much regarding my lack of Dragonmate wings since I'd discovered their disappearance. Morwen seemed more worried about it than I was. Once Priest Benigno had returned to us, Morwen disclosed the location of the tome the priest needed and then left to notify her mother of our plans.

"I have a gift for you that I hope will cheer you up," Morwen said. Her lips spread into a wide smile. It was the first true smile she'd given since I'd arrived.

I didn't have the heart to tell her that my lack of Dragonmate wings didn't bother me.

"And this gift is in the stables?"

Morwen remained silent, but her smile spread wider. I had no idea what this gift could be.

"I hope there are horses available, all things considered," the priest chimed in. "The Dragonseminary is a couple of hours north. It's in a more remote location to stay away from prying eyes."

Once a Dragonborn connected with the Dragongoddess Anahita, they were taken to a Dragonseminary, a school for Dragonborns. Most Dragonseminaries were located close to a city for convenience, but far enough away to ensure privacy.

I was still imagining what my time at a Dragonseminary would have been like, had my activation been under normal circumstances. When we turned down the curved path we were on, the stables came into view. The stables were constructed from sturdy timber and stone. Upon entering, we were greeted by the familiar scent of hay and the comforting sounds of contented horses. The interior was spacious and well-lit, allowing ample room for the horses to move around. Each stall was equipped with a plush bed of straw and a soft blanket. Above each stall hung a lantern emitting a gentle, warm light, ensuring that the stall was illuminated and warm. Along the northern wall of the stables was a row of troughs filled with fresh water and several baskets of crisp apples and carrots. On a western wall, racks held a variety of bridles, saddles, and grooming supplies. The Goddess Anahita loved horses, so to see these animals well taken care of in her city was certain.

I had seen many stables in my lifetime, but what truly set these stables apart were the magical touches. Runes of protection in the Dragonlanguage were etched into the walls to ensure the safety of the horses. It was marvelous. And so was the horse I spotted standing next to a trough.

"Zari!" I ran to my horse and threw my arms around her neck. I nestled into her, letting her warmth wash over me, providing me with a comfort I desperately needed.

My Kahina, Zari said. Love radiated from her. *I knew you would return.*

I am sure you did.

But you are not alone.

No, Morwen is with me. And that's Dragonpriest Benigno.

That is not what I meant. You have your mother with you.

Zari meant Nimerah. Somehow Zari knew I carried Nimerah's soul within me. I nuzzled more into her, relieved that even though I only had a small piece of my soul, I still felt the familiar connection I had with her.

You carry her soul along with yours.

Yes. When Amram took my magic through my mind, he took most of my soul. My mother gave me hers so that I could come back. As much as I love having a part of her with me, I need my soul back.

Seems to me that if he was able to take your soul through your mind, you can do the same.

I smiled. What she said made sense. I'd discuss it with Morwen later. *I feel like I haven't seen you in years, though.*

That would be accurate. I knew your mother when I was just a filly.

How old are you?

Old.

How is that possible?

Just one of life's many secrets, my Kahina.

My mother's doing, I'm sure.

Zari giggled. Well, she would have giggled if she wasn't a horse. *I also like your hair. You look just like her.*

Morwen walked up to Zari and patted the horse's neck. "Let's saddle up the horses and go see about this text."

We readied the horses, and once we were prepared, we set out to Lir Winslet beneath the lowering sun. I was thankful for the black leathers Morwen had given me. They clung to my body, providing more ease of movement and better coverage in case of an attack. She donned a similar set, but the leather she wore was her signature blue.

Priest Benigno had declined to change from his robe, but it didn't matter. If it came to a fight, he wouldn't be engaged in hand-to-hand combat.

As we rode onward, Morwen explained that the school sat within a heavily wooded area. It wasn't quite like the forests in the northern part of the kingdom, but we would still be surrounded by towering trees.

As soon as Morwen gave him an opening, Priest Benigno started on Lir Winslet's detailed history. "Its origins intertwine with the ancient worship of the Dragongoddess Anahita."

You don't say, I said to Zari.

She winked at me. *Now, that was definitely you and not your mother.*

I smiled. Maybe my mind was finding a way to balance itself with my mother's soul.

"Legend has it," Morwen said, interrupting the priest, "that there is an evil ghoul lurking beneath Lir Winslet."

I snorted.

Ignoring me, Morwen continued, "When the school was first built, a malevolent spirit known as the Dragonghoul was sealed away deep beneath the school by Anahita herself."

"So, that's where Anwir came from," I said jokingly.

Morwen laughed.

"The ghoul, so the story goes, was once a Dragonborn who devoted his allegiance to Amram in the war. But instead of fighting on the battlefield, he turned and ran. Amram, having a disgust for cowards, transformed the Dragonborn into a Dragonghoul. The ghoul still lingers beneath the school, bound by Amram's magic. If a student wanders too deep into the chambers, the ghoul will catch them and eat them alive!"

I laughed. "Oh, of course, it would!"

"Some claim to have seen a shadowy figure run past their windows at night, while others swear they've felt icy fingers brushing against their skin in the depths of the school's catacombs." Morwen turned in her saddle and looked me dead in the eyes. "Beware how far down you venture when we get there."

"Ha, ha, very funny," I said dryly. There was no way that legend was real. I'd never even heard of a Dragonghoul, but then again, I had once thought that Dragonheirs were just a story, too.

"That is just a story used to scare new students," Priest Benigno assured me. "Now, back to what I was saying."

I glanced at Morwen who shrugged. So, we were back to the priest's history lesson.

"Where was I? Um…Well, Lir Winslet has been dedicated to the study and mastery of water magic in the service of Anahita. Over the years, the school has grown and flourished, expanding its halls and welcoming students from far and wide.

"But mostly from this kingdom," Morwen added.

The priest prattled on without stopping. "In Lir Winslet, Dragonborns study not only water magic but also philosophy, history, and the natural world. Because…"

"True wisdom comes from understanding the connection of all things," Morwen recited. She'd apparently heard this history lesson before.

Priest Benigno's cheeks turned red. I held back a laugh.

Morwen leaned toward the priest, "We appreciate your knowledge and your willingness to share it in preparation of our arrival." This seemed to ease his mind.

We rode in silence the rest of the way. Between the quiet and Zari's gentle swaying gait, I was beginning to fall asleep when I heard Morwen say, "Welcome to Lir Winslet."

CHAPTER TWELVE

EMERA

Lir Winslet was a blend of elegant stone and sprawling, ivy-covered walls.

"It's beautiful," I said softly. I hoped no one noticed the hint of disappointment in my voice. I would never have the opportunity to attend Lir Winslet.

"Most of the students should be in class," Priest Benigno said.

"Wait. What?"

Morwen stopped her horse and turned to me. "Did you think it was abandoned?"

Zari halted. "No, I just figured with the attack on the city, it would have closed temporarily."

Morwen didn't say anything. There was a quiet pause as Priest Benigno stopped his horse.

"They don't know about the attack," I said slowly.

Morwen closed her eyes. "They do not."

The priest's eyes widened. "Princess! Why would you do that? They could have helped."

"How? They are still learning. They could have done more harm than good. There would have been more casualties."

"Then you are underestimating the school's ability to train them well." Priest Benigno crossed his arms over his chest, clearly upset.

"Hold on," I said, shaking my head. "Morwen is right. You must also take into consideration who will lead and protect the kingdom had the entire city fallen. It seems that Lir Winslet holds the future of the kingdom within its doors. It only makes sense that they remain protected in a time of uncertainty. However…" I faced Morwen. "You might have to prepare yourself. You could have a riot on your hands if they find out that you withheld the attack from them. I think you should tell them." Was that me speaking? Or my mother? I couldn't tell anymore.

Morwen considered my suggestion. "I am not sure now is a good time."

I shrugged my shoulders. "I don't think there will ever be a good time."

Morwen sighed. "Maybe you're right."

Priest Benigno lightly nudged his heels into the horse he rode. "I will locate the text. You two, at the very least, need to announce our arrival and intentions so as not to raise suspicion. Rumors are just as destructive as lies."

"One more thing. Zari made a suggestion regarding my soul," I said.

The priest's eyebrow lifted. "Zari? Your horse?"

"Yes. She's very smart actually. She essentially suggested that I enter Amram's mind and retrieve my soul that way."

Morwen shifted her weight in her saddle. "Makes sense, considering that's how he took it. I think I know someone at the school who might be able to help."

Priest Benigno nodded. "The more avenues we explore, the better. I'll look for the text, and you two can meet with whomever you think can help."

Just a few minutes later, we entered through the massive doors of Lir Winslet. "Want a tour?" Morwen asked.

"You're stalling," I pointed out. "And you never do that. You're Morwen Elderbrook. You always know what to say and when to say it. What's going on?"

Priest Benigno continued on, being a priest of Anahita, he could come and go as he pleased. Morwen and I paused outside the entrance.

"My father wanted to inform the school of the attack. He felt that we could use the students who had almost mastered their skills as reinforcements. I disagreed. In fact, I was the one to dissuade him."

"So, now you feel guilty."

"What if I was wrong?"

"But you weren't. Like I said, the future of this kingdom resides within these walls. They weren't ready to fight. They would have been at a great disadvantage."

"They should have been given that choice."

"You did what was best for the survival of your kingdom. Do not blame yourself for that."

Morwen straightened her back. "Maybe you're right. Okay. Let's go do this." Then she leaned in toward me and lowered her voice. "But we have time for a tour if you'd like one."

"Absolutely, I do."

We entered the school, and I gasped, and this time, no sign of recognition came from my mother's soul. So, Nimerah had never been to the school.

The interior was an impressive sight. Through the doors was a grand foyer, decorated with tapestries depicting Anahita and The Kingdom of Water's landscapes. I followed Morwen through the quiet corridors to a central courtyard. "This is where students gather between classes to socialize. A student cannot practice magic out here."

"Makes sense," I said.

"Now, let me take you to the heart of Lir Winslet: the Great Hall. This is where we hold assemblies, ceremonies, and important events." She led the way through large double doors into a grand hall, the walls lined with portraits of Dragonpriests and Priestesses as well as the king and queen. My heart sank upon seeing the king's face. Despite her calm resolve, I knew Morwen still grieved.

The doors to the hall opened again and in walked two Dragonpriestesses. "Princess Morwen. To what do we owe this pleasure of your visit?" one asked.

Morwen cleared her throat. "I come bearing unfortunate news."

* * *

Sitting there, facing the head Dragonpriest for Lir Winslet was slightly unnerving. I had done nothing wrong, but from the look on his face, it was like I'd decimated a building. His frustration wasn't necessarily directed at me but toward me.

We'd just informed him of our news, despite it being hours later. Dragonpriest Treveri insisted I, a Chaos Dragongoddess, have an in-depth tour of Lir Winslet. Following the tour, he'd made the cook prepare an elaborate meal in my honor. Guilt seeped through my veins. Morwen was the important person here, not me. Despite my feelings, Morwen made no indication that she was bothered. I imagined she felt somewhat relieved that the attention was off of her. She was able to meticulously plan out her end of the conversation.

I glanced at Morwen who still stood tall and confident before the aged Dragonpriest Treveri who sat at his dark oak desk. I, however, sat quietly, observing. Using my gift of telepathy, I hastily ventured into the priest's mind to gain a better understanding of how he'd react. Instead of being angry with Morwen about not being notified of the attack, he was furious that this Chaos Dragongoddess before him hadn't been there to protect the city.

"I don't understand," the priest said, his eyes focused on me. "Why did you not inform us of the dragon attack, Princess Morwen?"

"First, you may remove your gaze from Emera. She was not present when the city was targeted and had no part in the decision."

"And why was that?" His words cut sharp.

"Because I was dead," I said. Who did this guy think he was? Talking to a goddess like that?

The priest remained silent, but my words had the effect I wanted. His anger dissipated immediately, replaced by shock. Maybe we should have led with my death.

"Second, I chose not to inform you because I believed swift action was necessary. We did not have the time or the resources to notify you."

The priest's brow furrowed. He propped his elbows on the desk and clasped his hands in front of him. The billowy blue sleeves of his robe fell down his arms, revealing a scar that began at his wrist and continued halfway down his arm. "We could have offered assistance. There are many students who have mastered their magic that are graduating soon."

Morwen's jaw tightened. "I understand, Priest Treveri, but I also understand the severity of placing unprepared students in the path of a Dragon. The future of our kingdom was at stake," she said, "and I was not about to risk the lives of those who would be responsible for building that future should the palace have fallen."

Priest Treveri's features softening slightly. "That is commendable, Princess Morwen, but you must remember that you are not alone in this struggle."

"I appreciate that, Priest Treveri," Morwen said as she sat in a chair next to me, "but I will not apologize for acting swiftly and in the best interest of the kingdom." Morwen paused, letting the weight of their discussion hang in the air. She shifted in her chair, her expression now thoughtful yet resolute. "Priest Treveri," she began, her voice steady, "there is another matter of great urgency that we must discuss with you."

The priest raised an eyebrow, curiosity mingling with concern. "What can I help you with?"

Morwen glanced at me. So, this was the person she thought could help me. I cleared my throat. "I need to learn how to enter Amram's mind at will, safely, and siphon the god's magic."

The priest's eyes narrowed. His irritation with me was still obvious. "Walking into the mind of a malevolent god carries risks beyond measure. Most gods would never dare attempt such a task."

My focus remained steady on the priest. "I am not like most gods."

Morwen tried to hide her smirk but failed.

"Before I died, Amram siphoned all of my magic as well as most of my soul, making it easier to kill me. Simply put, I need them back. I cannot defeat him without either. Priest Benigno is searching for a text that will help while we venture down this course of action."

Priest Treveri pondered my words for a moment before responding. He leaned back in his seat. "A book might help, and I do know someone who can teach you, but…"

"But what?"

"He is not like us."

"How so?"

"His appearance is unnerving to say the least."

I waved my hand dismissively. "That is of no consequence."

"You might rethink that once you meet him."

Morwen sighed. "There is no time to be judgmental of one's appearance. We must get Emera into Amram's mind as soon as possible."

The priest stood and smoothed out his dark blue robes. They reminded me of Priest Benigno's, with silver stitching that mimicked the waves of the ocean. "Meet me in the courtyard at midnight."

"I appreciate the secrecy, Priest Treveri, but is it necessary?" Morwen asked as she stood.

"More than you know."

*　　　*　　　*

At midnight, Morwen and I entered the courtyard. This was following the brief conversation we had with Priest Benigno regarding the text he'd procured.

"It will take me a little bit of time to read through it," he had said. "Most of what I've seen so far does not pertain to our particular issue. A few more hours, and I think I'll have what I need."

Morwen and I both had bid him farewell, not bothering to mention Priest Treveri's secret teacher. I wanted to see if this person could actually help before letting Priest Benigno in on it. If whoever it was couldn't help me, then we needed whatever was in that text.

A few minutes after we'd entered the courtyard, Priest Treveri showed up. He carried a lit torch which I didn't think was needed because of how bright the moon was.

"Please, follow me," Priest Treveri said. With a solemn gesture, the Dragonpriest halted before a nondescript section of the courtyard's eastern wall. He mumbled words in the ancient Dragonlanguage and traced a series of shapes upon the stone surface. Suddenly, with a low rumble, a hidden doorway appeared and swung open, revealing a narrow staircase descending into darkness.

Morwen looked at me curiously, and we descended down the worn steps after the priest. His torchlight cast haunting shadows upon the walls as we continued deeper underground. The air grew colder and damper with each step, sending shivers down my spine.

"Where are you leading us, Priest Treveri?" Morwen asked, her voice shaking.

"No harm will come to you, Princess Morwen" the priest replied. Morwen must have trusted his words because she seemed to shake off her doubt. Then she straightened her back and didn't question him any further.

Finally, we entered a hidden chamber at the bottom of the stairs. The room was small and cramped, its walls lined with faded framed paintings. Cobwebs clung to the corners, and dust danced lazily in the faint light of a fire that blazed in a fireplace. A solitary bed sat against one wall, its wooden frame worn and weathered. A tattered blanket was haphazardly atop the bed. In another corner, a wooden table with a broken leg that was held together with twine. Papers and books littered its surface. The same could be said about the small table in the opposite corner, with the addition of a half-eaten plate of meat stacked on top.

At the center of the chamber, sitting in a rocking chair next to the fireplace, was a man with a hood draped over his eyes, low enough that I couldn't make out his face. As we approached the man, the Dragonpriest spoke in a voice that echoed through the chamber. "Endrit, you have visitors." The man turned to us and my blood ran cold. This was no man.

"You said the Ghoul was a legend," I hissed.

Morwen's eyes were wide, not with fear, but with shock. "It was just a story told to scare new students. I didn't actually believe it."

The sight of the Dragonghoul sent a chill through my bones, but I refused to show fear.

"You know that I don't answer to that name any longer, Treveri," the Ghoul rasped.

"Wait," I whispered to Morwen. "Did he just say Endrit? As in the God of Light?" My body froze as I laid eyes upon the once Dragongod who had lowered his hood. Endrit, who was supposedly killed for his betrayal of Amram, now sat before us as the school's infamous Dragonghoul. His once white and gold scales were now a sickly shade of green. His skin was wrinkled and marred with patches of red decaying flesh. His eyes were dull and lifeless like he had no

Dragonsoul. Where his nose had been were now two empty holes, void of bone.

I stepped forward. "My name is Emera."

The Ghoul's lips curled into a twisted semblance of a smile, revealing rows of teeth stained with decay. "I know who you are. Nice hair," it—he—said as he rocked back and forth.

I straightened my posture. But just because he looked horrifying, didn't mean he was evil. With a determined nod to Morwen, I stepped forward again, ready to confront the Ghoul. His lifeless eyes watched me with a haunting intensity, and for a moment, I thought he might set my soul ablaze with his light magic. If he had any left.

"Priest Treveri mentioned that you might be able to help me."

The Ghoul remained silent.

"I don't know what I can offer you in return," I continued, doing my best to disguise the desperation in my voice. "But if you help me, I will do whatever it takes to repay you."

He smiled again. Dragonpriest Treveri was right; the sight was unnerving.

The Ghoul angled his head. "You need my help to get your magic back. A dangerous task, even for a Chaos Dragon such as yourself."

"I will do whatever it takes." I waited for his response, but nothing came. "That is…if… you can help me."

The Ghoul threw his head back and laughed. The sound was indescribable. "Oh, I can. But be warned, sister. What you seek is dangerous, and the price of failure is steep." He pointed to his face.

My thoughts grabbed hold of a single word: sister. He was right. I was his sister, and regardless of what he looked like, I should act like one.

"Why did you betray our mother?" My question took him by surprise. He stared at me for a minute or two before standing and gesturing that we all sit down. Morwen sat on the Ghoul's bed, Priest Treveri took the rocking chair, and the Ghoul and I both sat at the table.

"I hated them," the Ghoul began.

"The humans." It was a statement, not a question.

The Ghoul let out a deep sigh, the flames in the fireplace flickered in his eyes. "Our mother created them, bestowed upon them her love and favor while the rest of us—even her own children—were discarded." I winced from his words. Guilt seized my heart. My mother's soul felt his anger.

The Ghoul's gaze hardened. "I tried to warn her. I was keenly aware of the darker aspects of human nature—greed, cruelty, and selfishness—that often overshadowed their positive attributes. Their unchecked influence could upset the balance of magic and nature."

"You judge them too harshly."

The Ghoul remained silent. Then he turned his head to gaze into the flames of the fire. "Maybe. Maybe not."

"Why go to Amram?"

"I thought he'd listen. Mother wouldn't see reason no matter how much I tried. Instead, she ignored me. Said I wasn't compassionate enough. So, I turned to Amram in the hope that he might help establish boundaries or limitations on the humans' behavior—to prevent them from causing harm or becoming too powerful in their own right."

"But he had other plans," Morwen surmised.

The Ghoul nodded. "He lied, and I believed him."

"So, you didn't know that he wanted to wipe out all of humanity?"

The Ghoul continued to stare at the fire as he said, "I did not want that outcome. Once I found out, I tried to convince him otherwise. When I couldn't, I tried to leave. He nearly incinerated me with chaos magic then banned me to a life of darkness."

"You could be dead."

The Ghoul whipped his head around. "What is worse than the god of light," he said, his voice growing louder with every word, "living in darkness for eternity?"

I leaned forward. "Help me get in, and I'll help you get out."

He laughed again, but this time I didn't wince. "Now that I would like to see."

"So, will you help her?" Morwen asked.

The Ghoul's lips curved upward into a menacing grin. "Okay, then."

CHAPTER THIRTEEN

CALIAN

We were part way through one of the Kingdom of Water's dense forests, when the canopy of trees above parted, revealing a moonlit clearing ahead. Despite being a semi-Dragongod, I was tired from our journey. Fin was plastered to my back, snoring loudly. My shoulder suddenly felt wet. I looked down to see a small spot of drool.

I sighed. I couldn't blame Fin. We'd traveled non-stop since Khaosar. We, including Dhruv, needed rest. But Dhruv would refuse to stop if I ordered him to. So, we kept going.

As we emerged into the open space, my senses immediately detected the presence of someone or something else.

"Dhruv," I said, my voice low. "Slow down. I think we've got trouble."

I let my eyes wander between the trees and through the thick brush. I expected to see menacing eyes from a nighttime creature, but there was nothing. The only movement came from the soft breeze that rustled the leaves. It wasn't a cold breeze, but it still sent a slight chill down my spine. Even Dhruv was nervous.

"Slow and steady," I said and patted his neck.

Dhruv walked a few steps forward. The path turned slightly left, obstructing our view for a moment. When we rounded the curve, twenty imposing men stood before us, the scales on their necks glinting in the moonlight.

"Mercenaries," I mumbled, taking note of the armor they wore and the weapons at their hips. "I don't have time for this." My eyes scanned the area but found no horses. "So, these men hid their horses. Unfortunate for them. Fortunate for us."

Dhruv snorted in agreement. He sensed the tension in the air but remained steady. With a flick of my wrist, I summoned a single flame in my palm and let it grow higher and wilder as we advanced on the mercenaries.

Fin choked out a final snore before sitting up. "What's going…" He slid off Dhruv, took a fighting stance, and readied his bow with an arrow.

The leader of the group, a towering figure with large muscles and white scales stepped forward. "Captain Calian Westbow. Your presence is an affront to Amram's will. Surrender now, and perhaps your death will be swift."

Fin and I exchanged glances and then laughed.

The leader's eyes blazed with fury. Good.

My magic hummed beneath my skin. "If it is a battle you seek, then a battle you shall have." The flame in my palm morphed into a large ball, and I heaved it at them. The ball hit its target: a scrawny man with missing teeth. He dropped to his knees, clearly surprised by the large hole I'd blasted through his torso. He fell, dead. The other men shifted nervously.

The leader roared, and the men advanced just as Fin let loose a volley of arrows, taking down a few of the mercenaries on the outside edges. As the others moved forward, I dismounted Dhruv and pushed my hands out, creating walls of fire that erupted from the ground and engulfed a few of the men in searing flames. Gusts of wind sent them tumbling backward, screaming in agony. The leader, who'd somersaulted away just in time, climbed back to his feet and ran toward me. The wall of flames died down, and the rest of his men spread out to try and surround us.

Fin continued his assault as the mercenaries unleashed a relentless barrage of elemental magic. His amulet protected him from the magic being thrown at him. But eventually, he'd run out of arrows.

Dhruv reared back and kicked his powerful hooves, knocking out a couple of idiot men that attempted to grab him. Streams of crackling lightning zig-zagged through the air, followed by torrents of icy shards and searing blasts of fire. I focused on wielding fire magic with, weaving flames that warded off some of the onslaught. However, amidst the chaos of the magical onslaught, sudden close movement caught me off guard. I turned to see the leader just as he pushed his blade into my stomach. I looked down to see blood dripping down my black leathers.

I looked up with a smirk on my face. "You missed," I said. Then I blasted a ball of fire at him, the impact sent him reeling backward. My body swayed, so I took a moment to regain my balance and pulled out the sword. My healing magic flared to life, and the wound was mended in no time.

While I was healing, Earth Dragonborns conjured massive boulders from the ground, hurling them toward Fin. I countered with waves of searing flames, but the boulders weren't deterred. Fin dove out of their way just before being hit.

"Don't be stupid, Cal," Fin scolded, jokingly. "You've got to use more chaos magic." He was right. I didn't have much, but it was enough to overpower any regular Dragonborn.

But I didn't have time to test that power. A bolt of lightning, conjured by one of the remaining mercenaries, struck true. A scream of agony tore from my throat as I watched the lightning sear through Dhruv's flesh. My horse's eyes fluttered before closing and falling to the ground.

"No!" I screamed.

Fin's eyes widened. "Go! I've got this"

I didn't argue. Heart-wrenching anger flooded my body as I ran toward Dhruv and knelt beside him. I glanced toward the night sky. "Please, Ragnar. Protect us." Then, with what little chaos magic I had, I called to all the stones and rocks in the forest and built a wall surrounding Dhruv and me. My hands trembled with grief and rage.

Beyond the wall, the elemental magic stopped. The mercenaries must have realized Fin was immune to their magic. The clanging of swords rang out around us. As Fin fought valiantly, heavy clouds blocked the moon, shrouding what little light we had. Raindrops fell suddenly, washing out any fire that still remained.

Tears streamed down my cheeks as I cradled Dhruv's head in my lap. His once powerful body lay twitching, his chest heaving with labored breaths. "Stay with me, boy," I whispered, my voice breaking. My hands trembled as I stroked his mane. The rain poured around us, soaking my skin.

Dhruv's eyes, usually so full of life and mischief, were dull and glassy. Pain was etched in every line of his face, and it all but broke me. He was more than just a horse to me; he was my companion, my friend.

"Hold on, Dhruv," I pleaded, my tears mingling with the rain. "You can't leave me, too." I took a deep breath and called to my healing magic, hoping it would be enough. A soft glow emitted from my hands, and I pushed as much power as I could muster into my magic. "Why isn't this working?" I said, my voice choking back the sob in my throat.

His breathing grew shallower, each exhale was a struggle. Regardless of how much healing magic I poured into him, I knew deep within my Dragonsoul that his life was slipping away from him. An overwhelming sense of helplessness washed over me. I had fought battles, faced down enemies with nothing but a sword, and even killed a powerful Dragongod, yet I was powerless to save my mate and now Dhruv from dying in my arms. As the final breath left Dhruv's body, I leaned down and pressed my forehead to his. Then the wall around me fell.

Fin appeared at my side, gasping for breath. "No," he panted. "Oh, I'm so sorry, Cal."

"They will pay with their lives," I whispered to him.

Lightning crashed around us. Deep within my body, a primal surge of power exploded. My body convulsed with raw chaos energy. My muscles rippled and bones shifted beneath my skin. Crimson scales erupted from my flesh, spreading like wildfire across my body as my limbs elongated and contorted, reshaping into powerful claws and massive wings. A row of spines sprouted from my back. While my once-human features twisted and elongated, an intense inferno blazed within me.

With a mighty beat of my newly formed wings, I rose into the air, looked directly at the mercenaries, and roared. There, standing several feet in front of the rest, was the leader. His smile faded slowly as he lowered his blade. Flames erupted from my jaw, engulfing him in a blanket of fire. There was nothing left of him when I stopped.

The remaining Dragonborn mercenaries screamed in fear at the sight of their disintegrated leader. I leaned my neck down and Fin climbed on. Then, with a deafening roar that echoed through the forest, I ascended into the air and hovered above them. Roaring once more, I released a wave of flames upon them. Only scorched bodies remained as I flew toward the City of Anahita.

*   *   *

Any other time, I would have been ecstatic at the idea of being able to shift into a Dragon form. But I had no joy in my heart. Emera was gone. Dhruv was gone. And as I walked into the City of Anahita with Fin, I could tell even through the darkness that the once vibrant city was gone. Hatred for Amram flared in my chest. He was the cause of all of this.

"I will take everything from him," I vowed to my horse and my mate as I stepped over debris. Yet amidst the crumbling buildings and overgrown streets, half of the palace remained intact. The other half was a mere shadow of its former glory. It had been one of my favorite places. King Calder Elderbrook was one of the kindest kings I'd ever met. His family didn't deserve this fate. With a heavy heart, I entered the palace. I didn't know what to say. Fin was right, we should have been here.

Once inside, we headed for the throne room. I was about to knock when the large doors opened, revealing Queen Baia.

Fin stepped forward. Queen Baia rushed forward and all-but threw her arms around him. Fin held her until the queen stepped back. She smoothed out the fabric of her dark blue skirt.

"It has been too long since we last crossed paths, Captain. Come." We followed the queen into a smaller room that looked somewhat like the war room back in the City of Vukan. However, this room didn't have a table with a map of Amram's attacks. It was cozier and more inviting, despite the state of the palace.

Queen Baia sat in a chair facing a large portrait of her family. I sat in the opposite chair and gazed at the portrait myself.

At the center of the painting, stood the king in robes of deep blue, representing the kingdom. Beside him stood the Queen, a vision of grace and beauty as usual. And between them stood their daughter, Morwen, a symbol of hope and the future. Despite her youth, there was a quiet strength in her demeanor.

"Fin. Captain Westbow," Queen Baia began, her voice steady but tinged with sorrow, "As you have probably guessed, my husband will not be joining us."

Fin nodded, silently processing the information.

"Queen Baia," I said, choking on the words. "I cannot begin to tell you how sorry I am. The amount of regret that I feel is…"

The queen held up a hand. "I am exhausted by the number of condolences I have received. Instead, I must tell you of the events that transpired here. Because I fear we were not the last city he will destroy."

I nodded, "He will march on the City of Tamasvi. I came to gather information. That, and other things.

"I will tell you what I saw."

I leaned back in the chair, listening intently as she began.

"It was a night unlike any other," Baia continued, her gaze distant as she recalled the chaos. "Dark clouds gathered in the sky. There was an unusual sense of dread throughout the city. The type of dread that just weighs on your bones. And then, without warning, they descended upon us—the Dragons." Her voice trembled slightly as she spoke. "I had never seen one before. To be honest, I was in awe at first. But then," Queen Baia went on, her voice growing stronger with each word. "They swooped down from the sky, their deafening roars echoing through the streets as they unleashed their fire."

Out of the corner of my eye, Fin's jaw tightened as he imagined the scene unfolding before him.

"There were three of them, one larger than the others. That one was a purple Dragon. I didn't know they existed anymore. The others were white and green. They targeted the palace first," Baia continued, her voice faltering slightly. "Calder stood his ground, but he was no match for them. The green one struck him down without mercy, and then turned to the city, leaving chaos and death in their wake."

A heavy silence hung in the air as the queen paused, her eyes moist with unshed tears.

"They spared no one, Captain," she whispered, her voice barely above a whisper. "Homes were reduced to rubble, and innocent lives were lost in the blink of an eye. Our city lies in ruins, and our people are left to pick up the pieces of their shattered lives." When she looked at Fin, her first tear fell. "Only a handful of humans survived. The Dragons hunted them down and…" She stopped speaking, unable to recount the horrors of the attack on the humans.

Fin clenched his fists as he struggled to contain his rage. "I swear on my life that I will hunt them down, and they will pay for what they've done. I will end them."

Queen Baia nodded; her eyes were filled with gratitude. "There is someone you should meet."

Fin frowned. "At this hour?"

"He's been unable to sleep since the attack, so I doubt he will mind." She motioned for us to follow her, so we did. We made our way up the grand staircase and down a long hallway. At this point, I found it odd that Morwen wasn't with her or that the queen hadn't mentioned her daughter at all.

"Your Majesty," I said, but the queen stopped outside of a room and knocked on the door, interrupting my question. After a few seconds, the door creaked open, and a human man with yellow hair appeared.

"Mr. Ren. I hope that we are not disturbing you."

The man's eyes were puffy and red. He'd been crying. "No, not at all," he said slowly.

"May we come in?"

"Of course, Your Majesty." He opened the door wider, and we followed Queen Baia into the man's room. It was unusual being in a stranger's bedchamber at this late hour, but these were unusual circumstances. Fin and I sat on a small couch while Mr. Ren and the queen sat in opposite chairs.

"Mr. Ren, I would like you to meet Fintan Archer. He is my daughter's betrothed and future King of the Kingdom of Water."

I almost choked on my own saliva. I'd never heard Queen Baia introduce Fin that way.

"And Fintan," the queen said, addressing my friend. "This is Mr. Ren. He is responsible for all the immaculate gowns I wear." The queen smiled, but it didn't meet her eyes.

Fin stood abruptly and thrust out his hand. "A pleasure to meet you, Mr. Ren."

"I…am…honored." Mr. Ren stammered, seemingly awe-struck by Fin's presence. He remained seated for a few more seconds before finally standing and shaking Fin's hand. His eyes met the queen's. She inhaled a quick breath and exhaled.

"Mr. Ren is staying here as my personal guest. His shop was destroyed in the attack while he was visiting the palace." She glanced at Mr. Ren who hung his head. She turned her attention back to Fin. "And his family was killed in the process."

Fin opened his mouth to respond, but he closed it. I, too, didn't know what to say.

"The humans of this kingdom—of every kingdom—know who you are," Mr. Ren said, his gaze still focused on the floor.

Queen Baia placed a gentle hand on Mr. Ren's knee. "Mr. Ren, like so many other humans, looks up to you. You are a symbol of strength and resilience for your people. They do not turn to the Dragonborns for protection; they turn to you."

Mr. Ren sniffled. "Knowing that a human is fighting the Dragon's for us… It means more than you can imagine."

We remained for a few more minutes, hearing Mr. Ren's stories of the humans who sang Fin's praises. Once we left the room, Fin cleared his throat. "Well, that's a lot of pressure, isn't it." His tone was serious. There was no hint of humor.

"Maybe so. But you can handle it."

Fin snorted as Queen Baia joined us in the hallway, having bid Mr. Ren a good night. Although, I figured it would be a while before he had another good night's rest.

"Your Majesty, where is Morwen?"

The queen's expression darkened at the mention of Morwen, her lips forming a thin line. "Morwen has gone to the Dragonseminary Lir Winslet," she said bluntly. "She left earlier today."

"Lir Winslet," I repeated. It had been quite a while since I'd walked through the Dragonseminary's halls, but I remembered where it was. I stood abruptly. "Then that is where we will go." I bowed, walked to the door, and opened it.

Queen Baia spoke out just before I left. "She went with Dragonpriest Benigno and the Dragongoddess Emera."

I paused, my heart pounding in my chest. It felt like the ground had shifted beneath my feet, leaving me unsteady and breathless. Emera? How could that be possible? My mind raced, a whirlwind of disbelief and hope swirling together. I watched her die, and yet here I was, hearing that she was alive.

My throat tightened with emotion as I tried to find my voice. Finally, I managed to stammer out a shaky thank you. Without waiting for a response from the queen, I turned and left, my legs carrying me away. The world outside seemed brighter and sharper knowing that Emera was alive. Mother said I would see her again, but truthfully, I didn't think she had meant in the living world. So, how was it possible? I had to find her, to see her with my own eyes, to believe that Queen Baia's words were true.

Fin and I ran through the city, and I used my air magic to throw any heavy rubble in my path. We ran as fast as we could until we reached a clearing large enough for me to transform into my Dragon form once more. Fin climbed up and held on tight as I lifted from the ground and flew quickly toward Lir Winslet.

Gliding effortlessly through the night sky, my mind raced with thoughts of Emera. The anticipation of getting to hold her in my arms was almost too much to bear. My heart pounded passionately. It hadn't beat that fast since I realized Emera and I were Dragonmates. I wanted—no, needed—to feel her warmth and hear her laughter.

Then my heart dropped. I had to tell Emera about Dhruv. I swallowed a lump that formed in my throat. It burned on the way down to the pit of my stomach. It was bittersweet. Losing Dhruv but getting Emera back.

I pushed my thoughts aside as I soared above the trees. I focused my attention on getting to Lir Winslet quickly. My keen eyes scanned all of my surroundings. Then, in the distance, I spotted a silhouette against the moonlit sky. For a moment, my heart stopped, thinking I was watching a Dragon.

"Do you see that?" Fin shouted.

I growled, hoping he understood what I meant.

"Considering how many Dragons Amram resurrected, my best guess was that it won't be friendly."

I growled again. Anxiously, I flew closer. I exhaled when the silhouette resolved into nothing more than a large bird, its violet wings outstretched as it soared gracefully through the night sky right before me. Its wings reminded me of Emera's Dragonscales. Gods, I missed her so much.

"Thank the gods," Fin said loudly with a sigh.

Once I saw Lir Winslet, I began my descent. I landed just beyond the Dragonseminary's entrance so as not to disturb the students and Dragonpriests. My massive form would no doubt send everyone scattering in fear. Once back in my human form, we strode toward Lir Winslet hopeful that Emera was somewhere within its walls.

CHAPTER FOURTEEN

EMERA

"You are weak."

"And you are rude. Seems like we're even."

The Ghoul's lips curled into a sinister grin. He sat at the head of a classroom at an instructor's refined wooden table, his weathered form hunched slightly over a stack of wrinkled parchment. His piercing gaze, illuminated by the flickering glow of a solitary candle in front of him, was fixated on me. I sat at a student's desk before him, Morwen occupying the desk to my left. I shifted impatiently in my chair, twirling my violet hair in my hands, but refusing to look away from his gaze.

"Not many people—even powerful Dragonborns—would attempt this," the Ghoul added.

"How fortunate that I am not just a powerful Dragonborn." The drumming of my heart quickened slightly with anticipation as I leaned forward. Morwen looked bored, which I thought was unlike her. She continued tracing the intricate carvings etched into the surface of the table with her fingers. Maybe she wasn't bored. Maybe she just didn't want to look at the Ghoul.

"How do we even begin?"

"With patience, cunning, and a healthy dose of audacity," he replied with an amused smirk.

The Ghoul picked up a tattered piece of parchment from the desk, its edges frayed and yellowed with age. "This, my dear, is the key to unlocking Amram's mind," the Ghoul explained, his voice barely above a whisper. "Are you sure you're ready to do this?"

"My readiness has no bearing on the situation."

At that moment, the door creaked open. We all turned to see Calian standing in the doorway.

"Who the Dragonhell are you?" the Ghoul snapped.

Calian's handsome face was etched with worry and longing as he stared at me. For a moment, he simply stood there. Then, without a word, he strode through the classroom and wrapped me in his arms, holding me close as if afraid I might leave him again.

"I thought I had lost you forever," he whispered gruffly, clearly holding back tears.

I stood there hesitatingly, uncertainty gnawing at my heart. My feelings were fragmented, and my thoughts were scattered. I knew I should feel something for this man.

But I didn't.

As the shadows from the candlelight lengthened, I pulled back slowly so that I didn't startle him. My gaze drifted over his handsome features, searching for something I couldn't quite grasp. All I felt was friendship and mild curiosity. The connection I once felt remained elusive.

"I... I'm sorry," I murmured, my voice barely above a whisper. "I am not who I once was."

He swallowed hard, the weight of my words hanging heavy in the space between us. "I don't know what you mean," he replied, his voice strained.

Morwen stepped forward. "She has Nimerah's soul, not her own. She's not herself."

He reached out to me, but I stepped back instinctively, a pang of guilt stabbing at my heart. I might not have felt love for him, but I did feel remorse.

"I'm sorry," I repeated. "I just...I don't know how to feel." I pulled back the collar of my shirt. Calian peered down, his eyes widening when he noticed my Dragonmate wings were gone. He then grabbed his shirt and hastily pulled the collar back. His wings were still there.

He nodded, a flicker of pain crossing his features before he masked it with a forced smile. "We'll fix this," he said, his voice cracking slightly. "I'm just glad that you're alive."

The Ghoul's chair screeched against the hardwood floor as he stood. "Can someone please tell me what is going on?"

Morwen leveled with the Ghoul. "This is Captain Calian Westbow. You might remember him as Vasuman, the son of Vukan."

"Morwen," Calian said, his voice filled with regret. "I'm so sorry that I wasn't…" His voice trailed off, struggling to produce the right words.

Morwen held up her hand. "You…and Fin…were right where you needed to be. I hope that your time in the City of Vukan was fruitful."

"Did I hear my name?"

We all turned to see Fin walking toward us. Morwen rushed to him, and they embraced. Then Fin pulled back slightly and cradled Morwen's face in his hands. "I will never forgive myself for not being there."

Morwen's voice was soft. "Then I will forgive you for the both of us. You had no way of knowing."

"But your father," Fin managed to say before Morwen placed her finger to his lips, silencing him, then replacing her fingers with her lips.

My eyes lingered on them before sliding to meet Calian's. The notion of love felt foreign to me now. Calian's eyes darted to the floor, and he ran his fingers through his hair.

The Ghoul cleared his throat and shot Calian a mischievous grin. "Vasuman, huh? Good to see you alive and kicking. But please tell me why I should care that you're interrupting us?"

"I'm Emera's mate," Calian growled.

I winced at the mention of the word. We weren't mates any longer. Fin took notice, the lines of his forehead creased with curiosity. "What's wrong?" Morwen leaned in and whispered an explanation in his ear. His eyes widened before he smiled. "So, you're Emera, but you're not? Whoa."

The Ghoul waved his hand for Fin to quiet down, his grin widening as his beady eyes danced between Calian and me. "Ah! How convenient!" he raised a finger and pressed it to his lips, looking at the ceiling like he was deep in thought. "We can use you. Now, we need to get moving up here. The sun comes up in a few hours, and regardless of your progress, I won't be here to see it."

"Who are you?" Calian demanded.

"Endrit the God of Light." I caught myself. "*Former* God of Light. He was cursed by Amram, so now he is the Ghoul. He has agreed to educate me on entering a mind at will and stealing magic."

"Amram's magic to be precise," Morwen added.

"So, what is the plan, Ghoul?" I asked.

He chuckled darkly. "The plan, my dear sister, is simple. You will traipse into the recesses of your mate's mind, seeking out the relics that represent his magic and his soul."

"That doesn't seem too bad," I said.

The Ghoul smirked again. "Then you will siphon them from his body."

Fin scrunched his nose. "That seems aggressive."

"Agreed. I won't do it."

The Ghoul's smirk faded, replaced with irritation. "Then you've already failed, and I am leaving."

Calian took a step forward. "Wait!" He turned to me. "Em, it's okay. I trust you."

But I didn't trust myself. If I'd learned anything about my mother's soul in the time since I'd been resurrected, it was that she would do whatever it took to defeat Amram. And if that meant siphoning Calian's soul in the process…

I shuddered at the thought.

Morwen raised an eyebrow, intrigued. "And what will Emera do with these relics once she's found them? You said siphon his magic and soul, but surely, that means she must manipulate or destroy the relics."

The Ghoul's grin turned positively wicked. "Perceptive. She'll pluck them from the depths of his consciousness and wield them like the treasures they are," he explained, his voice tinged with excitement. "But first, we must navigate the labyrinth of this young man's mind."

"Fin," Calian said, throwing his chin toward the door, "be the lookout."

Fin nodded, kissed Morwen on the cheek, and made his way back toward the entrance of the room.

Meanwhile, the Ghoul moved two desks, making them face one another. With a wave of his hand, the Ghoul gestured for Calian and I to sit. We did as he demanded.

"Close your eyes," the Ghoul instructed.

"Wait!"

The Ghoul's eyes narrowed. "What now?"

"How do you know all this?"

"Because this is how I died."

"But you're standing in front of me."

"I am just a shell of my former self. I have no soul, no magic. Amram took it all from me through a Dragonmeld. He made me watch from within."

I nodded, accepting his answer. I did as he asked and closed my eyes, calling to my water magic, letting it flow within me to keep me calm.

"Focus your thoughts," the Ghoul whispered in my ear. I almost jumped at how close he had become without me noticing.

I fueled my magic with every ounce of energy I had. It took control and forced my eyes open.

Morwen sucked in a quick breath. "Your eyes. They're…"

"Pure chaos," the Ghoul said.

"Violet mixed with lightning," Morwen murmured, her voice just loud enough for me to hear.

My magic created thin violet threads that stretched out to Calian and coiled around him. The threads seeped into his skin, and the Dragonmeld had begun.

At first, I was shrouded in darkness. I looked left and then right, searching for his memories. The only Dragonmeld I'd ever done was in Erjon's mind, and he opened up fully. Memories ran on display almost instantaneously. Calian's mind wasn't like that. It took several minutes before I finally located a single flame twisting and turning in the distance. I walked toward it, each step an echo.

As I made my way toward the flame, it grew taller and brighter. The darkness flowed into color; a landscape formed around me. I found myself transported to a world of gritty streets and alleyways. I didn't know much about his past, just that Hestia had saved him from torture so long ago. But there was a gap between Calian being at the palace and him living on the streets.

I coughed from the air that was thick with the scent of smoke and grime. Sounds of bustling activity echoed off the walls of the surrounding buildings, yet I was the only person there.

"Okay," I whispered to myself. "Relics."

"Yes, find the relics." The Ghoul's voice was distant.

"Your eyes may be open, but your mind has closed your vision so that you can only see where you are now. Do not forget that we are here…In case things go…awry."

"Got it."

I cautiously put one foot in front of the other into the narrow, winding streets, lined with shoddy buildings with flickering lights in their windows. Trash littered the ground, blown about by the ever-present gusts of wind that sweep through the town. Or city. I couldn't tell from where I stood. But amidst the darkness of the streets, there were pockets of light. Warm, inviting light.

As I advanced through the maze of alleyways, the weight of Calian's past pressed down on me. My empathic magic sparked to life. There was pain and struggle, but also resilience and determination, each emotion woven into the very fabric of the streets.

Then I saw him.

He stumbled through the crowd, his shoulders hunched and his expression weary. His clothes were threadbare, his eyes hollow with hunger and fatigue.

Calian approached a baker's shop, his gaze lingering on the mouthwatering display of pastries and bread that were on display in the window. Calian hesitated for a moment before slipping inside the shop. Through my empathic magic, I felt the weight of his hunger and desperation as he approached the counter. But he didn't ask for bread.

"If you're that hungry, why don't you buy a loaf?" I asked him. But because this was a memory, he didn't respond. Instead, his stomach growled with need.

Right as he turned to go, someone stepped in through the door. I released a quick breath. Elio.

I knew they had a tumultuous past. Would they exchange words? Would they throw their fists at one another? It was neither. Instead, there was a flicker of compassion in Elio's eyes as he studied Calian's face. Elio reached into his pocket and pulled out a couple of silver coins. He placed them in Calian's hand, nodded, and went to the counter to make his own purchases before exiting. Calian didn't argue. He marched up to the counter and purchased two loaves of bread with one of his silver coins.

I followed him out of the bakery and down a darkened alley. I was drawn deeper into the recesses of his past, following close behind him as he navigated the streets of the city. He hastily pulled off pieces of bread and stuffed them in his mouth. As he ate, his pace quickened as if he was guided by a sense of purpose.

With each twist and turn, the familiar sights and sounds of the city faded into the background until all that remained was the oppressive silence of the night. At last, Calian came to a stop before a nondescript doorway. Without hesitation, he opened it and disappeared from sight.

"Okay, here we go," I said to no one and followed him.

I stood in a musty, damp hallway. My breathing quickened along with the fast cadence of my heartbeat. I couldn't see Calian, but there was no other way to go, so I continued onward. A faint glow grew brighter and brighter the further I traversed down the hallway. When I reached the end, I stood behind a curtain, the light piercing through its holes and past its edges. With trembling hands, I pushed aside the curtain and stepped inside, my eyes widening in astonishment.

Before me lay a hidden sanctuary, a secret refuge nestled within the heart of Calian's memories. The walls were adorned with tapestries and trinkets, each one representing a piece of Calian's personality.

How was I going to figure out which ones were the relics?

In the center of the room, a small fire burned brightly, casting a warm, comforting glow over the makeshift furnishings that filled the space. And there, sitting in a chair before the flickering flames, was Calian, his expression was one of utter despair.

Heat filled my body from the unsurmountable anger I had for Queen Hestia. Prophecy be damned! How could she do this to her only son? How could she toss him onto the streets to live like this? I might not be his mate anymore, but that didn't mean I had lost compassion for him.

But then he turned his head, and our eyes met. For the first time since I'd seen him, a small surge of emotion washed over me. Despite the erased Dragonmate wings, *there was a confusingly profound sense of connection between us. I remembered the electric feeling when we'd met, but this time it felt foreign and unusual. Like my body was trying to jolt our connection back to life.*

I took a few deep breaths to steady myself. My breathing eased as I gazed into his dark eyes. A single curl of his dark wavy hair hung over them. He brushed it away and ran his fingers through his hair. Then he took me by surprise with just three little words.

"Who are you?" he asked, his voice filled with suspicion.

Okay, what? Did I just hallucinate? I looked left, then right. No one else was in the room. I pointed at myself and said, "Me?"

Calian leveled his stare. "Who else? You're the only other person here."

"Um...Yes...I suppose you're right," I stammered. My feet remained frozen in place.

Calian's eyes widened in recognition, a flicker of confusion crossing his face before he composed himself. "Who are you?" he asked. He strained his vision to see me more clearly in the dim light. He stood from his chair and faced me fully. His brows furrowed. "Better yet, what are you?"

I felt a pang of disbelief. He wasn't an all-powerful Chaos Dragon. He wasn't supposed to recognize me. Wasn't that how it worked? Erjon never did when I entered his mind. "I'm...I'm just passing through," I managed to get out, my gaze darting around the room for the relics. Find them, get them, and get out.

Summoning my water magic, I drenched my bewilderment with tranquility. It coursed through my veins, and I felt at peace. I had a mission to complete, and it didn't involve this. "Calian, I need your help."

"You didn't answer my question," he said gruffly.

I held up my hands in surrender. "I mean no harm."

"You're a Chaos Dragon. I know what you're capable of." A ball of flame formed suddenly in his hand.

"I just need your help. That is all."

"Help with what?" he asked cautiously, letting the ball expand larger, brighter.

I ignored his silent warning and took a step forward. "I'm searching for two relics," I explained. "Each one is a representative of who you are." I decided to withhold that one relic contained his magic and the other his Dragonsoul.

It was apparent from the skepticism written all over his face that he thought I was a lunatic. "So, judging by your reaction when I saw you, you came here to steal from me."

Was I sweating? Yeah, I think I was sweating. This was not going to plan.

"I don't want to steal them. I want to look at them."

For a moment, Calian hesitated, and he scanned the room. "You just want to see them?"

"Yes."

"How do you know what they look like?"

I dropped my hands and sighed. "I don't."

Then, slowly, he nodded. "Alright, I," he agreed, a small smile playing on his lips. "Lead the way." He extinguished the flame in his hand and gestured toward the room.

I had no clue what I was looking for. Two relics. That represented him. Calian leaned against the wall - his usual stance - and watched me with keen interest. I studied the room and its treasures. A wooden box, a key, the silver coin Elio had given him, a ring...

A ring.

A simple yet elegant ring, probably passed down through generations of Calian's family, sat on a small side table next to his wooden bed. I picked it up and inspected it. It was made of polished silver, its surface adorned with intricate engravings that spiral around the band.

At the center of the ring was a single, luminous gemstone, a vibrant violet that radiated with an inner light. Its deep purple hue reminded me of the endless expanse of the night sky, flecked with tiny twinkling stars. On each side of the gemstone were two small pearls, adding to its elegance. It was the most beautiful ring I'd ever seen.

Calian appeared at my side, looking at the ring. I felt his emotions welling up within him, so I reached my magic out to him to gain a better understanding. At first, I felt a profound sense of connection to his past. For him, the ring was more than just a piece of jewelry; it was a symbol of his identity.

"Where did you get this?" I asked him even though I didn't expect him to tell me.

"I awoke one day, lying in the middle of the street. It was on my finger. I don't remember much about that day to be honest, nor do I remember what happened before it."

Okay, so I was wrong. This version of Calian, the one before Anwir got a hold of him, must have been more open and trusting. "I think this might be one," I said in a hushed tone. I stood there for a minute, not sure about what to do. So, I slipped it on my finger. I held my breath and waited.

"Were you expecting something to happen?" He reached out to touch the ring.

"I don't know. Maybe."

Then it happened, the room grew still, suspended in time. Calian stood frozen beside me, his arm extended in the air. I waved my hand in front of him, but there was no reaction.

With a deep breath, I closed my eyes, allowing my chaos magic to surge forth. It hummed and crackled around me, and I felt the connection between my soul—mine, not Nimerah's—and the ring. Calian's Dragonsoul came to me willingly. A rush of power coursed through me, tingling along my skin with whispers from Calian. My breath hitched in my throat. Intertwined with that power was something more intimate, more intense. His soul continued to flow into me like a gentle stream. I could drown in it.

The light in the room began to fade. I looked at Calian. His appearance was changing. He became increasingly pale. I was taking too much! I pulled at the ring with all my might, but it wouldn't come off. Sweat prickled at my hairline and my breathing became labored. Panic had set in.

I continued to tug at the ring while shouting, "Wake me up! Ghoul! Morwen! I'm taking too much!"

Finally, the ring slid off.

When my vision cleared, I saw Calian lying on the floor. The familiar jolt of electric energy was back. But so was the panic I felt in his mind.

"What have I done?"

CHAPTER FIFTEEN

EMERA

I stood over Calian, back in the classroom, my heart pounding in my chest as I realized the gravity of what I had done. I had siphoned so much of his soul, that the coloring of his skin, once vibrant and full of life, was now gaunt and sickly.

The Ghoul walked slowly toward us, with a mesmerized look on his face. It was as if he was drawn by the scent of death. His eyes sparkled with what I could only describe as a ravenous hunger. He stopped and hovered over Calian, his bony fingers reaching out as if to claim my mate.

"No!" I growled, summoning a gust of wind to throw back the Ghoul into a row of tables at the center of the classroom.

His body collided with a couple of chairs and then went careening into a table. I looked down at my hand and considered my instinctual reaction. I still didn't feel the Dragonmates' bond between us, but there was something buried deep within my mind that indicated it was still there.

Fin sprang into action, positioning himself between where the Ghoul lay and Calian. He faced the Ghoul with an arrow nocked and pointed at the creature's head. "Don't even consider doing that again."

The Ghoul held up his hands. "I'm sorry. I didn't mean anything by it. It's just a product of who I am, who I've become." He dropped his head, ashamed of his actions.

I looked back at Calian, determination coursing through my body. "You will not die today." With my hands on his chest, I channeled my healing magic. It traveled through my fingertips and seeped into Calian's skin. The familiar glow of my healing magic pulsed beneath my palms, but Calian didn't move. His breathing became more shallow.

Morwen closed her eyes and murmured a prayer to Anahita. Through her prayer, I felt her tranquil magic course beneath my skin, cooling my body and offering a sense of calm. Her magic allowed me to gather my thoughts.

I wasn't sure what I needed to do. Think, Em. What would you have done before you died? The thought surprised me, but maybe the drop of my own soul was trying to tell me something.

"Let's try it," I mumbled to myself. I leaned down, pulled my hair away from my face, and placed my lips lightly onto his. Then, with a sudden gasp, Calian's eyes fluttered open and he let out a small grumble. I leaned back and watched him as he sat up. At first, his eyes were clouded and unfocused, but as he blinked away the haze, clarity returned, and he looked up at me with a mixture of confusion and relief.

"Em? What...What happened?" His voice was strong, and a healthy color had returned to his face.

"You're alive," I said and sighed with relief. "I thought I'd killed you."

Our moment of relief was shattered by the sudden intrusion of Dragonpriest Treveri. The heavy wooden doors of the room burst open, revealing the disheveled priest, his robes torn and his face pale with fear. He was visibly shaken. What had happened? Calian and I both scrambled to our feet.

"Thank the heavens I found you!" the priest exclaimed, his voice quivering. "There's... there's a Dragon attacking Lir Winslet!"

Dread seized my body, and my mind raced with a thousand thoughts. A dragon, here?

"What color is it?" Fin asked.

"Excuse me," the priest asked.

"What color is it?" Fin said more assertively.

Color drained from the priest's face. His brow creased as he searched his memory. "Uh…Green…I think?"

Calian's eyes narrowed. "There's a Dragon attacking your seminary, and you couldn't even bother to take notice of what color it is?"

"Not when I have young Dragonborns to alert and get to safety," the priest snapped. Beneath his attitude was fear, and I couldn't blame him for it. He had every right to be scared.

Calian's expression turned grim when he looked at me. "We thought we saw a Dragon as I flew here, but it was just a violet bird." He kicked a desk. "Valda can shapeshift! A violet bird with feathers like scales? How could I have been that stupid?"

I grabbed his shoulder and turned him toward me. "What do you mean you flew here? You can fly?"

He took several deep breaths before answering as if he were trying to steady himself. Then he ran his hand through his hair, combing back a few curls from in front of his eyes. It was then that I caught a glimpse of tears. They pooled within his eyes and glistened beneath his black lashes.

"What's wrong?" I asked.

He cleared his throat, desperately trying to stay composed. "I flew here because I couldn't ride."

For a brief moment, I wasn't sure what he meant. But then it sank in. "No," I said softly. I shook my head and placed my hand on my heart, acknowledging the weight of the news. It was sad, undeniably so, but the sharp pain I expected wasn't there. Dhruv was gone. Oh, Zari would be heartbroken.

"I was attacked on my way here by a group of mercenaries sent by Amram. Dhruv fought gallantly, but he was killed. It must have been the fuel I needed to transform into a Dragon." He looked directly into my eyes. "And after I did, I burned them all."

"As you should have," I replied.

Calian studied me, confusion written all over his face. "How can you be so calm about this?" he said, his voice gruff with disbelief. His eyes said it all. He didn't understand why I didn't feel as much remorse as he did.

I sighed, meeting his eyes and trying to find the right words. "It's not that I don't recognize or understand the severity of this loss. Try as I might, I don't feel the same way toward anyone that I used to. The bonds I have with all of you are different now, filtered through my mother's soul. It's hard to explain."

Anger flashed in his eyes. "Try me," he barked.

I leveled my stare. "I'm not the same person you remember."

Fin appeared at Calian's side, resting his hand on his friend's shoulder. "This is a conversation for another time. We need to stop the Dragon."

I turned to the Ghoul. "I know you don't want to be seen, but as much as you seem to despise this place, it is your home. We need you."

The Ghoul placed a finger to his lips and thought for a moment.

"So…Will you help us?"

He smirked. "I thought you'd never ask." He pulled out a dagger he had sheathed on his hip.

I didn't even look behind me as I rushed to the door and out into the corridor. My chaos magic pulsed through my body and hummed beneath my skin, begging to be released. Morwen, Fin, and Calian fell into position behind me, their hands spread wide, ready to produce their magic. Then all of us, including the Ghoul, raced through the corridors of the Dragonseminary, our footsteps drowned by the panic of the students. They all scattered like leaves in a storm, some fleeing in terror while others stood their ground, summoning elemental magic to defend the seminary.

"Tell everyone to stay inside!" I shouted above the noise to Priest Treveri. "And find Priest Benigno! We'll handle this!" The Priest, though visibly shaken, turned to the students and began ordering them into the sub-level classrooms. There was an occasional cry of "Ghoul!" And then other cries of "The Ghoul is real!" But most were too distracted by the Dragon to notice, or maybe they didn't even care. I hoped it was the latter. I hoped the Ghoul would be able to roam freely on campus one day.

We passed some students who remained vigilant in their desire to help, but I was able to persuade them to retreat with my empathic abilities. Besides, a little extra dose of fear wouldn't hurt. They weren't ready to face a Dragon. Their bravery would lead to their deaths.

When we reached the entrance hall, the full extent of the havoc unfolded before us. Smoke billowed from shattered windows, and the scent of burning wood filled the air. An entire wall had caved in, claiming the tables and chairs beneath it.

And right in the center of the Dragonseminary grounds, the massive green Dragon roared and stomped his colossal feet at a young Dragonborn.

Zari! We're here.

I was trying to distract him, my Kahina.

You did a fantastic job. Now, please, get to safety.

As you wish. Please, be careful. I do not want to lose you again, my Kahina.

Morwen stood in the open doorway. "We have to stop him before he destroys everything else."

Calian nodded, his jaw set in a determined line.

Fin angled his head toward the Ghoul, who remained silent and waiting. "We'll be the distraction," he said with a bit of force behind his words.

The Ghoul grinned, his teeth shining in a feral snarl. "Consider it done."

And with that, we stepped out into the smoky night air. Fin and the Ghoul continued forward as the rest of us spread out, taking positions on each side of the Dragon. I recognized it instantly.

"Bud," I whispered. For as docile as I'd imagined Bud before, he surely wasn't now. He roared in challenge, his emerald scales glinting in the flames that were spread sporadically throughout the grass and seminary. He reared back and opened his mouth, gushing forth more flames.

The Ghoul and Fin both sprang into action and charged forward. Bud turned around, emitting a deafening roar that echoed through the air. Fin let loose a couple of arrows, but they bounced off the beast's scales. Then Bud swiped his tail. Fin dove out of the way just in time. Then the Ghoul attacked again, his movements swift and purposeful. With a quick lunge, he dodged Bud's fiery breath and plunged his dagger into the soft flesh of the Dragon's throat.

A bellow of pain erupted from Bud, and he thrashed wildly, his massive wings beating the air.

Fin climbed to his feet and let loose another couple of arrows at Bud's underbelly. The Ghoul weaved, rolled, and lunged, slicing the Dragon's hide with his blade. With each arrow and each strike from the Ghoul, blood seeped from Bud's wounds. I stood somewhat dumbfounded. Most blades couldn't penetrate a Dragon's scaled hide, but this one did with ease.

The Ghoul rounded Bud's backside with his blade ready for another blow, but he was met with Bud's tail. The cracking of bones could be heard from where I stood, some twenty feet away. I winced as the Ghoul hit the ground hard. He didn't move. Fin rushed over to the Ghoul's side to check if the creature was alive.

"Calian!" I yelled. "Heal him. I've got this!"

Calian ran toward the Ghoul and slid to his side. He thrust out his palms and healing magic flowed instantly into the Ghoul's chest.

While Calian healed the Ghoul and Fin stood as a barrier to protect them, Morwen raised her hands, conjuring a swirling tornado of water that surged forth like a wave. It crashed into Bud with enough force that the green giant lost his balance and fell to the ground, soaked in water.

I stood with my hands out wide, my palms facing upward. I looked into the sky and called to my chaos magic. Within seconds, purple lightning streaked into the sky and downward into Bud's body. The purple lightning sent shockwaves of energy through the Dragon, and it roared in defiance. But it was no use. The beast convulsed from the intense electric energy that shocked his body.

Finally, he stopped twitching. Even as he lay dying, his gaze locked onto mine. Then he transformed. Green smoke filled the air around him, blocking him from our view. Once it cleared, a naked man with light hair and light weathered skin was revealed. His lips were twisted into a scowl, and his eyes were cold and calculating, betraying a soul tainted by cruelty. He was nothing like I thought he'd be. With a name like Bud, I surmised he'd have a more innocent appearance regardless of if he was one of Amram's lackeys. Instead, a thin-lipped sneer curled at the corners of his mouth, as if relishing my surprise.

"This...was but...a distraction," Bud stammered, sending a chill down my spine. "Valda and Irmak...are headed to the...City of Tamasvi as we...speak. Good luck...stopping them." Then the Dragon took one final breath before closing his eyes for eternity.

"What did he say?" Calian asked behind me.

"Valda is about to attack the City of Tamasvi."

"Then we need to get out of here.

CHAPTER SIXTEEN

EMERA

We bid Dragonpriest Treveri and the Ghoul good-bye immediately. The Ghoul seemed all too eager to get rid of us. He was still reeling from the fact that some of the students had come out to meet him. According to them, the seminary was abuzz with talk about the Ghoul, and how amazing it was that he actually existed. One student ushered the Ghoul inside, asking if he would be willing to share the story of his life. Despite the heavy anxiety that weighed on my heart, I chuckled at the look on the Ghoul's face.

Priest Benigno ran out of the seminary, the tome he'd been reading was clutched in his hand. "Are you all right?"

he asked breathlessly as he glanced back and forth between Morwen and me.

"Yes, and we have to leave. Now," I said anxiously.

Morwen, with her voice soft, said, "But you, dear priest, should remain here and assist the seminary."

"I, uh, think that's a wonderful idea," he replied meekly. "But before you leave, I must tell you some important information I learned from the text. I didn't locate anything specific to withdrawing souls, however, I did discover that when you walk into the mind of a god, you can die there. Tread carefully, Emera."

"I appreciate your help *and* your concern. "Fortunately, the Ghoul's help paid off, and I know how to look for my soul," I said with a tight smile. "I will heed your warning when I attempt to enter Amram's mind."

"Right. Good luck." The priest bowed slightly before turning and heading back into the school. I ran to Zari.

"You will take Fin and Morwen to the City of Anahita so that they can warn Queen Baia of what is about to transpire. Calian and I will fly to the City of Tamasvi at once."

As you wish, my Kahina.

And, Zari, please be careful. I reached deep within me for the pain I knew I should have felt. *Because…Well…I don't know how to say this. Dhruv is gone.*

Zari just stared at me, unmoving. *What do you mean?*

He was killed.

She angled her head as if trying to get a better look at me. *That's not possible.*

I'm afraid it is. He was taken down by a group of mercenaries.

No, you misunderstand me, my Kahina. It is impossible for…

But her words were cut off from my mind once I saw the Dragons. Two of them, one violet and one blue. "Valda," I seethed.

As the Dragons flew overhead, no doubt inspecting the damage done by the Dragon, and its human body lying dead in the grass, my demeanor shifted instantly.

"We leave now!" I yelled. I backed away quickly from Zari until I had the space I needed. My skin rippled and shimmered, morphing into scales that glimmered like thousands of tiny violet gemstones. Powerful muscles bulged beneath my clothing as my limbs elongated and contorted, taking on my Dragon form. My eyes blazed with an intense energy as my human features gave way to a snout lined with razor-sharp teeth. Wings unfurled from my back with a resounding snap, casting a shadow over the ground below. In mere moments, where I once stood as a woman, I now stood as a Dragon. It may have been my imagination, but I felt bigger. Was it my mother's soul?

I reached my mind out to Morwen, but she, Fin, and Zari were already headed toward the City of Anahita. I looked beside me to see Calian. His form was smaller than mine but still magnificent.

You're bigger, he said. But not aloud. He was in my mind.

You can speak to me.

Apparently. Must be a Dragonmate thing.

Calian, as I've said—

I know what you said. I don't believe it.

I shook my massive head and focused my eyes on the sky above. Then, as the early morning light painted the sky with hues of pink and gold, we lifted into the air with powerful beats of our wings and flew toward the City of Tamasvi. Our scales shimmered in the dawn's light, and for a moment, I forgot about our mission and only saw us as we were: two beautiful Dragons soaring through the heavens.

But my vision of us was short-lived when a roar thundered throughout the sky.

The Dragon that Bud had called Irmak.

The destination was clear in my mind now. We streaked across the sky with a sense of urgency, our forms cutting through the crisp air. A great distance ahead of us, were the two small silhouettes of Valda and Irmak. Calian and I flew faster, both of our eyes locking on our enemies. With every flap of our wings, we closed the distance, but I feared we wouldn't be able to catch them. Finally, we neared the edge of the Kingdom of Water. In the distance, I could see the light fading the closer it got to the Kingdom of Darkness.

Why didn't I think of it before? *I've got an idea,* I told Calian.

Lay it on me.

To get to the city quickly and out-pace Valda and her pal, Irmak, I need to shift into my human form and access my power of teleportation. I'd try this in my Dragon form, but I don't think I could teleport you with me.

So, you want to land on the ground and teleport?

Not on the ground. On you. I'll hover over you and shift, so you'll need to catch me. Once I land on your back, I'll teleport us to the city.

Have you ever teleported something as large as me?

No.

Have you ever teleported anyone?

Also, no.

That's reassuring.

I can do this, Calian.

A low rumble vibrated his throat. *Fine.*

Calian slowed his flight so that I could hover more steadily over him. I focused my breathing and began my transformation. I had to be more careful this time and not shift so fast. I knew I needed to slow the process and focus on one area at a time, leaving my wings last. But even then, that would need to be fast enough so that I didn't break my back. On top of all that, I needed to make sure I was fully clothed.

With a push of my chaos magic, my Dragon form shifted and contorted in the air. My scales melted away first. Then muscles rippled and bones realigned as the rest of my human form took shape. Just after my body became human, my wings folded inwards, sinking into my back as if they were never there. I fell, landing on Calian with a thud.

"Ugh!" I gasped from the jolt that rippled through my body.

You all right? Calian asked. I didn't have to hear his voice to know that he was worried.

I'm all right, I assured him. I looked down and sucked in a quick breath. I had transformed without injury, and I was fully clothed. Elated, I celebrated my success by taking a deep breath and feeling the cool night air fill my lungs. For a moment, I felt weightless with the wind rushing past my ears, whipping my hair around my face. Calian's powerful wings beat against the air as my fingers gripped tightly to his scales. His body was warm beneath me; his muscles flexed beneath my touch. I pressed myself down on his back, my heart racing with exhilaration.

"Are you ready?" I yelled, my voice barely audible over the rushing wind.

Calian let out a low rumble, a sound that vibrated through my entire body. I took that as a yes.

Closing my eyes, I focused all my magic on the image of the City of Tamasvi. I'd never attempted magic on such a grand scale, but I didn't see any other way to beat them. With my eyes closed, I took a deep breath, and with a sudden jolt, we were gone.

When I opened my eyes, we were suspended over the city. Calian glided down and landed at its center. I slid off, finding myself standing in the heart of the city, surrounded by the towering buildings and the bustling crowds of people. Calian raised his head, his massive form causing people to run screaming into the nearest building. I let out a long breath and shook my head. I'd managed to teleport us to a wide-open space at the center of the city. There would surely be panic, considering that other cities were being decimated by Dragons.

I turned to Calian. "We made it," I said. "But I need to get you some clothes quickly. A large Dragon landing in the city is sure to cause a bit more of a panic." I scanned the area and caught a glimpse of a shop on the corner of our street. I teleported there, grabbed what I thought would fit Calian, told the owner I'd be back, and then transported away. I laid the clothes next to Calian. City guards came running toward us just as he began his transformation. Red smoke started to fill the space between us. It engulfed Calian's massive Dragon form until he was completely hidden from sight. When the red smoke cleared, he stood there naked.

"You should probably hurry," I said. I turned away and saw a mother cover her young child's eyes, a look of horror on her face.

A couple of minutes later, Calian was dressed in all black. I'd grabbed leather clothing, new and stiff but solid. Beneath the leather vest was a simple tunic with sturdy fabric; nothing flashy. But it fit him just right, like it was made for him. Even the boots.

"Looks like I did okay," I said.

"More than okay. It all fits great. And look at you."

I looked down at the leather attire that covered my body. Embossed patterns of deep violet scales adorned the leathers and matching boots, looking almost like natural Dragon scales. The leathers themselves were form-fitting, tailored to my body to provide maximum mobility while still offering ample protection. I raised my arms and saw the reinforced stitching along the seams that would ensure durability.

"Interestingly, I didn't really think about it. Must be another result of my mother's soul." I jumped, took a fighting stance, and threw a few punches in the air. "These leathers are light and flexible. They move with me, like a second skin."

"Maybe they are like a second skin," Calian offered. "Think about it. Your Dragonskin and scales transformed into leather. It's like you created your own personal armor. And they match your hair." He reached out and touched a lock of my violet hair. "I like it. It suits you."

I pulled back from his touch, a sense of unease pooling in the pit of my stomach. "As much as I'm enjoying this moment, we're here for a reason. We need to see King Orpheus."

Calian's smile faded, and he looked past my shoulder toward the palace. "I hope we've made it in time."

I hoped so as well because the City of Tamasvi was a city unlike any other, where darkness and shadows reigned supreme in every corner and alleyway. Lofty towers rose high in the star-studded sky of the city's eternal night.

Lanterns flickered with soft golden glows, casting pools of dim light that danced upon the cobblestone streets below. Everywhere I looked, the architecture of Tamasvi took my breath away. Towering structures adorned with intricate carvings depicting the night sky and beyond. Despite the perpetual darkness, life thrived within the city. Market stalls lined the winding streets, their wares illuminated by the glow of the enchanted lanterns.

"Are you ready to teleport there?"

I bit my lip before responding, "I'm not sure I can. I don't know what the palace looks like. And I'd prefer not to teleport to the king in case…Well…In case he's in a compromising place."

"Fair enough. Follow me. It's not far."

We passed the Temple of Tamasvi. It was a grand structure dedicated to my sister. Its spires reached toward the two large moons that were suspended in the sky.

"I wonder if there will ever be a temple dedicated to me," I said, studying the grand appearance of the temple. I hadn't intended on saying it aloud, but the words were out before I could stop them.

"If it were me, I wouldn't want one," Calian murmured beside me.

"Really?"

"I don't deserve their praise. I've done terrible things in my time."

My eyebrow raised involuntarily. "You are worthy of every praise." Before he could answer, I pointed up into the sky. "Look!" My breath caught in my throat, and I was completely entranced by the ethereal glow from the moons. The sky beyond them was painted in hues of black, purple, and dark blue. We continued our way toward the palace, ignoring the suspicious looks of the people who walked the streets. Instead, I focused on the warm air that carried the scent of jasmine and incense. The lovely aroma had almost calmed my heart. Almost.

Standing outside of the city's palace was quite the experience. This was my sister's palace, and it was a magnificent sight to behold. The outside was crafted from dark obsidian glass that seemed to drink in the surrounding darkness. At the right angle, the glass looked deep blue instead of black.

Tall, slender spires rose toward the heavens. Each spire was adorned with celestial carvings, adding to the palace's beauty. The glass walls shimmered spectacularly, reflecting the twinkling stars above.

But it was not the structure of the palace that impressed me the most. Embedded within the dark glass were numerous gemstones of every purple, black, and blue hue imaginable, each one sparkling brilliantly.

"It's breathtaking," I said, feeling a sense of peace.

"Agreed. As much as I'd love to stay here and drink it all in, we can't. We must go inside." Then he nodded at the two guards like he'd known them all their lives. They returned the gesture and opened both doors. Once I stepped inside, I was in a whole other world. We were greeted by the gentle music of cascading waterfalls. Rich tapestries decorated the walls while ornate chandeliers with hanging obsidian crystals hung from the ceilings, casting prisms of light across the marble floors we stood on.

Calian took my hand. "This way." He led me to the throne room at the heart of the palace. When we entered, my heart skipped a beat.

"Stunning."

"Absolutely."

I glanced at him, smiling, but he wasn't looking at the ceiling. He was looking at me. A fleeting flutter of my heart caused me to pause. His eyes were just as mesmerizing as the palace. Maybe more.

"Captain Westbow?"

I turned from Calian and made eye contact with a person I expected to be King Orpheus. The king sat on the throne crafted from the rare Nightfire Opal. It was elegant, a true testament to my sister. It was designed with sinuous curves and flowing lines that evoked the fluidity of shadows. Intricate patterns were carved into the surface of the opal, forming constellations of the night sky.

"King Orpheus, it is good to see you again." Calian strode across the marble floor and knelt before the king. I quickly followed and did the same.

I remained kneeling until a hand appeared before me. "You bow to no one," King Orpheus said. I took his hand, and he gently pulled me to my feet. "What brings a Chaos Dragongoddess to my feet?"

"Your city will soon be under attack."

"Hmm," he said, stroking a short beard that framed his wise face. It was neatly trimmed and added a touch of ruggedness to his features. It was almost the same color as his hair, which was pale yellow and tied at the base of his neck. Like Kedron, the king preferred to wear all black. The pearls in place of buttons were a nice touch. In the short amount of time I'd been in the throne room, I had already surmised that King Orpheus was a figure of quiet contemplation as he surveyed the affairs of his kingdom.

"Your Majesty," I said, doing my best to maintain a steady voice. "The Dragongoddess Valda is on her way now."

The king's expression remained impassive, though a flicker of concern flashed in his black eyes. "Tell me more," he said, his demeanor relaxed yet alert.

Calian stepped forward. "They will stop at nothing to see your kingdom reduced to ashes. Especially once they discover we are here."

The king's gaze hardened. "This moment was inevitable. Once we heard about the attack on Anahita, we've been preparing. Our people are ready to be moved, and our military forces are on standby." He addressed his advisors, who had been standing quietly to his left. "Women and children go into the caves first. All soldiers are to be at their positions immediately. Do so as discreetly as possible so there is no panic. And find General Brangwen." The advisors nodded and scuffled out of the throne room.

King Orpheus remained calm and steady. "Come."

We followed the king down the hallway to a small room with a long table, a map spread across its top. A map of the unnamed world hung on the wall. It was massive, taking up almost the entirety of the wall. The king gestured toward the table. "Please, sit."

Calian did as the king requested, but I stood before the map, my heart sinking like a stone each time I noted a city marked by a crimson blot. Those were the cities burned by Amram's army. Each mark represented lives lost and homes reduced to rubble. Tears welled in my eyes, but I refused to let them fall. Instead, I traced a trembling finger along the jagged lines that defined the path of destruction. Anger simmered within me so much that my hand clenched into a fist, the nails digging into my palm as I struggled to contain the rage I felt.

A hand suddenly rested on my shoulder. I turned, expecting to see Calian, but instead, I peered into the face of Kedron.

"I like what you've done with the hair," he said with a sheepish grin.

"It's so good to see you," I breathed.

Another person behind him cleared their throat. I looked past Kedron to see whom I assumed was General Brangwen, considering the armor he was wearing. He was a mountain of a man. His face bore the scars of battle, and his eyes were sharp and piercing, holding no nonsense. In a deep, gruff voice, the General said what we were all thinking. "The faster we make a decision on how to proceed, the faster we can get out of this palace and kill some Dragons."

CHAPTER SEVENTEEN

CALIAN

General Brangwen stood at the table and unrolled a map that detailed the landscape of the kingdom. His brow furrowed in deep concentration. He cleared his throat, breaking the heavy silence that hung over the room.

"My scout," he glanced at Kedron, "told me they stopped just at the border."

Kedron nodded. "Valda and the blue Dragon are there with an army of Dragonborns."

King Orpheus nodded solemnly, his gaze fixed on the maps spread out before him. "Moving any army that quickly means they have some method of travel that we aren't aware of. We cannot afford to underestimate them."

I raked a hand through my hair. "And if they haven't moved on the city just yet, we can assume they're gathering more forces."

King Orpheus, his scaled hands clasped before him, finally spoke. "The Dragons are powerful, but they are not invincible."

General Brangwen looked at Emera and me. "Our first objective is to neutralize the Dragons' aerial advantage. We'll deploy our archers with arrows, but we'll need your assistance in the air."

Emera nodded approvingly. "We will do our part to get the Dragons on the ground. Valda will be a challenge." She looked at me. "She's mine."

I leaned back in the chair, doing my best to appear confident and relaxed about the situation. I wasn't. The nerves were settling in, and my empty stomach was suddenly queasy. "Then I'll take Irmak."

Emera continued, addressing the others. "Eventually, we'll get Valda and Irmak on the ground, dead or alive."

King Orpheus's eyes flashed. "Hopefully, dead."

"And we will march on their Dragonborns."

Kedron and I exchanged a knowing glance. This was going to be difficult.

General Brangwen scanned the maps. "Black," he said, addressing Kedron, "I need you to use your teleportation abilities to scout the enemy's movements. Head to the border and gather whatever intelligence you can."

Emera's scowl was evidence that she did not agree with the order.

Kedron nodded, but his expression gave away nothing. "I will leave immediately." He stood and headed for the door. Emera did the same, clearly wanting to stop Kedron from leaving. But before he could even make it past the table, the door swung open, and a cloaked figure slipped inside. All eyes turned to the unexpected visitor who lowered their hood, revealing a woman with lustrous hair that matched the near-white color of Kedron's.

General Brangwen's eyes raised in surprise. "Nyx, I thought you were getting the women and children to safety?"

The sorceress stepped forward. "My father was able to get most of them hidden within the caves below the city. Neighboring towns and villages have been warned. I figured it was a good time to pop in and share some information I've gathered."

"Does it involve a dress?" I huffed. The room went silent, and I was met with confused glances from everyone in the room.

Nyx smiled before letting out a thunderous laugh. "Not today, Captain."

Emera leaned in front of my face, her brows raised with curiosity.

"It's a long story."

"Not that long," Nyx quipped.

"Maybe, but it's not one that needs to be shared at this moment."

Nyx plopped down in a vacant seat. "Now, that, I can agree on." Then she mouthed the word later to Emera. Despite Emera not being my mate—at the moment—she chuckled. Then she cleared her throat, and her face turned serious once more.

General Brangwen eyed her warily, his fingers drumming on the hilt of his sword. "What information do you have for us?"

Nyx inclined her head in acknowledgment. "My sources tell me there are movements at Castle Umbra, the outpost that's just inside the northern border. I imagine that's where the Dragons are."

"There were thirty men at that castle," the general nearly shouted.

"Not anymore," Nyx replied lightly. She started inspecting her nails that were painted pitch black.

The king's eyes narrowed as he considered the sorceress's words. "And who is this source?"

Nyx met his gaze without hesitation. "I understand your skepticism, Your Majesty. But I assure you, these are legitimate sources, and I hope you will not think less of me when I refuse to disclose their identities."

My respect for Nyx grew tenfold.

Finally, Kedron spoke up. "I will teleport with Nyx to the northern border. Together, we will gather whatever information we can and return."

Kedron and Nyx locked eyes, a silent understanding passing between them. Nyx stood and crossed to her twin. Kedron took her hand, and with a flourish of magic, they vanished from the war room.

"You look worried," the king said.

I knew he wasn't talking about me because my face remained neutral. I glanced at the general. He was hunched over the table, too deep in thought to be worried. So, that left Emera. Sure enough, her shoulders were tense, and her nose wrinkled like she'd smelled something awful. "I just wonder how wise it is to send Kedron away at this time."

General Brangwen stood straight. Emera had essentially questioned his order, and he didn't take kindly to it. I admitted to myself that he did well to hide the anger which warmed his cheeks. But he wasn't perfect. I saw it, and knowing Emera, she did, too. "I trust Kedron's abilities," he said pointedly.

"As do I, General, but…"

The general crossed his arms before him. "But what?" he interrupted with an edge to his tone.

I sat straight, readying myself to defend my mate.

Emera stood and leaned forward, spreading her fingers wide on the table's surface. "Time is against us. We don't have the luxury of waiting for Kedron to return. You're used to strategizing and planning out attacks, but I fear it will be too late by that point. We must act now."

"Black can—"

King Orpheus stood, interrupting the general. "I agree. Gather the men. We ride to Castle Umbra immediately." And with that, he turned and left the warm room, leaving the general grappling for words. He turned to Emera with fury written all over his face. Then he stomped out of the room like a petulant child.

Emera plopped down in the chair and released a forceful breath. "That was not my intention."

"Regardless of your intention, you were right." I stood and offered her my hand. Her eyes met mine, showing a vulnerability that stirred something deep within me. She hesitated but then gently placed her hand mine. "This might actually be the last…"

She held up her other hand. "We're not foreseeing the outcome before the battle has even started."

"Okay."

*   *   *

We'd been preparing for a few hours, and as the next one approached, a knot of tension tightened in my chest. We would be riding out any minute now. Well, our men would be riding. I would be flying. I closed my eyes for a moment, attempting to block out the chaos around me. I thought of my loved ones, wishing they were here to help, and yet, glad that they weren't. They were safe in other parts of the unnamed world, hopefully.

"Get to the front of the line!" General Brangwen commanded, forcing me out of my stupor. He was yelling and cursing at his men to get in formation.

The city was vacated, almost ghostly. All the citizens were able to escape into the underground caverns. I could only imagine their distress from the impending attack on the city. We now stood just in front of the city walls, waiting for the order to move.

The general continued to ready his men, obviously anxious about how long it was taking. I glanced at Emera but looked away sheepishly. She was a commanding presence. The soldiers bowed when she walked by. Some even threw themselves at her feet. They'd heard the rumors. Emera, daughter of Nimerah, walked among them. Whereas I felt suffocated by the weight of responsibility pressing down upon me, she took it all in stride. I assumed most of that was due to her mother's soul being within her. Then again, the woman had been killed and resurrected. Maybe the battle wasn't comparable to that.

General Brangwen was giving his final command as I turned and looked out into the distance. Soon, we'd be marching toward victory or defeat.

Suddenly, a thunderous roar echoed throughout the city like a warning bell. My heart leaped into my throat as I scanned the skies, searching for the source of the disturbance. Was it Valda? Irmak? Then I saw it; a colossal red dragon soared into view.

"Father," I breathed with a sigh of relief. The God of Fire descended upon the city with haste.

The soldiers watched in awe and a little bit of terror as Vukan landed before us, his immense body forcing the ground to tremble. My father's eyes burned with an intensity that sent a shiver down my spine. Something was wrong.

With a mighty roar, smoke permeated the area around my father, blanketing him from view. He emerged from the smoke in his human form—in leathers like Emera's. My father surveyed the area, and once our eyes connected, he ran. I took off toward him, meeting him halfway.

"Looks like you could use some help. That blue Dragon named Irmak was notorious during the war for drowning his victims."

I clenched my fists, my anger rising like a tide within me.

Just then, Kedron appeared out of thin air right beside me, his sister standing next to him.

"It's time," he said immediately. "Once they realized Emera was here, they accelerated their plans."

Emera jogged up to us, braiding her violet hair out of her face. "What's going on?"

Nyx outlined the grim reality of our situation. "Valda wasn't all too pleased to hear that you were alive and kicking. Something about a failed assassination."

I raised a brow at my mate.

I'll tell you after, she said in my head.

"Anyway," Nyx continued, planting a hand on her hip. "Because of you, they're anxious to burn this city to the ground."

"Watch your tone," I growled.

Nyx ignored me. "Thank the gods for Cal's daddy coming to our aid." She winked at my father, and his cheeks turned crimson.

"We need reinforcements," Vukan said. The god was born of fire, but even he knew that they were outnumbered and outmatched.

"I can teleport to the Kingdom of Fire," Kedron offered.

"There is no way you'll return in time."

We all turned to see King Orpheus standing behind Nyx.

The King of Kingdom of Darkness stood tall and imposing, clad in armor that was crafted in darkened steel. His pauldrons were impressive, detailed with spikes along the edges. Each spike was meticulously sharpened to a deadly point. Even his gauntlets were adorned with jagged edges to deliver crushing blows.

I needed that armor. What I wore paled in comparison. Because I was transforming into my Dragon form, I still wore my fighting leathers. There was no reason to wear armor. Earlier, had attempted to teach me how to transform back into human form with clothes, but I made sure Kedron packed a bag of clothes and boots for me, just in case.

Don't worry, Emera said in my mind, detecting my apprehension. *You'll be fully clothed when you transform.*

I snorted. She had way too much confidence in me.

You used to have that confidence yourself, she replied.

And what if I'm not fully clothed?

She shrugged, her face serious. *Then you'll fight the Dragons while naked.*

Funny, I retorted.

I wasn't joking.

I looked to the sky and took a ragged breath then combed my fingers through my tousled hair. The moons above cast their light upon the restless soldiers. I could have gotten lost in their glow, but a sharp blast of horns cut through the dark air, jolting everyone into action. I stumbled out in the open where my father had landed. Emera and the God of Fire joined me. But before I made the transformation, I glanced back at the soldiers.

Instead of marching forward, they were scrambling, armor clanking as they rushed out of formation and to their posts. The orders spread like wildfire—four dragons had been sighted. Plans changed, and the army had to get into the towers and fortify the city. Panic bubbled up in my chest, threatening to overwhelm me, but then I locked eyes onto Emera. Her words rang through my mind. You used to have confidence. I'd shrugged it off, but she was right. I was Captain Calian Westbow. I didn't follow orders, I commanded them. I was Vasuman, son of Vukan, the God of Fire. I didn't show mercy to my enemies, I slayed them. This night would be no different.

I knew what I had to do. I had trained for this moment, prepared for the day when I would meet enemy Dragons on the battlefield. And now, with an army on the horizon, there was no time to waste. With a nod and a shared breath, Emera, my father, and I let our magic flow through us. Red and violet smoke billowed around us. Scales erupted from my skin and wings burst forth from my back. I let out a triumphant roar. Transforming into a Dragon was exhilarating and terrifying all at once. The rush of power coursed through my veins as the smoke cleared and I took flight, my Dragon form cutting through the night sky with ease.

I banked left and gazed down upon Emera. She let out a fearsome roar before launching herself into the air. She was brave and beautiful. Love swelled within my heart for my mate. I refused to believe after all this we weren't mates anymore.

My father flew close to my right, his massive form, blocking out one of the moons. He angled his large head toward me and nodded. He was ready.

Below us, the City of Tamasvi's soldiers were readying themselves, weapons raised for the battle. The archers stood in the taller towers with arrows nocked and aimed at the four figures that loomed in distance.

As we soared overhead, the first glimpses of the enemy came more clearly into view. Valda and Irmak, flanked by two other Dragons, led the charge. Brandgwen and King Orpheus sat atop their horses, their swords extended in one hand and magic read in the other.

This is going to be difficult, I told Emera.

Yes, it will. But we're not alone. We have each other, and that's all we need.

Let's hope you're right.

We flew out under the cloak of night. As we closed the gap between the other Dragons and us, I knew there would be no exchange of words. There would be no taunting, only fighting. Their roars echoed through the night as they flew toward us.

I caught a glimpse of my father. *Be ready*, he said.

Ready as I'll ever be. I heard him as clearly as Emera. Maybe it wasn't a mate thing, like I'd initially thought? Maybe it was a Dragon form thing? Or a family thing?

His snout parted, exposing his razor-sharp teeth. He was smiling.

Irmak flew closer, his blue scales shimmering beneath the glow of the moons. When he got within range, I opened my mouth and unleashed a torrent of blazing fire from my jaws. The searing fire illuminated the darkness as it streaked toward Irmak. But the blue Dragon was swift, dodging the fiery onslaught easily.

He turned toward me, and in retaliation, released a blast of fire from his mouth. I met the attack head-on, my own flames colliding with his in a display of power and fury. The night sky was ablaze, the very air crackling with intensity. I had no time to see how Emera or my father were doing. I couldn't even peer down at the soldiers that fought below, defending their city.

With a mighty sweep of my tail, I lashed out at Irmak, the impact sending him hurtling through the air. He regained composure and flew toward me. He responded in kind, his own tail whipping through the darkness with deadly precision. His tail connected with the side of my body. Tremors rippled through my limbs.

Then, with a deafening clash, we collided, our claws locking in a battle of strength and will. We were tangled with each other, wings unable to get purchase in the air. We started to free-fall, continuing to kick and scrape each other's scales as we hurtled toward the ground. Each blow was met with equal force, neither of us were willing to yield an inch.

As the ground grew closer and closer, Irmak pushed away, shoving me away from him. He opened my mouth and roared. Instead of fire hitting me in the snout, I was blinded by a wave of cold water. I roared in agony while twisting and turning in the air, but I couldn't regain flight. My thoughts were of Emera when I crashed into the ground.

CHAPTER EIGHTEEN

EMERA

Well, if it isn't Emera back from the dead. Valda's words slithered their way into my mind.

Hello, Valda.

We both hovered in the air above the raging battle below, staring into each other's vibrant purple eyes. Calian and Irmak were already engaged in fighting while Vukan's flames tore through the expanse of the night sky toward the remaining two Dragons. Vukan was the size of both the Dragons put together, and more powerful, so I figured he'd be done quickly. Calian on the other hand...? I so desperately wanted to find him, but I knew if I took my eyes off of Valda for even a second, I'd be dead.

Your mate didn't do you any favors, but he put in a valiant effort.

Valda stared silently at me, her eyes narrowing. After a minute, she responded. My mate?

Nile?

She said nothing.

Nile Ford? Kingdom of Water?

She looked away. *Nope. Still got nothing.*

Her feigned ignorance annoyed me. *One-eyed man who hated me?*

She looked back at me but said nothing. Finally, after a couple of minutes, her eyes widened, pretending to realize who I was speaking about. *Oh, that arrogant Dragonborn? Her mouth opened and she forced out a laugh. He wasn't my mate. He wanted my father's favor so desperately; it was kind of pathetic. So, I let him believe we were. Even put some fake Dragonmate wings on him.*

Well, he's dead now…So…

Her eyes flashed with pain. I didn't need my empathic abilities to tell me that she'd been lying. She and Nile had been mates. And I'd just revealed that he was dead. Probably not the smartest move.

She angled her neck, and I saw it. The slow tremble that vibrated the scales covering her throat. She opened her mouth just as I dove to miss her blast of pure chaos magic. But the chaos caught the tip of my tail as I glided downward. The pain was worse than fire. I roared in agony and angled my head to get a look at the damage. Three spikes and several scales were gone, exposing my flesh.

The chase began. Valda beat her large wings and turned then headed toward me. I called to my healing magic, which thankfully healed the wounds on my tail. But if her chaos blasted through my heart? There was no coming back from that.

I continued my descent and flew as fast as I could toward the ground. Then I straightened my flight and soared just above the battle of Dragonborns. I saw Kedron wield his dark magic to hide himself from his opponent's view. Then he reappeared and stabbed his opponent in the back. I turned and witnessed King Orpheus create thick black tendrils that wrapped around his opponent's neck, strangling the Dragonborn. My eyes scanned the rest of the battle, hoping to see Nyx or Brangwen, but I didn't. My eyes lifted toward the skies, but I couldn't see Calian either. Where was he?

With a quick beat of my wings, I ascended upward. Valda raced past me and pulled up just in time to keep from slamming into the ground. But as she glided over the battle below, she unleashed a torrent of fire magic, incinerating an entire group of Darknessian soldiers. As I watched, adrenaline surged through my veins. I twisted my massive body to get a better view of her destruction. Her scales shimmered in the flames below, cunning and power rippling off of them. But I was not afraid. I'd been to the afterlife and back.

While Valda flew higher, I took a few seconds to search for Vukan and Calian. To my left, I caught a fleeting glimpse of Vukan as he battled valiantly against two white Dragons. His flames blazed like an inferno, swallowing one of the Dragons. Its body fell to the ground below. The other charged, but Vukan maneuvered his body before the white Dragon's blinding light met Vukan's eyes.

I looked to my right, desperate to see Calian. My heart clenched with worry as I failed to locate him. He was supposed to be engaged in combat with Irmak, but I couldn't see the blue Dragon either. The uncertainty gnawed at me, followed by a heavy fear that took over my body. Something was wrong.

Valda stopped and hovered.

Come get me! I shouted into her mind.

Her teeth pulled back and exposed her villainous grin. Suddenly, a blow of icy shards hit me from behind and I catapulted toward the ground. Irmak attacked me with a ferocious roar, his claws slashing through the air like scythes as I fell. I turned my body, righting myself in the air, and met his onslaught head-on. Our bodies collided. We clashed with a force so strong that a wave of energy rippled through the air. When the wave hit Valda, it sent her spiraling backward.

Irmak and I threw our heads at each other, each trying to gain purchase with our teeth and claws, whipping out tails to bash through defenses. He matched my every move with uncanny precision, testing the limits of my strength and speed. He'd been training to fight Dragons in mid-air longer than I'd been flying, so it didn't come as a shock that he was better than me, despite me being more powerful. As we locked in a deadly embrace, the searing heat of his breath warmed my scales, threatening to consume me.

Despite his relentless assault, I refused to back down. I thought back to the chaos magic Valda had used on me. If she could use it, then I definitely could. Drawing upon the depths of my inner magic, my chaos hummed beneath my scales. Once it spread through my entire body, it pulsed momentarily. Then, I unleashed a blast so powerful that there was nothing left of Irmak but his bones.

Irmak's bones fell to the ground, landing on at least a dozen or so of Amram's Dragonborns that had been held back as reinforcements. I regained my balance and jettisoned higher into the air toward Valda. I was weakened by the amount of chaos magic I used, but I wasn't about to show her that.

I flew until we faced each other. Our eyes locked on to one another's and for a brief second, I saw it: fear. Unadulterated fear. Then she narrowed her eyes, beat her wings, and let out a blood-curdling roar. Everyone on the ground froze in place and looked upward.

Valda's wings beat in rhythm to keep her suspended where she was.

Impressive.

Now you're alone. Three against one.

Three?

I scanned the sky. Vukan was flying toward me, but that was it. There were no other Dragons in sight.

Cal.

All's fair. A Dragon for a Dragon.

Instead of searching the sky, I looked down and searched the ground. It took me only a minute to see Calian's mangled Dragon form.

No! My roar thundered through the heavens, and everyone below me cowered.

Yes, she hissed, taking pleasure in my pain. *You think I care about Irmak's death? Think again, Emera. I don't need him. My father doesn't need him. But Captain Westbow. Oh, I think you do need him.* A chuckle rumbled in her throat.

I stared at the ground. My head told me to focus on Valda, that she was just trying to buy herself time. But my heart urged me to check on Calian. The small piece of my soul pushed my mother's aside. I was desperate to see him, feel him, hear him.

Suddenly, the air shifted, and my instincts told me to drop quickly, so I did. I tucked in my wings and fell. Chaos magic flew overhead, almost blasting a hole in my head.

A thunderous roar came from above. I extended my wings and swooped upward. Vukan had made it. He was engaged in battle with Valda.

Without thinking twice, I dove downward as fast as my wings would allow me. I landed on the ground and almost instantly, I transformed back into human form with my scale-like armor I'd created before. There was no time to celebrate how quickly I'd transformed. I needed to get to Calian.

Elemental magic was hurled throughout the air. The clashing of swords and screaming of soldiers were deafening. I stumbled, somersaulted, twisted, and leaped until I cleared the main area of battle. I didn't think, I just moved. There was only one thought that consumed my mind: Calian, lying motionless on the scorched earth.

Tears blurred my vision as I ran up and knelt beside him. Calian's Dragon form was battered and broken, his once-glorious wings were limp and lifeless. Every fiber of my being screamed in anguish, and my hands trembled with fear and desperation.

"Calian, please," I whispered, my voice barely a breath against the roar of battle. "You have to hold on. I can't lose you."

But he remained still, his breathing shallow and labored, his body ravaged by the wounds inflicted by Irmak. With every passing moment, I could feel the darkness closing in around him, threatening to snuff out the light that burned within his soul.

Summoning every ounce of my strength, I reached out with trembling hands, willing my healing magic that flowed through my veins to mend his broken body. A soft glow enveloped below my palms as I poured my energy into him. With tears streaming down my cheeks, I whispered through clenched teeth, "You will not die. Not now." Then I pushed the last remaining bit of energy and magic I had into him.

Calian's large eyes fluttered open. Red smoke filled the space between us. When it cleared, he was there, weak and exhausted, but dressed in the same type of form-fitting leather as me. It was a supple yet durable leather like mine, only his was dyed a deep shade of red, like the color of blood. His leathers were embossed with patterns of scales, too, but overlaid with patterns of swirling flames. His boots were not of the same color. They were black.

"You did it," I said softly. My limbs were weak, and I fought to keep my eyes open.

Calian pulled me into his arms. "I did. And…look…" He pointed to a slight tear in my leathers, just above my heart. A pair of purple wings appeared. They were faded, but they were there.

I smiled faintly.

Calian's brow furrowed. "You used too much magic. You need to rest."

"I can't…Your father…He's fighting…Valda…And he…will lose." Every word was a struggle.

"You are going to lay here until Kedron can get you out. I will be back." He lowered my head and rested it gently on the ground. Then he stood and took off running. It was the fastest I'd ever seen him run. My strength waned with each passing minute, but I refused to lay there and do nothing. With immense effort, I climbed to my feet.

"Keep going," I urged myself through gritted teeth. I struggled to maintain my footing as I trudged toward the ongoing battle. My foot caught on a large stone, and I fell forward. But a familiar hand reached out and grabbed me. Kedron pulled me upright.

"We need to get you to safety. You're in no shape to fight."

"No. I am staying."

"This is no time to be stubborn, Emera. You're going to get yourself killed. So, I am taking you to the caves whether you like it or not." I'd never heard Kedron be that forceful. I gave in and nodded weakly, my energy now completely spent. My knees buckled from exhaustion, so Kedron slid his arms around me to hold me up. I caught a glimpse of a large red Dragon flying upward just before Kedron teleported.

In Kedron's darkness, we were transported to the safety of the underground caves. As my feet touched solid ground once more, I felt a wave of relief wash over me. The cool, damp air of the caverns was a welcome respite from the searing heat of battle.

I closed my eyes. "Go," I told Kedron. "I will find my way. You must get back. You must help them." I tried to hide the trembling in my voice, but it was no use. Then the tears fell.

Kedron took my hand. "I will do everything that I can."

I released a sob after he'd teleported away. Part of me debated whether or not I should remain where Kedron left me, but deep down, I needed someone—anyone—to keep my mind off of what was going on above the surface.

I closed my eyes, only intending on resting for a minute, to gain whatever strength I could. But when they opened them again, panic rose in the form of bile, crowding my throat. How long was I out? My stomach churned. I bent over and heaved the contents of my stomach. With a quick thought, a small pool of water formed in my palms. I poured the cool liquid into my mouth and sloshed it around to break up the bile in my mouth and throat. I spit it out quickly then looked around me. I then called to my light magic, and a beam of light shot out of my palm into the dark. Despite not wanting to sleep, the quick nap left me with a small amount of strength. But if I didn't rest for a lengthier period of time soon, I'd quickly lose what little amount of magic I had gotten back.

The little bit of light illuminated the path before me. The city's underground caves boasted a maze of twisting tunnels and cavernous chambers. Slender diamonds hung from the ceiling like jagged teeth, their sharp points glinting in my light. The walls were lined with shimmering crystals.

But it was not just the natural beauty of the caves that caught my attention. Scattered throughout the caverns were the remnants of a long-forgotten civilization. My eyes widened. There were ruins in these caves. Crumbling stone pillars rose from the partially sunken floor, worn away by the passage of time. I ran my fingers along the stone walls, tracing indecipherable pictures of what could have been an ancient language. An urge to explore crept up within me, but I resisted and pushed it down.

Placing one foot in front of the other, I slowly walked toward a glowing light in the distance. As I navigated forward, the beam of flickering light in my palm cast eerie shadows upon the walls. The shadows seemed to take on the form of my mate and others. My heart weighed heavy with guilt for Calian and Kedron and everyone else that was above fighting.

"Okay. Here's the plan," I said aloud to no one. "Find the humans who sought refuge in the caverns, and rest with them. Once I have my strength back—enough to fight with the others—I will teleport out of the caves and end Valda's life once and for all."

It seemed like a good enough plan, and one that I hoped I could carry out sooner rather than later. All I could do now was pray that the others were still alive.

The light grew bright as I neared a large chamber. When I walked through an ancient archway, hundreds of faces appeared. Approaching them cautiously, I offered a small smile of reassurance to the humans and Dragonborns. "I mean you no harm. I'm Emera."

A human man with piercing blue eyes looked at me, his brows furrowed. "We know who you are, Goddess. But why are you down here?"

A human woman, about the same age as my human mother, Cordelia, stood at the man's side. "Yes. Why are you not above fighting with the others?" she demanded.

My smile faded. "I was able to kill one of the Dragons, but it took a lot of power and magic to do so. I was teleported down here, so that I could safely regenerate my strength. Once I have done so, I will return immediately."

The woman tossed her long black braid behind her and folded her arms over her black blouse. "But you're a goddess. Aren't you supposed to be all-powerful?"

"Even goddesses have their limits. I can use what little magic I have left and die up there, leaving the city even more defenseless. Or, I can remain down here, replenish my magic, and go kill another Dragon."

The woman held up her hand and sighed. "I'm sorry. It's just…Well…We never imagined we would find ourselves in this situation," she admitted. I didn't miss the hint of anger in her voice.

"I understand," I replied, my voice soft and empathic. "But you're safe here. We'll do everything we can to protect you."

A flicker of determination mingled with weariness sparked in her eyes. "Safe? You see, Goddess, the Kingdom of Darkness—this city—is our sanctuary, a beacon of hope within this hateful world. For generations, we tried to live in peace."

I knew where this was leading. I'd heard it before. Seen it before.

"However, as the Dragonborns' grew and grew, everything changed," she continued, her voice growing bitter with resentment. "They saw us as nothing more than pests in their quest for dominance, treating us with contempt and cruelty." She recounted tales of oppression and persecution, of families torn apart and homes destroyed in the name of the Dragonborn.

"We are not all from this kingdom. Many are from the Kingdoms of Light and Earth. We were forced to flee our homes, to seek refuge here. My family and I are a part of those people. We were from the Kingdom of Earth, once living in a thriving community, nestled in the heart of the Arden Forest. Once King Tellus came to power, everything changed. Sure, he tried to appear like he was tolerant. If a stranger walked into the City of Dhara, they might think of him as a great king and friend to humans. But that was all smoke and mirrors."

Her words painted a harrowing picture of what I'd seen when Calian and I had visited the City of Dhara to find Avani. She was right. Within the darkest chambers of my mind, the memory materialized. I had been in awe of how humans and Dragonborns walked along the streets together.

The woman held back her tears. "I'll never forget the day they came for us," she said, her voice quivering. She glanced down at a small boy beside her. Her son. "They stormed through our streets like a force of nature, their magic was used to reduce everything in their path to rubble."

The little boy grabbed his mother's hand as she spoke, her voice choked with grief. "They took everything from us—our homes, our loved ones, our very way of life." Her words echoed off the cavern walls.

"So, we packed everything we could and left. But even here, it seems we are not safe. The god Amram and his Dragonborns will stop at nothing to eliminate our kind."

As I listened to her words, my heart ached with a profound sense of sorrow and guilt. I had not been blind to the suffering of those who had fallen victim to the tyranny of my kind, because at one time, I believed I was human, and that suffering could have just as easily been directed at me. But looking back. No one I knew did anything to fix the imbalance of power. Not even my own parents, who were indeed human.

The woman nodded at her son, and he let go of her hand.

"What is your name?"

"Petra."

"I understand more than you know, Petra," I said softly. "I, too, was once a human, before I became a Dragon."

Her eyes widened in surprise, and hushed voices rose around us. "You...You were?" she asked, her voice tinged with disbelief.

I nodded. "I know the injustices you've faced, the cruelty of the Dragonborns. And I vow to do everything in my power to make things right."

"As will I."

We all turned. As I stood there, grappling with the weight of the world upon my shoulders, an elderly man, hunched over his walking stick, wobbled toward the woman and me. When he got closer, I saw the silver scales along the sides of his neck. He was a Dragonborn.

"Farley, you should not be walking." Petra held out a hand to the older man. He brushed his gray hair out of his face, took Petra's hand, and attempted to straighten his back.

"You are Emera, daughter of Nimerah, yes?" he asked with a gravelly voice. I nodded in response. Then he dropped his walking stick and reached out his hand, "Then you are able to siphon my magic. Take it," he urged. "Use it to fuel your own."

Petra's eyes widened in alarm. "Farley! She could kill you."

"Doubtful," he said. He gazed into my eyes as I took his hand.

"I won't kill you, but I cannot guarantee there will be much magic left."

The old Dragonborn laughed. "There better not be. I am much older than I look."

I chuckled. "I gathered that."

He smiled gently. "It has been a long, fulfilling life. One with love, friendship, and laughter. But not much to do with magic, I assure you."

I grabbed hold of the arm he extended toward me, closed my eyes, and I started the Dragonmeld.

There was no darkness. The man stood plainly before me. He held out his hand, and in his palm was a tiny pebble. His relic. I opened my palm, and he placed the pebble in it. Suddenly, a surge of energy pushed into my hand, and I welcomed it, letting it course through me. I breathed deeply, drinking in the power Farley was giving me. I let it stir within my body before it rushed through my veins, filling every space of me and igniting a fire within my soul that burned brighter than ever before.

My eyes opened, and I let go of his arm. Chaos magic burned through me, begging to be released. It was done, and I hadn't killed him. Relief flooded through my veins.

"You see? I am still myself. Just no magic."

My mouth gaped open when I gazed down upon his hands, now smooth and void of any scales. "But. I didn't…"

"I did," he said with a smile. "I gave it all. It's the least I can do to end this war."

I bowed to Farley and nodded at Petra. "Then I must do as I vowed."

"Good luck, Emera, daughter of Nimerah."

Petra shook her head at Farley. "No." Then she turned to me. "Good luck, Emera, Goddess of Chaos."

Gratitude warmed my soul. I walked back into the dark tunnel, the echoes of their words ringing in my ears like a rallying cry. I closed my eyes, took a deep breath, and teleported back to the world above.

CHAPTER NINETEEN

EMERA

I teleported into the middle of the battlefield where swords clashed, and arrows flew. Soldiers paused mid-swing, staring at me in bewilderment. Some of them retreated from where they stood while others turned back toward the bloodshed. My plan was to transform immediately, but two Dragonborns came at me from each side. I dodged a ball of fire and a sharp piece of ice they threw at me.

"You think yourself powerful, goddess?" the fire Dragonborn spat, his voice laced with arrogance as he hurled a barrage of flames toward me. "You're nothing but a traitor."

Beside him, the water Dragonborn joined in, his voice a cold whisper. "You may wield chaos, but you are no match for all who fight here."

"Wanna bet?" With a flick of my wrist, I sent vines of earth energy toward them. They quickly ensnared their bodies, pinning their arms to their sides. "Too easy," I taunted.

The fire Dragonborn roared with fury, his flames flickering in defiance as he struggled against the binds of my magic. The flames suddenly engulfed his arms, and he howled in pain. Beside him, the water Dragonborn released a stream of water, attempting to extinguish the flames that were now closing in around him.

"So arrogant." With a wave of my hand, I sent pure chaos crashing over them, breaking the vines. They staggered back, their bodies flaking away before my eyes. The water Dragonborn met his demise with a chilling silence, his breath freezing mid-air before there was nothing left of him. The fire Dragonborn tried to run away, but his legs flaked away first before the rest of his body turned to pieces and then nothing.

I didn't like to kill. In fact, I loathed it. But in war, it was necessary, and there was no other means to get around it. I kept repeating that to myself as I looked for an open area to transform and took off running. I sprinted through the combat, with swords being swung around me and arrows flying through the air. My heart pounded in my chest, adrenaline coursing through my veins as I dodged and weaved between soldiers and enemy Dragonborns, each step bringing me closer to the open space I desperately needed.

Chaos magic flared to life and built to a crescendo within me, and the urge to unleash my Dragon form clawed at the edges of my consciousness. But I had to wait and bide my time until I reached the safety of the open field. If I transformed here, I wouldn't just kill our enemies, I'd kill our allies.

As I pushed forward, my eyes caught a glimpse of General Brangwen sitting atop his horse, his blade cutting through any Dragonborn that dared to get within his reach. Suddenly, his horse was startled by a large ball of flame that was hurled at it. The steed reared on its hind legs, and the general fell to the ground, landing on his stomach. Just as the general turned over, a blade pierced his armor. General Brangwen had fallen.

Time seemed to slow as I witnessed his death. Anguish gripped my heart, but I forced myself to keep moving, knowing that he fought valiantly until the end. I pressed onward through the throes of battle. The noise faded into the background as I finally broke free into the open field. There, with the sky stretching endlessly above me, the transformation began.

Power surged through me, my muscles contorted and elongated as scales erupted from my skin. Wings unfurled from my back, catching the wind as I rose into the air. I let out a thunderous roar that echoed throughout the sky.

As I soared higher into the sky, the drumming of my heart quickened with anticipation and dread. Below me, the battlefield seemed to stretch on and on, but I tore my eyes off of it and into the sky around me, focusing on finding Calian and joining him in the battle against Valda. As I flew over a row of trees, I spotted them in what appeared to be a swirling cloud of combat. Fire and chaos were everywhere, highlighting the sky like an elemental storm. Calian and Valda's bodies clashed, and their roars reverberated through the air. When they parted, I saw Vukan between them.

But as I drew nearer, I sensed something was wrong. Vukan was sluggish, which wasn't typical of his usual agility. A pit formed in my stomach once I saw the gaping hole in his side, a wound undoubtedly inflicted by Valda.

With a rush of adrenaline, I raced toward them, my wings beating faster and faster through the dark sky. I came up behind Valda and unleashed a blast of searing flames at her back. The flames hit their mark, and she recoiled, hissing in fury as I hovered beside Calian and Vukan. When she realized who hit her from behind, she vanished into thin air.

Calian was at my side. *Did she just teleport?*

I swung my massive neck back and forth, but I couldn't see her anywhere.

Appears so.

Well, three to one is not favorable odds. Even for her.

You look better. It didn't take as long as I thought it would.

It's a story worth sharing when we're not fighting a powerful Chaos Dragon.

If she returns, do you mind doing...whatever it was you did last time?

Gladly.

But before I began boosting my chaos magic, preparing myself for Valda, my eyes met Vukan's. His movements were slower, and his breaths came in ragged gasps as he fought to maintain his position. The wound on the god's side was severe.

Your father needs to land, or he'll die.

You try telling him that. He won't listen to me.

I searched for Vukan's mind. When I found it, I was hit with pain. I shook my head to repel the pain he was passing onto me. *You need to retreat.*

You need me up here.

We need you down there.

Screams of torture traveled upward from the battle below.

All three of us looked down. There she was, commanding her magic and killing everyone.

Uh, like I said. We need you down there.

Calian dove down and landed with great force that all of the soldiers and Dragonborns on the ground struggled to maintain balance. A large dust cloud from his landing mixed with the red smoke of his transformation. Vukan and I followed.

After we'd landed and transformed into our human forms, I looked at Vukan. "I can heal you," I called out over the noise of combat. I raced toward him.

He shook his head. "You must help Vasuman."

I ignored him and held my hand out, thrusting my healing magic into his side. "He will never forgive me if I let you die."

"That is not close to the truth, and you know it."

I peered directly into his eyes and held my gaze. "I would never forgive myself."

He cracked a sheepish smile.

"There."

The God of Fire glanced down at his side.

"All better."

And I thought he would be. If it wasn't for Valda who suddenly teleported behind him and blasted chaos magic into Vukan's back.

Calian! I screamed in my mind as Valda teleported away.

Vukan slumped into me. I wrapped my arms around him tightly and held him up. Calian appeared in the distance, running as fast as he could toward us. I released a quick breath, relieved that he was still alive. But then I scolded myself. How could I feel relief at this moment. My mate's father, the God of Fire, was dying.

Calian rushed to me and took hold of his father. He brought Vukan down slowly to the ground. As he cradled his father in his arms, Calian finally felt the weight of Vukan's fading existence. The once powerful god struggled to draw breath, his chest gaping open from the blast of chaos magic.

"Father..." Calian's voice shook, and his eyes glazed with tears. He had just gotten his father back.

"I'm here, my son," Vukan whispered. The God of Fire weakly reached out a hand, his fingers trembling as they brushed against his son's cheek. "My son," he rasped, his voice barely a whisper. "I'm sorry…"

"Don't speak, Father," Calian pleaded. "Save your strength. Em will heal you."

"Oh, I don't think so." Valda sauntered into view. The air crackled with energy, and before I could comprehend what was happening, a blast of chaos magic tore through the sky, aimed directly at Calian. Instinctively, I pushed him aside and threw up a shield of wind. The magic bounced off of the shield, but the force of it sent me sprawling to the ground.

"Emera!" Calian cried out. He still held his father in his arms. I was not going to let Valda take that moment from him.

I staggered to my feet, my muscles aching as I faced Valda.

"You will not interfere, Em," she sneered and unleashed another wave of chaos magic toward me.

I dove out of the way and rolled to my feet. "And neither will you." I sent my own blast of chaos magic toward her. Valda fell to the ground. While she climbed to her feet, I reached out to Calian in silent communication. *Heal him.*

I didn't wait for a response. I needed to get Valda away from Calian and Vukan.

"Hold on," I heard Calian say. Light began to flow from his hands into Vukan's wound.

Emera. Vukan whispered in my mind, his voice barely audible. *Take care of him.*

Tears welled in my eyes as I nodded, my eyes still locked onto Valda. My throat was tight, doing its best to push down the fiery sobs that were building inside it. "I will," I promised, my voice barely a whisper. I didn't know if he heard me.

I teleported just after Vukan whispered his final words in Calian's ear. I appeared behind Valda, simultaneously drawing my blade and thrusting it in her back. She shrieked and teleported before I was able to hit her with another round of chaos magic. "Ugh!" I yelled in frustration. As Zepherin taught me, I lowered into a fighting stance, waiting for her to reappear. In the distance, I saw a Dragon with two others following it, but it wasn't Valda. The Dragon roared loudly, and I knew then that we had back-up. Risna swooped overhead then glided down to the ground, landing beside us. The other two Dragons followed her lead and landed, forming a wall around us. Fin hopped off of Risna's back, his eyes widening as he took in the scene before him. I shook my head then ran to Calian and skidded to a halt.

With a final, labored breath, Vukan's hand fell limp at his side, his once bright crimson eyes dimming as the spark of life left him. Calian let out a strangled cry, his grief echoing beneath the moons while he clung to his father's lifeless body.

I dropped to my knees and wrapped my arms around him, offering what little comfort I could. Calian lowered his father to the ground. He then turned and buried his head in my chest. I held him there as he cried. Tears swelled and streamed down my cheeks. As we wept, I vowed to honor Vukan's memory and ensure that his son carried on his father's legacy.

*　*　*

Once word spread that Valda retreated, the rest of Valda's army of Dragonborns surrendered. Those of King Orpheus's army that were still alive, shackled the enemy Dragonborns in enchanted chains that inhibited magical abilities before marching them back into the city and imprisoning them behind enchanted bars. Thankfully, the city was mostly untouched since the fighting between us Dragons had occurred above it. The Darknessian soldiers were able to defend the city so that enemy soldiers didn't penetrate the outer wall.

An occasional shingle was missing from a roof, a window was shattered from a stray arrow, and a few buildings had the remnants of fire blasts. But each building still stood tall, and the palace was just as magnificent as ever. It was mid-afternoon at that point, but the darkness over the city remained.

Nyx and Kedron were joined by their father in the city square. The three had worked tirelessly the entire morning to help citizens move from the caves back into their homes. Now, they sat and drank tankards of ale, doing their best to calm their nerves. Nyx still had blood soaked in her hair from the battle. Kedron's leather attire was ripped in several places. Perran Black just looked lost.

I, on the other hand, had used my time to quickly change into clean clothes and prepare Vukan for travel. His body remained below the palace in a chamber that was cooled by a subterranean river. The plan was to take him back to the Kingdom of Fire where he could be properly buried.

Calian was nowhere to be found during any of it. He'd decided to take a walk and clear his head. My heart ached for him when I realized everything he'd been through up until this point. His life hadn't been easy from the start. He was brought up as a skilled Dragon Slayer, only to be tortured to the brink of death. Then, his mother suspended his age in time - somehow - and kicked him out on the streets. Following that, Anwir got a hold of him and raised Calian on the wrong side of the prophecy. Anwir even captured Calian and tortured his adopted son. Calian's life seemed to take a turn for the better once he found his father. But now?

The deep breath I hadn't realized I was holding finally burst from my mouth. I needed to find my mate. Seconds turned into minutes and minutes turned into a couple of hours. As I stepped into the midnight garden behind the palace, the air was heavy with the scent of night-blooming flowers, and the moon cast an ethereal glow over the garden's winding pathways. My heart tightened when I finally caught sight of Calian sitting alone on a black stone bench, his face cradled in his hands.

"Calian?" I whispered, my voice barely a breath in the quiet of the night.

He looked up, his eyes meeting mine, and I saw the pain reflected in their depths. Without a word, I sat beside him, the cold stone seeping through the fabric of my night dress.

We sat in silence for a moment, the only sound the gentle rustle of the flowers in the breeze.

Finally, summoning the courage to break the stillness, I asked the question that had been weighing heavily on my heart. "Calian, what did Vukan say to you before he...before he passed?"

Calian's gaze turned inward. "He told me to be strong," he murmured. He cleared his throat, clearly fighting back a sob. He took a deep breath, gathering the strength to speak of his father's final words. "He said..." Calian's voice wavered, his emotions threatening to overwhelm him. "He said to always cherish my love for you, to hold onto it fiercely, for it's the most precious gift life offers. That in times of sorrow, it's love and compassion that sustain us, that bind us together."

Tears welled in my eyes as I listened.

"And he asked me to take care of my mother," Calian added, his voice finally breaking as tears cascaded down his cheeks. "To be her strength, her comfort, in the days to come."

My heart ached at the rawness in his voice, at the pain he was enduring. Gently, I reached out and took his hand in mine, offering what little solace I could. I didn't say anything more. Not even as he leaned over and rested his head on my shoulder. Together, we sat beneath the watchful gaze of the moons, two souls finding solace in each other's presence.

CHAPTER TWENTY

ERJON

I stood at the altar beside my mate, our hands interlocked. She gazed up at me, a warm smile spread on her beautiful face. Despite my devotion to her, I found it difficult to smile. According to Eteri's scouts, Dragons would arrive any moment. Our union was not merely a celebration of our love as Dragonmates but a strategic alliance, a consolidation of power in the face of imminent threat.

The ceremony was devoid of extravagance, for time was a luxury we could not afford. Avani and Zepherin stood witness, both in full gray Arian armor, ready for an attack. Their presence was also a silent assurance of support. Eteri stood before me in her armor, the Kingdom of Air crest etched into her chest plate. I had donned my regular fighting leathers with chain mail on top. I detested wearing full-plate armor. It was restrictive of my movements.

Dragonpriest Zeru cleared his throat and smoothed out his gray robe. "Let us begin."

I swallowed. Despite having rehearsed my vows several times the night before, I found myself to be nervous. I quickly squashed the irrelevant feeling. "My dearest Eteri. My love for you knows no bounds. In a time, such as this, our bond must transcend our personal desires, for the survival of our realm depends on our unity. A unity I will cherish until my dying breath."

Eteri's smile widened even more, and she squeezed my hands. "My dearest Erjon. In you, I have a Dragonmate whose steadfastness mirrors the strength of the Mystral Mountains and whose intellect rivals the brilliance of the stars over the highest snow-capped peaks. With you by my side, I have learned that love is not merely a fleeting emotion as you would call it, but a guiding light that illuminates even the darkest of paths.

Needless to say, she was better at writing vows than I was.

"In times of uncertainty, I vow to stand with you, Erjon. To offer solace in moments of despair and unwavering *support in times of need." She looked past me in the sky. "No matter how long we have together."*

A distant roar resonated through the walls of the small room. Amram's Dragons had come.

"For us, and our people," she said.

We turned to Zeru, and he nodded. "Erjon, Eteri, your union is not merely a union of two souls but a merging of destinies. May your bond be as resilient as the mountains and as steadfast as the stars above them," Zarith continued. "In love and in war, may you find strength in each other's embrace, and may your union bring prosperity to our land."

Eteri and I leaned in and sealed our union with a kiss. It was a fleeting moment because a sudden commotion shattered the tranquility of the ceremony. Another deafening roar shook the walls, and we all turned to the window just in time to see a massive dragon land in the palace courtyard.

I addressed the priest. "Dragonpriest Zeru. We thank you for your services, but as you can see, the ceremony has concluded. It would serve you well to retreat to the mountains through the tunnels beneath the palace."

The priest did not acknowledge my words, which was quite fine with me. Nothing he could have said would help the situation. Instead, he turned and ran just as chaos erupted around us through panicked cries of the palace staff.

We raced out of the room and out onto the grand balcony, our magic at the ready, to see a large Water Dragon appear above us.

The Dragon's tail lashed out, crashing through one of the palace's highest towers. I instinctively shielded Eteri and used my air magic to blow away the falling debris. The Dragon's eyes shifted. It locked onto the grand balcony where we stood and unleashed its flames. All four of us dodged the inferno mere seconds before being incinerated. As we climbed to our feet, I noticed Eteri standing too close to the balcony's edge, beckoning the Dragon closer. One hand was on the hilt of her blade while the other conjured a furious force of wind. Fear rose within me. What was she thinking? She was too close to the edge. Too close to the Dragon.

"Eteri, no!" I yelled over the cacophony of devastation below. The other Dragon had arrived.

My beloved turned to me, and that is when I knew I had made a grave error. I had drawn her attention away from the Dragon. In a devastating swoop, the dragon snatched her up in its jaws and devoured her before my horrified eyes.

Queen Hestia snapped her fingers, and I was back in the Kingdom of Fire.

We had arrived a few days ago. The final trek of our journey had been uneventful for the most part. Now, I sat opposite the queen in a sitting room, the remnants of her Dragonmeld still spinning through my head. For a brief second, my ability to suppress my emotions faltered, and anger rose within me. I desired vengeance.

A single tear slid down my cheek. I reached up and wiped it off with the back of my hand. I had not cried since Tuuli's death.

"You will see her again," Hestia said softly.

I retracted the other tear that threatened to fall. "I presume this is when you will tell me that I will see her again in death. Since she had a pure Dragonsoul, I would say you are correct. However, there is no determining when that will happen. It could be a hundred years before I see her in the DragonEmpyrean."

Hestia shifted in her seat. This particular movement would have alarmed any other person. Not I. "Do not withhold information to spare my feelings, Queen Hestia. It is a senseless act."

"Very well." She crossed one leg over the other, the sheerness of her pants exposing her human skin. I found the queen's garments to be absurd. Was it appropriate for the weather? Undoubtedly so. Was it appropriate for a queen? No.

"Not one hundred years. If my visions are correct, it will be much sooner than that."

"So, I will die in this war." It wasn't a question. Just an observation.

"Not necessarily. Again, I see potential outcomes. In regard to your life, the time fluctuates, but the outcome is always the same."

"I do not fear death."

She looked down as the right side of her lips raised slightly. "I do not doubt that for one second." She raised her eyes to mine. "You have an important role in ending this war."

Her statement confused me, and I was not easily confused.

She opened her mouth to say more, but the door burst open. General Sunniva stepped into the room. "They're here."

Hestia's eyes clouded for a few seconds. When they cleared, her eyes widened. Then she raised her hand slowly to cover her gaping mouth. At closer inspection, one eye was more moistened than the other, harvesting a single tear. Without so much as a glance in my general direction, the queen stood abruptly and ran out of the room. My eyes locked onto the general's, requesting an explanation. Her shoulders sagged slightly. Then her eyes dropped, and she left me there.

I knew those looks, the pain within them. Pushing my logic aside, I ran after them both. As I stepped into the opulent palace courtyard, my eyes landed first on Fin and Morwen. Fin's Dragon, Risna, was already flying upward and beyond the palace. The two Dragonmates held hands as they walked toward the carriage.

My eyes followed theirs to the royal carriage from the Kingdom of Darkness. Kedron sat atop a black mare beside the carriage as if on guard. My mind quickly assessed the situation before me. Queen Hestia stood frozen some twenty feet or so from the carriage.

Instinctively, panic stirred within me. I climbed down the palace steps, strode past the queen, and stopped beside the carriage. I glanced at Kedron. He dropped his gaze and shook his head. Someone was in that carriage. And they weren't alive.

I had lost my parents, Emera, and my mate. Whom had I lost this time? Putting my emotional barrier in place, I took a deep breath and drew back the curtain of the carriage. I peered inside slowly. There laid a figure, motionless beneath a white covering. For a brief moment, I feared it was King Orpheus, but as my eyes traced the outline of the body underneath, I realized it could not have been him.

Suddenly, a resounding roar caused us all to look upward. A large red Dragon with sharp horns and crimson scales appeared overhead. It swooped once around the palace before making its descent into the courtyard, which was just big enough for it to land in while not destroying anything.

Upon landing, the ground shook, and a red cloud of magic engulfed the Dragon. When it dissipated, Captain Westbow stood, wearing some unusual scale-like armor. If he was the red Dragon…then… My gaze darted hastily around the courtyard, searching for a familiar face. But I did not see him. I did not see the God of Fire.

Hestia appeared at my side. Calian ran toward her and attempted to intervene, but it was of no use. He reached out toward her, but she brushed him aside with a determined stride. As she neared the carriage, my heart sank. I knew what she would find beneath that sheet, and I dreaded the inevitable moment when her eyes would meet with the truth.

With a swift motion, the queen opened the carriage door and then pulled back the sheet, revealing the lifeless form of Vukan lying within. A ripple of whispers spread outward, followed by gasps and cries of shock and sorrow from the assembled crowd of citizens and palace workers.

In that moment, the queen's grief echoed through the courtyard. She dropped to her knees and held her face in her hands. Calian knelt beside her and attempted to comfort her. I could not help but wonder what twist of fate led to this tragic death.

Once again, my emotions pounded against the barrier I had built around them. The pounding grew more intense until a sudden disturbance shattered the somber atmosphere. A magnificent violet Dragon soared overhead, its wings casting a shadow over all of us below. We were already too much in shock to react to a potential threat, but as it turned out, it would have been unnecessary. A deafening, yet somehow melodious roar, pierced the air, echoing off the palace walls. Besides the queen and Calian, we all watched in awe as the Dragon, with graceful precision, landed in the courtyard.

The Dragon's form began to shift and change. Violet smoke filled the space around it, and when it dissipated, Emera stood tall. Her appearance was different. Instead of fiery red hair, her locks were deep purple. Her skin was radiant beneath the afternoon sun, and her eyes glowed violet.

For a moment, time seemed to stand still. Despite the tragedy that had befallen us, a surge of joy welled within me at the sight of my friend having been returned from the dead.

Emera's gaze met mine across the courtyard, and a flicker of recognition passed between us. Though her expression remained solemn, I detected a glimmer of reassurance in her eyes—a silent promise that we would find each other and share our stories.

As the queen's cries of grief echoed around us, I felt a sense of gratitude wash over me. For in this moment of darkness and despair, Emera's presence was a beacon of hope.

An unexpected gust of wind blew through the crowd. Zepherin and his men touched down just beyond the courtyard and came running. They had left just a short time earlier for a training exercise.

"When we saw the Dragons, we turned around right away." He twisted and turned, failing to locate any Dragons.

"There is nothing to fear here. The Dragons turned out to be Risna, Calian, and Emera."

"Emera?"

I pointed toward the carriage where Emera was kneeling on the other side of Hestia. She was rubbing the queen's back.

"Well. Maybe we can win this war after all."

"Maybe," I mused. "But Emera was defeated before. Who is to say she cannot be defeated again?"

Zepherin shrugged. "You've got to be optimistic, little brother. Even in times such as these."

He meant when gods die.

AMRAM

I inhaled the damp and musty air of the palace dungeons and smiled. It was the only part of the palace that was reminiscent of my earlier abode before the war. A single torchlight flickered weakly, casting shifting shadows along the stone walls as I strolled by the numerous cells. I focused on the sound of my footsteps against the stone floor while the queen's voice droned on beside me. I'd attempted to roam the dungeon alone, but it seemed I couldn't go anywhere without the queen hovering nearby like an annoying gnat that needed to be squashed.

"You know," she said, her irksome voice testing my patience, "we haven't heard from Valda in quite some time.

Surely, you must have some back-up plan. I can always send my soldiers to do your bidding."

I clenched my fists, fighting the urge to silence her with my chaos magic. One small blast was all it would take. "That shall not be necessary. Your soldiers are needed here." How had I allowed this tedious woman to accompany me? Her endless prattling had grown intolerable.

"As for Valda, she will arrive when she arrives," I replied curtly. "And I have no intention of sharing my plans."

"Oh, come now," she persisted. "We are allies, aren't we? I've offered my home and my kingdom to you. Surely, I can be trusted with such vital information."

Allies. The word soured in my mind. This queen, with her false charm and endless questions, was nothing more than a pawn—a means to an end. I turned to face her, my eyes narrowing as I took in her oblivious smile.

"Leora," I said, forcing civility into my voice, "Despite your…hospitality…my plans are not of your concern. Focus on your kingdom's affairs so that I can focus on the world."

She dropped her facade for a second, exposing the snake she truly was beneath. Then she quickly regained her composure. "I would hope that my kingdom's affairs would also be on your mind since you're a guest here."

Guest. The word was an insult coming from her lips. My patience, already worn thin, broke. Without a word, I seized her wrist and dragged her toward an empty cell. She yelped in surprise, but I paid no heed. I spun her around and shoved her up against the wall.

"What are you doing?" she seethed, struggling against me. "I am your ally."

I leaned close to her, my lips faintly brushing against her ear. "You are nothing." Then I teleported out of the cell and slammed the iron door shut. The sound of the lock clicking into place was music to my ears. "This is the consequence of overstepping your bounds," I said coldly, my eyes boring into hers through the bars. "Perhaps a little time in solitude will teach you the value of knowing your place."

She stared at me, fury burning behind her eyes. "You can't do this. I am a queen!"

A cruel smile played upon my lips. "You were a queen," I corrected. "Now you are simply a prisoner."

She screamed and emitted a beam of blinding light toward me. I teleported away from her and once I reappeared, threw a gust of wind that knocked her into the wall. She fell to the ground with a resounding thud and stayed there, unmoving.

I massaged my temples in an attempt to relieve the headache she'd given me. I kept massaging them until Valda appeared before me.

My daughter paused, taking in the sight of Queen Leora lying unconscious on the floor of her cell. "Finally, had enough, Father?"

"Obviously."

Valda cackled. "Better you than me. I would have just ended her life."

I rolled my eyes. My daughter was so brash sometimes. "And what use would she be to me then?"

"Well, the palace would certainly be quieter."

"That is until her kingdom revolts against me."

Valda leaned against the cell. "At which time we'd annihilate them." She inspected her nails. How in the world had I raised such a vain child.

"I'd prefer to focus my efforts on the true enemy."

"Yes, the humans."

I cleared my throat. "Yes, exactly."

Valda dropped her hand and angled her head. "That is whom you're speaking about, correct?"

I turned and walked toward the dungeon's exit. "But of course." Then I teleported to the throne room.

Valda reappeared just seconds after I'd sat on the throne. "Unless you're really talking about Emera Edevane, Father."

I leaned to the left armrest and propped my chin up. "Don't hold back on account of me."

Valda sauntered toward me. "You seem awfully caught up in destroying her. More so than the humans we originally set out to destroy."

"Emera is the one who stands in our way. As long as she remains alive, I will never have full control of the world. Your failure at the Kingdom of Darkness is evidence that she's grown powerful."

Valda's brows furrowed and her breathing quickened. "You heard."

I sat up straight. "You should know by now, dear daughter, that I hear everything. Now, please tell me something useful."

Valda rolled back her shoulders and stood tall. "I know where your amulet is."

I leaned forward. "How? Where?"

"I have my ways, father," she said, smiling. "Kedron Black, the Dragonheir of Darkness, has it."

If I had emotions, joy would have filled my black heart. "Find it and bring it to me."

CHAPTER TWENTY-ONE

CALIAN

My mother and I stood at the entrance of my father's temple. My heart was heavy with grief as I mentally prepared for what we were about to do. My father's body had already been taken in, but my mother and I still lingered outside the temple's entrance in silence.

"I think it's time," I said softly.

My mother didn't answer. Neither of us wanted to enter. My reasons extended beyond not wanting to be reminded of my father. I had never set foot in this temple, at least, not that I could remember. I was denied entry when I lived on the streets.

"Or I can do this alone."

She turned to me, finally breaking her silence with a sigh. "Absolutely not."

I pressed my lips together and nodded.

The Queen of the Kingdom of Fire grabbed the handle to the Temple of Vukan and pulled the door open. Stepping through the arched entrance, we were immediately enveloped by the sunlight that filtered through narrow, stained-glass windows high up on the stone walls. These windows depicted mostly my father, but my mother and even Vasuman—the Dragon Slayer —were present. Aside from the windows, the walls were also covered in tapestries dedicated to my father and his history. My face was woven into the scenes as well, making me cringe every time I gazed into my unfeeling eyes. The air inside was thick with incense, the sacred scent filling my lungs with each breath. It was supposed to be calming, but I just wanted to choke.

"So, this is why I wasn't allowed in here," I said to myself, my voice barely above a whisper.

"I couldn't have you seeing your face."

"You couldn't have me doing much," I mumbled.

My mother stopped and faced me. "I did what I had to do to ensure the survival of this world. Your grandfather's prophecy was all the hope I had left to see that your father's death wasn't in vain."

"I don't blame you."

"Your mannerisms suggest otherwise."

I contemplated her words as we stood there. "Maybe so."

Without a word, she turned away from me and continued walking down the long aisle. I followed behind her, taking notice of the towering stone pillars, their surfaces worn smooth by the touch of countless visitors. The pillars supported a vaulted ceiling that disappeared into shadow.

"How did you do it?"

My mother stopped but didn't turn.

Then I peered in front of me. At the heart of the temple stood the altar, not of simple stone but a slab of pure ruby, polished to a reflective finish. It was inlaid with golden gems that blazed like flames, forming an inner inferno that seemed to flare with life. Behind the altar stood a massive statue of my father in his Dragon form, carved from a single block of white marble. The god's eyes looked up at us with compassion, and his outstretched hands seemed to offer welcome.

My mother stood by my side, her face a mask of sorrow. She had always exuded strength, but today, she seemed fragile. A Dragonpriest, an old man with a long white beard and kind eyes, stood next to my father's cold, lifeless form.

I took a deep breath and stepped forward, my boots rustling against the stone floor. "Are you ready?" I asked, my voice barely above a whisper.

She nodded, her eyes never leaving my father's still form.

I turned to the priest, who was watching us with a solemn expression. "Can you explain the burial process?" I asked, my voice wavering slightly. My mother probably knew the ritual, but I didn't.

The priest bowed his head respectfully before speaking. "Of course. The burial process for a god is a sacred and intricate ritual." He grabbed hold of a bottle from a small table to his right. "First, we will anoint his body with oils to preserve his form for eternity." He sat the bottle back down and grabbed the silk fabric next to it. "Then, we will wrap him in this covering, a fabric woven from the finest crimson threads, to protect his soul on its journey to the DragonEmpyrean. At that point, you and the queen will view him privately." He paused, looking at me to ensure I understood. I nodded for him to continue. "Next, we will place his body in the golden sarcophagus, which will be sealed with the symbols of his element. These symbols will ensure that his body remains undisturbed. Finally, the…" His voice drifted as he slowly swept his focus from me to my mother.

My mother reached out and touched my father's hand, her fingers trembling. "I will recite the Rite of Ascension," she said softly.

The priest smiled gently and bowed. "I must take my leave and prepare for tonight." With that, he turned and exited through a small wooden door at the back of the temple.

"And what of his legacy?" I asked.

My mother turned to me with tears streaming down her face. She reached out and grasped my arm. "His legacy will live on through you, Calian. His memory will continue to guide and protect us."

I took a deep breath and looked at my father's body. "I hope so."

Mother took my hand. "Please, come sit with me." She led me to a small room at the back of the temple. Soft sunlight filtered through a small, stained-glass window, casting an array of gentle colors on the stone floor. It was sparse, yet serene. I imagined Erjon taking refuge in this room, healing his wounds from recent losses.

A small wooden shrine of my father's Dragon form stood against a wall with small offerings, undoubtedly placed there by the Dragonpriests. I meandered over to a tall bookshelf where scrolls of scriptures rested neatly. As I lingered there, breathing in the scent of ancient parchment, oak wood, and incense sticks, my mother cleared her throat. "I've always enjoyed sitting in this room. It is where I can truly find solitude and engage in deep self-reflection."

I sat at a small table, its satin cushions a vibrant red with cold accents. "I can see how that would be useful."

She wiped a strand of hair away from her gentle face. "I used a combination of an enchanted slumber potion and a mind stasis spell after your wounds were healed," she said. "It was the only way to ensure you would remain safe and undisturbed for as long as necessary."

I frowned, trying to piece together what she was saying. "A slumber potion and a stasis spell? How does that even work?"

"First, I brewed the potion," she explained, her hands splayed out on the table. "It was a mixture of rare ingredients—midnight fire flowers, scorch berries, a drop of dunescourge poison, and a vial of my blood."

"Poison? Blood?"

"Poison to slow your heart rate and chaos magic to maintain the comatose state were needed. Once you drank the potion and fell into a deep sleep, I cast the mind stasis spell," she continued. "I used my amulet, channeling a Dragonmeld through it to cast a web of stasis around your consciousness. This web kept your mind in a state of temporal suspension, ensuring you remained in that deep sleep until it was time to wake you…It also suppressed your memory, which will come back little by little over time."

Sweat warmed my palms. I rubbed my hands across my thighs to rid myself of the moisture. "So, I was frozen in time with no recollection of who I was."

She shifted her weight in the chair. "Yes," she confirmed.

"And then when I came to, you kicked me out?" Heat flared beneath my cheeks. Despite understanding her motives, deep down I remained infuriated by her apparent indifference to the matter.

"Something like that." She released a heavy breath and let her eyes wander around the vacant room. "I spent many nights in this room. It almost became a second home." She laughed softly. "At one point, the priests and priestesses brought in a cot. The palace haunted me day and night. Here," she gestured around her, "was peaceful."

"Did you stop?"

"I still come here occasionally, but after I adopted Shula, the trips became less frequent."

Jealousy gnawed at my insides.

"Day in and day out, Shula kept your presence alive. She assured me every day that you would return to me. That you would understand the sacrifices I made. She said you would forgive my transgressions."

I dragged my hand through my hair. "I do…most of the time. It will…take time. It's just…who I am."

A smile tugged at her lips. "Just like your father."

I stood and turned toward the door. Then I spun around, a thought bursting from my lips. "What about your age? Surely, the citizens took notice that you didn't age."

"They assumed I'd been blessed by your father. That his death led to my immortality. Not too far off." She tapped at the amulet she wore. "A piece of your grandfather's soul is within this gem, which was gifted to me upon his death. It holds his healing magic. When I feel tired or weary, I put it on, and it restores my health.

I felt my eyes widen. "And if you don't put it on."

"I think you know what would happen."

I nodded. "Are you coming?"

Mother closed her eyes and inhaled deeply. "No. I think I'll stay in solitude a bit longer."

I lingered in the temple a bit longer, exploring the rooms and introducing myself to the priests and priestesses, thanking them for the care they took with my father. The sun had already set, but since my mother decided to remain in solitude for the evening, the formal dinner was called off.

So, I took off in search of Emera. I found my mate, along with Erjon and the others, in the dining hall engaged in a hushed conversation as they ate their meal.

The conversation stopped after I shut the door. I couldn't blame them. It was an awkward situation all around. I had failed in my quest to get Anahita's help. Then I'd been nearly killed by another Dragon. And after that, my father was killed. I was a walking, talking mess of a man.

The feet of the dining chair scraped across the surface of the floor as I pulled it away from the table and sat next to Emera.

"Where were you?" she whispered.

"Catching up with a friend from my past." She didn't press the issue. Only smiled and turned her attention back to our peers.

"I'll have someone bring you a plate," Zepherin said. He scooted his chair back and started to stand, but I held a hand up to stop him. Slowly, he lowered back into his seat.

I watched Erjon eat in silence for several minutes while the others picked up their conversation. The weight of my own self-pity suffocated me like a blanket that threatened to smother me. I couldn't shake the sudden nagging feeling of guilt that gnawed at the edges of my mind. A bitter taste of shame lingered on my tongue as I watched the Dragonheir of Air. I had allowed myself to drown in my anger, knowing Erjon had suffered just as much. His pain was just as raw. We both nursed a gaping wound that no amount of time could heal. Yet here he was, keeping his emotions in check. I wanted to burn down the city.

"I'm sorry," I said.

The chatter ceased. Emera leaned into me. "What was that?"

My eyes locked onto Erjon's. I cleared my throat. "I'm sorry for your loss."

Erjon's back straightened. He looked down, then back at me. "And I am sorry for yours."

There was an insurmountable silence between us all. No one ate. Everyone just stared ahead.

I sighed. "I am sick of death."

We all turned to Avani. She still stared at her plate of food; the fork she held trembled as it remained suspended in the air.

Zepherin sat his fork down and sighed. "Same."

Avani stared at us all. "Look around you. Everyone here has lost someone." She paused. "Well, maybe except Fin."

Fin opened his mouth to respond, but he closed it.

I brushed the stray curls out of my eyes. "That may be true, but Fin has the weight of humanity on him."

Fin's brows furrowed as he stared at his plate, yet he remained silent.

Avani leaned forward. "How do you figure?" It was a genuine question with no animosity behind it.

"Everybody here, take a look at your hands. See those scales? Now look at Fin's hands. He's the only human here. Sure, other humans have joined the cause within the other cities. Kedron has retrieved valuable information regarding rebellions and attacks. But the only human who's been fighting with us since this started, the only one brave enough to stand up to Amram and to battle Dragons again and again, is Fin." I turned to my oldest friend. "The humans look at you as their savior. Not Emera. Not me." I gestured toward everyone else at the table. "Not them. You."

"He's right." We all turned to see Shula standing at the other end of the table. She walked around it, pulled out a chair beside Zeph, and sat down. "The humans of this kingdom - of every kingdom—know who you are," she continued, her voice steady and clear. "They sing your praises, not theirs."

Fin's hazel eyes scanned the faces around him, observing their reactions. I didn't have to read his mind to know he was thinking of Mr. Ren back in the Kingdom of Water.

"Shula is correct." Kedron's voice cut through the silence, drawing all eyes to him. He set his glass of water down with a decisive clink.

Morwen nodded, a small smile playing on her lips. "Everyone here is important, but it's the humans who truly matter in this war."

Emera stood. "Up until now, we've been so concerned with protecting the kingdoms that we have failed to remain vigilant in our duty to protect the humans." She turned to Fin. "Our people. They have been at the back of our minds, including mine. But not yours, Fin. You've continued to keep them at the forefront, to fight for them. They see the strength in you. That's why they rally behind you."

The room fell silent as everyone absorbed her words. Emera's words carried weight, and it was clear she spoke from her heart.

Around the table, nods of agreement and murmurs of support rippled through the group. The tension that had hung over the dining hall dissipated.

We stayed in the dining hall for another hour, the time slipping by as we ate, drank, and made a valiant effort to maintain our spirits. The weight of our worries seemed to linger, but we immersed ourselves in the camaraderie of shared laughter and stories. Fin entertained us with a tale of a particularly clumsy soldier he'd trained, his animated gestures causing ripples of laughter around the table. Erjon, ever the skeptic, added his occasional commentary which, despite his best efforts, added a touch of dry humor to whatever story was being told.

Emera's laughter, though genuine, had a slightly strained edge, as if she was constantly aware that she was not quite herself. I caught her glancing down at her plate a few times.

As the hour drew to a close, the conversation dwindled, and the reality of our situation crept back into our minds. My father's death, Queen Eteri's death, and the impending battle for the unnamed world. We exchanged knowing looks, silently acknowledging that the time for lightheartedness had passed.

"I think it best that I retire for the evening," Erjon said. He pushed away from the table, bowed slightly, and left the room.

Morwen rose from her chair. "I am inclined to agree with Erjon."

Emera leaned closer toward me. "We need to talk, privately. All four of us." She glanced at Fin and Kedron. Fin was already standing from his seat to join Morwen.

"Let's use the war room," I suggested, my voice low. It was secure, removed from the prying ears and eyes of servants and other palace workers. Emera nodded.

I stood, catching Kedron's attention with a discreet nod. "A moment, please," I said. Then I intercepted Fin and Morwen before they'd exited the hall.

"I apologize, Mor, but Em needs a word with Fin, Kedron, and me." She raised a single brow slightly. "But I'm sure you can join us as well."

Morwen shook her head. "No need. I am fatigued to say the least." She leaned toward Fin and pressed her lips lightly against his cheek. I couldn't ignore the pang of jealousy in my core.

Once Morwen was out of hearing range, Fin turned to me with a scowl on his face, clearly agitated. "This better be good."

I just shrugged and headed toward the war room to join Emera and Kedron, who had already left the dining hall.

Once the heavy door thudded shut behind us, Emera started speaking. "I know that you all are exhausted. But we need to discuss the amulets."

Fin sighed. "Really, Em? Now?"

"Yes, now."

Fin didn't budge from where he stood. "I know that it's really your mother speaking for you, so I say this with all the love in the world. No." He turned back to the door and reached for the handle.

"Fintan, please," Emera said softly, yet firmly. "This is important."

With a heavy sigh, Fin pivoted on his heel and sat in a chair with a huff. Then he leaned back in his chair and glanced toward the door, frustration evident in the tight set of his jaw.

Her calling Fin by his full name didn't go unnoticed. Just another reminder that Emera wasn't exactly herself.

Kedron watched the exchange, his brow furrowed, but he remained silent, his fingers lightly tracing the buttons of his black jacket.

Emera took a deep breath, her eyes sweeping across us. "The amulets. We know that they repel magic. We thought they were meant for humans only, but that's not the case. Nimerah's is different."

Kedron leaned forward, placing his hands on the table. "What's special about it?"

Emera touched the amulet hanging around her neck. "I know what needs to be done with it. But first, we must think about what to do with Amram's. I think we have to hide it.

He wants it, so there has to be more to it than just aiding a human's life. It's too dangerous to keep out in the open."

Fin stood abruptly, pacing the length of the room. "So, what's the plan? How do we hide something like that?"

I followed Fin's movements with my eyes as Emera turned to Kedron. "We need to find a place where no one will think to look. Somewhere secure, and only known to us."

"No," I said. "Too risky. It needs to be somewhere only Kedron knows."

"Okay, then," Emera replied.

"I have a few ideas," Kedron replied, holding out his hand.

Emera took off the amulet and gave it to Kedron. He put it on and tucked it under his shirt. Something about the exchange put me on edge, like I was forgetting something important, but I just couldn't place it. So much had happened in the last few days that everything was muddled.

Fin stopped pacing abruptly. "What can possibly be different with Amram's that he is so hell-bent on finding it?"

"Maybe I can help with that."

We all turned to see my mother standing at the door. I rose from my seat quickly. "Mother. I thought you'd be in bed by now."

She smiled, but it didn't reach her eyes. "Can't sleep."

A knot formed in my throat. Of course, she couldn't.

"Quite understandable," Em whispered.

"So, what's going on with Amram's amulet?" Fin asked. He plopped down in a chair and massaged his temples.

She crossed over to the table and sat down. With her arms outstretched, she motioned for us all to grab hands. "Why don't I show you?"

Fin leaned back, clearly unsure of joining us in a Dragonmeld.

"Scared?" I joked.

He crossed his arms. "Of you all seeing into my mind? Yes. And I'm not ashamed to admit it."

Emera scoffed. "No one is going to go traipsing into your mind, Fintan."

Fin uncrossed his arms and sat up straight. "Maybe not you. But I wouldn't put it past your mate."

I fought to keep my face neutral. Mate. My heart plunged into my stomach. I cleared my throat. "I promise not to take a stroll in your mind, Fin."

"I'll shoot several arrows in your heart if you do."

"Someone's touchy," I said with a chuckle. "Usually it's me."

Fin cocked his head to the side, thinking about my words. "True. I'm just frazzled, I guess. Is that even a word? Frazzled?"

Kedron nodded. "Yes."

My mother straightened her back and rolled back her shoulders. "Let's begin. Everyone, close your eyes. I haven't done a meld of this magnitude in a very long time. It takes concentration and as much mental power as I can muster." Our eyes connected. She was talking to me. Was this how she wiped my memory? Through an advanced Dragonmeld?

Before I could ask her, she focused her attention on Kedron. "Mr. Perran, someone must stay back, meaning, someone must remain in the present and of sound mind in case anyone should enter this room."

Kedron released his hands and stood. "Gladly." His relief didn't go unnoticed by Fin who wrinkled his nose.

Just as I looked back at my mother, my eyes clamped shut, and my consciousness was pulled from my body. All of us were collectively plunged into darkness.

When the darkness lifted, we found ourselves in the Kingdom of Light, standing at the back of the throne room. It was the exact location I'd been placed in during my previous Dragonmeld.

Amram sat on the throne. Beside him was Valda, inspecting her nails.

"Father," Valda said lazily. "You were telling me about the amulet earlier as if I should know what's so special about it."

"My dear daughter, special is an understatement. Unlike Ragnar's that protects humans and Nimerah's which protects a human or Dragonborn, my amulet holds my soul. It ensures that I will never be killed."

Emera inhaled sharply, her eyes locked on Amram. "It's worse than I imagined."

Amram continued, unaware of our presence. At least, he appeared that way. "With it, I can live forever, ruling with the power I deserve."

Valda's expression changed from indifference to fascination. "Father, you sly Dragon. You told me the amulet was just a burden, a responsibility."

Amram's eyes flashed with annoyance. "I said what I had to. The truth is, its power will allow me to transcend mortality. No one, not even Emera Edevane, will stand in my way."

Emera's face hardened. "Challenge accepted," she murmured.

Fin clenched his fists. "He can't get the amulet. If he does, everything we've fought for will be for nothing. He'll rule for eternity. Humans will suffer."

"Valda, you must help me retrieve the amulet. Together, we will be unstoppable."

"It shall be done."

"See to it quickly. I have a rebellion to squash." Then, as he'd done before, he turned his head and stared at us.

"Mother!" I yelled.

Valda whipped her head around and smiled when she saw us. She started running toward us. Suddenly, we plunged into darkness. Amram's voice grew fainter as the light faded. "You will not enter here again!" he seethed.

I opened my eyes, relieved to be back in the war room, the familiar walls grounding us after the Dragonmeld experience. Mother sat before us, her expression grave. "You've seen the truth," she said.

"We have," Emera answered.

Fin raised his hand. "Question. How did Amram know we were there?"

I closed my eyes and massaged my temples. "I just assumed it's because he knows everything."

My mother sat up straight with a strained smile. She was exhausted. "Amram is all-powerful…"

"Not quite," Emera pointed out.

"Of course, but even so, he has an acute awareness of the fabric of our reality and his own consciousness. Every intrusion or alteration, such as if I connected with his mind and projected you inside, it would be immediately noticeable to him... Well, almost immediately."

CHAPTER TWENTY-TWO

EMERA

Erjon and I walked side by side toward the library, the floor beneath us echoing our footsteps in the dimly lit hallway. Many of our friends had retired for the evening, but I couldn't. It was time for me to get my soul back.

"How are you feeling, Emera?" he asked, his voice as measured and even as always.

I chuckled, the sound light and airy compared to his steady tone. "You really want to know how I'm feeling?"

His expression remained unchanged. "Most certainly," he replied. "You are about to perform a Dragonmeld. A dangerous one, I might add."

I shook my head. "You're afraid I will fail."

Erjon halted abruptly and turned to me, and his brows furrowed intensely. "I am afraid you will die. Forever this time."

Recalling the Priest Benigno's warning, I clutched my chest and all-but gulped down a small lump that formed in my throat. My empathic tendrils went to work, sliding out of me and wrapping themselves around Erjon. The tendrils pulled at his emotions which were buried deep within him. Erjon was scared.

"I thought by now you would have more faith in me," I said gently.

Erjon's eyes darted hastily across my face as he grasped for control of his emotions. "You are currently walking an uncharted path. No Dragonborn has dared enter the mind of a Dragongod."

I locked onto his gaze and removed my empathic tendrils. "I am not just any Dragonborn. I am a goddess."

Erjon paused, thinking. "A true goddess knows how to balance their emotions. If you let your emotions consume you at any point during this meld, it could…" He stopped, leaving his thoughts dangling in the air. I'd never seen Erjon like this.

"Emotions aren't a weakness, Erjon." I reached out and touched his arm lightly. "You might see them as a distraction, but they give us strength, too."

He remained silent, only nodding. His throat bobbed as he struggled to maintain an impassive expression.

We walked on in silence for a while, the library drawing closer with every step. I knew Erjon's mind was turning over my words, just as mine was trying to find the right ones to ease his trepidation. As we reached the library's entrance, Erjon turned to me, his eyes softer than before. "Perhaps you are more of a goddess than I give you credit for."

I smiled, knowing that in his own way, Erjon had given me a compliment. "Perhaps."

We made our way to the back end of the library. I placed the candles we'd brought with us on a nearby table while Erjon made sure we were alone.

"Let us begin." Erjon's words were soft, barely more than a whisper.

I nodded.

Erjon stood beside me and placed his hand on my shoulder. We figured if I was going to enter Amram's mind, I would need all the magic I could get. Erjon would stay connected to me, and I could siphon his magic in case I needed more power. We'd discussed having Calian with us, but my mate had so much at stake that it could become a dangerous distraction. And although Hestia had offered her assistance, I turned it down. She needed time to mourn. Erjon and I could accomplish this task on our own.

As I'd previously done with the Ghoul at the Dragonseminary, I closed my eyes and let my mind wander into darkness. I inhaled an elongated breath through my nose and released it slowly.

The air was heavy, thick with the scent of decay. I forced my eyes open and found myself standing in a vast landscape with gnarled trees void of foliage. It was twisted and warped like what someone would see in nightmares. Jagged mountains loomed in the distance, their peaks glowing with a deep purple light.

"Amram," I whispered. The beating of my heart spiked. This place was not real, yet it felt disturbingly tangible.

A shiver ran down my spine. Water magic flooded my veins, providing me with a much-needed cool relief of tranquility. First thing: my soul. I collected my empathic abilities and pulled them to the surface. Golden tendrils slid out of my hands and traveled as far as I could see, searching for the faint pulse of my soul, my very essence. Power surged into the golden tendrils, carrying them farther into Amram's mind until they finally detected the presence of my soul.

With one cautious step after another, I followed the path of my tendrils. The sky above was a swirling vortex of storm clouds, lightning crackling throughout them. Each step I took echoed, as if the very ground was mocking my presence. I rolled my shoulders back and persisted, knowing that Amram's mind was designed to disorient and terrify intruders. I refused to let it break me.

As the tendrils guided me onward, I encountered twisted shapes and shadowy figures. They were remnants of Amram's darkest memories and fears. They hissed and snarled, as I walked by, their eyes glowing with malice.

Suddenly, one of the shadows shifted, contorting and expanding until it took on a more defined form. My heart pounded in my chest, and I stared in wonder as I watched one of Amram's memories take shape. I now stood on a celestial plane, a vast expanse of shimmering light and swirling colors. The ground beneath me was a mixture of radiant patterns. The sky above was an endless canvas of stars, their light casting a silver glow over everything. It was a place of creation, a realm where the chaos blurred the boundaries between thought and reality. I looked ahead and standing before me were Amram, Nemerah, and Ragnar. A breath caught in my throat when I saw my mother. She looked divine, her features embracing the setting around her. Then I took notice of Amram's concerned expression.

My mother's eyes sparkled as she spoke to him. "We have the power to create life, Amram. To shape beings in our image. Think of what we could achieve with humans— creatures capable of growth, learning, and innovation. Our children and our children's children will live in a world with companions without magic. Those companions will balance the Dragons' existence.

Amram's face remained unchanged. "But Nemerah, creating humans could introduce havoc into the world. They could bring about suffering and destruction. You say they will help maintain balance, but I do not believe it."

Ragnar, standing firmly beside Nemerah, nodded in agreement with her. "Amram, Nemerah's vision could lead to a new era of enlightenment. Isn't that what you strive for? Think about it. Humans could become our greatest creation, capable of wonders even we can't foresee."

Amram scoffed. "Without magic? What wonders would they be capable of without any connection to the elements?"

Nimerah smiled. "One does not need magic to do wondrous things. Power can come from our thoughts, our determination, and our compassion."

The tension in the room grew with each passing second. Amram's eyes shifted between Nimerah and Ragnar. "And what if they stray from the path of enlightenment?"

Nemerah stepped closer to Amram, her voice softening but remaining steady. "We have to believe in the potential for goodness. They will have the capacity to learn from their mistakes. Then they will rise to heights we can't even imagine."

Amram's eyes hardened. "You place too much faith in the unknown, Nimerah. We must tread carefully. The consequences of such a creation could be...deadly."

Ragnar's voice rumbled with conviction as he slapped Amram on the back. "Sometimes, Amram, the greatest risks bring the greatest rewards."

The scene blurred then cleared. I was in another area of the realm. Nimerah and Ragnar were no longer with me. Instead, a small child with flowing violet hair stood next to Amram.

"Valda," I whispered.

Her form was small and delicate yet full of a youthful energy that lit up the space around her. It reminded me of when she posed as Dwyn. A small ache bloomed in my chest.

"Father," she said, her voice ringing with innocent excitement, "Is it true? Are we really going to have new companions?"

Amram turned to her, his expression softening at the sight of his daughter. It was unusual to see. "Yes, Valda, we have the power to create new beings."

Valda's eyes sparkled with delight, and she clapped her hands and jumped. "Oh, Father, that sounds wonderful! We could teach them so many things. I could have friends to play with. Imagine all the fun we could have, creating and exploring!"

Amram's face darkened, an all-too-familiar look of annoyance twisted his features. "Valda, creating humans is not something to take lightly. They won't just be companions. They will be lesser than us. They will have no magic or intelligence. They'll be useless."

Valda looked up at him, puzzled.

Amram knelt down to her level. "They could hurt each other, cause suffering, and bring destruction to our world."

Valda sniffled, her voice trembling. "I don't want them to hurt us. I don't want them to destroy our world."

Amram pulled her into a comforting embrace, his own heart heavy with the weight of his decision. "They won't, my dear." Then he looked right at me. "Not if I have anything to say about it."

The scene blurred once more, the edges dissolving into the shadows once more. I found myself back amidst the twisted shapes, their eyes still watching, but now with a hint of understanding. Again, they advanced toward me to cause harm. I raised my hand, conjuring a barrier of chaos magic that rippled then shined around me. The figures recoiled, but they still attempted to break my defense.

My tendrils suddenly pulled me forward as if begging me to walk faster. I picked up my pace just as the landscape shifted and changed around me. The mountains melted into a dense, tangled forest of blackened, gnarled trees. Their branches reached out like skeletal hands, clawing at the air. I managed to weave through them, my heart pounding in my chest.

Then, a clearing opened up before me. In the center stood a massive, obsidian tower, its surface glistening like stars reflecting off the restless waves of the Kaimana Sea. Its structure rose high, its jagged spires piercing the sky, a dark silhouette against the backdrop of a crimson light.

The tower's exterior was adorned with intricate carvings in the shapes of Dragonscales and grotesque creatures that seemed to always face the traveler even when viewed from a different angle. Shadows danced along the vines that wound their way up the sides.

I cautiously walked on the narrow path of blackened stones that led to the tower. The pull of my soul grew stronger, almost overwhelming, compelling me to move forward despite the thick aura of evil that seemed to glow from the structure. It was as if the tower itself was alive, a sentient being beckoning me into its depths.

As I neared the entrance, the air grew colder, and the faint sounds of whispers reached my ears. The scent of damp ground and the decay of flesh filled my nostrils, causing me to gag.

Breathe in, breathe out. Breathe in, breathe out.

Large iron doors were before me, their imposing presence a final barrier between the safety of outside and the unknown horrors inside. I took the remaining steps forward and stood before doors which seemed to hum, inviting—more like luring—me in. Above the entrance, a sinister sigil glowed faintly—a dragon's eye—and its gaze followed me as I placed my hand on the cold, rough surface of the door. The moment my fingers brushed against the iron, the doors slowly creaked open, revealing nothing but darkness beyond me. The pull of my soul was now a relentless force, urging me to step forward into the heart of the tower.

I stepped forward, pushing open the heavy iron doors. Inside, the air was colder. How that was possible, I didn't know. The air was filled with the scent of blood and soot. With a snap of my fingers, I created light, revealing a long corridor.

"Here we go." My footsteps were heavy as I walked down the corridor. Each wall was lined with the heads of the Dragongods and goddesses, but their faces were twisted into grotesque-looking ghouls. All except for Amram's head which was a perfect replica of his face. Except his eyes. They were hollow and lifeless.

I paused when I noticed the head of Endrit mounted on the wall. Despite the grotesque twisting and deformities, the face unmistakably belonged to Endrit rather than the Ghoul I'd met at the Dragonseminary. I leaned in and inspected his features. A chill ran down my spine, and I shuddered before forcing myself to move on.

After several more steps, the end of the corridor opened into a large chamber. In the center, atop a pile of bones, was a crystal gem suspended in the air, glowing with a soft violet light. My soul. Warmth radiated from its pristine edges, desperately yearning to be within me. I peered left and then right. The chamber was empty. But as I stepped closer to my soul, a deep, rumbling laugh filled the chamber.

"Emera, darling," Amram's voice rang around me. "Did you really think it would be this easy?"

I turned. Behind me, Amram's head detached from the wall, forming into the shape of the Dragongod himself. His eyes were no longer hollow but burned with deadly malice as he regarded me with a sneer. He stalked forward, his deep violet robe swaying lightly against the stone floor.

I clenched my fists, summoning my chaos energy within me. "I came for what is mine, Uncle. I will not leave without it."

He stood mere inches from me. "So brave." He raised his hand and tucked a stray strand of my purple hair behind my ear. Then his lips spread into a cruel smile. Before he could outmaneuver my attack, I raised my hands and released a blow of chaos magic at him. I caught a glimpse of shock on his face as he flew backward down the corridor.

I focused my will and teleported instantly to my soul. There it was, encased in the gem. I reached for it, my fingers trembling with anticipation. The moment my fingertips brushed the gem's flawless design, an overwhelming light burst through me, filling every corner of my mind.

I wrapped my hand around the gem tightly, feeling its warmth and energy seep into my skin. It pulsed with life, and as I held it, the gem dissolved into pure energy, merging seamlessly with my body. My soul flowed back into me in a powerful rush.

A sense of completeness washed over me as my soul settled into place, filling the void that had left me hollow for so long. The emptiness vanished, replaced by a profound sense of unity and wholeness. I felt my mother's presence, her warmth and her love, intertwining with mine, reinforcing my strength and power.

In the distance, I heard Amram's roar of rage, a sound that had once struck fear into my heart. But now, even though he was only some twenty feet away from me, the sound was diminished and weak.

His mind, the labyrinth of shadows and nightmares he had constructed, crumbled around me. The twisted shapes and shadowy figures disintegrated, their hisses and snarls fading away into nothing but darkness.

The darkness dissipated, and I felt myself back in my own body. The connection to Amram's mind was severed completely once I put my mental blocks back into place. My power was stronger due to the merging of two Chaos Dragon souls.

When I opened my eyes, Erjon stared back at me. He nodded with a faint smile as he slid his hand off my shoulder. Then he motioned toward the door. Calian leaned against it with his arms crossed in front of him. When our eyes met, his eyes widened and pushed away from the door.

"Em?" he murmured. "Are you…"

For the first time since I'd returned to the living world, my heart soared at the sound of his voice. He rushed toward me and knelt beside the chair. I extended my hands toward him and cradled his face, my fingers trembling with emotion. "I'm me," I whispered, my voice barely more than a breath. "I am completely me."

In that moment, I saw the depth of Calian's love reflected in his eyes. My soul embraced the electric feeling that sparked between us. I took a quick glimpse down beneath my shirt and smiled when a hint of vibrant purple showed above my heart. My Dragonmate wings were back.

Calian took my face in his hands, his touch gentle yet reassuring. "I missed you," he breathed.

"Me, too." A single tear fell down my cheek. "I mean, I missed you, too."

He smiled and pulled me in for a passionate kiss. For a brief moment, we were hidden from all our troubles. Everything outside of us was suspended in time. Nothing mattered but the two of us.

Erjon cleared his throat, pulling me back to reality. "I take it, you are you again?"

I smiled. "I am more than just me. I am whole. I am complete."

An all-too-familiar sound vibrated the walls of the palace.

"Good," Calian said. "Because it sounds like they're here." He ran to the window and peered out into the afternoon sky. "Valda," he said, his tone heavy. "And she's not alone—Gawen and a Water Dragon are with him."

"I'm ready," I said. My chaos magic sparked to life.

He leveled his gaze at me. "Calm down. I know you're ready for a fight."

I smirked, a sassy retort ready on my lips, but Erjon interjected before I could speak. "Provoking them would result in disastrous consequences."

I opened my mouth to argue that I could annihilate all three now that I had both souls, but I was interrupted by the door bursting open. Fin ran in followed closely by Morwen.

"Your mother," he said to Calian. "She's on her way out there."

Calian didn't respond. Instead, he teleported out of the room. My mouth gaped open, and I looked at Fin who shrugged with a smile. "Did you know he could do that?" I asked.

"Nope. Our little boy is growing up."

Morwen rolled her eyes. "Not the time, Fin. Let's go." And with that, she took off running. Instead of following them, I teleported outside, reappearing beside Calian who stood gallantly, waiting for Valda and the two other Dragons to land. We were a way away from the city. It was going to take the others some time to join us.

"Are you ready?" I asked my mate.

"As I'll ever be."

"This is so sudden. The Winged Warriors are still on their scouting mission. Hopefully, Shula is assembling her soldiers."

Calian turned to me and placed his hands on my shoulders. "We've got this. We've got you. Two souls, remember?"

He was right. Where had my confidence gone? My water magic soothed my body, letting me regain the composure I'd momentarily lost.

Valda landed as did Gawen and the blue Dragon.

I took the moment to study the faces of my friends whom I finally heard behind me on horseback. This could turn into a deadly battle. Were they ready? I twisted my torso slightly, looking over my shoulder at them. I found it interesting that Valda didn't advance until the others arrived. Interesting but not shocking. She was always one for a show.

The clip-clop of the horse's hooves ceased, followed by the multiple thuds of feet hitting the ground. Morwen's demeanor was as soothing as the waters she commanded, which contrasted sharply with Avani's tense readiness for fighting. Avani's hands were out and prepared to yield earth magic as she walked forward. Her emerald fighting leathers matched Morwen's cerulean leathers in appearance, but hers seemed to shimmer a little more. Or maybe that was just her confidence. Regardless, it shone brightly. Even next to Kedron whose shadows moved silently around him.

Then there was Hestia, whom I'd hoped had stayed behind. But of course, she didn't. She surveyed Valda with a sharp, strategic eye. The woman had been through so much in her lifetime. I hated seeing her out here, willingly facing a powerful Dragon. She should be inside with her husband, laughing and enjoying his company. She should be drinking wine with Shula. Speaking of Shula, I hoped the general was getting her soldiers into formation. They were supposed to surround the city and let us take care of the Dragons. It's the plan we'd formed when Calian was taking care of funeral arrangements for Vukan.

I angled my head toward the Dragons as they transformed. Each was able to create the same scale-like armor that Calian and I could. Valda's appeared black, but when she turned, I caught the quick shimmer of violet. Gawen's was his typical white which contrasted against the Water Dragon's sapphire blue. All three were beautiful creatures. Beautiful and terrifying. My relief at there only being three of them was short-lived. In the distance, another Dragon appeared.

Calian walked forward, placing himself directly between Valda and the queen. I wasn't about to let him lead this fight alone, so I joined him.

Valda smiled, exposing her perfect white teeth. "It's such a gorgeous day. Don't you think, Em?" I couldn't wait to bash her teeth in.

"And what are you doing here, exactly? Seems like you're walking into a wolf's den without any…" I let my voice trail off as I deliberately looked from Gawen to the Water Dragon and then to the other Dragon—a green one—in the sky. "Without any real back-up."

Gawen's face remained unchanged. He continued to stare blankly ahead, his long white hair blowing in the gentle mid-afternoon breeze. The Water Dragon on the other hand. She was more than upset at my words. She bent her knees and brought her hands in front of her. A swirl of water formed in her palms, growing bigger and bigger.

Valda held up her hand. "Are you really going to let her get to you so easily, Kaveri?"

Good. We had a name for Queen Eteri's killer. I glanced back in time to see Erjon join us. The Dragonheir of Air stopped suddenly, having noticed Kaveri standing next to Gawen. His expression gave away nothing, but I knew him. Despite his cool facade, he was seething inside.

Valda cleared her throat, forcing me to look at her. "I am here for my father's amulet," she declared, her fierce eyes scanning everyone before her. "There will be no need for bloodshed today." She held out her hand. "Hand it over, and you may all continue with your pathetic lives unharmed."

"Pathetic lives?" Fin was beside me, his bow and arrows ready, clad in black leather. His hood was drawn up, enhancing his appearance as an assassin not to be messed with.

Valda laughed. "Yours is for certain, foolish human."

The other Dragon, a green one, finally arrived. It glided to the ground and landed. But it didn't transform. Its form was similar to Gawen's but smaller and with fewer horns and spikes.

Before I could intervene, all my friends were lined up alongside Calian and me. Only Hestia remained behind us. I fought to keep my face impassive, studying Valda with a keen eye. Beside me, Calian's fists clenched, and the air surrounding him heated with his rising anger. Erjon, however, remained outwardly calm, though his mind was undoubtedly racing through scenarios and outcomes. Most of which I assumed were of him eviscerating Kaveri.

Morwen called out to Valda. "And if we refuse? What then, Valda? Do you promise peace today only to wage war tomorrow with your father?"

Avani's stance hardened, the ground beneath her seeming to rumble slightly in response to her power.

Valda smirked. "My intentions are clear, Princess. This is a simple transaction. I seek what is rightfully mine. You have it, I want it. No one has to die today."

Hestia stepped forward then, her regal bearing unflinching under the dragon's gaze. "Like no one was supposed to die in Anahita? Or in Tamasvi?"

"She's purposefully provoking Valda," I whispered to Calian. His mother was going to start a war right in her own city if she didn't stop.

The queen's emotions will get her killed, I thought silently, my eyes still forward. Chaos energy flowered through my veins, filling my body. It danced beneath my skin, waiting for the moment to be unleashed upon the Dragons before us.

Queen Hestia continued. "You might think we're at your mercy, but you're also at the mercy of our decision. Choose your next words wisely."

"With pleasure," Valda sang.

CHAPTER TWENTY-THREE

ERJON

The tension in the air reached its peak. Valda and her henchmen shifted into their Dragon forms, their massive bodies expanding in front of our eyes.

Calian, ever protective, turned sharply toward his mother. "Get to safety, now!" he commanded.

Suddenly, the green Dragon charged, its body a blur as it cut through the space between us. It maneuvered with such speed and agility that it successfully isolated Emera and Calian from the rest of us, trapping them against a large sandstone structure that jutted from the hard sand beneath our feet.

In that same moment, Kedron acted decisively. I watched as he gripped Queen Hestia's arm and teleported away from the immediate danger. Kedron was as smart as he was quiet. I appreciated him for that.

My focus was abruptly pulled back to Kaveri. It turned its attention toward me, its eyes locking onto mine with a disturbing recognition. Heart pounding, I thrust my air magic from my hands to launch myself into the sky and enhance my speed. The Dragon pursued relentlessly, each flap of its wings sending powerful gusts that threatened to throw me off balance.

Out of the corner of my eye, I caught sight of Avani and Morwen as they stared down Valda with more bravado than they were warranted. Avani commanded the earth, causing the ground itself to rise up in defense while Morwen manipulated water, blasting it toward the Chaos Dragon.

My instincts kicked in, and I focused on my own dire situation. I could not afford to get caught up in the others' battles.

I located a large dune just outside of the city's walls. If I could fly to it and then land there, I would have a better vantage point. A large shadow darkened the sky just above me. Gawen soared by. Then, I was almost knocked over as Fin raced by on a yellow mare.

Water rained down upon me as the Water Dragon attacked. I stopped and turned. It was not my finest decision. The Dragon swooped mere inches from my face. I narrowly escaped the beast's snapping jaws by using a sharp burst of air to propel myself beyond its reach, but it was too much, and I crashed into the ground. It ascended back into the sky and then turned downward. Then it landed. We were now in a standoff. The scorching desert sun beat down on the endless sands as I stood, facing Kaveri. Her massive form towered over me, ready to strike at any given moment. A bead of sweat trickled down my silver scales. The heat radiated off the sand beneath my feet, but my focus remained solely on the Dragon before me.

With a deep breath, I summoned my air magic and let it swirl within my body.

The dragon let out a deafening roar, a torrent of water spewing from its gaping jaws toward me. I reacted swiftly, conjuring a powerful gust of wind to deflect it. The water splashed harmlessly against the sand, evaporating in the intense heat. But the dragon was relentless. It lunged forward, its sharp claws slicing through the air toward me. I pushed air magic out of my palms and propelled myself up and over the Dragon. It whipped its tail toward me. But I pushed more air out of my palms and veered out the way just in time.

From above, I steadied myself and then retaliated with blasts of air, sending cold, sharp gusts toward the dragon in an attempt to keep her pinned to the ground. But the Dragon seemed unbothered.

Then, in a flash of movement, the dragon seized its opportunity. One of its outstretched wings knocked into my chest. I careened out of control but was able to conjure enough air to keep myself from hitting the ground. But by the time I was able to focus on my surroundings, the Dragon had pinned me to the scorching sand with its massive claws. I struggled against its immense strength, but it was futile.

Breathless and defeated, I gazed into the Dragon's eyes. For a brief moment, I saw Eteri's held within them.

Erjon, I could almost hear her say. *Logic might suggest you give up. Don't do it. Don't yield.*

A spark of rage ignited within my chest. It grew, crept into my mind, and then pounded on the mental barrier I used to keep my emotions at bay. It kept pounding louder and louder until it finally succeeded. Down came the barrier, setting my emotions free. The rage intensified and consumed me.

"Ah!" I yelled and with an unexpected force of power, I pushed air from my palms, propelling the Dragon off me and onto its back.

Then I jettisoned into the air, high above the Dragon as it rolled onto its feet. But I refused to waste any more time on this beast. My body shimmered with a silver glow as I harnessed my air magic and unleashed a furious wind, pressing the Dragon flat against the ground. I pushed more and more air into the Dragon's back until my ears were met with a sickening crunch. Blood trickled out of the Dragon's nostrils, proof that she was dead.

Slowly, the air from my palms let up, and I glided downward until my feet hit the sand below. Placing my hand to my chest, I breathed deeply. My chest rose and fell, relief fleeting through my veins. The Dragon lay motionless at my feet. Until it started to shake. A slight tremble through the ground made me sway. The Dragon was definitely dead; its eyes were still void of life.

I glanced up. "Round two," I murmured to myself.

Three other monstrous Dragons—having arrived after the fighting started—landed before me, their enormous forms casting ominous silhouettes as they sauntered forward. The largest one with gleaming silver scales lowered its head beside Kaveri's Dragon form and sniffed it. A growl erupted from its throat while it fixated its lethal eyes on me. Its lips spread wide, revealing rows of sharp jagged teeth stained with the blood of battle. Then it advanced.

I sighed. "Now would be a good time for someone to assist me."

I needed reinforcements. Looking left then right, I searched the area for Avani or Morwen. I located them in the distance, occupied with Valda. I scanned the area for Emera and Calian. But it was to no avail. They were lost in the mix of the battle. The green Dragon laid dead in the distance. I strained my vision to locate Fin, but he was nowhere to be seen. Neither was Gawen. My gaze drifted back to the Dragons that towered overhead.

"Looks like it is all of you and just me." With my knees bent in a fighting stance, air began swirling around my wrists.

The second Dragon chuckled. I shook my head and threw the preposterous thought out of my mind. Dragons chuckling? Their anatomy was not built for it. But then the others chuckled, too.

The ball of my foot connected with the ground first. Then my heel. Then the other foot. Slowly, I backed away from my spot, never breaking eye contact with the Dragons.

Something in the distance caught their attention, causing them to raise their thick necks. Each Dragon twisted and turned toward an unknown sound. I closed my eyes and steadied my breathing. The sound grew louder and louder. It reminded me of a pack of Lightenion wolves.

"No. Please no." Begging had never been much of a practice, but this seemed like an appropriate time to do so.

My back hit a wall or some other structure, and pain shot down my spine. The Dragons seemed focused on the impending presence of whatever was out there, so I took the opportunity to drop my hand and feel behind me. My fingers pressed lightly against hot rough edges. With a determined breath, I glanced over my shoulder. A large boulder was behind me.

"Just keep looking at whatever is out there." I mumbled to the Dragons. It was reckless, but for some odd reason, it was reassuring to me. The Dragon's necks were all twisted back, their heads facing the open desert. While they remained distracted, I darted quickly behind the boulder. Lifting onto the tips of my toes, I strained to see if whatever made the noise was closer. It was definitely louder.

Exhaustion clung to me like a second skin, each breath I drew was laced with weariness. My limbs were heavy, and my mind fogged from the intense battle I had just survived.

The massive green Earth Dragon turned back toward me. Its eyes sparked with joy. Joy of killing me when Kaveri could not.

I raised my hands, calling upon the air around me, manipulating it into fierce, cutting winds. I directed the gusts toward the Dragon, attempting to throw it off balance, but I was weak, and the beast was undeterred, barely flinching as it continued to advance with deliberate, heavy steps.

As the Dragon prepared to strike me down, a chilling howl pierced the air, momentarily distracting it. My heart leapt as I recognized the sound—definitely Lightenion Wolves. Howls erupted again beyond the Dragon.

Then she emerged. General Shula was charging across the golden sands atop a magnificent wolf, her presence as fearsome as the army that followed her. The other riders, each partnered with their own wolf, moved as a seamless unit.

With a warrior's cry, Shula directed her wolf at the green Dragon. The animal was a blur of speed and ferocity, its eyes alight with the thrill of battle. It darted swiftly around the Dragon's massive form, avoiding the swipes of the beast's colossal claws.

Just as the Dragon reared back, preparing to unleash a crushing blow, Shula shouted, "Go, Orcus!" She dove off her wolf as it leaped into the air, aiming for the Dragon's throat. The beast's scales, though tough, were no match for the wolf's dagger-like teeth that sunk into its hide. The dragon roared in agony. It twisted violently, its massive body contorting in an attempt to dislodge the wolf clamped securely at its throat. Sand was disrupted under its frantic movements, flying into the air like swirling dust clouds.

Yet, the wolf named Orcus maintained its grip. As the Dragon thrashed, its tail sweeping through the air, Orcus adjusted its stance, its teeth sinking deeper, unrelenting. The struggle was intense, but the wolf held on, bringing the Dragon down. After one last whimper of pain, the green Dragon was dead.

The atmosphere fell silent, except for the wolves' panting and the soft rustle of the wind. Shula walked back over to her wolf, her gaze meeting mine with a nod of respect. Then she mounted Orcus and took off to aid the others. But they didn't need to. The other two Dragons were dead, and Valda was flying away in retreat.

Looking left, right, then above me, I lowered myself slowly to the ground and crouched there behind the rock to catch my breath. I closed my eyes momentarily but opened them when something large landed in front of me. It was a white Dragon with its back facing me. Gawen. There, staring the Dragon down, was Fin, his amulet glowing faintly against his chest. I wanted to move, but my limbs were weak and my power drained. I would be of no help until my strength was replenished. Until then, Fin was on his own.

Every step Fin took was deliberate as he stalked toward Gawen, his gaze never veering away from the Dragon. His eyes flashed and then I saw it: the unknown world's deadliest assassin. I had heard stories of an assassin that disappeared into the shadows. An assassin that traveled the unknown world, not calling any kingdom his home. But from my time knowing him, the assassin had never risen to the surface. Fin was the joking sort of human who never took things seriously. But this was a serious matter. With a quick motion, Fin notched an arrow and released it. I watched as it sliced through the air.

And through a sudden cloud of white smoke.

The smoke cleared and Gawen stood in his human form, but fully covered in his Dragon scales. I had never seen a Dragon shift so quickly. Despite him being the enemy, I was impressed. He also had a bow and quiver of arrows next to him, which must have been strapped to his Dragon form.

Gawen smirked at Fin. "You missed."

Fin smiled lazily. "You're in human form, aren't you?"

Realization dawned on Gawen's face. He'd played right into Fin's trap. He lifted his arms and cast a beam of blinding white light across the space between them.

Fin stood his ground. The amulet around his neck grew brighter until it formed a shield against Gawen's light. Gawen's eyes widened in surprise, and Fin's lips curved upward into a wolf-like grin. In a heartbeat, the assassin's fingers flew, swiftly notching another arrow and releasing it. The shaft cut through the air and lodged itself into Gawen's shoulder.

Gawen's roar of pain shook the ground beneath me. He yanked the arrow out, blood trickling down his arm. "You'll pay for that," he hissed. He growled and shifted back into his Dragon form, his massive wings unfurling and creating a gust of wind that sent sand and dust flying. Fin and I covered our eyes as Gawen soared into the sky, his scales shimmering in the sunlight. Fin then lowered his arms and watched Gawen, his expression unreadable.

The Dragon circled above, then dove toward Fin with astonishing speed. Fin rolled to the side, barely avoiding Gawen's dagger-spiked tail. Fin would survive a magical attack, but not one from a Dragon. He drew another arrow and fired it at the Dragon. He proceeded to fire multiple arrows in rapid succession. Each arrow struck Gawen's wing, and the Dragon let out another roar of pain, veering off course and crashing to the ground.

Gawen struggled to his feet, his wing injured but not incapacitated. He shifted back to human form. Once the smoke cleared, his eyes blazed with fury. He knew he would have to fight Fin without magic. He held onto his bow and quiver of arrows once more.

With a swift motion, Fin dashed forward, drawing a dagger from his hip. He closed the distance between them in the blink of an eye and slashed at Gawen's chest. Gawen blocked the attack with his forearm, but Fin was relentless, his movements becoming a blur.

Gawen countered with a series of powerful strikes, his fists glowing with white magic. But Fin ducked and weaved, his agility allowing him to evade each one of Gawen's throws. Both of them moved with incredible speed, but even a powerful Dragon was no match for Fin, whose speed and agility appeared unmatched. Every time Gawen thought he had the upper hand, Fin would slip through his defenses.

Finally, Fin saw his opening. He fainted to the left, drawing Gawen's guard away, then spun around and drove his dagger into Gawen's side. Gawen gasped as blood poured from the wound. Fin twisted the blade, and Gawen's knees buckled.

"You'll never win," Gawen managed to choke out.

Fin leaned in close, his eyes cold. "Funny. Because it seems that I already have."

With one final, swift motion, Fin drew his dagger out and slashed Gawen's throat. The Dragon fell to the ground, his eyes glazing over as life left his body. Fin stood over him, breathing heavily. The amulet's glow faded with each ragged breath Fin took.

I rose to my feet, my strength slowly returning. "Fin…" I called out.

He turned to me, his usual grin returning to his face. "Oh, no, Erjon. Don't get up on my account. I've got it all under control."

I rolled my eyes.

Fin's mouth gaped open. "Why, Erjon. You just showed some real emotion." He placed his hand over his heart. "I am honored that you feel safe enough around me to let down your emotional barrier wall-thingy."

"I cannot comprehend what you just said."

Fin smiled and then scanned the area, searching for Morwen. I could not help but feel a deep sense of awe and gratitude. Fin, a mere human, had faced a powerful Dragon in this world and emerged victorious. Despite his usual carefree demeanor, he had shown me the true extent of his abilities. Even without the amulet, just watching Fin told me he could have defeated Gawen.

"There she is," Fin said and took off running. He had found Morwen, but I still could not see Emera. My breath remained locked in my lungs until I saw her violet hair as she emerged on the other side of a dead Dragon. A quick sigh burst from my throat. "She's alive," I assured myself.

CHAPTER TWENTY-FOUR

CALIAN

My heavy footsteps left slight imprints on the carpet as I walked down the aisle of the temple. The ornate columns before me seemed to rise endlessly, their surfaces glowing faintly in the soft light cast by flickering candles that rested on the windowsills. A burning lump formed in my throat, and I tried to push it down. But I couldn't. No matter how hard I tried to suppress my feelings, my heart weighed heavily with grief.

To my left, Emera, walked silently, her footsteps soft and silent. Her downcast eyes were filled with tears. Her royal red robe—mandatory attire for a Firan funeral—billowed slightly with each step. Her violet scales shimmered each time we passed a flaming candle. I thanked the gods she was with me. My mate was a pillar of stability for me in this moment.

To my right, my mother walked with regal grace, though she wore a mask of pain and loss. She reached up and adjusted her golden crown, adorned with the finest rubies I'd ever seen. Each one was handcrafted to resemble a Dragonscale. Together, the scales formed flames. The crown's twin sat upon my head. I couldn't help but feel ridiculous and completely out of place.

Emera intertwined her fingers with mine and squeezed my hand tightly. Air filled my lungs and swirled around within them before exiting my mouth in a heavy sigh. We were already halfway down the aisle. Halfway to my father's dead body. My body temperature spiked and anger flared within me.

Breathe in, breathe out. Breathe in, breathe out. Emera's words soared through my mind, a result of us being mates. I didn't answer. I just did as she said. After six failed attempts at steadying my breathing and my heartbeat, I gave up.

The temple was silent except for our footsteps and the occasional crackle of flames from the torches that hung on the walls behind the altar. I let my eyes wander over the vacant pews, not wanting to look ahead. Mother had prepared me for the uncomfortable silence. It was a long-standing creed in the Kingdom of Fire that a royal funeral service was private—immediate family only.

My mother, who was a few steps ahead, stopped. We were at the altar. My father was only an arms-length away from me. A storm of emotions raged within me. Yes, my heart was heavy with grief, but beneath that overwhelming sorrow, a seething anger burned hotter than any flame I could conjure. My father, the God of Fire, was deceased because of me, and the injustice of it all gnawed at my very soul.

The warmth of the eternal flame, the symbol of my father's presence in the DragonEmpyrean, failed to comfort me. Instead, it was a cruel reminder of what had been taken from me. My fists clenched at my sides, nails digging into my palms as I fought to squash the fury threatening to consume me. Each breath I took felt like inhaling embers. My chest tightened from the rage and sorrow that burned through my body.

Mother knelt before the altar and bowed her head. After a silent prayer, she stood and reached out to my father. Her hand, trembling slightly, hesitated and then rested on the red velvet blanket draped over his human form. Her eyes, glazed by her unshed tears, shifted from the eternal flame to the crimson red fabric. She took a deep breath, held it in her chest, and exhaled quietly.

"My beloved. Unfortunately, our fates have been intertwined in turmoil from the moment we met. I found you, I lost you, you came back to me, and now I have lost you for good." The corner of her mouth curved upward. "Despite your best efforts, our journey together is far from over." She leaned over him and whispered. "I have seen it, my darling." Then her tears fell silently. She even cried with a grace that I couldn't muster. Her tears glistened like the jewels in her crown, her sorrow a quiet, dignified thing. But I didn't want dignity. I wanted to scream, to rage against the unfairness of it all. My father, my guiding light, my mentor—gone. It wasn't right. It wasn't fair.

Emera sniffled behind me, and I blinked back my own tears as I watched my mother's knees buckle. She gripped the altar and pressed her hand to her chest. "I will miss you. Your infectious laughter, your endless wisdom, and your unwavering love. The throne feels empty without you beside me; the palace feels colder." Her tears dripped from her jawline to the floor. Then she stood, turned toward me, and looked deep into my eyes. "Our son will carry your legacy forward, and through him, your fire will never die." Then her palm cupped my cheek. A smile spread across her face, but it didn't reach her eyes. Then she turned away from me. My eyes followed her as she backed away several steps and let me have my moment.

Emera's eyes met mine. I jerked my chin toward my father, urging her to have her moment. I wanted to speak with him last.

She stepped closer, her fingers steady as they brushed against the cold marble of the altar. "Oh, Vukan," she whispered, her voice breaking. She lifted the cloth covering my father and looked down at his face, peaceful in death. A tear slipped down her cheek, but she didn't bother to wipe it away. "I'll look after them, Vukan," she vowed. "Just as I promised." She stepped back and joined my mother.

My turn.

The silence was oppressive, the weight of my grief almost too much to bear. I closed my eyes, willing myself to remember his smile, to feel the warmth that had always surrounded him. But I couldn't. After a few more seconds, I opened my eyes and forced myself to look upon my father's body. His face was serene, like his Dragonsoul was finally at rest. Mine, however, was not. "Why?" I choked out. "We had just found each other. This…This…It's so unfair!" I slammed my fists down upon the altar. The table shook, but my father's body remained still.

Suddenly, the temple was suffocating me. I clawed at the collar of my shirt, desperate for it to stretch out and let me breathe. My chest rose up and down fast as I gasped for air. My father was dead because of me. My mother's pain was because of me. All of this was because of me. Because I had failed so many years ago.

Emera's voice pierced my racing thoughts. "Calian. You need to stop. You are not to blame." She placed her slender hand on my back, massaging it in a circular motion. A cool sensation seeped through the robe, through my skin, and through my blood.

"Please do not use your magic on me. I do not want it." Her magic withdrew instantly.

"I only wish to help you understand that you are not to blame."

Mother stepped toward me. "Is that what you think?"

I looked away from them both. Shame and guilt warmed my cheeks. I was embarrassed.

My mother threw her hands in the air. "For gods' sake, Calian, you are not responsible for the fates of others. How long will it take you to realize that?"

"She is right," Emera said softly.

"You're godsdamn right that I'm right."

I winced. I'd never seen my mother this angry.

She leaned her head back, took a deep breath, then faced me. "You're stubborn like him." She paused, contemplating her words. "He held the world on his shoulders, and I had to remind him several times throughout our lives together that he wasn't a Chaos Dragon, therefore, the unnamed world was not his to watch and care for. Even before his death, I had to remind him that Amram's return wasn't his fault. And you're just like him. Even when you were young."

"I wouldn't know that would I?" I snapped.

My mother leaned back slightly, her eyes wide like I'd slapped her. "I did what I had to do."

"Toss me on the streets? Lock me out of my mind and throw away the key?"

Emera shifted uncomfortably.

"This is not the place for this conversation. I do not have the time, nor the energy."

"With all the Dragonmelds, I'd say so."

She whirled around, her eyes blazing with fury. "I am doing what I can to help prevent war."

"Really? When was the last time your so-called Dragonsight had a vision?"

"Cal," Emera said with a warning tone. I ignored her.

Mother pursed her lips and remained silent.

"Exactly."

"They said you were hot-tempered," she said softly. "I didn't believe them until now."

"Guess that's what happens when you're abandoned by your mother."

Emera inhaled sharply.

Both my mother's expression and her voice remained calm. She stretched her arms out wide. "You want to do this here? Now?"

I crossed my arms in front of my chest. "Yes," I huffed.

"Fine." She reached out, and before I could say a word, pressed her fingers to my forehead, but I shimmied away just in time.

"I don't want to be sucked into another one of your Dragonmelds. I want you to talk to me!" I yelled. My words echoed off the temple walls.

"I think I'll leave you two alone," Emera said softly.

"No. I want you to stay." My words sounded like a command, but I didn't mean them that way. I looked to her, my eyes pleading for her to remain with me. She nodded but didn't say anything.

Mother sighed. "Before the night of your birth, your grandfather came to me." She took my hand and led me to the first pew. Emera remained standing.

I leaned forward. "Go on," I replied heatedly.

She took a deep breath, her gaze distant as if she was looking into the past. "It was that night that he claimed to have witnessed a new prophecy. He told me that one day, I would have to cast you out into the world with no memory of me or your past. By casting you out, I would ensure the survival of humanity."

I lowered my voice. "Was it easy?"

Her eyes widened, and she shook her head. "Absolutely not. It was the hardest decision I have ever made. To send you away without knowing who you truly were. At first, I refused. But Ragnar assured me it was necessary, that your journey was intertwined with the fate of many."

Emera spoke softly. "How did you find the strength to do it?"

My mother's lips trembled. "I found strength in my love for my son," Her eyes met mine. "And in the belief that you would become the man you were destined to be. Ragnar told me that one day, you would return to me. I didn't think it would be so soon to be honest. Ragnar claimed it would be after the defeat of a terrible enemy. But Amram still lives."

"Many other Dragons do not," Emera offered.

My mother nodded. "That is true. Ragnar's words were more like guidelines. We never knew the full extent of their meaning."

A flood of emotions surged within me—anger for being tossed on the streets, sorrow for the blame I placed on my mother. Pure, unadulterated hatred for Amram. The god hadn't just disrupted Emera's life but mine and everyone else's.

She reached out and took my hand. "Every choice I made was for you and the survival of my kingdom. I will not apologize for them. Just like every choice you make is for the safety of the unnamed world. For those choices, you should never apologize. Do not hold any blame or guilt. They are unwarranted."

The anger within me fizzled. I leaned over and kissed her cheek. "I know."

"Good." She let go of my hand.

"What now?" Emera asked.

Two Dragonpriests entered the temple.

I leaned my head back and stared at the ceiling. "We wait."

The priests pushed in a golden sarcophagus, decorated with swirling red, orange, and yellow flames constructed by various colored gems. It only took them a few minutes to transfer my father's body from the altar to the sarcophagus. After that, they strode toward the front of the temple, opened the doors, and ushered in the people, Dragonborns and humans, that came for the public part of my father's funeral.

Within ten or so minutes, the temple was filled. I glanced around, taking in the faces of those who had come to pay their respects. Fin and Morwen sat next to Avani just a few rows behind us. Erjon sat with Zeph behind them. I didn't see Kedron, but he was probably sitting in the back somewhere, keeping to himself like he had been doing lately. Shula finally entered, having made sure the temple was secure. She joined us in the front row, sitting on the other side of my mother.

As the Dragonpriest from earlier stepped forward to begin the ceremony, I felt a pang of emptiness. I didn't hear what he said. The effort to suppress my anger, sadness, and guilt drowned out the words. It wasn't until my mother rose to perform the Rite of Ascension, or whatever it was she called it, that I sat up straight and focused on her voice.

She cleared her throat and then gazed out into the crowd. "By the eternal flames that warm our souls, I, Queen Hestia of the Kingdom of Fire, stand before you to honor our fallen god, Vukan, the God of Fire, whose flame once graced our kingdom."

She then stretched out her arms and lifted her gaze to the ceiling. "Our god, my husband, has departed the living world. In his honor, I light the eternal flame. Let it burn brightly in remembrance of our God of Fire, who so often guided our souls and provided strength during our times of need."

With the final words, she lowered her arms, ignited a match, and lit the ceremonial flame next to the altar. My throat held my breath captive as I watched the light flicker several times before it grew. Then it blazed brightly, and my mouth parted, releasing the hot, heavy breath of air.

"So let it be written, so let it be done. In the name of Vukan, the God of Fire, and our eternal flame." With her head held high and not a tear on her face, she took her seat next to Shula.

No one clapped. No one spoke. The Rite of Ascension was complete.

CHAPTER TWENTY-FIVE

EMERA

The morning sky was a fresh canvas, painted in the softest hues of dawn. Light pinks and oranges blended seamlessly with the deep blues of the receding night. Wisps of clouds caught the sunlight, glowing like threads of gold against the sky. The air was cool and crisp.

Avani and I followed Shula toward some secret location. The only information she'd given us was that we were headed toward a military training facility, and we were in for a treat. Calian and Fin had agreed with her, having already witnessed whatever it was she talked about. Shula had seemed excited about revealing whatever it was, which was the most excitement anyone had shown since Vukan's funeral two days ago.

Morwen, Avani, and I walked a few paces behind Shula as we strolled past several sparring rings and down a narrow, winding path that stretched beyond the barracks. Shula kept glancing back over her shoulder to make sure we were following, a sly smile dancing on her lips. Each time she peeked over her shoulder, my heart flipped and flopped from anticipation. Was she going to show me something that would help defeat Amram? And if so, why now? Why not earlier?

The path seemed to stretch on endlessly, but finally, we approached a heavily guarded and fortified enclosure. Avani and I stopped abruptly.

"What is this?" Avani asked.

"More like, what's in there?" Morwen said softly.

As we neared the entrance, my shoulders tensed. I wasn't dressed for any type of military training. In fact, I felt silly wearing this type of fashion from the Kingdom of Fire. Aside from Shula and her military garments, the rest of us wore ensembles of gauzy red tops that exposed our stomachs, off-the-shoulder sleeves constructed of sheer fabric, and high-waisted, billowing pants, gathered at the ankles with gold cuffs. The pants from my upper thigh downward were also sheer, mirroring the structure of the top. I understood that the clothes, from the flowing fabric to the golden accents, symbolized royal status, but if a Dragon showed, we would have to change. I'd argued that point with Calian, but he dismissed it, and for good reason. Queen Hestia had been through so much, and these clothes were a part of her heritage. Wearing them was our way of honoring her.

The guards' expressions warmed at the sight of Shula, their stances becoming more relaxed than when we'd approached. Morwen, Avani, and I exchanged uneasy glances. The initial excitement I'd felt was replaced by a tight knot of anxiety in the pit of my stomach. Morwen was right. What was behind this barrier?

"Welcome to Wolf's Hold," Shula said. "It's the training grounds for our war wolves."

Avani cocked her head to the side. Then, her eyes widened with excitement. "War wolves? Are you serious?"

"Very serious," Shula said with a wide smile. She turned to the two guards and nodded. Silently, they opened the gate, allowing us to step inside. Avani all-but ran past the guards and stopped. Her eyes widened like saucers as she scanned the area, the training yards and barracks.

Shula placed a hand on Avani's shoulder and said, "Let me show you." We followed the general along a path. Finally, we arrived at an enormous training arena, surrounded by elevated platforms where spectators could watch.

"It's an arena," Morwen whispered in awe.

Avani studied the area. "It's incredible." She walked around it, inspecting everything from the sand to the thick metal gates that led elsewhere. "I assume you use this for mock battles and training exercises."

"Under the supervision of our riders," Shula answered.

I turned abruptly. "Riders?"

Avani's eyes widened with excitement. "You ride them?"

Shula smiled. "Come on, you haven't seen the best part."

We exited the arena and headed toward a group of metal buildings. Avani kept pace with Shula, clearly excited about all of this. We stopped just outside the largest one. Shula pressed her palm on the entrance and whispered, "Vylar." After a sharp click, she turned the handle and opened the door.

Morwen remained silent at my side, observing.

"These are the shelters that house the wolves and their riders."

Avani rushed through the entrance.

"Most of them aren't here. Around this time every afternoon, the riders take their wolves out into the desert. Let the wolves stretch their legs. But there is one that tends to stay behind. Well, as long as I stay behind."

I stepped inside. The interior was spacious enough for both the rider and the wolf. And there, lounging on the floor was a huge Lightenion wolf with shimmering white fur.

"This is Orcus," Shula said.

Avani smiled. "He's incredible."

Morwen turned to Shula. "How do you keep yourself safe?"

Shula paused before answering, like she wasn't sure how we'd respond. "I can speak to my wolf telepathically."

Avani's trance broke, and she whipped her head toward Shula. "That's..."

"Incredible?" I finished and giggled at how mesmerized Avani was with all this.

Morwen sat at a small table, unbothered by the presence of the wolf. "How is that possible for a human?"

Shula inhaled and exhaled slowly. She was at war with herself. I saw it in her eyes. "I cannot go into detail, but it is my mother's magic. She was gifted a kernel of chaos magic when she was married. That is all I will tell you."

"Explains why Calian is so strong," Morwen pointed out.

My mouth gaped open. It did. Calian had a trace of chaos magic in him. I would definitely be speaking with him later about it. For now, I was too enthralled by the fact that Shula trained wolves and rode one into battle.

Shula stared at us in disbelief. "You're not going to pressure me to tell you more?"

Morwen and I exchanged looks. "Why would we?" she asked.

I smiled. "I'll just get it out of Calian later."

"That's fair," Shula said.

A rustling noise drew all of our attention to Avani and Orcus. Avani stepped forward, her eyes fixed on Orcus. The wolf's golden eyes watched her intently but made no sound or movement. Avani reached out her hand. "Easy now, friend," she murmured, her hand hovering just above the wolf's muzzle.

Orcus lifted his head and sniffed her outstretched hand cautiously. Despite him being twice her size, she held her ground. Slowly, she lowered her hand, gently touching the Orcus's nose. The wolf's posture relaxed, and it rose to its feet. It stepped closer and pressed its head against her hand. Avani smiled, her fingers sinking into the thick fur. Then she scratched behind his ears, and Orcus leaned into her and released a contented sigh.

"He likes you," Shula said. "He doesn't like most people."

With a soft chuckle, Avani dropped her hand. Orcus plopped back on the floor.

Avani locked eyes with Shula. "I want one."

*　　*　　*

By afternoon, the sky was a brilliant blue that stretched endlessly above. The sun bore down upon us, radiating a bright, golden light that bathed the kingdom in warmth. Fluffy white clouds drifted lazily across the sky, casting shadows on the ground. The light was vibrant and energizing, bearing down on Morwen and me as we left Wolf's Hold without Avani, who was adamant that she bond with a wolf. Shula had taken her to the holding pens while Morwen and I had made our way out. Our plan was to check in with Zeph and his group of Winged Warriors. They'd just returned from their scouting mission, and I was curious to see if they'd gotten any new information regarding the Kingdom of Air.

As I walked alongside Morwen, I was both nervous and honored from the exchange I'd had with Orcus before I'd left Wolf's Hold. While the others had visited, relishing the opportunity for a little bit of normalcy in a world of chaos. At one point, much to my surprise, Orcus had—much to my surprise—approached me. Mind-to-mind, he had told me the wolves' version of our history, and how they had been forced to fight in the war against their will. They had been waiting for a time to right the wrongs of their past. I had listened eagerly as he had spoken of their ancestors' traitorous acts. The wolves had waited for me. To take their rightful place in the war and follow the daughter of Nimerah into a new and better world. I would do my best to live up to their expectations.

I found Zeph in his usual spot, on a bench outside of the weaponry shed, eating. If Zeph wasn't training, he was eating. He gulped down some water before taking another hasty bite of bread, his eyes closed as he savored it in his mouth. He'd probably mate with food if he could.

"Emera," he greeted me between a bite of cheese. "And Morwen. Cal and Fin are out flying."

I sat beside him. "Were you able to obtain any new information?"

Zeph's expression grew serious, and he shook his head. "Unfortunately, no. The Dragons still hold the kingdom firmly under their control."

I sighed.

Zeph swallowed his last bite of apple and threw the core on the ground. Morwen looked at the apple core and then slid her gaze to Zeph. He shrugged. "For the ants. Or birds. Or whatever animal is looking for a snack."

She rolled her eyes and smiled.

"But," Zeph began. "There are rumors of a group of rebels hiding in the Mystral Mountains. Unfortunately, none of my men were able to locate them. But we were able to talk to a couple of citizens who fled the city. They claimed there are rebels planning a resistance, hoping to take the City of Ilmari, and essentially, the kingdom back."

"Do you think these rumors are true?"

"Hard to say. But the mountains would provide a strategic advantage, offering both protection and a hell-of-a vantage point."

"Then we need to find these rebels and offer our support."

Morwen looked toward the sky as Risna flew overhead. "Once we are able to defeat Amram, you mean."

"Right."

*　　*　　*

The sun dipped toward the horizon, ushering in the evening sky. It cast mesmerizing rays of amber and crimson.

Soon, it would mirror the colors of the kingdom, becoming a fiery spectacle of oranges and reds, as if the heavens were ablaze. Clouds were tinted with warm hues of sunset but would soon fade to dusky blues. In just a few hours, the world would witness the beauty of the night.

Morwen remained with Zeph for a quick sparring match. How she was going to fight in her clothes, I didn't know. I bowed out and walked to the palace and out to the back toward the garden. As I stepped outside, the scent of blooming flowers filled the air, and the sound of a gently trickling fountain provided me with a sense of serenity I so desperately needed.

Much to my surprise, I found Erjon seated on a stone bench near the rose garden, his eyes closed in meditation. Since Vukan's funeral, he and Kedron kept mostly to themselves. At least Erjon came down for dinner. And come to think of it, I hadn't seen Kedron lately. Granted, that wasn't unusual for Kedron who often teleported to other places for solitude.

I approached Erjon quietly, not wanting to disturb his peace, but he opened his eyes and looked up at me before I could slip past him.

"Your thunderous footsteps gave you away."

"Funny." I lowered myself beside him on the bench. "How are you?"

He looked taken aback by my question. He opened his mouth slowly, clearly unsure of what to say. "I am managing."

"Aren't we all."

He nodded. After a few minutes of complete silence, he cleared his throat. "And you?"

I smiled. "I am okay. Despite what has happened."

"War is cruel."

"Exactly." I took a deep breath, unsure of where to begin. "I've been worried about you."

Erjon's eyes widened, then he sighed heavily. "My thoughts have consumed me lately."

My heart sank, a mix of grief and anger welling up inside me. "I hate that you have endured so much pain."

"Not any more than you or Calian."

"Maybe."

There was another elongated pause. "We knew the attack was coming," Erjon said, his eyes still facing forward. "We went through with the ceremony anyway." He held up his left hand, revealing a single silver band on his third finger. How had I not noticed until now?

I clenched my fists and fought back the sudden tears that blurred my vision. "They will pay for what they've done."

He placed a hand on my shoulder. I looked at it and then slowly lifted my eyes to his. It was the most affection he'd ever shown me. "They will, Emera." He dropped his hand. I watched it slide down my arm and fall back into his lap. "Eteri named me as her successor before she was killed," he whispered. "I am now the king, but no one outside the palace knows yet. I wanted to tell you first."

The weight of his words settled heavily on me. "Erjon, that's... I don't know what to say."

"I did not want this responsibility," he admitted, his gaze still distant. "But I will do my best to lead my people." A single tear trailed down his cheek. "I am fearful. I cannot do it alone."

And for the first time since I'd met Erjon, he leaned his head onto my shoulder and wept.

"You will be a wonderful ruler," I said firmly, taking his hand in mine. "I know it is now what you want, but I am always here to support you. Always."

He squeezed my hand as he continued to cry, his shoulders shaking with each ragged breath he took. After a few minutes, he sat straight and wiped his tears. We sat and watched the sun dip below the horizon. He never let go of my hand.

* * *

I paused by the window of the dining hall. The night sky was awe-inspiring. It had deepened to a velvety black, dotted with stars like sparkling diamonds. The moon, in all its wonder, cast a gentle, silvery glow. Yes, this was truly my favorite time.

Dinner had been uneventful. Everyone was off in different places, trying to keep their sanity, so I had grabbed a quick bite. I now made my way up the stairs. Within a couple minutes, I stood outside Calian's door. It had been a while since we had any quality time together. An uneasy feeling bubbled up inside of me. Today was perfect. Something in my mind told me that this was the calm before the storm.

The faint light from inside spilled through the cracks of the large oak door, casting a warm glow on the carpet. I inhaled, holding my breath as I knocked gently. My heart pounded in my chest. I didn't even know if he was back yet. He could still be…

Then the door opened, interrupting my thoughts, and Calian's face appeared. His dark eyes lit up with a genuine smile when he saw me. "Em," he said warmly. His flight must have done the trick. He seemed more relaxed than this morning. He stepped aside to let me in.

I crossed the threshold into his world, his smoky spiced scent wrapped itself around me like a cocoon. His chamber was cozy. Along the northern wall were shelves built around the hearth, lined with ancient tomes on each side of a small fire crackling in the fireplace. I felt a sense of calm wash over me as I stood in front of it, warming my hands. Despite being in the desert, the nights were cool.

Calian closed the door behind him. "Is everything alright?"

"Everything's fine," I assured him. I took a seat on a large chair covered in smooth tan velvet. Its arms and legs were carved to mimic flames.

He stood before me, and I peered up into his eyes. I could swim in them. He lowered to one knee. "What's on your mind?"

"Just wondering when you were going to tell me you have chaos magic. I would hope by now we were past keeping secrets."

"Secrets? This wasn't a secret. I was fully prepared to share this with you."

"When?"

"I didn't know, alright?" he snapped, clearly frustrated. He stood quickly and walked to the window, his eyes intense. "Everything was falling apart, and I didn't want to add to your burden."

The air between us seemed to shift, the tension thick and suffocating. Anger radiated from his body, and I could see the turmoil in his eyes.

I held my ground. "I needed to know, Calian. We're supposed to face these things together. We're mates. Or did you forget?"

His eyes snapped back to mine. "Of course, not. In fact, I've wanted to be alone with you ever since we got here. But so much got in the way."

I closed my eyes and let my water magic fill my body to calm me.

He sighed, and his shoulders slumped forward slightly. "I'm sorry, Em."

I stood and quietly moved across the room, reaching out to touch his arm. "You're right. We've been through so much. I just want to help you."

"I know."

The air between us seemed to shift. Warmth radiated from his body.

"Did you really come to pick a fight with me?" He took one more step toward me, making our shared space more intimate. He reached up and tucked a stray strand of hair behind my ear.

My chest rose up and down with each heavy breath I took. "No." I leaned in, my heart fluttering as my mate's fingers traced a gentle path up my arm. His touch was light, but it sent the familiar jolt of electric energy coursing through me.

"Emera," he whispered, his eyes fixed on mine.

My knees started to buckle. "Yes?"

Calian's gaze held mine, and for a moment, the world outside ceased to exist. He smiled and pulled me into his arms. The feel of his body against mine sent an unfamiliar wave of warmth through me, causing me to sigh and lean into his embrace. "I've missed being alone with you," he murmured, his breath tickling my ear.

"Me, too," I whispered back, my fingers tracing the lines of his jaw. Suddenly, he pulled back, then tipped his head down to mine and our lips met. The warmth of his lips against mine ignited a fire within my core, and I pressed closer, deepening the kiss.

His arms tightened around me, and I pressed into his chest. The feel of his body against mine sent another wave of fire through me. He pulled back slightly. "I've missed this," he murmured, his breath tickling my ear. Then our lips met again. This time, our kisses grew more passionate, more urgent. I didn't want them to end. Then his hands moved to cup my face, his thumbs gently caressing my cheeks. "Stay with me," he whispered against my lips.

This was it. Nerves overtook me, and I trembled. This was the moment I hadn't been ready for…Until now. I was no longer the girl from Medora. Now, I was a woman. Now, I was ready. "Yes."

His dark eyes sparkled. "Forever," he breathed.

"Yes," I breathed, "forever."

AMRAM

The news of Valda's return had reached me moments ago by Anwir. We had just gotten an update regarding the other kingdoms. King Tellus still sat on his throne, barking orders to purge the kingdom of all humans. He was a blubbering fool, but I needed the forest. Then I'd learned that a rebellion was forming in the mountains behind the City of Ilmari. I thoroughly enjoyed the idea of a rebellion fighting back. And losing. Finally, my spies confirmed that the Kingdom of Water was now mine, having sent a new wave of Dragons to seize it. There were fewer casualties this time, which turned my mouth sour. The more human deaths the better, in my opinion.

Now, I awaited Valda's arrival with Anwir lounging on a chair behind me. The fool complained of his foot hurting, but I knew he was just a lazy snake that didn't want to stand. I was in no mood for his whining, so I ignored the chair he'd placed behind the throne.

"Out of sight, out of mind," I reassured myself quietly.

The doors creaked open, and Valda entered, her violet eyes sparkling with triumph. In front of her, shackled in chains that contained a Dragon's magic, was Kedron Black, the so-called Dragonheir of Darkness. His almost white hair covered his eyes as he walked toward me, hunched over by the force of Valda's hand pressing down on his back.

But I didn't need to see his eyes. Around his neck was the amulet I'd been desperately seeking.

"Father," Valda sang. "A present." Then she pushed the Dragonheir forward. He landed on his face just below the last step.

I rose from my throne and descended the steps until I stood next to the boy. My eyes never left the amulet.

"Well done, Valda," Anwir said behind me, having vacated his foolish chair.

I ignored him and smiled at Valda. "Daughter, you have exceeded my expectations."

With a fistful of the boy's hair, I yanked his neck back so that I could see his eyes. They were black as night, which was a stark contrast to the bright red blood that trickled from his nostrils. Droplets of blood dripped onto the pristine floor. The boy stared at me with defiance despite the shackles that bound him.

A cold smile spread across my lips as I lowered myself to his level. "Anything you wish to say, boy?"

His dark eyes remained fixed on mine as he pressed his lips together in a firm line.

I laughed and reached for the amulet, gripping it tightly before tearing it from the Dragonheir's neck. It was just as I'd remembered. A simple, unassuming piece at first glance, but it was so much more. A surge of power from the gem warmed my hand. Yes, this was it. This was the amulet that contained a part of my Dragonsoul, the key to my immortal life. But the sensation of power vanished as quickly as it had come.

Something was wrong.

"Father? Isn't that the amulet you've been droning on and on about?"

Ignoring Valda's disrespect, I examined the amulet closely, suspicion gnawing at me. It was too light, too dull. It felt...wrong.

Then I saw the flaw. A tiny fracture at the base of the gem, which was impossible, considering the gem I'd used. This was not my amulet; this was a worthless replica. Fury spiked through me.

"You dare deceive me!" I roared, my voice vibrating the walls of the throne room. The Dragonheir's defiance wavered slightly, but he managed a smug, knowing smile that only fueled my rage further. Without hesitation, I summoned my chaos magic, my hand sparked with energy. In one swift motion, I blasted the Dragonheir right in the chest with chaos. His eyes widened in shock and pain before he crumpled to the ground, lifeless. Then I crushed the fake amulet in my hand, the shards falling to the ground like worthless dust.

Valda stood silently beside me, her eyes wide but composed.

"I will find the real amulet," I thundered.

She nodded but her expression remained impassive. "Yes, Father."

I stepped over the boy's lifeless body, my anger simmering beneath the surface. The real amulet was still out there, and I knew who had it.

Anwir rushed in front of me and dropped to his knee. "Then we will eliminate the humans quickly."

I chuckled, low and cruelly, then placed my hand on Anwir's shoulder and squeezed. "I don't want to simply end their lives, Anwir, I want them to suffer."

Then I looked straight ahead and stared straight into my daughter's eyes, into her soul. My eyes narrowed. "I want them to know fear."

CHAPTER TWENTY-SIX

CALIAN

The scent of freshly baked bread and sizzling ham delighted my nostrils as Emera and I made our way into the breakfast hall. The long dining table was already occupied by the time we arrived, with plates and mugs cluttering the surface.

"Well, don't you two look refreshed and ready to conquer the world," Fin joked while Emera sat down opposite of him. I took a seat beside her.

Morwen, sitting next to Fin, elbowed her mate, but Fin was undeterred. "In fact, Em, you're simply glowing." My friend leaned over the table. "Y'know? I have a way of making Morwen glow like that."

A gust of air knocked into Fin. He, along with his chair, fell backward and crashed into the floor. He rolled to his stomach, climbed to his feet, and dusted off his black leather pants.

Everyone looked at Erjon, sitting beside Emera, who only shrugged before eating another spoonful of eggs.

I narrowed my eyes and threw Fin a pointed glare. "Let's remember our manners."

"Of course, dear." Fin picked up his chair and sat down, his usual mischievous grin plastered on his face. "I am so glad that you finally decided to grace us with your presence." He picked up a banana and started to peel it.

I snorted. "Couldn't miss another one of your riveting tales, could I?" I glanced at Morwen. "How many stories has he told already? Three? Four?"

It was Erjon who responded. "Too many to count."

Emera giggled and reached over to the platter of crispy bacon and sausages, their savory aroma making my mouth water. I cut a slice from one of the golden-brown loaves then slathered on a bit of rich, dark honey.

"Where's Shula?"

Avani looked up from her plate. "With the wolves."

I nodded. In the midst of the abundance of food, Em and I continued to fill our plates as the discussion about Dragons came up.

"Alright," Avani said, grabbing a roll and tearing into it. "What are we going to do when Amram finally decides to drop by?"

Fin chuckled, leaning back in his chair. "I say we offer him some of this food."

Morwen sighed. "That's your solution, Fin? Feed him, and hope he goes away?"

Avani leveled her gaze at Fin. "As great as that sounds, we should probably have a back-up plan."

Erjon put down his fork. "She is right. We should consider all possibilities and prepare accordingly. Just in case Amram overindulges and gets a stomachache from all this food."

Fin's mouth gaped open. "Erjon. Did you just make a joke?"

Erjon raised an eyebrow, causing Fin to clap.

I turned to Emera. "I say you blast your chaos magic and incinerate him like you did with the Dragon at Tamasvi."

"That was my first thought, but we can't rely solely on that. It takes a lot of energy for me to do it. I'm essentially useless afterward for a while. Should I miss it, or it does not work, I couldn't help you. I'm not sure for how long. When

I didn't have my soul, I was down for an hour or two before I had help getting my strength back. Even a goddess has limits."

Avani rubbed her hands together. "I'll reinforce the walls with my earth magic. It might buy us some time for the Firan soldiers to take their places."

I looked at everyone. "We're all still in agreement that the soldiers guard the city first and foremost. Leave the fighting to us?"

Erjon rubbed his chin thoughtfully. "I am not so certain that is the best course of action. This kingdom is Amram's final chance to eliminate us all. He will bring all the Dragons he has risen with the exception of those guarding the other cities. Most soldiers from the remaining kingdoms, along with human rebels, have been forced into hiding. We will not have reinforcements. Vukan must spare some of its guards to aid us in battle."

Emera leaned forward, her eyes sharp and shoulders tense. "Amram is mine. I don't care who you all choose to fight. He is mine."

I rested my hand on her arm. "Noted. Zeph has agreed that the Winged Warriors will remain in the air for aerial attacks."

As we continued to discuss our strategy, the doors opened. I expected to see my mother, since she had yet to join us from her morning meditation, but was surprised when I turned my head just as Nyx strolled in. She was a force to be reckoned with, clad in her all-black leather attire adorned with straps and buckles everywhere. How long did it take the woman to get dressed?

Nyx's presence commanded immediate attention. Her near-white hair fell in waves to her waist. Her dark eyes were a stark contrast to her vibrant red lips. The male servants in the hall ogled at her and the way she swung her hips as she walked. I remembered that suggestive sway and rolled my eyes.

Three Darknessan soldiers followed her in. Despite their robust size, I was certain she could handle them effortlessly on her own. Her eyes surveyed the room, smooth yet calculating, missing nothing. She was King Orpheus's top spy after all.

Nyx's gaze finally settled on me, and she smiled. Then she addressed the room. "Captain Westbow, I have brought with me some of King Orpheus's finest soldiers. We couldn't spare as many as I'd hoped. Despite our victory, my kingdom remains on high alert."

Emera took a sip of water. "As it should."

Before anyone could say something else, Nyx's gaze swept over the room. Her brow furrowed slightly as she scanned the faces around the table. "Where's Keddie?" she asked.

I glanced around, hoping to catch sight of his familiar face, but he was nowhere to be found. The realization settled in, a knot of worry tightening in my chest. When was the last time I'd seen him? I'd been so busy lately that I hadn't checked on him.

A hush fell over the room as we all exchanged glances. Kedron's absence felt particularly ominous.

"He was with us after the battle," Fin said. "But come to think of it, I haven't seen him since."

I met Nyx's worried eyes. "Kedron likes to teleport away for short periods of time. No one questions him. He'll turn up. He always does." I hoped my voice was more confident than I felt. A nagging pain filled my chest as murmurs of agreement rippled through the hall. It wasn't like Kedron to disappear for days on end, especially not when the world was in such turmoil. My mind raced with possibilities, none of them comforting.

Nyx's expression shifted from concern to anger. After studying everyone's faces, she turned sharply to face me, her eyes blazing. "No one bothered to check on him?" Her voice was sharp, her playful demeanor having vanished completely. "Amram could attack you at any minute, and Kedron goes missing without anyone noticing?"

Fin spoke softly. "As Calian said, Kedron tends to do this, Nyx. He teleports away randomly. It's nothing new. We can't be expected to keep tabs on him every moment. He's a grown man."

Nyx's glare fixated on Fin, but before she could retort, Morwen intervened. "Come to think of it," she said, "I didn't see Kedron at the funeral." The room fell silent once more, the weight of her words sinking in.

Erjon stood, his chair lightly scraping the floor as he pushed it back. "Kedron's absences might be unpredictable, but he is not heartless. Missing such an important moment is unlike him."

Nyx's anger flared. "Then where is he?" she yelled. Her eyes bore into mine. It was clear that she trusted me to take care of her twin brother. Her Keddie. My mind raced, trying to piece together any clues, but Kedron was a quiet individual, and his habits were somewhat elusive.

Nyx placed her hands on her hips. "I'm going to find him. So, if any of you so-called friends of his would like to join me, please do."

The clanging of forks and scratching of chairs against the marble floor were clear indications that everyone was going to look. We were about to disperse from the hall entirely when a memory resurfaced. I inhaled a quick breath.

"Calian," Emera whispered. "You look pale. What is it? What do you know?"

Everyone stopped where they stood and turned toward us.

I swallowed hard, my eyes darting around the room before settling on Nyx.

"What do you know?" Nyx asked firmly.

I inhaled deeply and exhaled slowly. "I saw him," I finally whispered, struggling to keep my voice steady. "In one of my mother's Dragonmelds. Kedron... But... Her visions don't always come true, so I..." I gulped down the burning knot which had formed in my throat. I needed to get a grip. Even with the worst bit of news, I was usually straightforward. That's what everyone would expect from me.

Nyx's face shifted from confusion to pain. Then she spoke softly. "He's dead, isn't he?"

I remained silent. That was all the confirmation Nyx needed. The dining hall erupted. Gasps and murmurs of disbelief hovered around us, but the most piercing sound was Nyx's scream. It was raw and cut through the tension like a knife, a sound of pure agony and loss. She staggered back, her hands covering her face as if to shield herself from the devastation.

Erjon lowered his head and mumbled a silent prayer. Fin wrapped his arms around Morwen and held on tight like he was going to lose her. Emera dropped down in a chair and stared forward in disbelief.

Avani, however, rushed to Nyx's side. The two didn't know each other, but Avani didn't care. She wrapped her arms around Nyx's shoulder to comfort her. Nyx's shoulders shook with silent sobs, her body wracked with grief. If anyone knew grief like this, it was Avani. Although Emera told us that Senna had risen in peace, her death still stung. And now, so did Kedron's.

I stood frozen, my mind struggling to process it all. Kedron, so quiet, kind, and willing to do whatever was needed of him…was…gone. Just like the nagging pain in my stomach. It was gone, replaced by anger. My blood boiled.

"I am so tired of death," I hissed. I pushed back my shoulders. "We have lost many. But their sacrifices will not be in vain. Amram will know death like we do."

Emera's eyes were filled with guilt as she looked at Nyx.

I turned to my mate and placed my hand on her. "Do not, for one second, think that this is your fault. I see the wheels turning in your head."

"If I had just—"

I placed my finger on her lips. "No. This is all me. I was too wrapped up in my father's death to notice Kedron's absence and remember my mother's vision."

"Which is understandable."

"Not in war," I huffed. "The time for mourning will come after the war is over."

Nyx finally looked up, her eyes red and puffy yet determined. "I must go back to Tamasvi. My father needs to know. The soldiers will stay here in case Amram attacks." She then turned to her soldiers. "Do what the queen and her general command."

The soldiers exchanged uncertain looks, but Nyx's status left no room for argument. They bowed their heads to her and left.

Nyx looked back over her shoulder and her eyes met Calian's. "And Cal, go see Zari."

Fin and Morwen were still discussing Kedron's fate as Calian and I left the hall just shortly after Nyx and Avani. I wanted nothing more than to run outside and set the world on fire. I wanted nothing more than to go to Kedron's chamber, knock on the door, and hug him after he opened it. I wanted nothing more than the war to be over.

Emera joined me as I walked through the city and toward the front gate. We greeted the citizens with as much grace as we could muster despite the past hour's events. Each stranger's face I mumbled hello to was replaced with the ones that haunted me.

Rehema, Senna, Elio, Nimerah, Eteri, and Vukan. Had they all entered the DragonEmpyrean? Rehema, Senna, and Elio had, according to Emera. Eteri, Vukan, and now Kedron would.

Nimerah couldn't.

A heavy ache throbbed in my chest almost to the point where I couldn't breathe. It wasn't until I inhaled the familiar scent of hay and leather that I was able to calm my anger. I needed to focus on the here and now. I would avenge Kedron's death, but for now, I needed a clear head. So, I leaned against a stall and watched in silence as Emera approached Zari. When the horse saw Emera, it whinnied.

My mate buried her face into Zari's neck and rested there. "You are too good to me," she whispered.

From where I stood, my eyes scanned the stalls absentmindedly. A flash of black caught my eyes, and they widened. No. It wasn't possible.

"Dhruv?" I whispered, my voice barely audible.

There, in the stall next to Zari's, standing tall and alive as ever, was Dhruv. My horse's ears perked up at the sound of my voice. I glanced at Emera whose expression shifted from shock to pure, unadulterated joy.

"Dhruv!" I repeated, louder this time, and hurried forward. My hands trembled as I reached out to touch the steed's neck, my fingers running through his familiar black mane. Dhruv nickered softly and leaned into my touch.

"You…Y-y-you…died," I stammered, trying to keep my emotions at bay.

His large dark eyes met mine, and I was filled with questions. But then, I didn't care. I just shrugged, a smile tugging at my lips.

Em appeared at my side. "It seems Dhruv here is tougher than you gave him credit for."

Dhruv snorted in agreement then stomped his hooves, causing me to laugh before the tears fell. They streamed down my cheeks while I continued to stroke Dhruv's neck. I shook my head in bewilderment. "I can't believe it. I thought I'd lost him forever."

Emera fell silent.

"You okay?"

"Zari said that Dhruv dying isn't exactly possible."

I looked at her curiously. "Why not?"

There was another elongated pause.

"Zari says that Dhruv was born of darkness. There is a pool of black hidden deep within the Kingdom of Darkness. When Dhruv dies, he is resurrected within that pool."

I stared at Emera's horse. "That's somewhat creepy, Zari."

Emera giggled. "Maybe, but Zari did not create him. Ragnar, did."

It seemed that my grandfather was always looking out for me. I dipped my head back and gazed at the ceiling, hoping Ragnar would hear me. Thank you, I mouthed. Now, if only Kedron could be okay. I prayed that he was.

My joy, however, was short-lived when numerous screams erupted from outside the stables. One of the stable hands threw open the doors. Our eyes connected. "They're here," he said.

CHAPTER TWENTY-SEVEN

EMERA

The scorching desert sun beat down on us, casting long shadows across the sand outside the walls of the City of Vukan. I squinted against the blinding light into the distance, the heat shimmering in waves around us and dropped my hand to make sure Soul Reaper was secured at my hip. To my left, Calian sat atop Dhruv, wearing his red armor-like scales just as I donned my dark violet ones. He tightened his grip on Vultesh, his knuckles nearly bone white. To my right, Morwen, having changed into sapphire blue fighting leathers with light fitted metal plates strategically placed on top, whispered a silent prayer, her lips barely moving.

We all knew what was coming.

Suddenly, the ground rumbled beneath our feet, and a deafening roar thundered through the sky. A massive Dragon with jagged edges and sharp horns descended from the sky, its wings beating with immense strength.

"Valda," I murmured.

Calian adjusted his weight on Dhruv. "Do you see Amram?"

I shifted my eyes, transforming them into their Dragon form as I maintained my human self. I scanned the sky as far as I could, but I didn't see the evil god.

"Not yet."

Valda landed. The ground quaked, and the city walls behind us shuddered. Her scales glistened in the sunlight, revealing a dark purple glint to them. Flanking her were hundreds of Dragonborns, their armor gleaming. Some held weapons like blades and battle axes. Others held their arms out with magic at the ready.

Then came the chorus of roars. Hovering above Valda's army were dozens of Dragons circling, their shadows gliding over the ground. The sight was both awe-inspiring and terrifying.

"How can we beat that?" Avani whispered, her bravery cracking.

"We will find a way," I said, determined.

Beside me, Morwen's hand hovered near her sword, ready to draw it at a moment's notice. Avani tightened one of the buckles on her emerald fighting leathers. She, too, wore metal plates over the top of her chest and other vulnerable areas. Her eyes darted between the Dragonborn ranks, calculating and strategizing her attack.

I exchanged a glance with Calian, Fin, Morwen, Avani, and Erjon. This was it. The moment we had been preparing for, the moment that would decide the fate of humans. The fate of the unnamed world.

I rolled back my shoulders in an attempt to rid myself of the tension building in my muscles. Without warning, a shadow passed over us from behind. This time, it was a massive black Dragon, its scales shining like onyx in the harsh desert sunlight. The Dragon descended gracefully, landing powerfully next to Fin.

"Risna," I breathed.

Risna turned her head toward Fin and lowered it in a gesture of respect and an invitation. Without hesitation, Fin stepped forward and climbed onto her back. He moved with practiced ease—a result of their training with Calian. Once mounted, he reached for his bow and quiver of arrows, securing them in place behind his back.

Fin gave Calian a curt nod, his eyes scanning the army on the horizon. "We're ready," he called out, and he patted Risna's hide.

A low growl vibrated through Risna's throat, and Fin laughed. "She's feisty," he said.

I met Calian's gaze and nodded. He sheathed Vultesh, lifted his finger, and signaled Fin to move out. I looked left and right at my fellow companions. My friends. My family. "Hold here." No one argued.

As we neared Valda, dense purple smoke enveloped her Dragon form. When it cleared, she stepped through it, clad in armor-like scales. Zari and Dhruv stopped a mere ten feet from her without command. The goddess's eyes, two glowing orbs of dark amethyst, scanned the soldiers guarding the city walls before settling on us. I felt a chill run down my spine despite the desert heat. There were so many of them.

Fin leaned forward with a grin plastered on his face. With a loud, steady voice said, "Valda, what brings you to the City of Vukan?"

An inescapable chuckle escaped Valda's throat. "Fintan, I come only for peace," she said innocently. Our eyes met, and she winked.

Fin looked thoughtfully into the sky then slid his eyes back to Valda. "Hmm. Tell me more." His eyes narrowed, and I could swear that our lighthearted Fin wasn't who stared at Valda. "But make sure that a lowly human like me can understand you."

Valda's notorious wolf-like smile spread across her face, exposing her bright white teeth. "Sorry, Fin. When I said peace, I meant for those with pure blood. Not filth like yourself."

I took a deep breath, trying to steady my racing heart. Fin's hand crept slowly to his bow. "Well, what must we do to earn this peace?" I said, trying to diffuse the situation.

Valda's gaze pinned me in place, her eyes sparkling with joy. "You die."

The Dragonborn ranks shifted, and a tall, imposing figure with bright white scales stepped forward. His eyes, a vivid white, locked onto mine. "Prepare yourselves," he commanded his soldiers.

Suddenly, a shadow passed over us, and I looked up to see Zepherin and his Winged Warriors hovering in the air above us. Zepherin lowered to the ground. His eyes, sharp and piercing, surveyed the scene ahead of him.

Valda's smile widened. How that was possible, I couldn't say. "Zepherin," she said, taking a step forward. "General of the Kingdom of Air and leader of the Winged Warriors. No one ever told me you were so…deliciously handsome." Her expression turned into a child-like pout. "Sorry to hear about your queen."

Zepherin ignored her and faced Calian. "We are ready, Cal. The skies are ours."

Valda snorted.

With Zepherin and the Warriors above, I felt a surge of confidence, but it was short lived. We still didn't have the number of Dragons that Valda did.

You are not alone in this fight, Zari said.

A new roar echoed from above, deeper and more powerful than any of the other Dragons. I looked up to see a large Dragon soaring, its wings spread wide, casting an enormous shadow over us. It landed with a thunderous impact. The Dragon's body was sleeker and more elongated than the other Dragons; its scales shimmered like the deepest blue of the Kaimana Sea, and its eyes were pools of liquid sapphires. Then it turned its massive head toward Calian. On the back of its neck were fin-like crests that resembled those of ocean creatures. These crests ran down its back, forming a spiny ridge that extended to the tip of its tale where fins like delicate, translucent ribbons flowed from behind it. Its limbs ended in webbed claws that aided its swift and agile movement through water. It was breathtaking.

Sitting atop the Dragon was the Ghoul. He slid off the Dragon and winked at me.

Blue smoke began to swirl around the Dragon, enveloping it in a dense haze. The smoke thickened, obscuring the Dragon from our view, and within moments, its form shifted and changed. Then, from the heart of the smoke, a figure emerged. As the smoke dissipated, Anahita, the Goddess of Water, stepped forward, her stride confident and purposeful. She was covered in armor-like scales of the same blue as her Dragon form's hide. I gulped. Her presence was commanding, and her eyes were sharp and determined.

"Anahita," Valda greeted, but there was no warmth behind it. "I thought I left you cowering in your ruin of a village?" There was an edge to Valda's voice. She didn't like surprises.

Anahita ignored Valda's question. "You killed my brother."

Valda rolled her eyes. "I did no such thing. That was just a soldier."

Anahita leaned forward slightly. "No difference to me. Your life is mine." Valda gulped quietly. Was she more powerful? Yes. But Anahita was livid and thirsty for revenge. I would have been just as terrified. And I didn't even know her.

Then, the Goddess of Water met my gaze.

"She's all yours," I said, smiling.

I looked over to where the Ghoul was standing, knives at the ready. "Glad you could join us," I said.

"My pleasure," he replied. He grinned maliciously toward the waiting army.

We all turned when, with a creaking groan, the towering doors to the city of Vukan opened. From within the city emerged Shula riding Orcus, her wolf. Beside them trotted a pack of twenty or so large, fierce wolves, their eyes glowing bright white. Atop each wolf was a rider clad in armor with their helmets beneath their arms. I strained my neck to see closer, focusing my Dragon eyes to discern the slightest detail.

"They're not just Dragonborns. Most of them are human," I murmured.

"How can you tell?" Calian asked.

I faced him and pointed to my eyes. "I can see their faces. They don't have scales."

"Filth," Valda spat, disgusted.

They were a wondrous sight to behold. The human riders sat tall and proud, their eyes scanning our forces. Shula herself was a vision of strength in her heavy armor. She signaled left, then right. All the riders put on their helmets and spread out into a row behind Morwen, Avani, and Erjon.

Shula's gaze shifted to Morwen who looked at me.

They stand ready to defend their city, she told me through her mind.

The wolves howled, and their riders gripped their reins tightly, ready for the signal to charge. Except one. A lone wolf with no rider, a magnificent creature with sleek white fur and piercing blue eyes, broke away from the pack. It stalked over to Avani, its eyes locked onto hers.

For a moment, there was silence, and I was about to teleport to her and defend a wolf attack. But then, the wolf lowered its head and bowed in a gesture of respect and recognition. Avani's eyes smiled as she bowed her head as well. She stepped forward, and with a practiced ease, she climbed onto the wolf's back.

I drug my eyes from Avani, sitting proud on her wolf, to Valda who watched with keen interest, her eyes narrowing slightly. "So, a few Dragonheirs and some wolves. That's all you have? If it makes you feel any better, I'll give you a head start." Then she raised her hand overhead, signaling her army to wait. "I'll give you five minutes," she taunted. Then she laughed. It was shrill and cruel.

I offered my hand to the Ghoul and helped him mount Zari. Anahita transformed back into her glorious self. Then she and Risna, with Fin still on top, lifted into the air. The rest of us took off toward the city walls. I nodded at Shula and Avani as we trotted up to them.

"What—I mean who—are you?" Avani asked, her eyes the size of saucers.

I rolled my eyes. "Real subtle, Avani."

The Ghoul laughed.

"Endrit, the God of Light," Erjon said.

The Ghoul bowed but kept eye contact on Avani. "They say we gods crafted the strongest warriors, but I never believed it until now. You are exquisite."

Did I see that right? Did Avani just…blush? Her cheeks warmed to a slight pink coloring, and she turned her face to the side. Yes. She actually blushed.

"Focus," Shula barked.

Thank you, I mouthed.

Just then a loud thunderous noise came from behind us. We all looked toward the city walls of Vukan. There, standing in steadfast rows, were the Firan and Darknessan soldiers. Their faces were set with determination, prepared to defend the kingdom, and the unnamed world, to their last breath.

Anahita swooped overhead with Risna and Fin following behind her.

If I didn't know better, I would have guessed Morwen had stopped breathing. She became still and silent as she watched Anahita soar overhead. "Is it really her?"

"Yes," I said.

Morwen continued to marvel at Anahita while I addressed the rest of our group. "Spread out," I said.

Shula glanced at Avani, nodded, then slid her gaze back to me. "We'll focus on their Dragonborns." The general gestured behind her. "The Darknessan soldiers have been tasked with guarding the walls as a last defense. My Firan soldiers will join us."

"As will I."

Shula dipped her chin in respect. "Thank you."

"Anahita declared that Valda is hers. Stay away from that fight but keep your wits about you. Should Anahita need assistance…"

Morwen's horse whinnied. "We will be there," my friend said.

"That leaves the other Dragons to me," I told them, peering up into the sky. At that point, numerous Dragons still hovered in the air over Valda's army.

Calian shifted in his saddle. "Em, I can transform."

"No. You must stay on Dhruv with Vultesh. The others need a Dragongod on the ground."

"You mean demi-Dragongod."

I smiled. "Semantics." I guided Zari closer to him, leaned over, and kissed him on the cheek. "You must be ready. When Amram appears, I will join you on the ground."

A chorus of shouting erupted from across the desert. Valda's forces ran toward us.

"It's been an honor," I said. Then I slid off Zari, took her head in my hands, and pressed my forehead to hers. "You mean the world to me. Please stay safe."

I ask the same of you, my Kahina.

I winked at her. "I make no promises." Then, with chaos magic surging inside me, I took off running, shifted into my Dragon form, and lifted into the sky.

CHAPTER TWENTY-EIGHT

EMERA

The battle raged on. Numerous Dragonborns, humans, and Dragons lay dead on the ground already, their blood seeping into the sand. After killing several Dragons with one chaos burst and several Dragonborns on the ground with fire, I needed a moment to rest and recharge. I was powerful, but even a goddess had her limits after a chaos burst at that magnitude. With both souls, I'd be back and ready to take on Amram in just a few minutes.

I perched on a jagged peak of a desert cliff, looking down upon the chaotic battlefield below while my magic replenished itself. The desert stretched out beneath me, its golden sands now marred by the scars of war. The harsh sun beat down relentlessly on all of us, casting long shadows and turning the air into a wavering haze.

From my vantage point, I watched the clash of armies, a swirling mass of Dragonborns and humans. In the center of it all, I spotted Calian, his sword, Vultesh, glinting in the sun as my mate cut through his enemies. His movements were fluid and precise, a deadly dance of fire and sword, leaving a trail of bodies in his wake. Across the distance, Shula commanded her wolves, their synchronized attacks taking down enemy soldier after enemy soldier.

Just a few feet from Shula was Avani, moving with the group like she had always been there, summoning walls of stone to shield the riders and their wolves as well as the remaining Firan soldiers from incoming arrows. Her power was intense, the very ground obeying every one of her commands. A couple of Lightenion Dragonborns broke through the walls. Avani's wolf ran straight toward them and stopped just a few feet away. Then it jumped high in the air. Avani shot vines from her palms, wrapping the Dragonborns before they could fire at her with their light magic. They unsheathed their daggers and tried to cut the vines, but they weren't fast enough. Avani's wolf mauled them both in less than a minute.

I peered out into the distance, scanning the sky for any sign of Amram. Still nothing. So, I turned my focus to Zepherin and his Winged Warriors. Their impressive wings weaved in and out of the swarm of Dragons. They swooped down from above, their wings slicing through the air as they unleashed torrents of wind to scatter the Dragons, forcing them to the ground where groups of Firan soldiers awaited them. Once a Dragon was forced to land, soldiers would overwhelm it, and death would be quick.

A large white Dragon fell from the sky, its tail lashing as it flailed about. It seemed to be wrestling with something or someone as it fell. It twisted and turned, revealing the glint of a Warrior's blade. Then it stopped thrashing and hit the ground, causing the sand to somewhat explode upon impact. Once the dust and sand cleared, Zepherin leaped off the Dragon, his sword dripping with blood.

"Ahhhhh!" he shouted in triumph as he speared his sword into the sky. He looked up at me and winked before he jettisoned himself back into the sky.

Just then a tiny dot on the horizon caught my attention. Was this it? Was this Amram? I readied myself, my chaos magic having mostly returned to me. I wasn't completely charged; therefore, I couldn't incinerate it, but I could take it down in other ways.

I launched into the air. My scales shimmered with the small surge of chaotic energy that coursed through me. The wind rushed past me as I locked eyes with my opponent, a massive green Dragon with jagged horns and a menacing glare.

An inkling of recognition breezed through me. *I know you,* I thought.

The green Dragon appeared to agree. It nodded slightly, and the corners of its mouth tilted upward into a smirk. Then it roared, making the air seem to shake. I responded with a roar of my own, and it was definitely louder. With a powerful beat of my wings, I jolted forward, my claws outstretched and my mouth blazing with chaos magic.

The green Dragon met my charge with a ferocity that matched my own. We collided in mid-air, the impact sending shockwaves throughout the sky. Some of the other Dragons and Winged Warriors careened out of control before regaining their flights.

I flung my tail at the green Dragon. Our claws clashed and our jaws snapped, each of us seeking an advantage. His breath was a searing, venomous mist that burned my scales, but I countered with a burst of chaotic flames that made him recoil. We twisted and turned in the air as we suddenly plummeted, our wings tangled together. With a hefty blow of searing flames, I burned a hole through his forearm. He roared in agony and twisted, dislodging himself from our entanglement. He retreated and dove downward.

I swiped at him with my claws, raking them across his back as he swooped below me. He roared in pain and fury, retaliating with a tail swipe that caught me across the chest and sent me spiraling. The sky spun around me, but I quickly regained my bearings, using my wings to steady myself once more.

I drew on the little chaos magic left within me and unleashed a torrent of energy, a blazing stream of chaos and lightning that arced toward the Dragon. He twisted in mid-air, narrowly avoiding my attack, but the force of the blast hurled him back.

Seizing the moment, I dove toward him, my jaws wide open. I clamped down on his wing, my teeth piercing through his tough green scales. He growled and thrashed wildly, trying to shake me off, but I held on, my claws digging into his side. Soon they were moist from the blood that spilled out of the puncture wounds.

With a desperate rush of strength, the Dragon rolled in mid-air, twisting his body to dislodge me. His tail whipped around and hit me in the neck, one of his spikes piercing my scales. I was forced to release my grip, and we both plummeted toward the ground, only to pull up at the last moment, the wind rushing past us.

My neck throbbed from the pain of my wound, but I ignored it. We circled each other warily, both of us panting and bleeding. The Dragon's eyes were filled with what looked to be a mixture of hatred and…lust? Even as a Dragon, I wanted to gag. I definitely knew who this Dragon really was.

Anwir.

A growl rippled through my throat. If he was in Dragon form, then he was gifted that power. Pure, unfiltered anger swelled within me. With a final, furious roar, I charged at him. Our bodies collided with a bone-shaking impact, and we grappled in mid-air, our claws and teeth tearing at each other. Blinding pain shot down my back as one of his claws raked across my spine, but I ignored it, focusing all my strength and power on killing him.

I reached down deep within my core and drew on the deepest reserves of my chaos magic. It hummed beneath my scales, building and building until I unleashed it all. A devastating blast of chaos energy engulfed Anwir. A thunderous roar escaped his jaws, and his body convulsed as the energy tore through him. It wasn't enough to incinerate him mid-air, but it was enough to send him spiraling down to the ground. His body was smoking, and his eyes were wide with shock and pain when he hit the sand below. He attempted to stand but staggered forward and fell again. Then his wings stopped moving altogether.

I watched as green smoke billowed around him, my breath coming in ragged gasps and my body aching from our fight. With the small drop of healing magic I could muster, I closed my wounds and glided down to the ground.

Anwir was bloodied but able to get up on his feet. Green scales covered his flesh like armor, a trick that Valda must have taught him. He glanced back at me and then shifted his gaze forward. Before him was Avani, her back facing him. Her earth magic threw daggers of rock and split the ground beneath her enemies' feet as she fought. Anwir looked at me over his shoulder and smirked.

Oh, no. I don't know if I have enough power to transform quickly. *Zari! You must save her! Zari! Where are you?!* My eyes darted back and forth over the battlefield, but I couldn't see Zari.

My transformation process started, but it was slow. I wouldn't make it in time. And Avani was so focused on the fight, that she didn't see or hear Anwir stalk over to her. I opened my snout to roar, but only a shout came out. My transformation had already changed my vocal cords.

Anwir released wooden daggers out of his palms. The daggers sliced through the air. I braced myself, fearing that Avani would not be able to dodge them. I watched in horror as the first dagger was about to pierce her scales. Then purple smoke surrounded me.

A scream burst from my mouth. "No!"

When the smoke cleared, I saw the wooden daggers on the ground where Avani had stood, but she wasn't there. Where was she? I looked back at Anwir just as Avani appeared right behind him. Next to her, was a young man in all black with light shoulder-length hair that was almost white. My heart skipped a beat as I recognized him.

"Kedron," I breathed and sprinted toward them.

Anwir turned, shock written all over his face. Avani smiled and in the blink of an eye, she formed a rock in her hand and threw it at Anwir. The small rock hit him in the forehead with such force, that his eyes rolled back, and he slumped to the ground unconscious.

I finally reached Kedron. He turned to me just as I pulled him toward me and wrapped my arms around him tightly. "You're alive," I said.

"I'm alive," he said.

I loosened my arms and leaned back slightly. Around his neck was my mother's amulet. Then I stepped back out of his arms completely.

"Did you really think a little death could stop me?" he asked with a wry smile.

Avani threw Kedron a grateful smile. "Thank you for saving my life. Figure out what you want to do with him." She pointed at Anwir who was just starting to come to. "Now, if you two don't mind, I have a wolf to find." Then she took off running.

I looked back at Kedron. "How?"

"Queen Hestia had a vision just after I teleported her to safety. She saw Valda coming to capture me. Luckily, Hestia had been working on a replica of Amram's amulet, and she was able to give it to me. She also gave me Nimerah's, saying that you had given it to her for protection but that I needed it more."

"How did he not find it?"

Kedron smiled. "I hid it around my ankle so that they wouldn't notice it, and I was just in time because Valda showed up and put me in shackles before I could do anything. Thank you for having the foresight to give Hestia Nimerah's amulet. I wouldn't have survived without it."

I swallowed a lump that had formed in my throat. Kedron was alive.

"I'm sorry it took me so long to get back, even with the protection I was knocked unconscious and had to recover." He raised the amulet over his head and placed it in my hand.

"Don't be sorry. You're here. You're okay."

He gestured toward Anwir. "What do we do with him?"

I wanted to kill him. I wanted to run a blade through his throat. But Anwir was not my kill to make. "Take him into the dungeons. Shackle him and leave him there."

Anwir, having heard me, smirked, clearly pleased that he was going to live. "Thank you, Emera." He licked his lips.

I looked him dead in the eye. "I'll let Calian deal with him."

Anwir's smirk fell.

Kedron held out his hand. "Here, I brought you this. It seems more useful here than hidden." It was Amram's amulet. "It holds his soul. Kill him and destroy this. Then, he's gone for good."

I inspected the amulet in my hand before fastening it through one of my boot's buckles.

Kedron walked over to Anwir, grabbed the snake's shoulder, and teleported him away.

Knowing that Kedron was alive energized me. My magic replenished itself more quickly and I was able to transform and take to the skies. From the air I witnessed Fin and Risna taking down another Dragon before swooping low and shooting Dragonborns with a volley of arrows. I witnessed Shula and her wolves continue to shred Dragonborns apart without mercy. I witnessed Calian deliver killing blow after killing blow with Vultesh and his fire magic working together.

"We might just win this." I unleashed my chaos magic in the air, incinerating a couple of nearby enemy Dragons. I soared back over the wall of the city. There, standing with her arms outstretched and her eyes a milky haze, was Hestia. She pointed furiously and shouted orders, commanding soldiers on where to go and what to do based on her visions.

With several flaps of my massive wings, I hovered over the battlefield, directly above Anahita, Morwen, and Valda. Amram still hadn't arrived, so Valda was now my focus.

Anahita began a new assault. She knelt on the ground and dug her fingers into the parched earth. Deep from below the desert surface, a massive wave of water burst into the sky, forming a towering wall that crashed toward Valda with immense force.

Valda raised her hand, and with a flick, she unleashed a blast of chaos fire. The flames met the water wall, evaporating it into a thick cloud of steam with ease.

Morwen seized the opportunity created by the steam. I descended downward just as she channeled her power, turning the remnants of the water into razor-sharp shards of ice that she hurled at Valda.

Valda smirked, her eyes glowing a vivid violet. She countered with ease and melted the ice shards mid-air before they could reach her. "Is that the best you can do?" she taunted. She then retaliated by summoning a whirlwind that spun around her, drawing in the sand and debris from the desert floor.

I landed and transformed instantly. Anahita and Morwen were ready. I summoned a dark cloud filled with rain that poured directly on Valda, washing away her maelstrom of sand. Anahita's eyes flashed as she raised her arms, this time transforming the raindrops into a storm of icy needles. Morwen added her power, sending icy daggers toward Valda.

My breathing paused as Valda laughed and waved her arms, creating a barrier that shattered the icy needles on impact. With a swift motion, she sent a wave of flames rolling toward Anahita and Morwen, forcing them to leap aside. Anahita rolled gracefully, but Morwen struggled to get up. I ran to her side and helped my friend to her feet.

"Are you okay?"

"I'm not sure. I think I broke it." She held out her arm, inspecting it. When she rotated it, she cried out in pain.

"I can fix that."

"There's no time."

"We're wasting more time arguing about it. Let me heal you. Anahita can keep Valda busy."

Having read my mind, Anahita glanced at Morwen and nodded. She then took off running toward Valda, refusing to give up. I covered Morwen's arm with one hand and let my healing magic do its duty. Meanwhile, we watched Anahita summon a surge of water that spiraled around her. With my other hand, I generated a powerful wind that lifted Anahita's water into a swirling cyclone. As the cyclone grew, Anahita froze the outer layer, creating a deadly, spinning vortex of ice.

Valda's eyes widened, but she quickly regained her composure. Her chaos magic formed a pulsating barrier around herself. The icy cyclone crashed into the barrier with a thunderous roar, sending trembles through the ground. For a moment, it seemed like Valda was overwhelmed.

Morwen's arm healed. She held it to her and said, "I think we have her."

Upon her last words, Valda hurled the cyclone toward us. I shoved Morwen out of the way just as the icy wind hit me. I flew back and landed hard on my back. Valda teleported, appearing at my side and unsheathing Soul Reaper from my hip. She held it up and inspected it in the sun.

"Look what we have here." Then, in an instant, she melted the blade. Molten metal flowed into the sand, leaving the glowing gem in her palm. She contemplated it for a moment, then cocked her head and crushed it. She opened her palm, and the powder blew away in the breeze.

"No," I whispered, disbelief rolling through me. Then, a massive shadow loomed over the battlefield.

Amram had arrived.

CHAPTER TWENTY-NINE

EMERA

The unnamed world seemed to hold its breath as the battle suddenly paused, and an unnerving stillness settled over the blood-soaked landscape. A light breeze carrying the harsh smell of smoke and charred flesh drifted through the air, stinging my nostrils. The silence was deafening, a stark contrast to the cacophony of weapons and magic.

I teleported to Calian. Deep down in my gut, I knew this was the calm before the storm. The tension was palpable. Everyone, enemy Dragonborns included, were on high alert.

"Valda destroyed Soul Reaper." I pointed at the amulet inside my boot. "But Kedron gave me this."

"Kedron?"

I plastered a smile on my face. "He's alive."

Calian angled his head to face me. "So, we kill Amram and then destroy his amulet. But what about the blade?"

"I don't know. Maybe we don't need it?" I knew it was a false hope.

Amram roared, forcing us to look up at him. His scales were an ominous blend of black and violet, a mixture of the chaos that stirred in his soul. His eyes, black as coal, locked onto us. He was the predator. We were his prey.

"We can keep Amram focused on us and not anyone else by showing him the amulet."

"Sounds like a plan."

I grabbed the amulet and held it up in the air for Amram to see. "Is this what you want?" I yelled at the god.

Everyone on the ground remained rooted where they stood. Even the Dragons remained suspended in the air, not daring to disrupt the presence of their god. Amram's presence was overwhelming, a force of chaos that seemed to suffocate the very life from us. I fought to steady my breathing, to keep my mind focused. Then Amram roared again, and the battle resumed.

Magic was hurled around me. Swords were clanking with each blow. Arrows whooshed past. Then the ground shook as Amram landed. Violet smoke filled the air as he landed, and he transformed instantly into his human form. His dark purple robes with silver stitching blew in the wind, giving us a glimpse of the thick scaled-armor underneath. He took a few steps forward, his gaze shifting between Calian and me. The corner of his mouth turned upward into a cruel smirk. "Emera Edevane. How I hope your soul has settled in well. The ease in which you retrieved it was quite impressive." His voice was low and dangerous.

Calian raised Vultesh in a striking position next to his face. His knuckles were almost white for how tightly he gripped it. The volatile chaos magic within me stirred, ready to be unleashed. My mate and I stood side-by-side, a united front against the one who sought to destroy the world.

"You're not as powerful as you thought you were," I replied, my voice steady despite the anxiety gnawing at my insides.

I expected Amram to lash out, but he didn't. Instead, the god's wicked laughter echoed toward us, a chilling sound that sent a shiver down my spine. "So young. So naive. So weak."

I took a cautious step forward. "Young? I was born during the great war."

His face remained unchanged.

"Oh, you didn't know that?"

Calian snorted. "Seems like there's much you don't know."

"I know you have that amulet. And I want it back."

"Funny that you say I'm naive. Because I've learned a lot since being blessed with my magic. Like how to kill you for good."

Amram lifted his left eyebrow slightly. Anger sparked in his eyes, but he clearly fought to keep his face neutral.

"And as for weak? My mother's soul would beg to differ. You made a grave mistake when you killed her. You didn't take her soul. And because of that, she was able to give it to me. So, you see, with her soul and my soul joined together..." I summoned my chaos magic, and it erupted in my hands. "I'm more powerful than you."

Amram growled and threw a lethal blast of chaos magic at me. I teleported out of the way with ease. I reappeared several feet away just as the god launched himself into the air in his Dragon form, his wings beating with immense power. I looked at Calian and he nodded. This battle would be a fight to the death. And I wasn't dying again.

My heart pounded in my chest, a mixture of nervousness and exhilaration. But this time, instead of suppressing my emotions, I fueled my magic with them. It hummed beneath my chest and didn't waver, even as Amram soared through the ash and smoke-filled sky. He released a thunderous roar, a deafening sound that caused many on the ground to hunch over and cover their heads. Even the most powerful of Dragonborns feared Amram's wrath.

The Dragongod dove toward Calian and me. He sent a wave of chaos energy crashing toward us. I reacted instinctively, raising my hands to conjure a shield of air over Calian and me. The air pushed the chaos magic away effortlessly. Calian and I stood.

"Ready?" I asked him.

Calian nodded. He loosened his grip on Vultesh and laid it on the ground. "Let's bring this beast down."

"Now!" I shouted, and Calian unleashed a whirlwind of flames, his magic searing through the air and striking Amram's underbelly right as he swooped overhead. The god roared in pain and fury.

Taking advantage of the distraction, I focused my mind and drew upon the chaotic power that defined my magic. I reached my hands out, held them together, and slowly pulled them apart, forming a sphere of pure chaos between them. With a swift motion, I hurled it at Amram. The sphere exploded upon impact and sent the Dragon staggering back.

But I knew Amram would not be easily defeated. "Calian, cover me!' I called out, knowing we had to act quickly.

Calian nodded, raising his arms and summoning a wall of fire that encircled us, providing temporary protection. I closed my eyes, channeling my energy and letting it course throughout my body. The chaos vibrated within me, ready to be unleashed.

With another desperate roar, Amram dove toward us again, his jaws open wide to release a wave of water. He doused Calian's flames, and at that moment, I unleashed my power. Chaos magic exploded from my body and struck Amram. Time seemed to stand still as Amram fell to the ground. The impact shook the ground so much that we all fell to our feet. His massive form convulsed, then crumpled to the ground, motionless. I got to my feet and stood there, panting.

Calian appeared at my side. "How's that possible? He's still…intact."

"Maybe his scales are thicker?"

"But he appears dead."

Amram remained motionless.

Calian turned to me, his eyes serious. "Let's finish this." Then my mate took off running, Vultesh in his hand.

"Calian, stop! Something's not right!" Sure enough, a large golden glow enveloped Amram's body, healing the Dragon. The beast teleported, reappearing right in front of

Calian.

"No!" I screamed and teleported as quickly as I could. But when I reappeared next to Calian, it was too late. Amram already had his jaws around him. My breath caught in my chest as I watched in horror. Amram was going to eat my mate.

But suddenly, the God of Chaos whipped his head back and then forward, roaring in pain. The tip of Calian's sword appeared through the top of Amram's snout. The Dragon reared back, opened his jaws, and threw Calian into the distance. My mate's body hit a large sand boulder with a sickening crunch.

"Calian!" I screamed. His body lay twisted on the ground beside Amram. I squinted my eyes, desperately seeking the familiar glow of healing magic. After a few seconds, the glow, although faint, emitted from his chest. Relief washed through my body. Calian was alive. I needed to stall Amram so that my mate could regain his strength. Then, we'd try again.

Amram roared and the world shook. He turned his massive head toward me, and his eyes flashed with maniacal delight. I gulped as my pulse raced beneath my chest. I backed away from him, raised my hands, and channeled the chaos power that coursed through my veins. I let it hum beneath my skin. I can't release you yet, I thought. I need more. I reached down into the pits of my mother's soul and just as I summoned the final drops of chaos magic, my foot caught on a loose stone, and I stumbled. I hit the ground with a resounding thud, causing air to burst from my mouth upon impact. For a moment, time seemed to freeze as I laid there. Panic seized my chest. I was vulnerable and exposed to Amram. The ground trembled beneath me as Amram stalked closer, looming over me, his eyes gleaming.

I scrambled to my feet, desperately trying to regain my footing. But before I could stand upright, Amram attacked, his claws slashing through the air at my torso. I twisted and turned then barely managed to summon my darkness magic and teleport away. Amram did the same. Teleporting mere inches from where I reappeared. He swung his tail into my stomach, which sent me hurtling backward. I was on the ground again, my breath coming in ragged gasps as I struggled to calm myself.

With a final surge of strength, I summoned the last of my magic, letting it flow throughout my body. But even as I started to let the magic explode from within, a lethal wave of chaos magic came at me from Amram's snout. I closed my eyes, bracing myself for the inevitable end.

But it didn't come.

I slowly opened one eye and peeked through the side of it. Erjon stood between Amram's chaos magic and me. A large shield of violent wind flowed from his palms. For a moment, it seemed as though his shield would hold. But I could see the strain on his face and the sweat that streaked down his cheeks.

"Emera," Erjon said, his voice barely audible above the roar of the wind. "My hip." I

I glanced down and there, sheathed to his hip, was a blade.

"It's supposed to be important in ending the war. Grab it and teleport. Now. Be the goddess you were born to be. Do it! I can't hold on much longer."

I quickly grabbed the dagger and secured it at my side. Then, just as Erjon's strength began to waver, a rush of magic coursed through me. I grabbed his shirt and summoned my darkness magic, teleporting us several feet away behind a large boulder. When we reappeared, I let go of Erjon's shirt.

I hunched over and placed my hands on my knees. "Thank you," I said, my chest rising and falling heavily as I attempted to catch my breath.

But Erjon didn't respond.

Erjon laid on the ground, face down. I fell to my knees,

and reached for him, hoping he was just knocked unconscious from teleporting. "Erjon?" I asked, my voice cracking from panic. With my hand around his shoulder, I turned him over slowly. My heart fell.

My friend's eyes were empty.

There, in the middle of his chest, was a gaping hole from Amram's chaos magic. I closed my eyes, and the world around me stilled.

"I wasn't fast enough," I murmured. Tears stung my eyes, and my fingers trembled as I leaned down and shut his eyes. Then I kissed his cheek, fighting to hold back the sobs that threatened to rip my throat apart. I swallowed hard and wiped away the tears. "I will be back for you. I promise." Then I teleported back to the battlefield, materializing in a distant corner so that I could steady myself. Fury boiled within me. The image of Erjon's lifeless eyes fueled my rage even more.

I was going to kill Amram. And enjoy it. Erjon's distant words rang through my ears. "Balance your emotions, Em. Be a true Goddess of Chaos."

Amram spotted me. I drew in a heavy breath and teleported to him. His eyes flashed. *I warned you*, he said in my mind. *You cannot escape your fate, Emera.*

His words only fueled my anger more, stoking the spark

of the chaos magic within me. Movement caught my eye beyond Amram's colossal form. Calian was back on his feet, running toward us with Vultesh at the ready.

I grabbed the dagger Erjon had given me and inspected it. "It can't be," I said in disbelief. The dagger looked exactly like Soul Reaper. Erjon wouldn't lie. If he said this dagger would help, then every part of me knew that it would help end Amram's life. I shifted my eyes back to the god and smiled. "I'm a Goddess of Chaos…And my fate is to kill you."

Amram narrowed his eyes and lifted his head, his neck vibrating with chaos magic inside. But it didn't matter. He was not walking—or flying—out of here alive. With my palms facing upward, I let my chaos magic flow out of me. Lightning streaked through the skies. Power surged through my body, and heat flared behind my eyes as I stared at Amram. With a flick of my wrist, the jagged bolts cascaded down to my feet. Amram recoiled as the ground where he stood erupted in bursts of electrified energy, his monstrous form momentarily thrown off balance.

As I pressed forward, the Chaos Dragon's rage intensified. With a feral growl, Amram launched himself forward, blasting lethal chaos magic in my direction. I was not deterred. My body twisted and turned, dodged and weaved with fluid-like precision.

"Emera! Now!"

Calian leaped onto Amram's tail. The Dragon thrashed about wildly, trying to dislodge Calian. It was just the right amount of time I needed. I planted my feet, raised my arms, and summoned the largest bolt of lightning my magic allowed. I drained all of my magic and soul into it. The bolt zig-zagged from the sky. Calian had climbed up Amram's back, despite the Dragon's attempt to shake him off. With a boost of energy, Calian leaped into the air with Vultesh above him, the bolt connected with the blade just as Calian plunged it into Amram's skull. The Dragon's roar of agony echoed around us.

"My turn," I breathed. I ran as fast as I could, thunder roaring overhead and lightning crackling through the dark clouds. I pulled the second Soul Reaper out of its sheath. My feet skimmed the ground as I slid beneath Amram's body, just below his chest. "For Erjon," I whispered and thrust the dagger upward. The dagger hit its mark, puncturing Amram's scales and into his heart. The gem flashed a blinding violet, and I could feel it siphoning Amram's soul into its dark blade.

I teleported away, using the last drop of energy that filled my bones. I reappeared just a few feet away from the God of

Chaos, putting my hand on my chest to steady my breathing. There were no words spoken between Amram and I, but his gaze was locked on mine, filled with agony and disbelief. Slowly, the light faded from his eyes, and the Dragon fell to the ground, dead. The ground shook beneath my feet from the impact, causing me to stumble and fall to my knees. Despite the clanking of swords and cries of dying soldiers, I didn't move. I couldn't. I had no energy. No strength. No willpower to continue.

Calian slid to my side and wrapped me in his arms. He pulled me close to his chest. I longed for his familiar scent of wood and spice, but instead, my nostrils were filled with the metallic scent of blood. After a few minutes, he gently pushed me away and held Amram's amulet in his hands. He opened my palm and placed the amulet in it.

"Can you do it?"

I nodded firmly, knowing that if I exerted myself anymore, I'd surely lose consciousness. But I didn't care. I would die all over again if it meant Amram never returned. I turned the amulet over and over in my hand, inspecting its beauty as it pulsated with an eerie light. It was unlike my mother's or Ragnar's amulets. This one's surface was weathered and worn by the passage of time. The gem was a small thing, insignificant in the grand scheme of what we'd been through, yet it held within it the weight of Amram's immortal soul.

With a steady breath, I closed my fingers around the gem, feeling its edges pressing against my palm. There was a moment of stillness, a pause in the steady rhythm of the unnamed world. I focused my thoughts and gathered my power. And then, with a sudden surge of determination, I exerted my remaining strength upon the rock. For a moment, there was resistance, but then there was a sudden release of tension. I heard a sharp crack, like the sound of lightning crackling across the sky. The gem fractured beneath my fingers and crumbled into smaller pieces before blowing away in the wind. A triumphant breath escaped through my lips.

"It is done," I mumbled. "The rest of his soul is gone."

A scream pierced the air, a mixture of agony and rage as Valda's eyes fell onto Amram's lifeless body. The features of her face twisted into an expression of disbelief.

Even the battlefield, a cacophony of clashing steel and desperate cries, grew silent. Enemy Dragons, the few that remained, took one look at Amram lying dead on the sand and retreated. Enemy Dragonborns dropped their weapons, looked at each left and right, then ran after the Dragons. It could take years to find them all, but we would do so. They would pay for the lives they took, the blood they spilled.

Anahita took slow steps forward, her eyes fixed on Valda. I didn't need my empathic magic or my telepathic magic to know what she was feeling, what she was seeing. The memory of Vukan's death at the hands of the Valda fueled her power. Blue water magic glowed from her outstretched arms. With a powerful movement, the goddess raised her hands, summoning all of her elemental power. A mist formed around her, and with the flick of her wrist, the tiny droplets formed sharp, icy shards.

Valda's eyes remained focused on her father. Her chest rose and fell with each ragged breath she took. The wind grabbed hold of her raven hair and flailed all around her. She stood frozen as strands of hair whipped onto her face. Her arms were slack at her sides. The expression on her face said everything.

"She's giving up." I whispered to the gods. She had nothing else to live for. Her mate was gone. Now her father.

Anahita hurled the ice daggers at Valda. One after the other, they all found their mark, embedding themselves in her back. The once powerful goddess of chaos staggered forward a few steps before she collapsed to her knees. For a moment, the unnamed world seemed to hold its breath. Valda's eyes fluttered before they locked onto mine.

I approached her cautiously. In my hand was Erjon's dagger, its edges still tinted red from Amram's blood. Valda didn't call to her healing magic as I stood over her. "For all the pain you've caused," I murmured, my voice a low, dangerous whisper. Then, with a swift, merciless stroke, I plunged the dagger into her heart and watched it drain her soul.

As Valda's lifeless form laid on the hard sand, the battlefield seemed to exhale. Calian and the others formed a circle around Valda. I held out the blade in my hand and with my chaos magic, melted it.

"Never again will she walk this world." I glimpsed back at Amram over my shoulder. "Neither of them."

CHAPTER THIRTY

CALIAN

The grand dining hall was alive with the sounds of celebration. Additional long tables were brought in so that Shula's human riders could attend the feast. The tables were laden with a variety of lavish dishes, from roasted meats to exotic fruits, and goblets of wine that seem to flow endlessly. Even the servants were partaking in the festivities. Music filled the air, a lively tune played by a band of musicians at the far end of the hall.

I stood with my mother at the head of the main table, surrounded by those who fought and bled beside me. Emera sat to my right, conversing with Morwen and Fin. Her eyes sparkled with a rare light of joy. She took a quick glimpse at me and smiled. My heart soared within my chest. She looked exquisite in her gown. I wasn't one to take notice of women's fashion, but tonight was different. It was a silk masterpiece of elegance that shimmered with every move she made. The rich violet hue of the fabric reminded me of a twilight sky.

What really drew my eye was the neckline, a graceful off-the-shoulder design, adorned with tiny, sparkling gemstones that accentuated her collarbone and her purple Dragonmate wings tattooed right above her heart.

She turned in her seat, and I finally saw the back of the gown. There was lace. I growled, hoping no one would hear me. The entire gown was sensual and fit her like a glove with a voluminous skirt that cascaded to the floor in gentle waves. Despite how magnificent the dress was on her, I planned on tearing it off later. She looked sophisticated and timeless.

Emera must have read my mind because she blushed, turned, and locked onto me. She was my mate, soon-to-be wife, and I wouldn't have it any other way.

I leaned down and whispered in her ear. "You look radiant tonight. Happy birthday, my love."

Her eyes widened and sparkled with surprise. "How did you know?" she asked.

"I have my ways."

She laughed, and it was a glorious sound.

I chuckled and scanned the rest of the table. On the other side of my mother sat Kedron, and I praised the gods that he was alive. He chatted quietly with Nyx and Zeph, no doubt reminiscing about the warrior's great loss.

Erjon.

I swallowed the lump in my throat. I broke away from where I stood and made my way toward Zeph. His eyes were distant as he mourned the death of Erjon. Erjon's sacrifice saved Emera's life, and Zeph's grief was a palpable thing, a reminder of the price of our victory. I stood behind him, placing a comforting hand on his shoulder. "Erjon's bravery will never be forgotten, Zeph. He didn't just save Emera; he saved us all. His sacrifice will be written in the history books. I will make sure of it."

Zeph nodded, his eyes glistening with unshed tears. "Thank you, Cal. He would be honored to hear that."

Further down the table, Avani sat next to the Ghoul, giggling and blushing. Upon Amram's death, Endrit's soul returned to him, along with a pair of white Dragonmate wings above his heart. The same Dragonwings that Avani now had tattooed on her skin as well.

Avani stood and raised her goblet in a solemn toast. "To Senna," she declared, her voice carrying over the crowd.

Zeph stood and held up his goblet. "To Erjon," he added, his voice booming. He looked at Emera. When their eyes connected, they both smiled and nodded.

Despite his quiet nature, Kedron stood up and raised his goblet as well. "To Queen Eteri."

One by one, everyone at the table stood and raised their goblets before saying the name of the loved one they'd lost.

Fin toasted to Elio, Morwen toasted to her father, King Calder. We'd lost so many.

Emera stood and raised her goblet. "To Nimerah, my mother."

The moment was bittersweet as I reached down and grabbed my goblet. Then I raised it high. "To my father, Vukan."

My mother stepped forward, her knees shaking slightly. She was still drained from all the visions that plagued her during the battle. She raised her golden chalice. "To all the lives lost. Their lights guided us, even in the darkest times. We will continue our fight for peace in their memories." We all echoed her sentiment, our hearts heavy with the memories of our fallen loved ones.

Everyone took a drink, causing the room to become silent. My mother lowered her chalice and cleared her throat, demanding our attention. She smoothed out her gown which was gold with intricate embroidering mimicking swirling flames of fire. She took a deep breath, and with her voice steady and clear, she announced. "I renounce my title as Queen."

The crowd, me included, was stunned. No one said a word. No one moved. No one blinked.

Then she looked at me, her eyes filled with tears. "You are the king, my son. You will lead our people—Dragonborns and humans—into a future of peace." Her voice was firm yet gentle. There was no dissuading her.

I looked out into the crowd. Everyone waited on bated breath for me to respond. I swallowed the burning lump that had formed in my throat. "Only if Emera agrees to be my queen."

Emera's eyes widened as the crowd erupted into applause and cheers. As the celebrations continued around us, I went to my mate and cradled her face in my hands. I pulled her in and kissed her tenderly, surrounded by friends who had become family and the memories of those we'd lost. The war was over, but the journey of rebuilding peace had just begun.

I pulled back and gazed into her beautiful violet eyes. The music started up again, and I raised my goblet high. Emera did the same.

"To the future!" I shouted.

Fin raised his goblet. "To the future!"

The hall erupted in more cheers while a surge of hope and determination rushed through my body. I know my responsibilities are great, but I also know that I am not alone. I am surrounded by the strongest and most loyal friends anyone could ask for.

Mother appeared at my side and took my hand. Her eyes were filled with pride and love. "Lead with your heart, Calian. That's what will make you a great king."

*   *   *

Hours later, the grand hall above still echoed with laughter, clinking goblets, and the joyous sounds of a celebratory feast in full swing. Below, however, in the damp, cold depths of the castle, a different fire was about to be kindled.

I pushed open the heavy iron door to the dungeon. It creaked open, and the flickering light of torches cast long shadows on the rough stone walls. The air was thick with the stench of mildew.

Once I stepped into the dimly lit corridor, I called to my magic and formed a single flame in my palm. I let it grow until it illuminated the outlines of the prison cells. I quickened my pace, my steps resonating from the walls as I approached the very last cell.

Inside, Anwir sat hunched on the straw-covered floor, chains rattling as he shifted his weight. He looked up at me with his evil green eyes. His peppered, greasy hair fell over his gaunt face which twisted into a sneer at the sight of me. The shackles, which took away his magic, also siphoned his life-force. There was no denying my feelings. I relished in his torture.

But I was here to end it.

"Calian," Anwir rasped. "To what do I owe the pleasure? Shouldn't you be upstairs, basking in the glow of your own glory?"

I raised an eyebrow, a smirk playing on my lips. He had no clue what I had in store for him. "Oh, I do enjoy a good celebration, but I thought you might be in need of some conversation. It must get quite lonely down here."

The traitor laughed, a hollow, bitter sound. "Concerned for my well-being, are we? How touching."

I leaned back against the cold stone wall. "Hardly. I have questions. And only you have the answers."

Anwir's eyes narrowed. "And if I refuse?"

I leaned toward him and brought the flame in my palm closer to my face. "Even you know that fire can be...*persuasive*."

His sneer faltered for a moment, replaced by a hint of fear. He composed himself quickly, though, his defiance—and arrogance—returning. Did he really think he was going to walk out of here alive?

"Ask your questions, my boy. But don't expect me to play nice."

I took a step back away from the bars. "Did you know who I was when you found me?"

Anwir's eyes flashed with amusement. "That you were Vasuman, the Dragon Slayer? Sadly, no. Oh, but I knew you were special. You were a hundred times more powerful than any Dragonborn I'd ever seen. I figured with the right amount of training—"

"And brainwashing," I added, interrupting him.

He scoffed at me. "You're still blind to the truth, it seems."

My patience wore thin, the flame in my palm flaring brighter just like my annoyance. "Get on with it."

He sighed. "After a few months of watching you hone your magic, I knew there was more just waiting to be awakened within you. Then the Dragonheirs started being revealed, and I knew the time was near. At that point, you became a means to an end."

I narrowed my eyes at him, absorbing the information.

"I will not lie to you, Calian," he said, interrupting my thoughts. "If you know anything about me, you know that. And it wasn't personal. I wanted Emera from the moment I laid my eyes on her. I needed her." He chuckled. "Tell me. Is she just as delicious as she appears?"

I straightened my back abruptly, extinguishing the flame by closing my palm around it. "Thank you for your cooperation. Enjoy the rest of your stay."

Anwir snickered as he backed up into his cell. I stared at him in the faint glow of the torch on the wall behind me. Our eyes remained locked on one another. His smirk was still planted on his face.

I smiled slowly. As slowly as his smirk disappeared once realization dawned on him.

"W-W-What are you doing?"

I took a step forward, willing my expression into a mask of calm fury.

Anwir sneered, struggling against his shackles. "You think killing a defenseless man is justice?"

With a raise of my hand, the air around us shimmered with heat. "Yes."

With a swift, commanding gesture, my hand ignited, flames dancing around my fingers. With all my power, I willed the flames to grow brighter, hotter. Anwir's face twisted into an expression of pure fear as I thrust out my hand, sending a bolt of fire straight into his chest.

He screamed. But the fire didn't burn his skin; instead, it seeped into him, merging with his blood. Drops of sweat formed along his scales as the fire spread within him, an unbearable heat coursing through his veins. His eyes widened in terror as he realized what was happening.

"No... No, you can't! I took you off the streets. I trained you!" Anwir gasped, his body convulsing as the fire filled every limb. I closed my eyes and used my Dragonhearing to listen to his blood boiling, the heat intensifying with every heartbeat. He dropped to his knees and writhed in agony. His screams grew louder and louder. Steam rose from his skin, and his veins glowed a fiery red, visible even through his flesh.

"Stop it! Please, Calian, stop!" Anwir begged from the floor, his voice breaking.

I forced my face to remain impassive. "This is for Senna. This is for Emera. This is for me."

Anwir's body now convulsed violently. His skin blistered and cracked, and his eyes rolled back into his head. The boiling blood within him reached its peak, and with a final, shuddering gasp, his body went still. Smoke rose from his lifeless form, the air thick with the scent of his burned flesh.

I took a deep breath. There was no satisfaction in his death. It was necessary, but I didn't take pleasure in killing him.

Okay, maybe I did. But just a little. I turned away from the corpse and walked back down the corridor, leaving Anwir to the darkness once more. As I ascended the stairs, the sounds of the feast grew louder. So did the beating of my heart.

CHAPTER THIRTY-ONE

EMERA
~5 YEARS LATER~

Hushed murmurs and soft footsteps echoed through the corridor of the palace just outside my drawing room. The day was glorious. A full sun and blue skies overlooked the City of Vukan. I stared out at the city through my open window. Today was the day. Anticipation fluttered in my chest.

A light tapping against the door turned my attention away from the beautiful landscape beyond the palace window. Calian opened the ornate doors and stepped in. "Your Majesty," he said with a low bow. I giggled at his foolishness. "Yes?" I replied, my voice steady despite the butterflies dancing in my stomach.

"The High Dragon and High Human have arrived."

Before he could react, I rushed past Calian and burst out of the room, my heart pounding with a mixture of relief and longing. There, in the hall, stood Morwen and Fin. Without hesitation, I threw myself into Morwen's arms, wrapping her in a tight embrace.

"Emera," she whispered, her voice warm with affection as she returned my embrace, "it's been too long."

Tears pricked at the corners of my eyes as I pulled away, my gaze meeting hers. Despite the years that had passed since we last saw each other, our sisterly bond remained unbreakable.

Morwen glanced at her husband, Fin, who stood beside her with a fond smile. "You look like you haven't aged a bit, Em," he said.

"Really? Because you look really old."

He threw back his head and laughed. "Being a human will do that to you. We age faster than you Dragonborns, remember?"

"Oh, I remember," I said, chuckling.

"Nyx can slow down the process for me, but she can't stop it."

Morwen took his hand. "When you go, I go."

Calian appeared at my side. "No one's going anywhere."

I turned back to Fin. "Agreed." As I took in the sight of my dear friends standing before me, a sense of gratitude washed over me. Calian held out his hand, and Fin took it. But instead of shaking it, he pulled Calian in for a hug.

As the two men had their moment, Morwen and I smiled at one another. "How long has it been?" she asked. "It seems like ages."

I nodded, a wistful smile touching my lips. "It has been three years," I replied.

She sighed sadly. "The passage of time feels both fleeting and eternal in this world."

The men—more so Fin—finally released one another. Beside me, Calian nodded in agreement, his expression thoughtful. "So much has changed since then," he remarked.

Morwen glanced at Calian. "Indeed," she said.

Calian looked down the hall, but no one was there. He turned back to Fin. "How's the council? I heard you were able to hold your first meeting in the new Temple of Nimerah last fall."

"We did. The Council of Unity will convene there from now on. I'm grateful because the last place was musty and old."

Morwen lightly smacked Fin on the shoulder. "That is my mother's drawing room you're talking about."

"I know. And I stand by what I said."

Morwen and Fin were chosen as the Council's High Dragonborn and High Human, both the leader of their species.

The council was composed of six members of each species, carefully selected from the most respected and capable individuals within their respective kingdoms. Each member brought unique perspectives, skills, and experiences. The council's primary duty was to ensure harmony and cohesion across the new realm. They deliberated on matters of governance, trade, diplomacy, and defense, striving to address the needs and concerns of both Dragonborns and humans.

"And what about the new name?"

"How about we take this reunion to a better place than the hallway?" Calian said, intervening. "Might I suggest the gardens?"

Morwen raised an eyebrow. "Gardens?"

I smiled. "They were built last year. You're going to love them." I grabbed her hand and led her toward the back of the palace. We exited a large door.

Behind the towering walls of the royal palace was our sanctuary of tranquility and beauty. Enclosed by high stone walls decorated with intricate carvings depicting magic and Dragons, our garden represented our prosperity.

We stepped through ornate wrought-iron gates and were greeted by a symphony of colors and scents. Lush greenery flourished under the warm sun, scattered with vibrant floral blooms that thrived in the fertile soil—thanks to my earth magic.

Morwen's radiant smile spoke volumes. She strolled down the stone pathway as it wound its way through the garden. She paused at the bubbling fountains adorned with sculptures of each Dragongod—except Amram, of course. The water shimmered in the sunlight and cast rainbow-hued reflections on the surrounding plants.

At the heart of the garden stood the garden's centerpiece, a magnificent statue of a Nimerah amidst a cascade of water. Morwen rounded the fountain and paused, her eyes looking a few feet ahead of her.

Sitting in an alcove on a small stone bench, tucked away amidst the greenery, was a young child looking at a picture book.

Her hand brushed her lips as she stared wide-eyed at the child. She turned to me, and I nodded. I followed her while she made her way to the young boy with dark tousled hair, lavender eyes, and violet scales.

Morwen knelt before him. "Hello, there."

"Hi."

"My name is Morwen."

"I know. You're my auntie."

Morwen laughed. "Yes. I am. Unfortunately, it's been a long time since I've seen you, Erjon."

While Morwen spoke to my son, a slight breeze blew through the garden. I couldn't help but feel that Erjon was looking down upon us. When our son was born, Calian and I had decided to do away with the practice of naming a child after their element. It felt right, and our son wouldn't have been born if it weren't for Erjon's sacrifice.

The thought of Erjon brought a smile to my lips. Happily, Tamasvi visited us shortly after the war and informed us that both Eteri and Erjon had ascended into the DragonEmpyrean together.

"I know you're happy and at peace, my friend," I whispered into the sky.

"Em! Come join us." I whirled around to see Calian and Fin seated at a wooden table beneath a tall oak tree. Morwen and Erjon were reading the book, so I joined the men, taking a seat next to my mate.

"What is so important that you must tear me away from our son?"

"Little E is over there?" Fin straightened his back and strained his neck to catch a glimpse of Erjon. "How old is he now?"

"Four," I answered warmly.

He relaxed back into his chair. "And tell me again how he has scales, and you didn't until you cut yourself?"

"Nimerah's doing. She wanted to make sure I could pass as human while I grew up."

Fin stroked his chin. "So, like…the spell was lifted when your activation started."

I nodded. "Yeah, you could say that."

"Fin was just saying how the council had agreed upon a name for the unnamed world."

Fin leaned back slightly. "Yes. Despite the occasional disagreement, we decided on Yara-Syla."

"Yara-Syla?"

"Yara is a human name, meaning 'strong', and Syla is a name from the old Dragonlanguage meaning 'together'. So…"

A smile graced Morwen's lips. "It means we are stronger together." She walked up the path, holding Erjon's hand.

"It seems that you have everything under control."

Morwen nodded. "For now. Though my mother continues to rule the Kingdom of Water, her time on the throne is limited. When she passes, Fin and I will vacate our seats on the council, opening the door for two new high-ranking members to be voted on."

Fin pointed at us. "Which could be you."

Calian crossed his arms. "So, that's the real reason you came to see us, huh?" He narrowed his eyes, but his tone was playful.

Fin put his hand on this chest. "I am shocked, Calian Westbow, that you would even consider such a thought." He placed his hand on his chest. "I'm sorry. Calian Sunniva. I'm still getting used to you taking your mother's name."

My mate laughed. "Save the apology. Even I'm still getting used to it."

The men continued to joke around while I entertained the prospect of sitting on the Council once Morwen and Fin left. I knew that the decisions the Council made would shape the course of our world for generations to come. Generations of both Dragonborns and humans.

A voice from behind interrupted my thoughts. "Emera, darling."

We all turned to see both of my parents standing there, one with a platter of fruit and the other with fresh water mixed with a hint of lemon and mint leaves, which they sat on the table.

"Mr. and Mrs. Edevane," Fin squealed. My parents laughed as he quickly hugged them both followed by Morwen. However, Morwen was more reserved in her greeting.

Erjon decided it was time for Papa Struan to play hide and seek, so he skipped out of the garden and back into the palace. I nodded at my mother and father who both smiled and followed my son.

Fin picked up a strawberry and stuffed it into his mouth. "They're not going to join us?"

"We can all catch up at dinner tonight," I said with a chuckle. Fin and my parents had grown close over the years, considering I made sure Fin checked in on them often in my absence. Both he and Morwen made it their duty to visit every few months.

Calian took a sip of water. "Avani visited us just a month or so ago. She's doing well."

"Yes," Morwen replied lightly. "She's become quite the vintner. Her wine is divine. I bring in monthly shipments from her vineyard."

A faint smile touched my lips at the memory of Avani's spirited reaction to seeing Erjon. She hadn't been present for his birth, so she had never met him. I swore I could hear her squeal in my head.

Calian took another sip of water. "And what of her mate?"

Fin sighed. "They are quite the pair."

Calian set down his drink. "How's the reconstruction process going?"

Morwen smiled graciously. "The healers have been working night and day. It's truly remarkable. He looks like himself again. Granted, he still goes by the Ghoul," she added, shaking her head.

"Because it sounds much more bad ass than Endrit," Fin said.

"That's good," I said. "Oh! Zeph arrived on behalf of the Kingdom of Air, his duties as General are keeping him occupied."

Morwen's expression turned thoughtful. "Yes, I remember," she said. "Did he mention how the new queen was handling her court?"

"The queen is a relative of Eteri's, right?" Fin interrupted between mouthfuls of grapes.

Calian raised an eyebrow. "Wouldn't you know that, oh King of the Kingdom of Water?"

Fin shook his head. "Nope. I'm not king yet. But when I am, I'm just going to be there to sit on my throne and look pretty. I'll even have it written into law. All decisions will be made by Morwen."

Morwen rolled her eyes. "First of all, you're going to make a wonderful, compassionate king. Second, we won't have to worry about that for a while. My mother has everything under control and a long healthy life ahead of her."

My mind raced with the flurry of recent events, each one being proof to the ever-changing landscape of our world. The mention of the north brought to mind another recent development—one that filled me with a sense of both sorrow and relief. "And speaking of the north," I continued, "Kedron finally settled into Ragnar's palace in the Realm of the Dragondead. He oversees the graves of Amram, Valda, and the rest of those buried there to ensure they never return. He's even taken up archery so that he can use Ragnar's bow to protect the realm."

"Why do I feel like I'm missing out on so much?" Fin asked with raised arms.

Morwen rolled her eyes. "My dear, we have been busy."

We all exchanged more stories and reflections of our time apart. A soft smile spread across Morwen's face, and her eyes sparkled with a quiet joy. "It's truly remarkable to see how far we've come," she said.

Calian and I exchanged a loving glance before I looked back at both of my beloved friends. "Agreed."

ABOUT THE AUTHOR

From an early age, Sarah Edgerton had an active imagination, creating stories, make-believe worlds, and songs. Now, she's using that creativity to share stories with others.

Sarah currently lives in Kansas with her husband, Michael, and their two children, Dexter and Penelope. The family has a dog named Hugo and a cat named Ari. When not pursuing her writing career, Sarah teaches at her local middle school.

Sarah considers herself to be a geek. She loves Star Trek, The Mandalorian, and Marvel. If she's not reading or writing, she's watching movies and television shows, traveling, training for half marathons, or shopping.

For more information, including new book announcements, please go to www.sarahedgerton.com.